# FAST FRIENDS

*Recent Titles by Susan Dunlap*


COP OUT
DEATH AND TAXES
DIAMOND IN THE BUFF
SUDDEN EXPOSURE
TIME EXPIRED

# FAST FRIENDS

## Susan Dunlap

This first world edition published in Great Britain 2004 by
SEVERN HOUSE PUBLISHERS LTD of
9–15 High Street, Sutton, Surrey SM1 1DF.
This first world edition published in the USA 2004 by
SEVERN HOUSE PUBLISHERS INC of
595 Madison Avenue, New York, N.Y. 10022.

British Library Cataloguing in Publication Data

Dunlap, Susan
    Fast friends
    1.    Suspense fiction
    I.    Title
    813.5'4 [F]

    ISBN 0-7278-6112-3

Typeset by Palimpsest Book Production Ltd.,
Polmont, Stirlingshire, Scotland.
Printed and bound in Great Britain by
MPG Books Ltd., Bodmin, Cornwall.

*For Ann Campbell,*
*partner in small escapes, with Peet's*

# One

The one black and white photo was all Liza Silvestri had of Jay's youth, and he wasn't even in the picture. The white-bordered shot was simply a living room, the squat, plaid sofa already old, the plank coffee table partially blurred, and only the edge of the Formica dinette set visible in a corner. Jay once described it as red and white, but in the photo it was shades of gray.

But it wasn't just any living room; it was the beach house where his family had stayed every July, where when he was fifteen, he'd had a magic week of sex. Eager, all-consuming, and so innocent. If she could take him back there—to wherever there was—he'd be okay.

At the best of times, he was never still, grabbing for six ideas at once, foot tapping, eyes sparkling. For him life was a game. But the momentum had turned on him.

Now he was wired, exhausted, gray. He needed respite. Devising an escape was tough, even though escape was her forte. A sexy blonde wife who could create the kind of games that distracted him had been enough for three years, but now the tentacles of business grasped no matter where she took him.

*Escape* . . . the photo was Jay's passport to a time when his only thought was Ingrid, an older woman, eighteen to his fifteen, three cottages down the beach.

It had taken Liza a month, searching thrift shops from L.A. to Barstow, south to El Cajon, to replicate that room here in the loft that would soon hold Jay Silvestri Financial Management. Finding the sofa had been easy—sofas last, are reupholstered, and when they're beyond salvation, given to thrift stores. The coffee table turned out to be the sticker. But the coffee table was key. Without it the room would have been an appetizer before an empty plate.

1

"It had big wooden pegs," Jay had said, "lines of them going across. After that first afternoon with Ingrid I had purple bruises all over my shoulders and butt. I couldn't take off my shirt for a week." Liza hadn't asked why they chose the coffee table when there was a sofa a foot away—teenagers, she figured. She'd finally found a similar one in a shop aptly named The Last Ditch way out near Joshua Tree. The loft room that would be the receptionist's office became the "beach house." Here Jay would relax, away from the phone, in this unconverted loft in this building that was still virtually empty. He could languish all weekend in front of the nine-inch Philco—she'd had to call half way to San Francisco to find a man who could get that to work—eat pizza and "make out" on the coffee table. He could be fifteen again. She looked around at her creation, took a deep inhalation of brine and Sea & Ski—*eau de beach*—and smiled.

But Jay was already an hour late, and soon time would accordion and even if everything was perfect those perfect things would be too crammed together.

A clank in the hallway startled her. The freight elevator? There had never been hall noise when she and Jay had lain on the futon in the unfinished area that would be his office, kitchenette and bathroom—sweat cooling their bodies, fingers just beginning to roam again, eyes half-focused on the red, green, and white lights of the Los Angeles night reflected off the fog.

She listened for footsteps, but now she heard nothing. Planes were late all the time. If she'd brought the cell phone in from the car she'd know about his flight, but she could hardly break the one rule she'd insisted on: no phone.

The clank startled her. This one was real. She could hear Jay's shoes hitting the hard hall floor. It wasn't the slowness of the steps that surprised her, but the connected sounds, as if one step dragged into the next. If he took the elevator, instead of the stairs to the second floor, he really had to be exhausted.

But he was here, and there was still an hour and a half before 10:00, when the pizza would arrive.

He had to come into the room alone, see it as he had when he was fifteen. He had to take it in, fill himself full from this

2

room where he had been so safe, so at home, when the wonders of life were bubbling up before him. But she couldn't bear to miss the look on his face. She slipped behind the arch to his office-kitchen space, stood peeking around the wall, feeling like a child on Christmas Eve waiting for a glimpse of Santa.

His feet stopped; his key scratched into the lock. Her skin quivered; it was all she could do not to jump out shrieking, "Look at this! And this! And this!"

The door shoved open. He stepped inside and plunked his briefcase on the chest she'd put next to the door.

She wasn't breathing at all, couldn't. He had barely noticed the chest. Would he stumble into the room, flop on the couch and never corral the energy to look around him? If she had to explain, the joy would be gone, his escape would sink to duty. The pizza would be not the end to the perfect evening, but the respite from an hour and a half of awkwardness.

"Omigod!" His voice cracked. "Oh my God!"

He strode to the couch, stood before it staring as if it were a Picasso. He turned toward the end table and she couldn't make out his face. But that didn't matter now. She could see his shoulders relax, his arms move forward as if to embrace the room. It was all she could do to keep from running out.

"Oh my God, it's the house at the shore! I can't believe it! The old sofa! Is it really our sofa? Liza? Liza! Oh my God! And the Point Pleasant Beach sign like we stole from the beach. Oh my God!"

She ran through the arch. He bear-hugged her, lifting her like a child, squeezing the air out of her, splotching kisses on her forehead and ears, her nose and cheeks before he found her mouth, and all the time exclaiming, "Oh my God!"

When he put her down she was too breathless to talk, but that didn't matter because he hadn't stopped talking. "Look, there's the Philco. A Philco, Liza, how did you find that? When we had the house, even then the Philco was ancient. Jeez, does it work?" He was halfway to the nine-inch television when he wheeled around, his attention grabbed by the end table. "Those lamps! I didn't think there were two of them left on the planet. I broke one of ours myself. My mother was good and pissed about that, too. It wasn't our house, she told me. She must have told me six times. We were just renting

3

it We couldn't be breaking things. Oh, and . . ." He stopped, staring at the coffee table. A slow grin crept up his face. He slid his hand under Liza's arm and cupped her breast. "The coffee table! The coffee table—"

"—you hid under when you were three."

He laughed. "Right, and later—"

"—you sat on it and ate peanut butter crackers and watched cartoons on the black and white TV."

"Yeah, that too." He was laughing now, getting in rhythm with her teasing. "And what else, Liza? What else did I tell you before I mentioned Ingrid Carroll and the broken ashtray?"

She eased down onto the table, grinned up at him and pushed the ashtray off the edge.

"It's plastic! You got the ashtray made from plastic!" He balanced on the edge of the table, pulling his arms out of his jacket. "The old ashtray must've weighed five pounds and it was full of butts—everybody smoked then. But the sucker hit the floor and it bounced. Honest to God, bounced. When I got around to checking it, after Ingrid pretty much left me for dead, it was fine, but I was on my hands and knees till my parents got home and there was still soot in the rug." He yanked his arms free and ran a hand over the table. "Jeez, you even got a table with a row of those godawful wooden pegs. My back looked like I'd been attacked. The guys kept at me every time I took my T-shirt off."

She gave his arm a poke. "Yeah, and you were one proud fifteen-year-old, right?"

"Well . . ."

She sank against his body, feeling a softness, an ease of tension she barely recalled in him. His lips moved across her face but she held him off before he got to her lips. "We've got till ten o'clock—"

"And what, my parents come home?"

"Till the pizza's delivered."

"Like Ingrid and I had! God, I felt like such an adult when I strode to the door and paid the 'boy' who had to be older than me. Jeez, Liza, this is too much. This is a dream, isn't it?"

She pinched him, and stretched back on the table.

Metal rattled.

4

It was a moment before she connected the sound to the hall door. Knocking. She pushed up on her side. "Damn! I'm sorry, Jay. I told them not to come before ten. I told them a minute before ten and no tip."

"Don't worry, Sweet. We've got all weekend. And I'll give the boy a tip; but I'll chew him out first." He was already off the table and holding out a hand to haul her up. "I suppose there's beer in the cooler, too?"

"Aren't you underage?" She laughed and splatted through the arch, her bare feet cold now on the concrete. In the kitchenette she stood by the fire-escape window, the air cooling her skin. The flow of light from the living-room lamps reflected off her car keys and outlined the styrofoam cooler. Even with the pizza fiasco, and his plane being late, this evening was perfect. Worth every thrift shop in southern California. There'd be plenty of time. She looked up at the red and green and amber lights melting in the fog and smiled.

"—fucker!" It came from the door.

She stiffened. The male voices were low but "Goddamned fucking asshole" was clear. Not Jay's voice. She strained to hear him, but now she couldn't make out anything. But the door didn't slam. She should never have brought up the tip thing.

Something banged. She rushed to the arch.

Jay was backing away from the hall door. He had a gun. A man—big—faced him back-lit from the hall light. He had a gun, too. Not pizza. Fire shot out of his gun. Jay stumbled back. She put out her arms toward him. He sagged against the arch, slid around it and fell against her.


# Two

Liza jumped back. She tried to pull Jay through the archway but his blood-slicked body slipped out of her hands and she stumbled backward. His white shirt glistened, spouting red, white disappearing, red all over.

5

"Run!" His choked voice startled her. "Go!"

She couldn't leave him.

A thick gargling sound came from his throat, then words almost indistinguishable between his viscous breaths. "Richland . . . grade. Go—" Blood poured from his mouth, gushed from his neck. She tried to staunch it; new spurts tore open his neck. Blood everywhere, gallons of blood, all his blood. His head flopped to the side. Half his neck was gone.

It was only a moment, the silence that followed Jay's death.

"Search the place!" Then the beach-house room exploded in noise; shots so loud it sounded like the earth splitting apart. Shots going on and on and on. Men screaming, bodies crashing over furniture.

She stood behind the arch wall for an eternity, unable to help Jay, unable to desert him, frozen. She had to get Jay a doctor—but he was dead! She had to go, go fast. Call 911. But he was *dead*. DEAD!

The noise filled the other room but it no longer registered as gunshots, yells, shoes slapping floor. The volume blasted through thought. Words lost their form. Terror, grief turned to black. She had no thoughts, just buzzing in her head. She picked up the gun, Jay's new gun.

Silver sparkled by the cooler. Car keys.

Oblongs of light. Windows.

She grabbed the keys, thrust up the window she'd never been able to budge, climbed out onto the fire escape. The gun slipped out of her hand, smacked metal, clattered down, hit with a thud. She shot a glance down at the light-spotted darkness two stories below. So far down. Too far. Instinctively she began to climb. Metal rungs cut into her bare feet; rusting rails scraped her fingers and palms. The old metal structure shook with every step, rattling like . . . like the gun shots coming after Jay. She climbed faster, fingers clutching the keys.

Noise below. Great snores of traffic. Metallic spikes of music. Voices. Closer. From her window. Sharp. Gruff. The fire escape rattled. She hit the fifth-floor landing, passed the darkened window, caught the railing and raced on. Her breaths came fast, singeing the back of her mouth. Voices from below pierced her consciousness. Suddenly the collage of meaningless sounds reassembled. Voices separated from the splatter of noise, shifted into words, smacked her like a jockey's crop.

The fire escape ended.

She stopped. Thoughts spun in her head but she couldn't get hold of them. She looked over the edge of the roof, clambered over. Pebbles on the tar-and-gravel surface cut her bare feet. She stumbled, looked down, kicked at a sock that must have fallen out of . . . something.

Jay, was he dead? No, no; he couldn't be. Jay was *dead.*

She started for the far corner, stopped so abruptly her feet stung. No escape? Where to hide? No safety but the shadows here. She raced for the near corner in the dark below the next building. The fire escape rattled like thunder; heavy feet pounded, closer, closer. *The neighbors will hear; they'll call the cops.* She relaxed, just momentarily. She was fooling herself. This was an industrial area. There were no neighbors to notice anything, much less call the cops.

The voices were closer. Any second they'd be on the roof.

She pushed back into the corner. Her jeans and T-shirt were black. If she could cover her hair . . . and her feet . . .

A ladder led to the roof of the next building. It was still in shadows, but gray not black. She tossed the sock near it, and huddled in the darkest corner, kneeling, head almost in the gravel, arms crossed over her blond hair.

Shoes scraped against the gravel. The two men were panting ferociously. She peeked through her hair, squinting so they wouldn't shoot when they saw the whites of her eyes. She almost giggled, caught herself, let out a squeak.

Both of them stopped dead.

Light shone off the silver guns.

She held her breath. She could see only one pair of shoes, pant legs. Feet moving around a central point as the man surveyed this half of the roof. He was facing her, closing in. She was going to die. Like Jay. Oh, God, Jay. She clutched the keyring like a talisman.

The feet stopped. He was standing ten feet away. Did he not hear her teeth clattering against each other?

Five feet away! How could he not see her?

No flashlights. The men didn't have lights!

7

"Over here!" he yelled.

Pebbles shot into her scalp as the black shoes pushed off. The gravel under her shins, ground into her bones. She didn't dare move. Where did the next roof lead? To another roof, to a stairway, a dead end that would bring him back?

Maybe this was all part of some bizarre game and Jay wasn't really dead.

Jay's blood was real.

She shifted her head and watched till the last foot lifted onto the bottom rung. The man was huge, twice the size of Jay. His black-clad body stood out against the lighter night like an eighteen-wheeler coming out of the fog. He grunted and hoisted a leg up onto the next roof.

She pushed off and ran for the fire escape, raced down, hands sliding down the rusty railings. Her bare feet smashed into the grated landing. The fire escape thundered. She leapt for the flight of stairs, sliding on her hands, feet not touching the steps. Men shouted. A flight above? Two? Three? She was moving too fast to make out words. She turned again, slid down another flight of stairs. Her feet crashed into the grate. She turned—

The crack was ear-shattering. The ping a foot away.

Her arms went stiff; she slid down the stairs, swung into the turn.

Her breath caught. No more stairs. The sidewalk was twelve feet down. Frantically, she looked for a ladder. Nothing. Another shot—so close the blast of air iced her shoulder.

The fire escape thundered, shook.

The vibrations stopped. Everything was silent.

She felt the heat on her breast before she recognized the sound of the shot, the bullet ricocheting off the railing. Blood spurted bright, light against her black T-shirt.

She grabbed the grating, dangled her body through the hole where the ladder should have been, and dropped. Metal reverberated. She'd hit a garbage can. Some part of her body stung but she couldn't tell which.

*Where was Jay's gun?* She scanned the sidewalk.

Feet banged on the fire-escape stairs.

She looked behind the garbage cans, beside the stoop, the

8

patch of weeds that once was garden. There: in the dirt! She grabbed it.

Her car was ten yards away. She fumbled the keys out of her pocket and hit the remote, holding her breath till she heard the buzz. She was into the seat and starting the engine without realizing it. The wheels screeched as she cut into the lane and floored the gas.

For the first time she felt safe.

The back window shattered. The side window crackled like a Fourth of July sparkler. She pulled the wheel hard to the left and hung on. A truck loomed in front, she yanked the wheel to the right, passed it on the wrong side of the street. Her foot was stuck on the accelerator. There was no time to check the rearview mirror. She swung a wide right at the corner; horns blared.

She'd been to the loft on and off for two months, been on every street around here looking for props for the beach-house room. Suddenly nothing was familiar: any street could dead end. She was on a main road, four lanes with parking on both sides. All the stores were chains; she could have been anywhere. Behind her, cars were coming fast, cutting in and out of lanes. The two men could be driving any one of them.

The light ahead was red. With a final look in the rearview, she ran it. Brakes screeched; horns blared. More brakes squealed.

Overhead a sign said *405 West*. She hung a right onto the freeway. She was in the fast lane before she could check the rearview for headlights tailing her. She veered onto the 10, driving by rote, checking: rearview, road, speedometer, gas, rearview. Friday night on the 10; no one was going to stand out speeding.

Suddenly the cold hit her. She turned the heat all the way up. She was near the beach, almost home. She could call Jay—

Oh, God, Jay! Jay, bleeding on the cold floor.

She was doing eighty. The car hit the lane bumps as she reached for the cell phone. She only knew one cop but he was the last one she'd call. She had to do something; she just couldn't leave Jay there on the floor to— And she couldn't go back, not and stay alive. She swallowed hard, yanked the wheel, and remembered 911. The car hit the lane bumps on

9

the far side. As soon as the dispatcher started, Liza gave the loft address. "A man is dying in number three."

"Who's calling? Don't hang up!"

But she did. She couldn't make herself say the word *dead*, not about Jay. She could still see him grinning as he recognized the sofa, the coffee table. She could feel the ghosts of his kisses across her face. There was nothing she could tell the police. She needed to get home.

Going home would be crazy. If the killers found the loft— No one else knew it existed. Jay hadn't even put in a phone.

And the killers trailed Jay there.

She couldn't go home, not to the house in Malibu. That was the first place they'd look. They'd come in shooting.

She could call the cops to the house. *Some other woman* could and they'd protect her. Police cause problems; that she knew.

The exit for the coast road was coming up. She didn't think of the alternatives anymore. Suddenly the ultimate clarity was: she had to get home before the killers. She shot across three lanes and pulled off the freeway.

No one was on her tail. Slowing down, she navigated the familiar streets. She'd already gotten three "exceeding speed limits" this year; she couldn't chance being stopped now.

The house was on the beach. Roadside it was no more than a garage door and a six-foot-high wall. Beach-side it was two stories of glass with steps down to the Pacific.

She beamed open the garage, cut a Y and backed in, beaming the door shut so fast it nearly took off the hood.

She hefted the gun—the thing was huge. It almost threw her off-balance as she ran into the house. Squeaks came from behind the downstairs door. She had to get out of here. But she couldn't keep herself from going into the living room, from stopping in front of the fireplace, from looking at the couch and rug and chairs and coffee table with the fleece slippers she'd given Jay abandoned beneath. Slippers to keep him warm. Oh, God, his poor cold cold feet.

She shivered; her T-shirt stuck to her breast. Blood. Jay's blood. Or her own? She yanked off the shirt and her blood-caked jeans, threw them in a heap next to the sofa.

Jeans, a jumble of T-shirts, bathing suit lay on the sofa arm,

10

a bright yellow sweater on the seat cushion. Towel draped over a lamp. Three pairs of sandals, running shoes, socks, underwear, jeans. Jeez, she really was a slob. She loved knowing she could be a slob and no landlord could break in and evict her.

She had to get out of here. She toweled off the dried blood, jammed her legs into fresher black jeans, grabbed a white T-shirt.

The squeaking downstairs was louder. She checked for outside noises, wheels squealing, brakes, the gate banging open.

It was foolhardy to stop in the bedroom, but she couldn't help herself. Light from an outside lamp threw the room in shadows. It still smelled of liniment from Jay. Her eyes welled up. She stood, planted in the doorway, looking at the bed they lay in last Sunday long into the morning till the fog lifted and the sun striped across Jay's chest and face, and he lay, head turned toward her, smiling like life, their life, would go on forever.

The gate banged. She hadn't heard a car. She grabbed Jay's leather jacket, inhaled his smell from the collar, breathing deep to make it part of her, and ran to open the downstairs door. "Come on, Felton."

The black and white pot-bellied piglet grunted happily, following her, trotters clip-clopping on the floor. He veered into the living room, snuffled under the coffee table for crumbs.

"Felton! Come on!"

The piglet glanced up and returned to his crumbs.

Footsteps slapped the front walk.

She raced into the living room, bobbled the gun as she grabbed the squirming piglet and ran for the garage. It was ridiculous her attachment to him, this piglet the neighbors threw out. The warmth of his body, his sweet little pink snout burrowing into her chest almost made her bawl.

The front door to the house crashed on its hinges. She moved around the car, eased the driver's door open, slid in.

Shots cracked the air.

She hit the remote, floored the gas. The garage door banged the roof of the car as she flew out.

# Three

Liza flicked a glance in the rearview again. She was clear now. Behind her on the 405, five lanes of headlights did a line dance at 75 mph. She'd hit the freeway fast. Even so, the killers might have followed her. She'd double looped the first exit, shot around the entire clover leaf and back on in the same direction. She was sure she'd lost them. But just in case she'd looped off and on one more time when she veered onto the 405 South. No one followed.

Now it could have been any Friday night, skimming along in lane 3, ready to swing off at LAX and pick up Jay. Any Friday Jay wasn't dead.

A soulful squeak cut through her attempt at calm. She leaned over to comfort the sleepy piglet before she realized the sound came from her.

"We're okay," she said. "No one's on our tail. No one knows where we are. I'll just keep driving till I figure out what to do. I'll—"

The buzz of the phone jolted her halfway to the roof. She'd already said hello before she thought to keep quiet.

"Liza?"

"Who is this?"

"Francis Bentec. Is it true Jay's been shot?"

"How'd you get—"

"I'm the Assistant to the Commissioner of the Police in this city. The dispatcher got your number when you called. Tell me what happened?"

She didn't respond. Overhead the sign noted: *LAX 3 mi.*

"Liza, I'm Jay's friend. I want to help you. What can I tell you?" There was a different pitch to his voice now.

Liza'd never spoken to him on the phone; she couldn't judge this tone against his normal. She didn't trust him, but that was because he knew about her. She'd met him only once.

At first he'd stared like men always did. But soon she'd seen the threat in his eyes. After that when Jay'd had him to the house, she'd made a point of being out. *What can I tell you?* Why Jay bothered with you, that's what.

"Liza, where are you?"

The phone was shaking in her hand. She had to say something. "I don't know. Driving. Thinking."

"I'm in headquarters, downtown. You know where that is. How soon can you get here?"

*LAX 2½ mi.*

"Liza we need to talk to you."

"Why?"

"To find out who did this to Jay. Who was Jay involved with? Did he have business problems?"

"Business problems solved by two guys bursting in with assault weapons? What the hell kind of business are you talking about?" She was screaming; she who always sensed people's reaction before they opened their mouths; she who lived by watching for the safety zone. Here she was screaming at the Assistant to the Commissioner of the entire Los Angeles Police Department. She was losing it.

"I'm . . . asking . . . you, Liza."

She took a breath, forcing her throat to unclench. She had to get control of herself. Still, she could hear the hysteria in her voice as she said, "I don't know. Jay's business is his business." Bentec wouldn't believe that; no one ever did. But she was hardly going to tell him about their agreement to enjoy their life together and leave the unspoken unspoken. Jay hadn't asked about her past, even when Bentec just about threw it in his face. Jay was the only man who ever took her at face value, the only man who didn't find out more and cut her loose. She saw him again, grinning at the beach-house room—he must have had that same grin when he was five. She felt him again, crumbling against her, sliding on his blood.

Her eyes clouded with tears. She swiped them with the back of her hand. Bentec was hollering but his words were spewing out at the windshield now as she tried to clear her eyes. Felton was squealing. A sports utility cut in front of her nearly taking off her fender.

"Liza!"

"There's nothing I know. My husband is dead! Leave me alone. Go find the two gunmen."

"Can you identify them?"

"No."

"You must have seen them. You must remember something."

She saw the hall doorway; Jay stumbling back, grasping helplessly at the archway. She remembered too much. Her shoulders clamped in from the sides; her neck felt like she was being choked. "No," she forced out, "I can't identify them. They could be anyone."

"Liza, you need to get down here. We've got to find out how Jay got himself in this mess."

*Got himself in this mess!*

"Where are you going?"

*Got himself in this mess!* She smacked her fist so hard into the steering wheel the car jolted.

"Liza?"

"Mexico; that's where I'm going. I'm driving to Mexico. You want to talk to me, plan to speak Spanish." God, she was turning back into Liza Cummings, provoking the Assistant to the Police Commissioner.

"Liza, Liza, we don't suspect you of killing Jay."

"What?" She jerked the wheel right. A horn blared. She pulled back into her lane.

"You are not a suspect. We're just asking for your help. Jay was my friend, Liza."

*LAX — next exit.*

A suspect? What was the man talking about? The whole world was going crazy.

"Liza!"

She threw the phone behind the seat. The car veered across the lane marker; a horn blared; she yanked the wheel back. She'd only gone off like that once before and that time it was disastrous. But this, hanging up on a cop, an Assistant to the Commissioner, oh God. The phone rang. She was glad it was out of reach. Glad, like she'd be as soon as she was on a flight headed anywhere. She swung over three lanes into the LAX exit.

14

# Four

Inspector Francis Bentec smacked the receiver onto the cradle. She had hung up on him! Francis Bentec was not someone men dared hang up on, not even once. Even cons knew better. In his nineteen years on the Force he'd sent out tendrils to every station house, to snitches all over the city. No one twitched without his knowing. He'd worked damned hard creating his network. He'd played out favors carefully, left the debts outstanding and collected just enough interest on them to remind a lieutenant in Simi Valley, a detective in West L.A., that they owed him. Sworn officers all over the city understood the value of being Frank Bentec's friend. Cons all over the city got out of his way.

But Liza Silvestri had hung up on him. Fury colored Bentec's face and he was glad there was no one in his office to see him lose his cool. Where the hell was she? And what was this Mexico crap? He'd raised eyebrows insinuating himself in this investigation that should be no concern of the Assistant to the Commissioner. No one would question him, of course, but still he needed to get in and out quick. He needed her to tell him where things were, needed—

The phone rang. "Bentec."

"This is me, Heron." Heron, one of the thugs who screwed up.

"Where are you?"

"On the four-oh-five. We lost her."

Bentec felt his face flush again. He took a breath before speaking. "Heron, what kind of morons are you two? What the hell made you kill Silvestri? You were supposed to remind him to play nice, not shoot the bastard."

"He pulled a gun. We had no choice."

Bentec nodded. Heron was no fool. He wouldn't have used Heron if he were. "Right, but that still means instead of a

15

simple work-over I've got a corpse on my hands and detective division looking for the killer. Unless we get Liza Silvestri the search is going to spread, the search for the killer. Do I make myself clear, Heron?"

"We'll find her. Listen, he said something to her. He was on the floor slipping down in his blood—"

"What? What'd he say?"

"'Run' and 'Go,' and then something else."

"Something else? What the hell else?"

"Couldn't tell. Guy was choking on all the blood. Like he had a mouth fulla candies."

"Heron, you—"

"But she heard him, and she lit out of there. Look, Bentec—"

"Inspector," he said automatically.

"Inspector," Heron repeated as if he knew better than to not. "She's driving an old Mustang. We'll spot her. Don't worry about that . . . Inspector."

"I'm not worrying; you're the one who needs to worry, you understand that, Heron? Where are you, where on the four-oh-five?"

"This side of the airport."

"Well, where do you think she's headed then? Get to the airport, find her, and call me. Don't let her see you. Just keep her where we can find her. You understand?"

"Yeah, man, we'll get our eyes on her."

"Don't let her talk to anyone, and don't let her get away again."

Johnny Heron clicked off the phone and glared over at the driver. "Slow down, asshole, we don't need to get hauled in for speeding. If anything happens to us Bentec's not going to bother hauling our asses out of the fire."

Eddie slowed the Grand Am to 80. "Where we going?"

"Airport."

"We gonna watch the broad?"

"Not hardly."

"That's what Bentec said to do." There was a pronounced whine to Eddie's voice.

"Well, I got a better plan. We—"

"Count me out of your better plan, man. I seen what happens

16

to guys who cross Bentec. You spit on Bentec, and the next day you end up with your head in the toilet hoping you can hold your breath long enough to come up for air and say you're sorry. And, man, you don't even know who's holding your head down or how that guy's into Bentec."

"Eddie, calm down. Listen to me. We got insurance. In the airport we got a woman who heard something that Bentec's hot to find out. We squeeze her, then we got the hot topic, you understand? We eliminate her, then we're the only ones with the hot topic and our price goes up, way up. When you got what a guy wants, got it in your head, then you're in control, even when you're dealing with Frank Bentec."

"He'll find a way to get us. He'll get some cop or some snitch, or, I don't know man, but you know he'll get us, you know that. Even if we get ourselves out of L.A. he'll find us and we'll end up holding our breath in the toilet and—"

"Then we better find Silvestri, get the hot topic off her, and move fast."

# Five

*Short Term Parking.*
Liza Silvestri pulled up near the elevator vestibule. Why "short term," Jay always kidded her. "What? The owner of a house in Malibu can't afford valet parking?" Whatever her reasons were normally, tonight she'd turned in there from habit alone. Now she wished she'd chosen a spot closer than Saudi Arabia. She didn't want to leave the restored '65 Mustang—the car Jay gave her. "Pull yourself together! Do it, or you will die! You knew how to survive before Jay; do it!" The thrust of her words pushed her out of the car. She stuck the gun in the glove compartment—all she'd need would be to be caught in the metal detector—lifted Felton into his pig carrier, and ran for the elevator.

17

The vestibule was empty. Wind poured through the open doors on both sides. Her steps echoed off the cement. Elevator doors parted. She darted in. Safe. For two levels. The elevator lurched, hummed, stopped. She raced out, her shoes clacking as she ran through the empty tunnel. The killers could be waiting behind any display, behind potted plants, in alcoves, or around the corner of the escalator. This was the perfect place to pick her off. *I lost them on the freeway. They don't know where I am. I'm safe.* But she didn't believe that.

Arty neon lights changed color, painting Felton's carrier red, purple, blue, green. He smacked against the side, squealing miserably. She longed to stop and cuddle him till the fear faded.

She jumped on the escalator. Her stomach lurched as the stairs jerked up. In a minute she would be stepping off, walking to the counter, and buying a ticket to safety. She'd be choosing between window and aisle seats, and swearing that no one asked her to carry any packages on the flight, that her luggage had never been out of her sight. Her biggest problem would be convincing the clerk to let Felton ride on her lap.

The escalator leveled out. She took a deep breath, stepped off and headed for the ticket counter.

The counters were empty.

Empty!

The whole ticketing area was empty!

Behind the counters the lights were dimmed. The counters said only: *Closed. Closed. Closed. Closed. Closed. Closed.* The Departures screen listed no flights before 6 A.M.

She couldn't believe it. It was like a bad dream, a horror movie.

It was not yet 2 A.M. She couldn't stay here. The dark windows reflected her image; her every step was like a drumbeat. Felton groaned and she was sure the desolate sound was echoing throughout LAX. "Hush," she whispered. But he didn't hush. There was no fighting it. She pulled him out of his carrier and sat in a phone nook stroking his coarse hide, murmuring disconnected words, looking down at his little crinkled black and white face, his mobile pink snout sniffing with a million questions, rooting into her armpit, burying his face in the safety of her body.

The emptiness rose up around her, the silence broken only by the announcements for American flight four twenty-five from Dallas landing at gate something or other and Craig Leffers, Mister Craig Leffers to the white courtesy phone. She pressed farther back in the phone nook, knowing it was useless as a hiding place, knowing no alternative. She needed Jay.

She squeezed back tears. She couldn't let herself cry, not even for Jay, Jay who she loved so much, Jay with his blood gushing, Jay, oh God, Jay . . .

She'd been here so often, dropping him off, waiting while he bought a last minute ticket. She'd strolled to a gate, her arm in his. She'd stood right here and nestled into him, letting the last kiss sprong through her before he ran for his plane. She could feel his sweater-covered ribs, the vestigial prickling of his shaven cheek against hers. His thick dark hair still crushed from the cap he'd decided to wear.

But that wasn't at the airport; he never wore caps in L.A. That was at the Richland grade—had it been only a month ago? She could see his sleek sharp face drawn up laughing as he shook his head at the botch he'd made of the picnic plans. The great gush of rain on the rental car's windshield had curtained off the world, and their breaths clouded the inside. The torrent had created a wall of sound and after a while he'd abandoned the pretext of lunch and slipped his hand up under her sweater and pulled her over against him and—

Was she crazy? Here in the airport with killers after her and she was daydreaming about Jay's car picnic at the Richland grade. But it had been his last thought, the memory of that silly day when they made love in the car like teenagers. If Jay were here, he'd—

But Jay was dead.

Where could she go? To a friend's? She shoved off the thought. That kind of friend she didn't have. She'd never had. Friends asked questions. Jay had never prodded her or she him about things unmentioned; how could she have allowed anyone else to poke into their life?

There was nothing to hang onto, nowhere to turn, nobody she could trust. She stared at the ticket counter signs: *Closed. Closed. Closed. Closed.* She couldn't stop shivering.

19

But there was Ellen Baines. Ellen would come. She'd come because she had to, but she would come.

A bang resounded in the distance. She clutched Felton to her. There were no more bangs, but the cavernous departure hall wasn't silent either. Now, she heard plastic bumping, something—a mop—swishing, a distant loudspeaker whining about Craig Leffers, Mister Craig Leffers to the white courtesy phone, please. There was ample noise to cover careful footsteps. No way could she be alert enough to be safe.

Liza called the airlines and the ordinariness of the reservations process calmed her. By the time she'd made a hotel reservation and dialed Ellen Baines's number in Kansas City—it would be almost 4:30 A.M. there—she'd almost convinced herself that the hour, and her request, were reasonable. "Ellen?"

"Yes?"

"It's Liza Silvestri. Jay's been shot. He's dead. I've made you a plane reservation, United to San Francisco. The first flight out tomorrow morning. I got you a room at the Rosewood Hotel downtown. Will you come?"

It was a moment before Ellen said, "Yes, of course I'll come, Liza. Are you okay?"

"No. Yes. I don't know. But you're coming, right?"

"Yes, Liza. How could I not come?"

Her breath came in a great gush as if she'd been holding it since Jay died. "Thank you. God, Ellen, thank you."

The connection was gone and she'd replaced the receiver before it occurred to her that she'd said her husband was dead and Ellen Baines hadn't sounded surprised.

She couldn't worry about that now. She gave Felton a final hug, slipped him into the carrier, and walked purposefully onto the escalator. In five hours she'd be safely in San Francisco waiting for Ellen's plane.

The passageway was empty but it didn't frighten her now. Walking threw her into a rhythm, and going somewhere reminded her she had choices. By the time she got out of the elevator at the blue level she was considering which freeway to head for, trying to remember how much gas she had—not much, unless this weekend was different from all others—and to guess where she'd be most likely to find an open station in these pre-dawn hours. Trying to figure where she'd be safe.

20

In the vestibule she shifted Felton's carrier to her left hand and readied her car keys. Then she stepped from the bright, tiled elevator foyer into the drafty garage. Nothing else moved. Half the spaces were empty. She'd left her car at the end of a line, in the roadway really. *What's the worst that can happen, you'll be towed?* And she hadn't been towed. Not even ticketed. By now, despite the emptiness of the airport, travelers or employees had materialized from somewhere and driven off in the cars that had sat next to hers. The red Mustang looked as if she'd abandoned it in the middle of Wiltshire Boulevard.

Felton squealed. A "gotta go" squeal.

"Hang on, boy. I'll let you out the first time we see grass."

After a final visual sweep, she stepped out into the roadway, stopped, listening for an engine cranking up, for footsteps, for breathing. There was no sound but her own breath hitting the sides of her nose, her own heartbeat, her own pig breathing louder than she was.

She threw her shoulders back, strode across the cement to the car, half expecting bullets to whiz by from all directions. But there were no bullets, no assassins. She put the carrier down and opened the car door. The bullet-cracked glass shimmied. Shifting Felton's carrier across her onto the passenger seat, she slipped in, stuck the key in the ignition and turned it.

"Jeez," Jay would say, "you're worried about killers and you don't check under the hood? You could be blown up."

But that didn't happen. Nothing happened.

She turned the key and pressed the gas three more times before she got out, pulled up the hood and spotted tubes and wires, their yanked and ripped ends sticking up like arms severed in an explosion.

# Six

Ellen Baines was shaking when she put the phone down. It was 4:26 A.M.; the heat had been off for hours in her apartment, and snow had been coating Kansas City since dusk. But her shiver came from deeper than the skin. Liza! Poor Liza! She had never heard Liza sound so scared. No, wait, not "so scared." She had never seen Liza scared at all. Nothing frightened Liza, at least not in college. For Liza breaking the rules merely meant accepting the price. She'd spent more weekends "under house arrest" than any freshman girl in the history of the school. Most of the girls at St. Enid's College for Girls with No Better Alternative—which was one of Liza's names for the place—considered her a California snob. Snooty, abrupt, and much too beautiful. And they were right. Liza had hated the place—St. Enid's of the Frigid Youth (her February coinage), and that only made Ellen think better of her.

And now Liza's husband was dead, shot like a gangster! God, poor Liza. Ellen pulled her covers up around her shaking shoulders. Shot! She could hardly believe it, and yet she'd seen Jay Silvestri and she wasn't surprised . . . and yet, and yet, shot! Decent people don't get shot dead. Jesus! Poor Liza!

And poor Mom. She picked up the phone before she had time to reconsider. Mom would be up, getting ready to leave for St. Enid's cafeteria to start the water for oatmeal. Cooking for two hundred girls was too big a job for a woman her age even with help but Ellen knew there was no point in going through that again, particularly at four thirty in the morning. "Enough that I can stay near your brother," Mom would say and that would be the end of it.

"Mom, Liza's husband died," she blurted out before her mother could even speak. *Died*, not *was killed*, not *shot*.

"Oh, dear, Ellie, poor little Liza. How could that happen to her—she's so young?"

22

"Well, her husband was older, maybe ten years, maybe even more." Jeez, soon she'd be talking heart attack and clogged arteries. And clogged was one thing Jay Silvestri certainly wasn't. Oh, Jeez, Ellen, get a hold on yourself! What was Mom saying now?

". . . you know, Ellie, I still see her as that little orphan at Thanksgiving."

She forced herself out of the warm bed to the closet and yanked her suitcase off the shelf. She could see the picture in her mother's mind: Liza, the little blonde freshman her mother invited to Thanksgiving dinner because "the poor little thing" had nowhere to go. Mom always felt sorry for the "holiday orphans," which just proved how sweet and how naive she was. She never imagined that later those girls would giggle with their friends about their make-do Thanksgiving with Mrs. Baines, the lady who ladled out cream corn on the cafeteria line. It never occurred to her that the girls were not stiff from post-adolescent awkwardness but from concealing smirks at her shabby two-room suite the college provided, or the mismatched plates, or, worst of all, at her nervous fawning when Mr. Sleem, the cafeteria manager, made his inevitable appearance. Ellen yanked open her underwear drawer, grabbed a handful of pants and slammed them in the suitcase. Each year had brought a new wave of humiliation. Liza was a freshman her senior year, and Ellen had expected the worst.

"Ellie, remember how sweet Liza looked that Thanksgiving in that smart teal dress with the little silk jacket and those high heels that just about had her standing on her toes. Just like a little girl playing dress up."

Ellen added a bra to her pile, half slip, stockings and a pair of socks just in case. She'd been fooling herself to think she could call Mom for just two minutes, particularly talking about Liza. Liza, her favorite of the St. Enid's girls, could do no wrong.

"And that bottle of wine she brought, Ellie! You know I didn't know what to do, her being a big city girl and all. Should I serve her wine, underage and all? But I couldn't, could I, not with those two sophomore girls eyeing the bottles, Mr. Sleem sitting right there." A little laugh stopped her, and Ellen had to laugh too, even though they had been over the

23

Thanksgiving scene dozens of times. How had Liza managed to get that wine? Ellen had never asked.

In the end the disaster had not been the one she'd expected, but Mr. Sleem drinking almost the entire bottle himself, babbling endlessly, and ending up patting Mom's butt. She could still see Mom cringing.

Her stomach tightened now just as it had when she glanced over at Liza—a pat on the butt; that would amuse the freshman dorm all the way to Easter.

"That little smile on Liza's face, so sweet. You know, Ellie, I was watching Mr. Sleem then"—after ten years replaying this scene they could dip in at any point without explanation—"and he was still full of himself from patting my fanny. I could tell he thought Liza was smiling because he was such a cosmopolitan ladies' man. But when she handed him her little jacket, well . . ." Ellen knew Mom was blushing, even after all these years, feeling a bit guilty as they both pictured Mr. Sleem's round red face transfixed with sensual greed as he unconsciously rubbed the silk between his fingers, while eyeing one firm young white arm sliding into the left soft, slippery sleeve, the nubile breasts lift and dip as the blonde Lolita from L.A. twisted to enter her other arm into the waiting right sleeve. "What *was* he thinking?" Mom had asked later and been appalled when Ellen and Liza hooted.

What he hadn't been expecting was Liza twisting so quickly that she caught his hand between her arm and breast, her letting out a dainty cry, Mom gasping with true horror, and Ellen letting out a cry she could not in all the years of discussion after, ever quite define. And the two sophomores staring open-mouthed.

Ellen added a black dress—too dressy for a funeral but the only one she had, jeans, a green wool sweater. She didn't know which had startled her more—Liza's unthinking support of Mom, or Mr. Sleem's having been too drunk to remember the incident. Or more surprising yet the length of time it took for the rumours about Mr. Sleem to circulate. She didn't remind Mom of the wretched rest of that winter when nothing changed in Mom's life except her fears for Liza and for the one job she could get near to Eddie.

The three years in age was too great a gulf for friendship

24

then, but she and Liza did trade St. Enid's slurs in whispers or anonymous notes until Easter, when in a maneuver Ellen hadn't fully understood for years, Liza gave the Baineses freedom.

It was a gift so overwhelming her mother thanked God for Liza every night in her prayers, and Ellen never thought of Liza without seeing her own inadequacy, which, she had to admit, only made her feel more inadequate and not a small bit petty.

"But, Ellie, how could Liza's husband die? She never mentioned him being sick or anything. You know I keep in touch with Liza. Better than you do, hon."

"I know you do, Mom, and you keep me up on her. That's why Liza called me. I'm flying out there first thing this morning. That's why I'm calling you now."

"Does Liza need me to come, too? I could get off work. We owe it to her—"

"No, Mom. I can handle it."

"I'm sure you can, Ellie. All that paperwork about death and those miserable funeral directors, and lawyers and who knows what out there in California. You know Liza's not good at spotting pitfalls. She'll need you, honey."

"Yeah, Mom."

"You're not going because you feel you have to, are you?"

"No, Mom. I'll call you when I get back. Bye." She certainly did owe Liza, but she wasn't going out of debt. Ever since she'd seen Liza's husband last month at the St. Enid's West Coast Alumnae reunion in Portland she'd known the man was a sleaze. Look at how he led Harry Cooper on, huddled in a corner with him like he was really interested in Harry's arcane railroad talk. Harry did love railroading and, alas, he did go on. She'd zoned out more than once herself. And Jay Silvestri, well, clearly he was a fast-lane guy. He probably mocked Harry all the way back to L.A. Harry was such a lamb, and Liza's husband, well anyone could see the man was a predator and for him an innocent like Harry Cooper was mutton on the hoof. Of course she hadn't told Mom. But how could Liza not see the man was a snake?

She was shivering hard and now it was from the cold. The clock said 4:46 A.M. She dialed Harry Cooper and let the phone ring till his machine picked up. She wasn't surprised

25

he turned off the ringer at night; it was the sensible thing to do.

She walked to the apartment window and stared out at the best view in town. In the park snow covered the grass and outlined the more protected trees. Moonlight skated on the stream. Her view was really the nicest part of the four months she'd been in Kansas City.

But she hadn't expected more. She knew Harry Cooper was a "settled for." Harry Cooper loved her and that should be enough. She was no Liza Cummings. Not blonde, not beautiful. She was what she'd always been: the daughter of the woman who served the creamed corn at St. Enid's cafeteria. The kernel of reliability—that witticism from a date who thought she missed the insult.

She'd tried it on her own in Portland and look what happened. She should consider herself lucky that a reliable man, a sweet man like Harry wanted her enough to create a job for her in Kansas City.

It wasn't enough; the whole move here had been a mistake, but she couldn't go back to Portland, and besides, poor Harry, well, she couldn't do that to him. At least she was a good assistant for him, organized, alert, able to see through problems.

If Harry had told her what Silvestri said to him in Portland . . . but when she had asked he'd skewered her with, "Well, Ellen, if you didn't want me to find out what kind of slick operator your friend Liza married you shouldn't have egged me on to talk to him."

# Seven

Liza slammed the hood down on her ravaged engine, scrambled for her cell phone in the back of the car. 911? Police? No way. She punched 6 on speed dial, one of the exorbitantly priced airport limos. "E. Six. Double your rate if you're here first."

The parking lot was almost empty. In the corner farthest from the exit lane security guards used, a black car's engine roared. She punched 7. "E. Six. Double your rate if you're here first."

Tires squealed. The black car sped at her, veering left, cutting off her escape to the stairs.

Pain filled her chest, as if she'd already been shot. She forced herself to breathe, to move, to crouch next as she hit 8 and repeated the offer.

The black car stopped ten feet away. The driver's door jerked open. A shot cracked her windshield.

Wheels screeched. Headlights striped the cement. A white limo skidded around the corner, squealing to a halt by the man emerging from the black car. A black limo shot in from the exit lane.

Liza flung open the car door, grabbed the pig carrier and the gun and ran for the stairs, thrusting the gun in her purse as she raced down two flights, nearly slipping as she jerked around the corners, her centre of balance thrown off kilter by the weight of the squirming pig. The cell phone clanked to the floor but she couldn't stop. She yanked open the exit door and ran for the moving walkway, running on it, leaping off the other end and racing past the escalator into a whole different cavernous room.

Empty.

Empty except for two women behind rental car counters. She hesitated, eyeing them for any sign they'd been alerted about the false alarm. Their identical expressions said: It's the middle of the night; finally my shift is almost over; take your problem to her. Liza chose the counter closest to the outside door and filled out the paperwork.

Half an hour later she was headed north out of L.A., her purse stuffed between the seats, the gun butt within reach. "It was a good sign, this car," she assured Felton. Not such a great sign to have used her own credit card, but there'd been no choice.

If she could put enough distance between herself and L.A., that wouldn't matter. She wanted to drive so fast, yesterday would never catch up with her. In the anonymous car she felt almost safe. Like she did driving home to Malibu. The low, white house in Malibu had cloaked her with its reliability. But even it had never been enough to dislodge the claw that had grabbed her stomach for as long as she could remember.

Every afternoon in junior high when the last bell rang it began to dig in. With each step of her walk home it had pierced deeper. By the time she'd rounded the last corner she'd been doubled over, hand on her gut, head hanging. She'd had to stop and force her head up, and look down the street at her house to see if this was one of the times the furniture would be piled at the curb and the sheriff walking away from the door.

As much as she'd loved Jay she hadn't minded him being gone for weeks at a time. She had luxuriated in the silent house, filled with peace and certainty, without the shrieking laughter, the shrieking cries, the tears, hours upon hours of slurred regrets, the threats, the blood-caked bruises, breaking bottles, the smell of bourbon flowing from rug and chair, sweating through the pores of her parents, the town's drunks. In Jay's house in Malibu she had loved picking up the phone without fearing an angry neighbor, her acrid grandmother, or the police.

When she'd married Jay, she'd sworn not to think about those miserable years again. And Jay had understood. In their three years together he never asked. He hadn't complained, blamed, bemoaned, or bruised.

A happy interlude. Gone. Done. Over.

She was so cold. The rental car was cold. "Jay is dead," she forced herself to say aloud. Even if she wanted to she couldn't call Bentec at the police department. He wouldn't believe she knew nothing more about Jay's business than the title he put on his 1040.

"So what?" His business couldn't matter now. In business if you screwed up you got fired. You didn't get tracked down like a deer and shot.

Thoughts were coming too fast. She couldn't . . . she couldn't—anything. She told herself she'd pick up Ellen and they'd drive to the Richland grade and eat ham sandwiches like she and Jay did and everything would be all right.

The thought of Ellen calmed her. Ellen would know the safe thing to do. Everything would be okay when Ellen got here. It was Ellen who'd come up with the school motto: "St. Enid's, Never Think Outside the Lines." Liza smiled. Thinking safely inside the lines, that was just what she needed now. But that last time she saw her, at the reunion in Portland last month, Ellen was so aloof, and it was clear she didn't like Jay. Still, she was coming now and that was what mattered.

Outside the night seemed darker than night ever is, the road narrower, the pavement rougher. She stared hard ahead, relieved to focus on the drive. The road *was* narrower. Only two lanes going north. She watched for signs overhead, signs to the right, signs that would confirm her suspicion she'd taken the wrong arm on an interchange, that she was not on the 5, the fast road north, but had veered off onto the old road, I-99, that lurched through Fresno, Atwater, Modesto, Manteca. By the time she spotted a 99 sign, she was resigned. The road would take her to San Francisco, just more slowly. She had the time.

Still, it was not a good sign. It was not even enough to blot out the question of just what made Ellen dislike—no, not dislike—be suspicious of Jay. So Jay had been talking to her boyfriend, the old guy with the railroad, so what? St. Enid's reunions didn't offer much. She was lucky Jay had found anything at all to interest him.

Why did Jay agree to go?

But he didn't *agree* to go; he wanted to go. She had no interest in St. Enid's alumnae; there were no school memories she wanted to savor. Jay was the one who'd found the invitation in the mail, who'd insisted it would be a campy addition to the weekend. The reunion and the gun show in Idaho were just addenda to whatever he was up there for. And the picnic had been his gift to her for enduring the gun show.

What was he up there for? She didn't know. Of course, she didn't know. Why didn't you ask, Ellen would say. Liza's hands tightened on the steering wheel. The big bushy plants on the center divider waved threateningly, lurching nearer when the headlights hit them. The road was too narrow, only two lanes; it was too easy to be followed here.

Why didn't she ask? Ellen didn't understand what it was like to not have to worry about keeping secrets, to not watch your every word as if it were coming from the mouth of a

29

stranger who wasn't sharp enough be trusted. Ellen Baines had no way of understanding the joy of drinking a glass of wine without ratcheting her guard tighter, the relief of letting a lover see her body in the light and knowing he would ask no questions. Respecting Jay's reserve had been a small price for it. "Venture capitalist" had been a good enough description of Jay's work for cocktail talk. Helping start-ups get started sufficed for the business and professional set. Making it possible for orphan drugs to reach the sick took care of the liberals. What goddamn difference did it make if he chose not to discuss his business with her?

Because he was dead. Because killers had shot him, shot at her, followed her all the way to Malibu trying to kill her.

"Oh, shit!" Her face went hot with shame. She'd called Ellen without thinking. How could she have been so needy? So utterly selfish? If she got Ellen out here, Ellen could end up dead, too. How could she do this to Ellen? How could she do it to Mrs. Baines? Tears slipped down her cheeks. Of course she couldn't. She had to stop her. The skin around her eyes flushed at the thought of doing without Ellen, the thought of going on alone with killers after her. "I have to," she insisted aloud.

Ahead was a *Food Gas* sign. Liza yanked the wheel right, onto the off ramp and pulled up in front of the restaurant.

She raced for the double doors, in through the foyer. There were two phones and two men using them. She ducked into the safety of the ladies' room and pulled the stall door closed behind her.

When she came out of the stall a haggard middle-aged woman in clothes just like hers was staring at her . . . in the mirror. She hardly recognized the drawn gray-skinned face with the long blond hair. She was twenty-eight years old; she'd always been beautiful. Now she looked like an outtake from a B movie. Definitely a woman witnesses would remember if the killers came asking.

Warily, she eyed the food court. The counters were filled mostly with men. Again, she realized she had no idea what Jay's killers looked like. She bought popcorn and chocolate, looking over her shoulder as the clerk took an eternity to pick her change out of the cubicles in her drawer. Clutching the

30

money, she ran to the phone, almost dropping her handful of change as she felt around in her pocket for the card with Ellen's number.

Relief washed over her when Ellen said, "Hello."

"Ellen, don't come. I'm sorry. Listen, I'll explain . . ." It was not Ellen on the phone; it was her message recording. It announced she was out of town.

As Liza hung up, a wave of relief washed over her, followed by a sickening wave of guilt. They pushed her outside. In the pre-dawn light she checked the sidewalk—empty but for a teenaged couple with a squirming baby—and raced for her blue car. She let Felton out, shivering as he snuffled and shat. She watched the restaurant door, checked the parked cars.

The sky was no longer black, but gray; the air still night-cold. It was just before dawn, as it had been on the trips with Jay to the Sierra. She could almost hear Jay . . . She *could* hear Jay again. "Come on, Felton." She plunked Felton back in the car, ran for the phone and dialed home. It rang three times and there he was, telling the world the Silvestris were away from the phone. There was that little laugh in his voice, as he said, "a-waaay from the phone" like he had in the loft at the end of delicious nights a-waaay from the phone. She could see his nose wrinkling, his dark blue eyes crinkling with his grin, feel him slipping his hand around her ribs.

"You have one message."

Without thinking, she pushed the button.

"Liza, Francis Bentec. Call me. There's no hiding out. Don't think you fooled me with that bit about heading to Mexico. I know where you're going and what you're driving— a blue Firebird. You're over your head, Liza. Every patrol officer in L.A., every highway patrolman in the state is watching for you. I've got connections all over the state. There's no way you can disappear. Call me."

She dropped the phone and ran for the car. It was getting light out and her little shadow of safety was gone.

She drove with her gaze on the rearview mirror. She had to get out of California. Nevada was what?—a hundred miles to the east? Two, three hours over the mountains? The highway patrol didn't patrol on switchbacks in the Sierra. She could be safe . . .

Ellen was on her way. She couldn't just abandon Ellen at San Francisco airport.

At the first exit she turned off, away from the freeway and the highway patrol. She didn't even take the old highway. Instead she headed north on city streets.

# Eight

The little bitch was stonewalling. Just like her asshole husband, her dead asshole husband.

Assistant to the Commissioner Francis T. Bentec took a breath and reminded himself that L.A. was his city. Every patrol officer was keeping eyes peeled. Sworn officers in San Francisco P.D., Sacramento, Redding, Eureka, in the highway patrol, county sheriff's departments all over the state would be happy to redeem their chits from him, no questions asked. Things were under control.

He stood at the door of his office, "a modest office," Wyatt from the *Times* had described it, adding, "In the highly competitive arena of internal police politics it's surprising—make that refreshing—to find a man who opts for a small office at the end of the corridor so he can be handy to his boss." The office *was* small, plain, with no view but the delivery dock. It was around the corner, out of sight from Brown's, the Commissioner's. But Brown's convenience had been the last thing on Bentec's mind when he chose the space. And now his search for a secluded office was paying off. No one had reason to wander into the corridor, to overhear, to wonder why the Assistant to the Commissioner was still here after 3 A.M. No one would take a break from his case and wander in to shoot the breeze and ask, "By the way, how come you inserted yourself in the Silvestri homicide?"

Bentec leaned back. The chair cut into Bentec's thorax and an hour in the gym each day, done as religiously as his mother going to Mass, didn't provide enough muscle to cushion his back. He'd kept himself in shape even when it meant dragging into the gym after an all-night case. It hadn't taken a genius to realize that hard bodies rise faster, at least in the world of policing. The Commissioner wasn't about to front up a ball of flab for the TV cameras. At six foot, one-eighty-five, thick hair just graying at the temples—okay, a little help there—Frank Bentec was at ease in front of the cameras.

The gym had been a small part of his campaign for Assistant. Assistant was a stepping stone to the Commissioner's job, which would be a step to one of the real power politics jobs, or so he'd thought. Nineteen years, he'd spent dealing with scum, chancing his life against drug dealers armed better than a third world nation, armed way better than the Los Angeles Police Force. He'd watched them haul in millions, buy lawyers to break cases he'd busted his ass on. They answered to no one, while he reported to the Commissioner, Internal Affairs, the Civilian Police Review Commission, newspaper reporters, columnists, TV reporters and any old lady who called the department to bitch. He'd controlled himself, played the game, been the company boy. He'd gotten himself in line for Commissioner—just in time to see the Commissioner of the Police Department blamed for the Rodney King riots and bungling the O. J. Simpson case. The Commissioner was not a man of power, but a laughingstock.

The day the verdict landed, he made his decision. Keeping an eye out for the right trade to accumulate cash and chits had taken time. He'd turned down drug deals that had landed other cops in the dock; he'd set up stings of syndicate leaders and ending up not with them owning him, but owing him. He'd watched his mouth and his back.

And then Jay Silvestri appeared.

The shipments were small at first. He'd diverted one of the forty containers of weapons headed for melt-down. The deal he had insisted on had been that Silvestri ship it south across the border where the weapons would disappear into the Mexican underworld and never come back to shoot Bentec in the butt. Silvestri paid fast and well. Business had prospered. But this last shipment was a huge jump up, a haul of weapons worthy of an Israeli attack force. Bentec's share alone was five million.

Two days—was it only two days ago?—Bentec had checked

33

with Morales in Tijuana and discovered that Jay Silvestri's supposed buyer down there was no longer in the market because he was no longer alive. When he called Silvestri the asshole'd blown him off. Silvestri was sending the shipment north. No destination, no buyer named. Just north. Six million dollars of weapons could be going to Santa Barbara for all he knew! They could be on the streets of L.A. the next time he stepped outside! He had to slap Silvestri back in line quick. Who could have predicted Silvestri pulling a gun out of his briefcase? Or his wife, the little Lolita, seeing it?

Liza Silvestri, little Liza Cummings, she was the lynchpin of the whole deal. Strange guy, Silvestri, he had thought every single time he'd dealt with him. More to him than the surface gloss. Not what you want in a business associate. Silvestri intrigued him, irritated him and made himself into the kind of challenge that Bentec had rarely found since his move to the Commissioner's Office. Bentec liked a challenge, and he liked to win.

To celebrate their first big deal, he had challenged Silvestri to get them a couple of top-of-the-line hookers, ladies not known to L.A.P.D. He'd been curious, he told himself. Wanted to see what was out there. Good way to create a bond with Silvestri, to check out how Silvestri handled himself. Silvestri had delivered two knock-outs, one Asian, one black, so hot Bentec thought he'd have a coronary making up his mind. When Silvestri let him have both he'd been like a kid at Christmas. He'd been so eager, it scared him.

The second time Silvestri's great magnanimous gesture pissed him off. Silvestri was winning. He made his choice and left Silvestri with the other whore. But what was the matter with the guy? How could he sit in the living room of the hotel suite, smoking and chatting while the second bedroom lay fallow? He wasn't a fag. Why put himself through the agony? Was he so fucking controlled? Was he saving it for his wife? Bentec had done a double take. Maybe the guy really was saving it for his wife. That pleased him. The wife, then, she was his Achilles heel. He didn't know yet that she was Liza Cummings.

So he pushed Silvestri. The next time he insisted on using Silvestri's house in Malibu, the wife's house. He pressed him only so far—he was every bit as controlled as Silvestri—and didn't try to use the connubial bedroom. He didn't want Mrs. Silvestri to find a lipstick stain or a semen stain or any stain that would make her ask questions. Not yet, anyway. Not till he needed to pull the leash tighter on Silvestri. It was an elegant arrangement.

Too elegant. He'd been so sure of his hand on the choke collar that he gave Silvestri extra slack about the buyer. *The buyer insists on anonymity!* Shit! Any other time he would have laughed that out of the water. But—admit it—he'd been so confident that with his elegant scheme nothing could go wrong.

Until Silvestri's wife pulled in the garage unexpectedly and he'd had to grab his pants and his whores and run for the beach, clambering into clothes as he went. In the flurry he'd kicked his nine-millimeter somewhere under the damned bed, where he'd have needed to be a gorilla to reach it.

Then things went down one, two, three. First, he spotted Silvestri in his convertible with a knock-out blonde and he was only too pleased to pull alongside and command Silvestri to follow. Second, he discovered the blonde was Mrs. Silvestri, and that she had been the Lolita. For an instant he'd stood staring at the asp tattoo, thinking: Just how much of a threat was it going to be to expose adultery to a Lolita? Then he'd clicked on how useful the little lady's seamy history could be to him. He was still staring at the tattoo, watching her squirm. For days after, he waited for a phone call from Silvestri, ready to hear him squirm. Instead, Silvestri had offered him the five million dollar deal.

Now Silvestri was dead and his own nine-millimeter was lying under Silvestri's guest bed. And Heron had panicked when he heard Liza burst out of the garage; he'd forgotten all about the gun and went flying after her. Heron's second damned screw-up! Bentec smacked his fist into his desk. He had to find Liza Silvestri, to find the shipment's arrival time in Richland. Without that he wasn't going anywhere but to the gas chamber. And his own gun under Silvestri's bed would put him there.

Bentec took a minute to decide who to bring in on the search. Joe Potelli in Highway Patrol. Potelli had been the first guy outside L.A.P.D. he'd brought in on the deal. Allying with CHP had been the smart move then; it'd be the smart move now. He dialed.

"Potelli here." It was clear from Potelli's voice that he'd woken him up—it was nearly four in the morning.

"Hey, Joe. Frank Bentec, here. Remember the Pope Jewelry store case ten years ago or so?"

"Jesus, Frank, it's four o'clock in the fucking morning. Oh . . ." He'd be realizing Bentec wasn't calling to shoot the breeze. He'd be waiting for the connection. "You mean with the hot little blonde Lolita?"

"Yeah, that's the one."

"The little number with the tattoo, huh?"

He could tell Potelli was picturing the asp rising between those nubile breasts, its mouth open ready to take a bite out of the left one. Potelli'd be remembering that photo.

"Helluva artist." Potelli repeated the comment that had made the departmental rounds with the surveillance camera shot. Little Liza Cummings adorned more locker rooms than Wanted notices.

"Here's the thing, Joe. Guess who the girl, Liza Cummings, grew up to be—the wife of the guy who got his guts spread all over that unfinished loft downtown. She's Liza Silvestri now. And she's on the lam. I need—*we* need—to get her in custody and fast, you follow me? Priority one. And confidential."

"She armed and dangerous?"

"You know her history, Joe. Tell your men to take no chances. Call me the instant your guys spot her. She's the key to this case. If you get her, keep her locked up and silent, you follow me? She's driving a blue Firebird rental car, license number five vee pee el one nineteen. Most likely headed north."

Bentec could hear the swish of sheets—Potelli pushing himself up. Potelli realizing that the dead man was Bentec's connection to the shipment, realizing that the girl with the asp between her tits could take a twenty year bite out of him.

"Frank?"

"What?" He let an edge of irritation show through.

36

"Nothing," Potelli said in that nervous tone Bentec had come to expect when men considered challenging him and thought better of it. "Never mind, Frank. I'll get the word out."

# Nine

Ellen Baines pressed her knees against the magazine pouch and pushed back in her airline seat. Harry Cooper, who thought train travel was the civilized way to go, should only see her now, in Coach, wedged between the guy with the computer clacking on his tray table, his elbow poking over the armrests like an auxiliary wing, and the woman next to the window flapping pages of a natural supplements catalog. Ellen had made the mistake of glancing past her out the window. At that, the woman launched into a discussion of mercury build-up in the body tissues and cilantro extract tablets needed to leech it out. When Ellen closed her eyes the woman had raised her voice and launched into the history of how she and her husband found their calling in supplements.

Liza, Ellen reminded herself over the din, had never been a planner. Impetuosity was her charm, its debris the aftertaste she left. The first leg of this trip Liza had arranged had been First Class, and Ellen had to admit, she loved it. First Class, with its wide seats, foot rests, its fresh-squeezed orange juice, and coffee served on better china than she had at home. It was so Liza, that sweet generosity, with no thought that with her husband dead she might not have that kind of money anymore.

And so Liza to overlook the second leg. Just like in college—Liza'd done that one great impulsive favor and then almost canceled it out by climbing up the ivy and rapping on her dorm-room window at three in the morning. If the dorm mother had found out, both of them would have been expelled. Ellen felt a shiver down her back, only a little one now. After all, ten years had passed. And even back then she had thought to

37

check the ivy before anyone spotted the broken branches. Because she did think ahead.

If Liza'd thought ahead— But Liza didn't, not then, not now. And so, Ellen grumbled silently, she'd been the last passenger on this overbooked flight. She'd been held up at the door. Eyeing the jammed aisle, she'd said to the stewardess, "Are there any seats left or should I just crawl up in the overhead bin?"

"Fat chance of copping a bin."

Now, elbows pressed to her sides, and afraid to look in the direction of the windows, she downed the last of the Coke. Two cubes made one-hop landings on the laptop man's lap.

"Hey!" He swatted frantically.

"Sorry."

"Look, I'm trying to work here."

Pointedly, she shifted her elbow onto the armrest he had commandeered. "I know."

"There's little enough space—"

"I know."

"There's no leg room, not for a man—"

"My knees have been in the magazine pocket so long the stewardess will be picking them up as litter."

He glanced from his computer, to her legs and back.

Maybe, she thought, he would have jerked his attention back to the flickering screen even if she'd had legs like Liza's, but it would have taken more of an effort. And the man's pained expression would have been the result of self-control rather than remorse at a screen gone blank. So there it was: legs less sexy than a spreadsheet. In college they had been long thick legs. Newel posts with shoes. They had suited her long thick body, her straight brown hair and her square face with nose that looked too serviceable to ever be broken.

But that was ten years ago and life had slimmed her down. One of the things she'd learned by the time she left Portland was that the easiest way to lose weight is to diet. Unless you're in love, if you lose weight as a by product it's because you're sick or terrified or miserably depressed. She hadn't had to diet. And despite all that caused the loss of twenty-five pounds, it was still better to be lanky. She looked down at her knees;

38

they were covered with her brown skirt. Maybe even Liza's legs didn't garner stares when she was wearing brown. Maybe, but Ellen doubted it.

The crack of plastic on plastic startled her. The laptop was shut, the man gazing straight ahead. He lifted up and for a moment she thought he was headed to the bathroom, but the move was preliminary to reshuffling his cases under the seat. He settled a briefcase on the tray table and reached for the airline's phone over *her* tray table.

A bad flight should be the worst that happens, she reminded herself. Liza would be happy if it were the worst thing in her life. Oh, God! The thought of Liza pierced her anew, as if all the flight fuss had erased every pang she'd already had. She owed Liza, well, tons. Whatever she could do to help, she would do. She'd figure how to get Jay's body from the police, find an undertaker, a grave—or better yet cremation and dispersal at sea—Jay Silvestri bought a house on the ocean; he must have liked the ocean, why not spend eternity in it?

And definitely she would monitor that tone. What she could do for Liza was pretend her dead husband hadn't been a sleaze—at least till Liza realized he was. Surely Liza would want, would *need* to know why her husband had been shot.

Which was a good question. What could Jay Silvestri have been doing to get himself shot?

Maybe Harry gleaned some idea from that conversation with him in Portland. There was no answer when she had called Harry from the airport. It had been before 6:00 A.M. then, but she wouldn't have been surprised to find Harry at work. He'd already begged off from their first foray into opera Saturday—tonight, she realized. To get the tickets, he had moved heaven and earth, or as he'd put it "Union Pacific and Southern Pacific and all cars between engine and caboose." It wasn't his fault the UP strike had backed up everything on tracks west of the Mississippi and had him slogging sixteen hours a day to find alternate routes and extraordinary means to quick start two hundred metric tons of rice out of Stockton, ten thousand crates of frozen French fries out of Idaho. Senior Freight Manager at the major hub in K.C. was a damned big job, a big promotion from peripheral hub in Portland. At 50, Harry viewed it as his penultimate step up the ladder, or as he put it, forward to the engine. He was the best and he'd beam when she reminded him. She loved to see that smile on his serious face. But the price was that it spurred him on to route talk, his daring forays into rerouting, his victories over sun and snow, his war against slowdown. Even she found her eyes glazing. The move to Kansas City which Harry assumed would cement their relationship had spotlighted what she'd avoided seeing in Portland, that the relationship was already too solid, too bland and unvarying. It was a prison with the sweetest jailer in the world. She'd known it as soon as the moving van pulled away; she just couldn't bring herself to tell Harry.

But Jay Silvestri hadn't looked bored listening to Harry at the reunion. He didn't have the too-wide eyes and tight mouth she'd come to recognize on the faces of those trying desperately to appear interested. Silvestri really was interested. She'd heard him asking Harry to clarify something. He'd nodded as Harry repeated his theory about time variance as opposed to mileage.

Jay Silvestri was hardly a freight and sidings kind of guy. So why had he bothered with Harry? The reason had to be something about railroads. But what? Why? It just didn't make any sense. It certainly couldn't have been connected with him getting shot. But still . . . It made her uneasy. She'd try Harry again from her hotel.

Then she'd see what Liza knew, and what she really thought of Jay. Surely Liza could see what was obvious to everyone else . . . Then again, she did marry the man. Maybe she saw what she wanted to see. But she couldn't go on choosing her own view of reality. She'd have to start planning ahead instead of trusting to instinct.

Still, if Liza hadn't gone on instinct she never would have dared stride into the dean's office at St. Enid's and announce, "There is something very disturbing going on here." If she'd analyzed ahead she would have pictured Dean Ingles pooh-poohing her. It must have been instinct that led her to dress in black, with medium heels and the most subtle of make-up and give ancient Miss Ingles the feeling that if a sophisticated girl from Los Angeles found the situation disturbing it must be shocking indeed.

40

"Marcus! Jed Bakerman here," the laptop man shouted into the airplane phone.

Ellen jolted against his briefcase.

He nearly dropped the phone grabbing it. "I'm trying to do business here."

"I know. We all know."

She turned to the woman by the window whose catalog was open to a two-page spread on "The Miracle of Flax Seed for Health and Regularity," and whispered, "Talk about constipated! Sheesh."

She tapped the man. "I'm getting up now," clambered around him, and the phone cord and headed down the aisle.

Twenty minutes later when she was forced back to her place by landing preparations, the woman had moved to her seat, had her hand on the man's arm and was going on about putrefying residue in the colon lining.

"Stay where you are," Ellen said, climbing over the two of them.

She looked down at San Francisco Bay and across it the skyline of San Francisco, where Liza was waiting.

Liza had removed Mom's big fear of losing her job. Suddenly, Ellen had the freedom to leave home. She had taken it and moved to Portland. And if things hadn't worked out there, at least for one spring and summer life had been magic. Which were two seasons of magic she would never have had at St. Enid's. Would never have had without Liza.

The plane was late. Passengers dislodged carry-on luggage like freeing moose from bread boxes. When she made it to the gate Liza wasn't there. "I'll meet you at the gate, Ellen, no problem," Liza had insisted. But there had been a problem. Traffic? An accident? Or merely Liza not planning ahead?

Or was it worse, lots worse? Could Liza have been shot, too? Suddenly Liza's husband's death was becoming too real. It was all becoming too real and she realized she had grumbled and speculated, concentrated on memories and irritations, all to keep at bay the awful thought that whatever caused Jay's death could be threatening Liza.

There was a side of Liza she couldn't imagine, she knew that. If Liza was dead, too . . . A huge sense of sorrow, of waste swept through her. There was something so unfinished

41

about Liza, as if she were still the sweet, impulsive teenager standing at the door to the world. In an odd way Liza hadn't lived enough to die, not yet. Tears welled. She didn't move till a family jostled around her, pointing at the monitor and talking about the one-thirty flight from Seattle.

Liza wasn't dead. She couldn't be. Not the girl who tromped into Miss Ingles's office and announced she'd seen a very disturbing thing in the cafeteria kitchen, so unsettling that she couldn't bring herself to go into it. That she had come to St. Enid's to get away from that kind of atmosphere and now . . . Not the girl who had led Dean Ingles to the kitchen, positioned her outside the window where she would see Mr. Sleem's slimy hand squeezing Mom's butt, and where she couldn't help see poor Mom's humiliation.

Mr. Sleem was long gone now and Mom was cafeteria manager. And Liza could not be dead before there was a chance to make things okay for her.


# Ten


Liza's back felt like wet cement, her skin sandpaper. She could barely sit up, barely sit still. The numbers on her digital watch blurred. 2:32?

2:32 P.M.! Ellen's plane was due at 1:30! Now Ellen would be muttering, "Damn Liza, she never plans ahead!" And once again, she'd be right.

Had Ellen been waiting all this time? No, of course not, not Ellen. She'd have gone to the hotel. Liza took a deep breath. Maybe she should stop and call Ellen at the hotel. But she couldn't bear to get off the freeway and deal with city streets again. Not and get lost again as she had on and off all night paralleling Route 99. At dawn she'd decided to chance the freeway and then she'd made the wrong turn on the interchange with 580 to Oakland and San Francisco and was halfway to Sacramento before she realized it and miles farther before she could loop around. All the time, she'd had to keep an eye out for Bentec's highway patrol buddies looking for a blue Firebird.

With relief, she ditched car—and her trail—in San Francisco, hailed a cab and, being obsessively careful, headed not to Ellen's hotel but to the St. Francis. There'd be nothing to connect her to a room in the Rosewood Hotel in the name of Ellen Baines. The cab ride was less than ten minutes, but sitting in the back seat, looking out the window at the cable cars turnaround, the old-time trolleys, and afternoon shoppers, she felt herself regaining control. A bicycle messenger shot across the intersection inches in front of the cab, and the cabbie, a woman with a mop of gray curls, screeched to a stop, rolled down the window, and yelled, "Hey! You dropped something back there!" She caught Liza's eye in the mirror. "His brains."

Liza laughed. When the driver pulled up in front of the St. Francis, Liza doubled the tip, and said, "I'd appreciate you not mentioning the pig."

"No problem. Anyone asks, you're just another fare from the airport. I got assholes on bikes to think about; I can't be looking in the back seat. But listen, good luck, sister."

The cabbie's warmth invigorated her. As she lifted Felton from the seat she could tell she was a different woman than the frantic girl in jeans with the pig who'd thrown herself into the cab. She had learned to shift into the comfort of a role. By the time she was fifteen she was a pro. Then the policeman probably didn't realize she was that young when he stammered out, "There's been an accident. Cadillac over the edge of Coyote Canyon. Neither of your parents survived." It was she who had comforted him, she who had called her grandmother, she who never once mentioned the words drunk or suicide. She'd played her role so well he would never have guessed she'd already handled worse.

As the cab pulled off, she covered Felton with her jacket. In San Francisco the only thing that could make her stand out was her pig.

By the time she trudged up the half flight of steps to the Rosewood Hotel's etched-glass double doors, she was relieved to uncover her squirming bundle, and pause to accommodate the man opening them for her.

"Here, let me." He was tall, spare, boy-next-door handsome in a worked-at way. The blue of his crewneck matched his eyes. Eyes that disrobed her before she was over the threshold. She relaxed. This was one game she knew.

"Welcome to the Rosewood. How can I be of assistance, madam? May I take your pig?"

Him she did not offer a smile. His kind needed to be made to work for it. She put Felton on the floor and strolled to the counter.

The check-in clerk would never be a player. He was a set of squishy circles one atop another, the topmost of which held eyes stuck open at "too wide."

"My friend has already checked in. Ellen Baines. Would you tell her Liza is here?"

"Of course."

She could feel the tall guy's eyes on her back. Could she be gay? he'd be wondering. He'd be eyeing her butt and wondering whose hand would end up on it.

"Ms. Baines is on the phone," the clerk said.

"I'll just go up then."

"You can't do that."

Him she gave the smile. She was not going to get into discussing revealing room numbers to strangers. She scooped up Felton and held him out to the clerk. "Your management is probably fussy about pigs, even beautifully trained minia-ture pigs. I wouldn't dream of putting you on the spot about it. So, just keep him behind the desk while I go up and get her. We'll be down—" she winked—"in two shakes of a pig's tail. She's in room six, right?"

"No, sixteen."

"Thanks."

She turned, making the briefest of eye contact with the tall one, just enough to get him thinking that maybe she was not gay, after all. No point burning bridges unnecessarily. Then she headed for the stairs. Room sixteen was probably on the top floor, but she wasn't about to ask. The momentum was changing; both men had been leaning back taking her in, but now they were coming to the end of the arc and were about to swing forward into actions that would not be beneficial to her.

44

# Eleven

Frank Bentec levered himself out of his desk chair. His back was tight, his neck was stiff and his hands felt frozen into claws from holding the phone. He hadn't been off the line five minutes in the last hour, what with getting calls from the homicide unit at the crime scene, from the lab, from the clerk in Files running Liza Cummings Silvestri. He'd issued a directive that all departments report to him. Two days from now captains would be asking why the Assistant to the Commissioner had nosed his way in. By then, he'd be gone. The phone buzzed again. Potelli, wanting his hand held.

"Shift the perimeter north," he said, using jargon to calm Potelli. "She's been on the move for twelve hours, so figure twelve hours out of L.A. Take a couple off for sleep. She's got to be going north. I've hooked up with the Inspection stations at Needles, Blythe, Vidal Junction and Algodones; she hasn't tried crossing into Arizona. So either she's running north or she's holed up off-road somewhere, and if you recall her, Joe, she's not an off-road type of gal. No, trust me, she's moving north. We've covered every likely road out. I've got an A.P.B. to all the bridges and the park police. It's just a matter of time. So shift the perimeter all the way to Santa Rosa now and we'll be more than covered."

"Right, Frank," Potelli said a little sheepishly.

" 'S'okay. It's right to be careful here. We've got to be on top of this and make sure we get to her first, you follow me?"

"Oh yeah."

"Good, Joe. Check back in an hour if we don't have her before then." He could hear the fear in Potelli's voice, like a buzzing wire about to ignite a fire. He'd handled that potential blaze, but he was nowhere near as calm as he sounded.

But by now they should have had Liza Silvestri. She couldn't drive forever. *He* could barely keep awake. A civilian like

45

her—with luck she'd drive into a tree. But no, not die. He needed her. She would know the specifics needed for the transfer, the weapons for his six million dollars—his five million plus Silvestri's one million, which he could "inherit." Silvestri would have told her.

Even if he hadn't told her, she'd know. Wives always know where their husbands keep things, documents, addresses, phone numbers. She was headed north, north to the transfer point. If she didn't know about Richland, Washington, she would have taken the fast way out of California, to Mexico or east to Arizona or Nevada. But she was gutting it out, moving north, heading to Richland because she knew what to do when she got there.

The phone jarred him. "Inspector Bentec." It took him a moment to sift the accent and decipher the message—from a car-rental clerk. In regard to his request for information, Liza Silvestri had turned in her car at San Francisco.

"Thank you." Bentec reached for his Rolodex. San Francisco. That was manageable. He'd already alerted a couple guys in the department there. He'd get back to them with this news, get them on the horn to the cab and limo companies. For the first time in twelve hours Frank Bentec smiled. This was the part of the chase he loved. The hounds were closing. The fox had her tail to the wall. Now it was just a matter of getting her before the dogs starting nipping at her flanks.

# Twelve

"This whole trip," Ellen Baines grumbled, "it's like a step into a parallel universe." As, she realized, things always had been with bLiza. She hadn't been surprised when Liza didn't show at the airport. She'd even rented not a sensible compact car but a sports car to cheer her up. Now she was beginning to wonder if Liza would ever see it.

Where was Liza? If she was okay, why hadn't she called? And Harry, did Jay Silvestri suck him into whatever it was that got him killed? Could Harry be in danger? She shook her head against even the possibility, turned on the TV, yanked her suitcase onto the Rosewood Hotel's rose-print bedspread and started hauling out clothes. In tissue paper laid out in the middle was the chic black dress for Jay Silvestri's funeral, the one she'd been afraid would be too short and revealing for the opera with Harry. Harry. Was she really just away from him for a couple nights, or was this the end? She tried on the dress again, hoping for a few moments of distraction but even as she eyed herself in the mirror she couldn't shake the question of Harry. And of Jay Silvestri; he'd been talking to Harry, pumping him . . . Jay Silvestri—

Suddenly she realized the name was not being pronounced in her mind, but on the TV.

She grabbed the remote and turned up the sound and stared as the picture shifted from newsroom set to field reporter. A brunette with firm chin, sculpted cheekbones and too-bright blue eyes, was saying, "In a bizarre scene, last night the police found the bullet-ridden body of Jay Silvestri, a local venture capitalist, in the old Farley Building. According to police sources, Jay Silvestri was known as an up-and-coming businessman with a home on the beach in Malibu. Sources close to the investigation say Silvestri's loft space was listed as office space, but was furnished like a vacation house forty years ago. In a note of irony, Silvestri's body was found beneath a sign saying, 'Point *Pleasant* Beach.' Neighbors in Malibu have no explanation why a respected businessman maintained an apartment in a deserted building." Her tone said no explanation was necessary.

"Do the police have any leads, Connie?" the anchor asked. "Any other witnesses?"

"Women's clothing was found at the scene, but no one has come forward. Police are asking anyone who can shed light on this case, to contact Inspector Frank Bentec at the number on your screen. Silvestri's wife, Liza, is missing and police are, frankly, concerned."

"Oh, Jeez, poor Liza." Ellen grabbed for a pencil and wrote the police number on the hotel pad. Even the police suspected she was in danger. Or dead. Well, at least she could disabuse them of that last suspicion. She reached for the hotel phone guide, dialed 8 for long distance and was about to start the number. No wait! Not dead. And not in danger. "Women's clothing was found at the scene." The apartment was a love nest. Oh jeez, they thought Liza's husband was keeping another woman there. They thought— oh jeez—that Liza was the outraged wife and she shot him in his love nest. No wonder they were looking for her. No wonder . . . Oh jeez.

The phone was buzzing its demand for more numbers. She punched in Harry Cooper's. As she listened to the ring, she wondered why she had called; she didn't expect him to be home. But he was.

"Cooper here."

"Harry—"

"El! Where are you?"

"San Francisco."

"Honey, what're you doing out there? You ticked off with me? I know I've been working a lot—"

Did he really know she was leaving? At the least he suspected. Should she just make the break now and save—

"This work thing, El, it'll pass. It's just heavy right now. Once I get . . ."

She let him talk, taking in not his words but the soft, sad voice. She could picture him, fuzzy-haired, rumply-skinned, rubbing his fingers against his cheek and pulling the flesh as if he were a soft clay sculpture not quite set. He was soft all over, a man she could lean into on a cold night, like tonight was going to be. Why was he carrying on about his job now, with Liza's husband dead in his Point Pleasant Beach room? With a start she remembered that she had been annoyed about Harry's work and the opera tickets he'd been too busy to use. It all seemed so far away. "Harry, I'm not mad at you. Listen, huh?"

"You sure you're not mad?"

"Not if you listen! Harry, I'm out here to help Liza Silvestri. I just turned on the TV and saw her husband was shot in L.A." She couldn't bring herself to tell him about the love-nest room. Harry was not a man made for that. Whatever Harry had been discussing with Jay Silvestri in Portland it sure wasn't this.

48

A surge of relief swept through her; it shocked her how concerned she was about Harry. Of course Harry wasn't the type of man to abet a love nest. Harry would never be involved in a seedy apartment for seedy affairs. Whatever got Jay Silvestri killed had nothing to do with Harry. She wished he were here so she could hug him. She could barely keep the unseemly relief from her voice as she said, "It looks as if he kept an apartment for affairs, you know, with other women." Remembering the import of the newscast, she added, "Harry, I think the police think Liza shot him."

She expected the comforting rumble of Harry's voice, the cadence that said, "No need to worry," the low, easy tone that assured, "It'll all work out." But there was a whine of panic in his voice as he asked, "Did she?"

*Of course not!* was almost out of her mouth when she caught herself. "I don't know, Harry."

"Where is she?"

"She was supposed to meet me at the airport. She didn't show. Maybe—"

"Ellen, throw your stuff in a suitcase and check out."

She stared at the receiver as if the holes would mimic Harry's suddenly decisive expression. "Harry, I hate to leave her to deal with all of this on her own."

"She's not eighteen anymore."

"Still, I can't abandon her."

"Go. Right now!" She'd never heard him like that, even through all the hassles moving from Portland. "Jay Silvestri is quicksand. You could get pulled into worse than you think."

"Why, Harry? Pulled into what? I asked you and you wouldn't tell me. Harry, what was it Jay Silvestri said to you in Portland?"

But he wasn't listening. He was talking. "—so trust me, sweetie. Take your suitcase, get a cab to some hotel across town. Don't even stop to check out. Call me when you get there. Go!" He hung up.

"Whew!" That was so unlike Harry. She pressed 8 and his number. "Harry, Jay Silvestri was killed in a love nest. That was nothing to do with you. So tell me . . ." He was still talking, or rather his message was still talking. Okay, she'd

49

go ahead and change hotels and call him from the new one.

Her head was spinning; there was no solid ground at all. She was a practical woman, but her feet were slipping out from under her.

A knock on the door shocked her. Before she thought to ask who was there she'd opened it.

Liza was standing in the doorway.

Liza Silvestri smiled. For the first time in what seemed an eternity, she felt safe. Just like she had walking into Mrs. Baines's parlor, like she had climbing in through Ellen's dorm window. With Ellen here, things would be all right. She looked at Ellen, noted her reliable square face creased with worry, the suitcase she'd been too worried to unpack, and burst into tears.

Ellen Baines had not been looking at her luggage until Liza noticed it. Now Liza spotted the unpacked bags. What must she think? "Oh, Liza!" She wrapped her arms around her and that touch triggered an avalanche of sobs. She held Liza, murmuring syllables for their soft sound. She'd never been this close to Liza, hadn't realized how small Liza was, or maybe how tall she herself was. But Liza felt like a child in her arms, and when she swallowed hard and took a step back she looked like a red-faced little girl in her jeans and T-shirt and too big leather jacket.

"I thought . . . that was a . . . buzzer show." Liza nodded toward the television.

"Oh no." Ellen jumped to turn the set off before another report of Jay Silvestri's death appeared.

"You know, Ellen, like your mom and you watched." Liza swallowed.

She was trying too hard. Ellen wanted desperately to jump in and help but she couldn't figure what she meant. "Liza, what the hell are you talking about?"

Liza smiled, a real but wobbly smile. "A quiz show like you and your mom watched. You two loved them. And I was so jealous."

"Jealous? Liza, you were no slouch. You could have called out the answers as fast as I did."

"But your mom loved seeing you get them first. It was so sweet, her almost answering then catching herself so she could let you go first. She's so great."

Ellen forced a nod. Her mother knew the answers first? How could she have missed that all those years? How slow, how *dense* was she? Mom had let her win? How could . . .

Liza sank down on the bed next to her. "Ellen, I really hated to ask you to come out here. But, I have to tell you, now that you're here I am so so glad."

Ellen focused back on Liza, Liza who needed her now. "Me, too."

She let a beat pass, but they couldn't put reality off any longer. "Liza, the police want you to call them."

Liza felt like she'd been smacked. How could the police know she was here? She'd been so careful. How did they know about Ellen? "The police?"

"It was on the news," Liza heard her say. "On television. I wrote down the police number. I knew you'd want to call and give them whatever they need to find out, uh, what they need."

"They've got a lead on the killers?" Liza asked with desperate hope.

Ellen shook her head. "They're looking for you."

"For me! What about the men who shot him? Don't they even care about them?" If they were only after her, then Bentec was running things, hell-bent to find her, and no one gave a shit about the men who shot Jay. Her stomach clenched, and suddenly all she could see was the loft in L.A. at the moment Jay's fingers touched her skin. She felt the heat of him, smelled the sharp scent of him, heard the doorbell ring. "Oh God!" She sank back against the corner of a desk, using the pain to forestall the next moment—when the door opened, the gun fired. To keep the bullets from smashing into him.

Something pressed into her palm. She screamed.

"Liza, Liza, it's okay." Ellen's hand was on her hand and she looked down at the object in it—a tissue. Ellen was giving her a tissue.

"Here's the number. The police." Ellen held out a piece of paper.

She stared at it; the sheet with lines too wavy to read. "I can't call the police." She couldn't believe she'd said that out loud.

"What do you mean 'can't'?"

*The police are crooks! I don't know what they'd do to me.* She couldn't say that; Ellen would think she was crazy. Frantically she hunted for a story that would make Ellen stay—she'd always been able to come up with a story—but for once nothing surfaced but the truth. "I've got a juvenile record in L.A. The cop in charge remembers me. I can't trust him, believe me. Just take my word, Ellen."

"Liza, this is the police we're talking about. They're looking for you. You better call them before they find you."

"Why—"

"Because, Liza, they figure you walked into that love nest. They figure you saw your husband with another woman and you shot him."

"They said that?"

"The television reporter intimated that. But she had to get her information somewhere."

Liza stared. As shocked as she was, she could tell Ellen was more so. She swallowed, stared Ellen straight in the face—a challenge she never, never made—and said, "And what do you think? Do you think I killed him?"

"Of course not. I mean not unless you were . . . well, you had to or . . ."

Pain cut behind Liza's eyes, radiated out. She felt like her head was exploding. It was the same old thing, people finding out about her, cutting her loose. "Ellen, I thought you were my friend— Is this your idea of friendship?" Her voice was so low, sodden, it didn't even sound real. "Now you're saying I killed Jay—"

"*I'm* not saying that. Reporters, on television, are hinting at it. They're running the story here in San Francisco, hundreds of miles away from L.A. Maybe it's a slow news day or something, but this is a lot of press attention for a shooting. I'm sorry. I don't mean to sound so distant, but that's what you wanted me for, isn't it, to be logical. I thought you'd want me to handle the paperwork and things like that. Maybe help you close up the house. I never imagined . . ."

"No, of course not." Liza felt like she was in the eye of a hurricane now, cooler, a hundred times more logical than Ellen would ever be. The television report chilled her to the bone. Ellen thought it signified a racy story. Maybe so. Maybe her life was racy. But there was nothing in the loft to suggest that; nothing in a police call that would draw reporters running. The impetus here had to be Frank Bentec. Frank Bentec wasn't looking for the killers; he was looking for her. Frank Bentec had tendrils all over the state. He was everywhere. Maybe she should go back and face— No. Not that. Definitely, not that.

She needed time to think. And to sleep. And, oh God, she needed to get Ellen out of here before she got her caught in Frank Bentec's tendrils. She could see Mrs. Baines, dear Mrs. Baines putting an extra helping of chocolate cake on her plate because "a wiry little girl like you needs her sweets." Her stomach churned at the thought of what it would do to Mrs. Baines if anything happened to Ellen. She stared not at Ellen but the wall behind her, trying to blank out fear and longing, everything but what she had to do. "Ellen, I can't thank you enough for coming." Her voice sounded calm now. She kept staring at the wall. "Of course you're right. I'll call the police. But I've been driving all night. I need to get my head clear before I call them. You know the best thing you could do for me? Give me your room here. I need to sleep. Then I'll call the police. By tonight I'll be on a plane back home. Listen, I'm sorry to drag you out here, but maybe you can get a flight—"

"Liza, I'm not leaving you alone to—"

"I'm okay now, Ellen. There's nothing more you can do."

"Liza, what's going on here? I called Harry Cooper and when I told him I was with you he just about panicked. He wanted me to race out of here and go to another hotel. He has to know something about your husband, from their talk in Portland, something to make him react like that."

It was too much. Liza counted on instinct, on being able to react when she had to, but this double whammy when she was so exhausted flattened her. "I don't know."

53

"Why was he even in Portland?"

"Gun show. He went to a gun show." It was the truth. If she hadn't blurted it out she would never have realized that. She'd thought the gun show had been an addendum to Jay's real focus in Portland. Just like the reunion. Now she saw what she'd known but not admitted: Jay Silvestri didn't choose "campy" things like rural gun shows and school reunions for amusements. If he'd had business in Portland and wanted to add on a vacation, he'd have booked the best hotel in town, found the best fish house and the hottest club. If Jay opted for a gun show and the reunion, there had to be a reason. And the picnic at the Richland grade? She was so startled her exhaustion vanished.

"Gun show?"

But Liza wasn't about to go into that, not weird as that was. "Gun show."

"Harry doesn't know anything about guns. Your husband wouldn't have been huddled with Harry about guns."

"Ellen, I can't deal with peripheral things like that now. Look, I can't tell you how much it means to me that you've come, and that you'll lend me your room. But go now."

"I'm not going any—"

"Ellen, you're just in the way now."

"You need someone to help you, Liza."

Ellen's hand was shaking; the tissue she was holding looked like a white flag. There was something so awkward and sweet and so very innocent about her.

Liza took a breath and steeled herself to put on the toughest act she'd ever attempted. "Ellen, if you were able to handle things, you would have kept that slimy cafeteria boss, Sleem, off your mother's butt. You wouldn't have had to wait for me to do it." She had to swallow before she could add the coup de grâce. "You never could handle men. And my problem, Ellen, is all about men. Now go and let me get some sleep."

Liza didn't turn around as Ellen left. She couldn't bear to see her face, that face she would never see again. She stood in the empty room, alone.

# Thirteen

Devon Malloy threw the remote full force into the davenport. The soft thump of plastic into quilting was only
mildly satisfying, but he did not want to break the remote.
He could not afford the time to go out and buy a new one.

His whole adult life had been devoted to Hot Standby—
his one nod to melodrama coining the code name that never
escaped his lips. No children, wife an ex, mother he no longer
spoke to, a career he chose only for the access it gave him to
federal records. If the goddamned government vermin knew
about him they would have to admit he was the all-around
expert on the Hanford Nuclear Site, the most contaminated
acreage in the nation. Getting inside Hanford, opening the
stacks and throwing the government's lies in its face was his
life. It was just a matter of time. As in Free Cell on the
computer, and its 32,000 layouts; every player was defeated
by some layouts, everyone but himself . . . because he was
intelligent, disciplined and he restrained the urge to make a
move before he was certain his plan was foolproof.

He had his plan for Hanford; there was no way the government vermin would keep him out. Not with Silvestri's weapons
. . .He never dreamed he would attain firepower of that magni-
tude. Uzis, hand-held missile launchers, and up. Weapons that
would be the red carpet into Hanford.

And now the asshole Silvestri got himself killed.

Malloy retrieved the remote. He perched on the davenport
facing the blank screen and pressed the ON button to the point
just before it caught, released it, pressed again. The exercise
had become too easy; even so it served to distance him from
emotion about the slime— about Silvestri. He had once killed
a man without experiencing anything but the small concern
over the added complication the corpse created. Hours later
he had driven to a million dollar "ranch house" in Montana

55

and sweet-talked six rich dilettantes into ponying up a million each for the cause. Without hesitation or backward look, he had reeled out an elaborate story of money needed to support major civil unrest with the possibility of violence, something he could not rule out. The dilettantes liked that possibility of minor violence. It made them feel like they were in a militia, the living-room militia. He had gotten his six million in cash, in suitcases so heavy he could barely lift them. Silvestri had run him through hoops—no bearer's bonds, no gold, no wire transfers, only cash.

People called him cold, but he was not emotionless. He was a laser focused on Hanford. Tomorrow he would be laughing and crying, his body overflowing with the warmth of victory when he turned off the mixing pump inside the High Level Waste Storage tanks, let the gases build up, quickly, quickly, and watched them explode.

The rush he always got picturing the tanks splitting apart and the radioactive waste—uranium, iodine-131, strontium-90—spewing into the air uncontrolled, died before it warmed him. He had one shot at Hot Standby, tomorrow, and if he did not find out which train the shipment was on, the weapons would roll on to Pocatello or to Eastport and Canada.

One chance.

# Fourteen

Ellen leaned against the elevator wall. She felt as if the car were tumbling, swirling, as if reality had lost its moorings. She felt as she had in high school, in college, in Portland—the lumpy girl who couldn't handle men. The make-do, the last-minute date. Twenty-four hours ago she had been safe and settled in her apartment overlooking the Plaza, her biggest problem an unused opera ticket. Now she was in a strange city, about to wander out of a strange hotel, away from her friend who decided she wasn't good enough.

She shouldn't have left Liza in that condition. But what

choice did she have? Yeah Liza was upset; yeah things were awful; but still . . .

Liza was out of her life for good. She pushed the button for Lobby and the elderly car mumbled in its supports and began descending. What to do now? Fly home? Had Liza booked a return flight she'd have to change? Jeez, she was too tired to think straight. Tired and starved. The responsible thing to do was go to the police.

The elevator door opened at Lobby Level. Loud, male voices pierced the brocade decorum of the lobby. "Big," one of them insisted. "We have standards in this hotel. We do not have bigs."

Bigs?

*Pigs?*

Why were they carrying on about pigs? The hotel didn't even have a restaurant. Reality really had spun off its moorings.

"He can't stay in the lobby, rooting around for truffles."

San Francisco, indeed.

"Fine!" The man wasn't shouting. He had one of those whiny voices that cuts through noise. "Fine, Larry, just take him up to Ms. Baines's room and tell her we have some standards here."

*Ms. Baines's room!* The doors started to close. Ellen jammed her shoulder in the opening. The doors stuttered. She marched forward, dragging her suitcases.

The lobby was decorated for effect, not comfort—a mauve and gray room, with brocade sofas by an electric fire, carved mahogany chairs on either side of round writing tables lit by lamps with fringed shades. Marble-topped coffee tables with floral arrangements heavy on the weird and pointy. Intricate, and threadbare Oriental carpet. The check-in desk, a decorous marble and mahogany counter, was hidden away in the corner. No guests were present, only the uniformed bell captain and a lanky wavy-haired man with a lanky face, dressed in the San Francisco de rigueur of black turtleneck, tweed jacket, and jeans. There was a bulge under his arm and Ellen wondered if he was wearing a gun. Planted in front of the check-in counter the two men glared mightily at each other.

Ellen thrust her shoulders back, strode up, and poked her

57

suitcases between the two. "I am Ellen Baines, and I'm traveling alone. And I don't appreciate you taking anyone to my room."

All motion stopped, then the two men turned to her, puzzlement nearly transforming them into twins. Behind them, from inside the concierge's office came a squeak.

It was the bell captain who said, "I'm sorry, Ms. Baines, but we cannot allow livestock."

"Livestock?"

"It is a pig."

"*What* is a pig?"

The wavy-hair—Larry—was laughing now. He stepped forward. "Yeah, Daniel, what is a pig? You're working on a doctor of philosophy—just what is a pig?"

Daniel groaned.

"Now, Daniel, 'sounds like' won't do. This is a fine hotel and our guests expect their questions to be answered in words." Larry flashed her a grin. It was a conspiratorial grin produced by a mobile mouth. He leaned a forearm on the check-in counter. Daniel jerked back instinctively and his jaw tightened. In a battle of wits with Larry, the desk clerk was doomed.

She sensed the small wave of nausea before she realized its cause. Daniel. She could have stepped inside the poor little man's skin, his poor inadequate skin that covered his inadequate self. She knew the feeling only too well. Larry was a first-string kind of guy and if the elevator door opened and Liza Silvestri strolled out, he'd be striding over to her as naturally as vermouth to gin. They'd be heading out the etched-glass doors. Daniel would be left organizing his cards as if they were chapters in *War and Peace*. And she? She'd be relegated to the spot beside him, her flush of humiliation and fury cooled by the breeze from the closing etched-glass doors. Because she "never could handle men." Because she'd never be first choice; always make-do.

She turned her back on the tall, so-sure man with his Liza-like irresponsible banter. "I'm checking out—"

But the clerk was already reaching for the concierge door. He pulled it open. A black and white piglet trotted out, squeaking with each step.

Ellen stared. Reality really had lost its moorings.

The pig wrinkled his snout and headed purposefully for the brocade sofa.

Larry laughed. "This is one all-business pig."

Befuddled as she was, Ellen couldn't help laughing, too. "I'm no barnyard expert, but I know what pigs like to do—root. You may not want him rooting in your lobby."

The words were barely out of her mouth before Daniel was across the room and in the process of shooing ineffectually. She scooped up the pig. "Hey, easy, he's not going to contaminate you. He's only a little pig. And, I might add, not *my* pig."

Larry scratched the pig's snout, but it was her he was eyeing, and for a moment she knew how Liza must have felt all the time. Automatically, she shifted to avoid blocking his line of vision, even though there was no Liza-quality woman behind her. But he was definitely smiling at her.

Daniel's whine brought her back to herself. "Your guest—"

"Oh, Liza. Of course." Why was she not surprised that Liza Silvestri was avoiding the police and doing it with a pig? And that she was in danger of being left holding Liza's bacon?

The pig wrinkled his black and white snout. The end was pink, the white a skunk-like stripe up the middle, the black on the rest of its face and ears. It was a cutie and the poor frightened piglet did need her. The pig wrinkled its nose at her, as if the little guy understood that she was the one to count on.

Just like Liza understood. Well, she wasn't taking care of Liza or Liza's pig. She thrust the animal in Daniel's arms. "My friend will be down in a minute. She'll take her pig and leave. I'm checking out."

The clerk jerked back and would have dropped the pig if Ellen hadn't kept her hands on him. He turned as pink as the pig, and as if noting the familial color, the pig tried to nuzzle his neck. Daniel thrust him away like a vial of virus.

She hesitated and took him back, poor scared little fellow. She stood, knowing she should do something but unable to summon up the energy. She should check out. Find another hotel. Or arrange for a van to the airport and just sit there till the next flight to Kansas City. But if she went back now . . .

Or should she find out where the police station was and make a report? But suppose Liza was right about the police . . . Juvenile records were supposed to be sealed. Would the police really remember her this long? Of course, Liza . . . Well, men did remember. Maybe she *was* in danger from them.

She must have looked as overwhelmed as she felt; still it surprised her when Larry, the sexy one, put a hand on her shoulder. "You're too tired to make a decision about this pig. What you need is to sit down, eat something and get some time to pull yourself together. There's a quiet bar next door; they make a good roast beef sandwich. Come on, I'll take you over. Daniel can keep the pig till your friend comes for him."

Daniel stepped behind the counter. "Hey, no way am I—"

The piglet squealed.

Ellen looked down at his round squirming body. She felt so bad for him, and suddenly again for Liza, for herself, for this whole miserable mess.

"Food?" Larry's hand slid down to her arm. She thought of Harry and blushed, and felt stupid. If the man who directed her to food was a sexy guy, what difference did that make? Food and quiet were exactly what she needed before she could decide what to do about Liza and the police and a new hotel and calling Harry and . . . "You never could handle men," Liza had said. Well, she could damn well handle lunch with this one.

The pig wriggled again. She took a deep breath and corralled her concentration on the problem at hand. Giving the pig a little squeeze she plopped him against Daniel's chest.

"Hey, lady, you can't just walk out!"

She opened her wallet and pulled out a twenty. "Keep him till my friend leaves. And don't rush her; her husband just died and she needs time to rest and get herself together too."

The clerk made a show of avoiding looking at the twenty. He pulled himself up straighter and said, "Very well, as a kindness. But inasmuch as you are leaving I will need her name."

"Liza Silvestri."

# Fifteen

Liza stared first at the phone then at the television, her eyes blurring. She should do something, but she was so tired. She didn't know what to do.

But she knew what *not* to do. Calling Bentec headed the list of Not To Do.

She yanked the bedspread loose and pulled the fabric around her. It was stiff, made of some fake fiber that neither wrinkled nor warmed.

It had been fluke that she met Bentec at all, and bad luck he'd seen her that particular night a month ago. She and Jay were sitting at a red light on Venice Boulevard when Bentec's unmarked car pulled up next them. Jay'd been so smug about scoring a dinner reservation at Cleo when the normal wait was a year that he was noticing nothing around him. She couldn't help but smile remembering him going on and on about the underappreciated novelty of driving only city streets—as if she didn't realize how hard he was trying to cover up his déclassé glee. He'd been sitting in the convertible, his arm around her shoulder, his fingers tracing the deep neckline of the dress he'd just given her. The V-neck was two inches lower than anything in her closet, so low it revealed the snake tattoo that had seemed racy and daring when she got it at fourteen. Then the asp's open mouth arched lasciviously around her left breast made her feel sophisticated. It hadn't been long before she realized it was all too memorable. By the time she met Jay almost a decade later, she was keeping it covered to shield herself from remembering. In a city where showing cleavage was the norm, people assumed she had opted for provocative modesty.

But Jay had given her the dress and that one special night

61

she'd worn it. After all, she'd reasoned, their waiter at Cleo was hardly going to endanger his tip by looking down his nose at her. There'd be no one else to see it. And the black clingy fabric had looked every bit as terrific as Jay had predicted.

Jay'd had the top down on the Mustang, a CD of Betty Carter doing "Close Your Eyes" oozing from all four speakers. A horn yowled from the next car and the driver had motioned him to follow. Irritation had sparked Jay's face. "Five minutes, max, Babe," he'd said and cut across two lanes to the curb. He was on the sidewalk next to Bentec before the engine stopped.

Now she wished she could recall what Bentec had said to Jay. But all she remembered was his glance down at the tattoo, the leer he didn't bother to hide. It all happened in two seconds. Bentec made no comment to her, but she saw the truth. She had let herself believe the lawyers and social workers and the judge who insisted that juvenile records were sealed. The truth? Nothing is secret. A juvenile record like hers certainly wasn't secret. Frank Bentec had not been a cop on that case. But he had seen the surveillance photo, camera looking down on her naked fourteen-year-old breasts and the tattoo. He had seen it because that photo in the supposedly sealed case had been copied and recopied till it garnered leers in station-house locker rooms all over Los Angeles.

When she became Liza Silvestri she'd thought she was safe from Elizabeth Cummings's past.

Jay had seen her go pale. He'd cut Bentec short, drove to a boutique, bought her a lace turtleneck to wear to dinner, and never asked a question. The tattoo was gone now, gone too late, way too late.

If she had told Jay the whole story, would he have been prepared? Would he be alive now?

Frank Bentec could answer that question, but she knew better than to get anywhere near him. She pulled the bedspread tighter around her, but it did no good.

The dark TV screen stared accusingly. But Jay's death wasn't going to make it onto CNN. It would only be mentioned on a local channel—

But wait. *Local* would be L.A., and Ellen saw it here. Why

was it such big news it made San Francisco television? She shivered; the bedspread fell off and she didn't bother picking up its useless fibers.

The room had a mini bar. She could have one of those little bottles of gin or vodka or brandy. She could drink one after another till they drowned this day.

Or she could close her eyes for a few minutes. She'd be able to think if she weren't in such a fog of exhaustion.

She nudged off her shoes, pulled the blanket loose and slipped under it. She'd just rest for a few minutes. Then she'd decide what to do.

The door burst open. A man was back-lit by the hall light. *God, he's going to shoot Jay!* Liza's scream tore at her throat.

The man was running at her. She screamed louder. She tried to push Jay out of danger. She couldn't see Jay. There were blankets in her way. She wasn't in their loft but in a strange bedroom. In bed.

"Lady, lady, please! Please stop screaming. You're going to get me fired!"

She recognized him, the clerk she'd left watching Felton. The poor man was more terrified than she was. But the sound of the gun shots in the loft still resounded inside her flesh. She was too frozen to speak. It was all she could do to stop the momentum of her screams.

She could hear creaking—doors—outside in the hallway; mutterings she couldn't translate into words; feet pounding. The room was dark. How did it get dark? It was afternoon, a minute ago.

"Lady, are you okay?" The guy was shaking.

She forced a nod, but it was like moving a rusted lever. And still, inside, she could feel the icy terror of the loft and Jay's body sliding down hers to the floor. She had to focus, now. She moved a hand toward the clerk, held it out so he could not avoid taking it in his though the movement was clearly foreign to him. But it worked. The warmth of his hand, the touch of skin drew her away from her frigid inner body to the skin, the room, the present. Just in time. Another man— security, she knew how to spot them—strode through the doorway. "It's okay," she said. "I was having a nightmare."

63

Security looked from her to the clerk. "Yeah, well, what's he—"

"He came up to remind me about my pig." She gave him a weak smile. Her face still felt frozen. It was the best she could do. "I really appreciate that accommodation. Watching him for an hour makes a big difference. It's the reason my firm uses this hotel. But, I guess management's already told you that." She let go of the clerk's hand, pushed back the bedspread and swung her legs to the floor so the security man could see she was dressed. "I appreciate your concern." She shot him her best dismissive smile. If Jay were here he'd shake the man's hand, give him a fifty and shut the door. This guy'd have to make do with a smile.

As soon as the door closed behind him the clerk drew himself up to his full five foot eight. "Lady, this isn't your room. It isn't even your friend's room anymore. She checked out hours ago. You can't camp in here and—"

She didn't get up or even look at him. Putting a hand gently on his arm she said sweetly, "Hotels don't just fire clerks for breaking in on unaccompanied women, they blackball them. I just saved your bacon, honey."

"Yeah, but you still can't—"

She stood, stretched, caught him out of the corner of her eye watching her stretch. "I didn't intend to sleep. I've had a hard day. What time is it?"

"Nine fifteen."

"Nine fifteen at night? Omigod. It was just three in the afternoon. Felton, is he—"

"The pig?"

"Miniature pig. Is he—"

"Hungry, is what he is. What he *was*. He ate an entire tray of custards."

"Oh, no. Did it make him sick?" The look on his face said she'd asked the wrong question. She revised. "Is your kitchen okay?"

"Yeah after half the maintenance crew swabbed it out."

She rejected her first rejoinder. "Oh, I am sorry."

He nodded the most minimal of acceptances. "Lady, you and your pig, you can't stay here."

"Of course." She glanced around the beige room for Jay's

64

leather jacket. "I'm going to go to the airport and see my friend off."

There was a flicker of oddness on his bland face. Another woman would have missed that, but Liza was a natural at reading people. She could react to their thoughts before they knew they had them. It was how she'd survived. What made him doubt her plan? There was no way to avoid asking, "Did Ms. Baines leave me a message?"

"Nope." A smug nope.

"She just left?"

"Well, not just."

Liza clenched her teeth hard. The incidents of the day came back to her now like a line of drunks staggering home, the last one herself kicking Ellen out of her own room and goading her out of town. Cold shot through her; She was so alone, without Jay, without even Ellen. Her throat tightened.

She dug her fingernails into her palms. *Think about Ellen. Be glad she's getting away.*

She took a breath to bring herself back to the situation at hand, sat back on the bed and patted the spot next to her. "Okay, tell me what happened."

"I don't—"

"Of course you do. What happened?"

"She went with Larry Best."

"The tall guy I met in the lobby? The letch?"

"Yes."

"Where was she going?"

"To the bar next door . . ."

"And?"

"A hotel room he found for her."

"Which means his room?" Whew! What about the boring railroad guy? She really didn't know Ellen Baines at all.

The clerk shrugged.

"Where is his room?"

"I don't—"

"Yes, you know that, too. Where?"

"I can't tell you—"

She turned to face him head on. There was no charm in this look of hers. "You broke into my room. The security guard found you holding my hand. You were intimidating me.

65

I was too scared to tell him the truth. You . . ." There was no need to go farther. The color had drained from his face, leaving it the same shade as his uniform and him one five foot eight beige capsule of frustration. "Where did he take her?"

"The Orestes, on Nob Hill." He paused and she knew he was trying to decide whether to reveal something more. His face shifted not into a gotcha smirk but a more neutral expression. He hadn't given her the full story, but that was okay. This kind of story she could figure out on her own.

"Don't worry, lady, she'll be back. Her car's still here. I know, the key is at the desk."

The next move was clear but Liza let a beat pass. "Okay, I'm going to let you free of this whole thing. I'll take her the car. Come on, let's go so the maids can get this room done." She grabbed her things, finger-combed her hair and kept moving.

The elevator car came before she could pull her hand off the button. A couple in thick turtlenecks and suede jackets cut short their conversation and Liza and her clerk joined the silence.

In the four-floor ride she ran through three dead-end scenarios about the car key but when she reached the check-in counter the transaction required nothing more than putting out her hand. "Don't tell them I'm coming."

For the first time the clerk smiled. "No, ma'am."

She noted the pause before his smug answer and it made her uneasy. But her best move was to move. She picked up Felton, a sated, sleepy pig, and took the stairs to the garage.

She almost walked past the shiny black Camaro in slot 4. *Ellen* chose *that*? Her view of Ellen was really out of date. She unlocked the door, slid behind the wheel, and nestled Felton on her lap. Larry Best was a viper, but any woman with any common sense would spot that right off. Would Ellen? Ellen? Liza had brushed her out of the room so fast she hadn't really looked at her. But now, recalling the slender woman in the sharp black dress, she wondered just how out of date her image of Ellen was. No one would mistake this Ellen for the awkward St. Enid's girl. This woman wasted no time picking up a guy in San Francisco. She was sure out to make the most of her weekend away from her boyfriend. This woman wasn't *her* Ellen anymore. Liza scooped up the little black and white pig and sobbed. Tears gushed down her face, over the back of the pig, onto her hands. The loss of Ellen meshed with Jay's death with the loss of everything she had been. She felt as if she'd never be safe again.

Felton squealed.

"Sorry, boy, I didn't mean to squeeze you." She put him on the other seat, wiped her eyes and stared ahead at the cement wall, at the long empty roll of the future. It was almost a relief to think about just the next move. Gotta drive, but where? This car was essentially hers now. The last thing Ellen would be thinking of would be the car. If she did, Larry Best would assure her it was fine where it was. He was not a guy to be slowed down by parking limits. In San Francisco a car wasn't a necessity, it was a nuisance. Even this sporty number would be a terror for a woman like Ellen who didn't know how to drive on hills. Ellen wouldn't come for it at least until tomorrow, maybe not for days.

Guilt—fear?—stabbed her. But, really, what could she do about Ellen? She could hardly follow an adult woman to a man's hotel room. The best thing she could do for Ellen was to put distance between them.

She pulled Felton closer and scratched his wiry head. He wrinkled his snout and rooted gently against her stomach. She had a full tank of gas and a car no one would trace to her.

# Sixteen

As the black Camaro disappeared into traffic a tiny smile tweaked the tiny mouth of Rosewood Hotel clerk, Daniel Kurtz. Liza Silvestri thought she could manipulate him. Think again, bitch.

All his life he'd been the nerd women ignored while they

preened for the likes of Larry Best. Liza Silvestri thought she was so clever. Not this time. She thought Larry Best was just looking out for her friend, anxious to make sure she got a good meal. Fat chance. She thought he hadn't seen the TV report on the loft murder; thought he didn't know who she was. He shrugged with pleasure; she shouldn't have been such a bitch.

Daniel Kurtz dialed the Los Angeles Police Department and what surprised him was how quickly he was transferred to an Assistant to the Commissioner.

"Bentec here."

"You're handling the investigation of the guy who was shot in the loft?"

"Who's calling?"

"Larry Best." The name switch just popped out of his head. Cool.

"From?"

"Come on, Inspector, I know you can pull up my number."

"Make it easy for me, Larry."

Kurtz read off the hotel number.

"So, Larry, what do you have for me?"

"The wife."

"Really. Terrific. Just hold her there—"

"It's not that simple. Hey, is there a reward? I mean this is a murder and all."

"Larry, Larry. We'll have the guilty party in jail by morning. I'm just looking for a clean case here. But, I'll tell you what, I'll pass the word to my buddies at Ess Eff that you're a good guy."

Kurtz almost choked before getting out, "Don't bother."

"Your choice, Larry. So, Mrs. Silvestri, where is she?"

The cop was phony as they come, but Daniel didn't care. It just added to the kick of it all. "In a black Camaro. California plates." He read off the number.

"But where is she?" The cop's veneer was slipping.

"She left here five minutes ago."

"Headed where? Didn't you look?" The "asshole" was understood.

For the first time Daniel was nervous. Then he reminded himself that for this phone call he wasn't Daniel Kurtz but

Larry Best. "Listen, cop, I told you what I know. Push me and I won't give you the biggie."

It was a moment before he heard a voice so constricted it could have been a machine. "What is it, Larry?"

"The biggie?"

"Yes, Larry?"

"The Camaro, it was rented in the name of Ellen Baines. Mrs. Silvestri stole it."

# Seventeen

San Francisco, an unfamiliar city, made up of sharp hills and dead ends, situated at the tip of a peninsula, was the absolute worst place for a woman on the lam. Liza headed down, toward water—San Francisco Bay—and the bridge east to freedom.

She swung a hard left, headed under the freeway and up onto the ramp and found herself emerging in the fast lane. Her shoulders were knotted tight and she could barely turn her head. The Bay Bridge was like a tunnel, drab, low-ceilinged. Cars whooshed by on either side. A murky yellow light pushed in from beyond the railings. She felt like she was driving to the center of the earth. It was ten at night. The cars were probably headed home. "Headed to the same place they were yesterday," she said enviously. She tried to lighten up. "But, Felton, we're on an adventure. Right, Felton? Tomorrow we could be anywhere, half way to Richland, Washington, right?"

Felton gave a muffled snort. Disbelief? He was grunting in his sleep. She reached over and rubbed his back, and repeated, "Richland, Washington," as if it were a magical chant. Richland grade were Jay's last words; had he uttered them from more than sentiment?

"Richland it is, then," she said, aware of the quaver in her voice. She wouldn't get over Jay for a long time, but she had to go on living. At least her hours of sleep had given her a boost. Or maybe the charge came from facing down the hotel clerk. She hadn't done much of that when she was with Jay. Life with Jay was easy. Money oiled every creak. Her biggest challenge had been providing him ever more exotic and intriguing escapes from the pressures of work. Three months ago she'd rented an apartment and changed the theme each weekend. He'd loved that, the separate apartment just for sex. Then he'd rented the loft and hinted broadly that they could make the most of it before he remodeled it for an office. The first month she went on instinct, then she upped the ante, letting him give her a single word before he left on Monday. He'd grinned and said, "I do love word games."

"Star" had been last month. Jay had assumed she would create "Hollywood." Later, he had told her that even before he'd got on the plane he'd known "Hollywood" would be too ordinary. He'd considered a constellation on a blue ceiling and discarded that concept somewhere over Colorado. Maybe, a note on the apartment door leading to a blanket on the beach? He was closer though he hadn't realized it. She smiled at the memory. She brought the beach to the loft, covered half the reception room with sand and made the "ocean" of deep blue pasta stars for him to dive into as a champagne fountain provided the sound of the waves. He'd loved that, just as he'd loved the Point Pleasant beach house and the memories of Ingrid whatshername.

The bridge ended; freeway began.

She was not Jay Silvestri's playful little wife anymore. She'd better remember who she was before: the girl with the tattoo on her tit; the girl who almost always knew how to stay one jump ahead.

Ellen had had second thoughts the minute she hit the Rosewood Hotel steps, and third thoughts when Larry Best led her into the dark empty bar next door.

Rarely had she been so wrong. Larry Best wasn't some smooth-talker out to snow her, he was just an incredibly nice guy. He had insisted she have a salad with her sandwich, and hot tea instead of liquor. Not once had he pressed her about her trip, her friend, or even her relation to the pig. He hadn't waited demandingly for repartee she was too tired to create. He'd sat while she ate and entertained her with anecdotes about the city, the hotels, and the funny and bizarre things he came across in his security job for a block of small hotels and private parties. He could have been a younger, buff-er, amusing Harry Cooper whose conversation strayed beyond the topic of railroads. When she admitted she should just turn around and fly back to Kansas City, he'd reminded her of the time change and the probability it was already too late to catch a flight tonight. And then to top it off he'd found her another hotel room.

The suite at the new hotel, the Orestes, had Oriental carpet, two TVs, and a jacuzzi. It was far and away the best hotel accommodations she'd ever had. She'd hesitated before asking Larry what it was going to cost her. San Francisco was an expensive city. But the question hadn't been a problem, in fact it had been a bond.

"Great, isn't it?" Larry had said. "Best part is it's a comp from my friend. If, out of the blue, a busload of tourists should arrive at midnight demanding expensive rooms, well, then you'd be camping at the Y. Otherwise, enjoy."

"Wow, this is terrific. You've been terrific."

Larry had hesitated. He'd still been standing half in the hall as if it would have been presumptuous to barge into the room he'd gotten her. "Say no if you're too tired—I'll understand and just feel like a jerk for asking—but there's a reception at one of the great mansions in Pacific Heights tonight. I have to make a pass through to check on our security guys. I'd love to have you come. You're already dressed for it."

She'd almost forgotten she was wearing the cocktail dress.

"Security checking is awkward. I don't want to stand out," he hurried on. "I can't talk to the security people without tipping them off, which would defeat the whole purpose. If I talk to any of the guests I have to come up with a story, and then get free because I've got other places to go. But arriving with a 'date' smooths all of that over. Then we're in, chat up a few people, eat some finger food, one swing across the dance floor and we're history. I'll have you back in your room before ten. It'd be worth going with any dolt just to see the place. But listen, I'll understand if you can't."

She was so tired; so cobwebby, but she couldn't disappoint

him, this Harry-only-better. Would she be so accommodating
to a short, dumpy bore, she demanded silently? Was she
responding from kindness or to flattery? Or maybe, just
maybe, was she really attractive to this Liza-quality guy?
Larry Best, a free hotel room, and a reception at a mansion,
it seemed too good to be true.

The yellow fog almost disappeared on the raised freeway as
Liza passed by the big white hotel. Then the hills crowded in
from both sides, the fog pooled murky yellow on the roadway,
the lanes curved to the right, and the only option was a tunnel.
No exit; no turn about. Her hands went stiff on the wheel as
the car was drawn closer to the tubes, the drain pipes into the
dark. "I'm not afraid," she said aloud in the toughy voice
she'd perfected years ago. She was not a fearful person; she'd
learned to see through false danger. She'd fire-walked,
skydived, and hit over a hundred on the winding canyon roads
before she met Jay and could relax and feel safe. But now the
tunnel loomed . . . Or was what loomed what Jay hadn't told
her? What she had chosen not to question.

That night Bentec stared at her tattoo she was only worried
about being exposed. Later, at dinner, she had asked Jay why
the man asked—she didn't say ordered—him to follow. Bentec
was a cop arranging security on a business shipment, Jay'd
said. She had nodded, and put it out of her mind, but at some
level she'd known the picture was wrong, the colors reversed.
A security employee does not order his employer to the side
of the road.

Traffic was slowing. She had to keep moving, driving,
thinking, because there was something else wrong with that
night Bentec saw the tattoo. She was down to thirty miles per
hour, so slow she could see faces in the next lane. They were
dark.

"Oh. It's my windows. They're all tinted." She smiled, safe
in her dark, moving, box. The lanes to the left were closed,
cars shunted into the right bore. The bore was directly ahead,
a sooty, cement pipe. She entered the bore, focusing on the
safety of the white line, then forcing herself to note out the
cars passing in the next lane, to check the rearview mirror.
Maybe she'd never go back to L.A. at all. She could pretend

72

Jay was just on a business trip, like she did after her parents died, only with them she pretended they were in a rehab program and they'd emerge as the bright witty loving parents of her dreams.

Jay buying the lace turtleneck to cover her dress—that was what was wrong. It wasn't her Bentec had been threatening with his stare, it was Jay. If Bentec had exposed her past it wouldn't have been to harass her but as leverage against Jay. She felt as if she was sinking in mud. Her life was being ripped away as if it were a painting on brown wrapping paper—nothing more. She'd thought Jay was so sweet to understand her distress instantly, buy her the turtleneck, pay for her tattoo removal. What he'd understood was his own danger, what he'd paid for was his own security.

Tears clouded her eyes. She blinked them back. This was not the time to mourn. She had to think about Frank Bentec and why he wanted to have something on Jay.

In the distance the murky tunnel was giving way to a black spot that grew wider, taller, nearer. She cleared the tunnel and stepped on the gas.

She didn't see the police checkpoint till she was almost on top of it.

Ellen had pulled her hair back and clasped it at the nape of her neck, leaving so short a tail it could have been on Liza's pig. In Kansas City she would have looked silly, but this was San Francisco and she felt avant garde. Or at least she did when Larry voiced his appreciation. She had been a dumpy girl so long that the thrill of seeing herself sleek, and high-cheekboned hadn't worn off. As she stepped through the baronial doors of the elegant Victorian mansion she felt like a star, like this was all too good to be happening to her. She felt like Liza.

"Larry, come in. And who's this?" The man at the door took her hand. "I'm Ernst."

"Ellen," Larry said, "and hands off, my friend."

"What a great house," Ellen said and immediately felt her own banality.

But Ernst appeared delighted. "When we bought it five years ago it was chopped into four apartments, one drabber than the

73

next. For what we spent restoring it we could have bought an emerging nation. So, I live for compliments."

"You must live well then." She took a step toward the living room, a mix of English study and Thai temple, but Larry caught her arm.

"First the buffet. Ernst worries that his friends just come for the food. And—" he shot a grin at his host—"he could be right."

"The food? Not the house, or Ernst himself?"

"Come and see. You haven't eaten dinner, have you? Lucky you." With a nod to Ernst he guided her to a dining room the size of her apartment.

She laughed. "I was expecting a buffet table that ran the length of the room. Nothing so gauche here, huh?"

"Don't let Ernst hear that. He never serves more than three entrées. More would only be frustrating. The problem is stopping yourself from gorging on these three. Ah, Jeff," he called to a guy she would have spotted instantly as an artist. "Come meet someone from your home town."

As she extended her hand she wondered if this night would rate tops in the year or the decade. It won the "worry least called for" category so decisively the contest was closed in perpetuity.

So this was how it felt to be Liza.

It was too late to turn off. Liza was in line behind five other vehicles. The highway patrol had pulled one over. Could Bentec's grasp reach this far? They were letting the next car go. She squinted into the distance trying to make out the sex of the driver. If they were letting men through she was sunk. The driver's hair was long. A woman . . . probably. Probably this whole thing was a manhunt. That'd be okay, then, as soon as they saw she was alone.

The car three ahead was moving to the right, too. Oh shit, it was no manhunt, it was a sobriety stop. They were stopping every third car. They'd ask for the registration and the rental agreement, and the name on that was Ellen's. Frantically she checked the other lane, but it was useless. She'd been to traffic school and she knew that any move now would only draw attention to her. She could only pray.

And what so far today would make her think the gods cared? She wasn't surprised when the patrolman motioned her to the right.

"Evening, ma'am. This is a sobriety check. We'd appreciate your cooperation."

"Certainly." The smile she gave him was watery. She focused on him so it was not a police stop but just him and her. Her tone was light as she said, "What can I do for you?"

"Hand me your driver's license and registration, ma'am."

Her first urge was to hit the gas. The second was to explain about the rental car and how come it wasn't in her name. She squelched both, nodded pleasantly, opened the glove compartment and handed him the registration. She pulled her purse onto her lap. Heavy. The gun; she'd forgotten about Jay's gun. She held her hand over the opening, fished out her wallet and extricated the license. All she needed was to be found in a stolen car with a gun.

The wind was cold out here, colder than on the bridge. The patrolman stared at her license so intently she could almost see him recognizing her name from a "Wanted" list. When he asked for the rental agreement, she handed it over. She didn't plan her story; inspiration would come; it always had. That was one of the things that Jay loved about her. At parties, he'd introduce her by name alone, take in the other man's envy and then see what story she'd give him.

"Ms. Silvestri, is that you?"

"Yes?"

"The rental agreement is with an Ellen Baines—"

"Oh. Oh, yeah. Right. And I didn't sign on as a driver." Her hand batted back through her hair automatically. "The rental company is going to have a fit. But, you know, by the time they want to charge you for insurance and drop off fees and then add on more just so you can share the driving, well, Ellen and I just didn't do it." Jay would have sneered at her lack of imagination. His rule was: no element of truth. But tonight, the world had gone inside out. She wasn't looking at the patrolman but she could feel his reaction. He wanted to believe her, but he couldn't just wave on someone who might be stealing a car.

"I'm going to require proof—"

75

"Of course." She particularly restrained herself from saying "officer," the word that in these situations meant "guilty." "You can call Ellen. She's staying at the Orestes, in San Francisco."

It was a mistake. He was suspicious now. "And where are you headed, ma'am?" The "at this hour, driving away from San Francisco" hung in the air.

Liza let out a big, disgusted sigh. "I'm taking her fucking pig to some people out here for the night because in the Orestes they only think of pigs as pre-bacon."

Time slowed. The patrolman could have been a cartoon character and instead of flipping the pages to create normal speed, she was turning them one by one, watching his eyes rise up millimeter by millimeter. His thought-balloons lined up like Pacific storms in January. Finally, she got to the last page. His gaze descended, his shoulders relaxed. He peered across her at Felton.

And Felton carried the show with a wriggle of nose and a porker-sized oink. Not a grunt or snort, but a true oink.

The highway patrolman grinned. "Well, I guess you're demanding professional courtesy, huh—uh—"

"Felton."

"Well, Felton. We don't get called pigs much anymore."

"Felton would feel you should regret that," she said, resting her hand on the window sill so he could return her papers.

"Drive carefully."

"I will," now she added with bravado, "officer."

"Wilkins," a man called from behind them.

The patrolman turned toward the voice.

"We just got a notice out of El A Pee Dee . . ."

She hit the gas, and shot in front of a truck leaving the checkpoint. An exit was five hundred yards away. She stayed in front of the truck till the last moment, then swung right, cutting off a van. The driver didn't honk, thank God. As she followed the off ramp turn, she caught a glimpse of men running at the checkpoint. It could have nothing to do with her, she told herself. Sure.

She turned right and, after a bit, right again into a residential neighborhood, slowed and eyed one house after the next till she found one with five newspapers and no cars in the driveway. She pulled in and doused the lights. It was going to be a long cold night.

Ellen didn't hear the band till she went downstairs. The drinks were beginning to smooth sharp edges and soften the center of things. She had a place to stay for the night and nothing to do till morning, so why not just enjoy this party, like Larry said? Why not just enjoy having this hunk of a guy introducing her to everyone like she was a star? If it seemed too good to be true—maybe that meant her standards needed to rise. She had the feeling she should be doing something, or not doing something, but she couldn't summon up the concentration to remember what.

All too soon, they had to leave. Security checkers didn't get paid for having a good time, Larry said with a sigh. And he did know how tired she was.

Soft waves of music from a symphony of speakers all over his car eased the transition. He made a nest for her between the bucket seats and gently pulled her head against his shoulder. His hair tickled at the side of her eye. She would have flicked it away but the effort to lift her arm and then to find the spot was too much. It was all she could do not to splat into the door when Larry made a hard left. Her right foot was wedged against the door, the other pressed hard into the dash. Her knees were sticking up at angles that she knew would seem less charming if she was sober. She was floating on a carpet and wasn't about to consider a thought that would leave dirty footprints. She'd had a coat when she came but didn't remember picking it up on the way out of the party. Had Larry? Didn't matter. His arm lay loosely on hers, and she was warm. Plenty warm.

She leaned back and looked out at the white lights of San Francisco lazing by, listened to a cello moan the length of her spine.

The lights changed from white on black to bright yellow. The hotel entryway. The music cut off; waves of thick, brusk silence batted her ears. Before she realized it Larry bounced her down onto her seat, and was out of the car and opening the door for her. His hand slipped around her waist so smoothly she almost felt as if she were getting out of the car on her own.

"I'm a little drun—"

"It's okay, Ellen, we're almost there."

"I'm sorry, I—"

"You're not going to be sick, are you?" he asked. There was a surprising edge to his voice and quickly she answered no.

He wrapped his arm more tightly around her.

Clusters of lobby lights sparkled. The rug was spongy under her feet. She heard Larry's voice but she knew he wasn't talking to her. She heard: "Yeah, guys, I've got her here."

The freeway sign offered Liza San Francisco, Route 80 North and Route 980 South. She'd spent two hours winding on back roads after she decided she'd rather face the entire Los Angeles Police Department than freeze to death in the San Francisco suburbs. San Francisco? That, she'd done. What about these 80s? If the highway patrol was really after her they were only going to be looking back in the suburbs she'd abandoned.

The turn-offs were popping up fast. With a sigh she kept on toward the Bay Bridge and San Francisco. It was the conservative choice and she hated herself for it, but maybe she should just haul the damn car back to the hotel and park it where she got it. It could spend its weekend in San Francisco waiting for Ellen to finish partying and take it back to the airport. Better yet, why not be a sport and take it to Ellen at her new hotel? Ellen had dropped everything to fly out here for her. And for that she ended up being skewered by her great "friend" Liza. That was for her own safety, Liza reminded herself, but the memory of Ellen's shocked expression still rebuked her. Taking the car to her new hotel would be the decent thing. A great wad of desperation filled her throat; she swallowed hard against her need of someone to trust—and to give that someone even a small reason to care about her.

The Bay Bridge shocked her. The lower level leaving the city was a dark wedge of under road, but this top level, it was beautiful. White lights hung off the suspension wires. Ahead was downtown San Francisco and even after midnight skyscrapers were lit like limousines driving to the stars. Sparkling in the night . . . the night.

Shaking her head against the sudden exhaustion, she pulled off the freeway at Fifth Street, spotted a cab and waved him down. "I need to get to the Orestes?"

"Yeah? How much is going on it?"

"Puh-lease. You think a hooker's dressed like this?" She could have said, built like this, but breast talk with strange men always led to problems. She could tell by the little twitch of his beard and the way his eyes sunk momentarily that he was still hopeful. There was a brattiness she knew came through in her stance—shoulders back, breasts forward as if to stretch the fabric of the T-shirt, breasts too small but trying extra hard. Let me prove I'm a big girl, her whole stance said. And it was a rare man who didn't react.

But the cabbie had a living to make. He merely gave directions.

She thanked him, but she was pissed and for a few minutes her anger kept her awake. By the time she spotted the Orestes, her eyes were closing and she couldn't bear to think of the hassle looming after she gave up the car.

She almost missed the turn into the hotel, a covered circular drive, so small three parked cars would be a jam. Only one was parked there and she was willing to bet the staff made sure there were never more than two. It was that kind of place. Potted trees, not palms or ficuses, but exotic flowering trees much too fragile for the damp cold. The trees wouldn't survive there as long as the guests. Through the glass doors she could see the lobby, spare with Japanese antiques and a lone orchid in front of a copper waterfall. She glanced down at her jeans and T-shirt, shrugged and stepped out of the car.

The bellman was coming toward her. If he was anywhere near as worn out as she, he wouldn't even notice her clothes.

"I'm here for one of your guests, Ellen Baines. I'm returning her car."

He could have been the cabbie's twin reaction-wise, but he knew enough to say nothing. He wasn't the type to endanger his work and his tips. He—Shawn, his tag said—was stocky, with curly red-blond hair poking out under his uniform cap. She could see him going to night school, playing touch football in the park, hoisting a few beers in a hangout that knew his name, getting this bellman job through a friend, and graying with it. He was holding out his hand for the car keys.

Instinctively she snapped them back. "That's okay, Shawn, I'll take them to her room," she said in the dismissive tone she'd learned being Mrs. Silvestri, the clipped syllables that said "you can look, but not familiarly." When she was with Jay men didn't presume to visually undress her. There was a clutching in her stomach she hadn't felt in years.

Shawn stepped back. "She's not here."

"She checked out?"

"No, she just went out. You can leave the keys. I'll see she gets them."

Something wasn't right about this guy but she was too muddy-headed to see what or even to rate her options. "I'll just wait for Ellen in her room then."

"Larry's not going to like—" He flushed—he'd given away the game and he knew she knew it.

She didn't bother with intermediary steps. If she interrupted Ellen and Larry's romantic interlude, they'd just be more eager to help her on her way.

"Give me the room number. Not the key, just the number. I'll knock. And if Larry's there I'll tell him I got it from Daniel at the Rosewood hotel."

He hesitated.

"There's my car. If I steal the towels you can sell it."

Still, he didn't move.

"Hey, Shawn, it's going to be dawn soon. I can wait for the manager and discuss this with him."

He checked a sheet. "One twenty-seven, and leave the towels."

She peered through the car window. Felton was curled into as much of a ball as a pig could be. His snout was pressed into the upholstery, but she could hear little snorfle sounds. Rooting dreams. It was almost obscene. He was a happy, sleeping pig.

Pocketing the car keys, she headed down the hall. 127 was at the far end. She knocked. "Room Service."

The door opened.

It wasn't Larry.

It was a dark-haired man the size of the door. "Yeah? Hey, you're not room service."

"Maybe she is, Ev. She looks like the second course."

The room was dim. There was no smoke, but the air was thick. A lamp threw pale shadows onto the floor. Onto the backs of four men. Onto the bed where another man sat next to Ellen. Onto Ellen, who looked scared out of her mind.

Liza felt the weight of Jay's gun in her purse, but she trusted herself more than it. She stiffened against her fear, became again the drunks' daughter ready to beard the neighbors, the bill-collectors, the cops. "Ellen," she said, careful not to raise her voice. "Get up. We're leaving!"

A bottle on the table looked empty. Another was on the floor. The men were different sizes, but they were all way bigger than she was. "Hey, what the—" one of them started. The others were moving slowly. They were looking to Larry.

He was staring down at her, back to them. They couldn't see his neck tightening, his hands bracing as if to choke, the glistening sweat on his forehead. It wasn't just sex he was about to be out, but money. Larry Best was not a horny date, he was a procurer. He spoke in a voice as controlled as hers: "She's staying as is."

"Think again, Larry Best. Think hard. How much of your life do you want to give up?"

He was across the room, in her face now. "What, are you going to call the cops? Hey, the cops are already after you."

He was a head taller. She stared him in the eye. "Then call my bluff, Larry." He wanted to, she knew that, but there was a wild quality about her at the best of times and when she was enraged even she didn't know whether she could control it. He was nearly snorting in her face. But across the room it was so quiet she couldn't read his clients at all. And she didn't dare take her eyes off Larry Best. She could feel the heat of him, of his overwhelming need to smack her. "I'm already news. You touch me and you and your business in this room will be, too. It'll be news all the way to Cincinnati, Tuscaloosa or El Centro, wherever these Johns are from."

Nothing moved, no eyes, no breath. She didn't dare break her gaze. Larry Best couldn't afford to blink.

81

He was saved by one of the other guys. "Forget her! She's just another cunt."

Larry shrugged in agreement. "Okay, we're out of here."

Liza didn't budge. "No, not you. Ellen. Ellen, get up, and get your things. Now!"

Ellen moved like a zombie, so slow Liza could hear the walls breathe. She looked like a piece of cardboard before there were any creases for joints. What all had Larry Best poured down her? She was trying to steer a path well clear of any of the men, as if any one of them might snap a hand out and grab her. Liza could sense her terror; she had to keep herself from leaping across the room, wrapping her own safe arm around Ellen and pulling her out. She stayed put, froze her face and her stance. Ellen was almost staggering, looking around blankly. Forget the suitcase, the purse, whatever, she wanted to tell her, but she couldn't chance confusing her. Nor could she make a sweep of the place for Ellen's things. Once she stepped inside the circle of men the rules would shift and all the power would be theirs. She was running on automatic now, barking directions. "Get your purse, Ellen." "Did you have a coat?"

Ellen nodded toward a chair in which one of the men sat. He was leaning back against it and the look on his round face said: You want me to move, make me.

Liza eyed Larry. "Bring me her coat and suitcase."

"Hey, I don't have—"

"Yes, you do have to and you have to do it right now."

Again his clients saved him. The coat and suitcase arrived at the door simultaneously with Ellen. Liza checked Ellen only out of the side of her gaze; she focused on the suitcase, coat and purse, lifted them through the door and shut it. Larry et al. could open the door and hassle them down the hall, but she was betting not one of them would make the move. They had face-saving and financial renegotiations to occupy them. Liza hoisted Ellen's belongings and headed to the lobby.

It wasn't till she had the key back from Shawn, Ellen in the car and the car headed onto the street that Ellen spoke. "Thanks." The word was barely audible. A small word, but Liza knew it encompassed everything she couldn't say.

"Yeah."

Silence settled like mud around them. Liza started to pull up to the curb, ready to wrap her arms around Ellen and let her cry or scream or whatever, like her mother did when Liza got the door shut against the neighbors or the cops. But Ellen shrieked, "No!"

She pulled back into traffic. "Do you need a doctor, Ellen?"

"No. Just a brain."

"So they didn't—"

"No—no thanks to me. I knew it was too good to be true. Jeez, how could I have been such a fool? If it hadn't been for you. . . Jeez, Liza, you were incredible. How did you ever get to be so brave? You were amazing."

"Hey, Ellen, don't blame yourself. Blame Larry Best, the fucking asshole predator. Slimy bastard."

"But I should have known."

"Listen, you don't run in this kind of circle, but I've seen guys like Larry and I didn't think pimp either. It's their trustworthy aura that makes the whole thing work for them. If Larry Best came over like a pimp he'd be working the Tenderloin. Feel stupid if you must. But it's over. You're safe now."

The car topped a hill and roared across the intersection against the light. Brakes squealed. A male voice yelled. She ignored it. "It's okay. Trust me. In a few minutes we'll be out of San Francisco entirely. When we cross the Golden Gate look back and see that you are okay and you are leaving it all behind you."

As they crossed the Golden Gate Bridge, Felton grunted from the back seat, settled and snored. Once again Liza thanked the gods of planning that there were no toll booths for those leaving the city.

"Ellen, we're out of San Francisco. We are safe now. No one knows where we are." She leaned across the seat and hugged Ellen. "We are two free women and pig!"

# Eighteen

Assistant to the Commissioner Francis Bentec eyed the phone on his desk but did not lift the receiver. He had called SFPD as soon as he hung up with the hotel clerk in San Francisco, the kid who didn't have the sense to look out the window and see where Liza Silvestri was headed. But common sense said she'd go north over the Golden Gate Bridge and on to Richland.

He had prodded Chan at SFPD to put a car on the entrance to the Golden Gate Bridge, and then he'd waited. Chan had called back every half hour to report no sighting till a stolen Jeep raced onto the bridge at ninety miles per hour and pulled the patrol car with it and Chan's man forgot about Liza Silvestri.

Two hours and no sighting of her. Either Chan's man had missed her before the ninety-mile-an-hour chase, or she hadn't headed straight north.

She could be trying to out-fox him by doubling back and going to ground in the Santa Cruz mountains with the other loonies, but boxing herself in like that would be a high-stakes chance to take, and he doubted she'd try. With most women he'd say a flat out No. But he'd pulled the whole file on Liza Cummings, and with her he wasn't so sure. She'd been one gutsy little Lolita. Most of the guys saw that surveillance shot—that asp going for her perky breast—and labelled her a saucy little tart. That's how the state painted her in the juvie hearings. He'd known right away that there was more asp than victim to little Liza Cummings. She would double back all right, if she felt the odds were with her. She was one hot number who could live off the lay of the land.

The frustration could have left him flailing, but Frank Bentec prided himself on control. Nineteen years on the Force, he'd dealt with plenty of frustration. He'd learned to grab naps whenever he could and never let emotion stand in his way. Three times those calls of Chan's had jerked him awake.

He wasn't any closer to Liza Silvestri now but at least after an hour and a half's sleep he was rested enough to think. And his conclusion remained sure. She had to be headed north to Richland. That was the only thing that made sense.

The phone rang, this time with a call from Potelli. "Frank, CHP had her in a sobriety check on twenty-four east of San Francisco—"

"Had, as in 'don't have anymore'?"

"Yeah. Don't ask. That's not the worst. It was two hours ago. Frank?" Potelli was scared.

"Where was she headed?"

"East on twenty-four. But none of my guys spotted her farther east, or on six-eighty. Twenty-four ends at six-eighty. She wouldn't have any other choice."

Bentec let a beat pass. "But she did, didn't she, Joe, because she's not on six-eighty. Look, I'm going to be straight with you here. Getting her is vital. Without her the whole operation fails."

"Yeah, Frank, I know and—"

"It not only fails; it boomerangs. So don't figure it's just you don't get her, you don't get money. Her husband's already dead. You want to join him?"

Potelli was silent. Bentec knew this was the first time he'd faced the truth.

"Get a man on every road. You've got the make and model she's driving. Make damned sure your guys find her."

"Yeah, right," Potelli coughed out. "Listen, though, if she's headed north out of state, then everything's okay. After Red Bluff there's only I-five inland. If she doubles back to the coast there's only one-oh-one. Or Route one, the coast road, but that would take her forever. Listen, we're still fine, Frank. Count on it."

Bentec didn't bother to answer. He pushed Off.

The phone rang again immediately. "Bentec."

"Heron."

"Where are you?"

"In L.A. We drove up and down the ninety-nine all night, man, and not only did we not see her, we didn't see any blue

Firebirds. I mean, it's crazy to expect us to, you know. Like a needle in a haystack."

Bentec tapped his finger on the phone, stopping Heron's nervous rant. He had two dangerous loose ends here in L.A. and now he saw how they could be tied up with one move. "Listen, Heron, you screwed up twice, twice in one night. You killed Silvestri and you let his wife escape. I'm not a man to give second chances, but you've never screwed up before, so for you I'm making an exception. Do this right and you're square with me, you understand?"

"Yeah, sure, Inspector."

"Go to Silvestri's house in Malibu. Break the front door— there's an alarm so you're going to have to move fast. Go straight ahead, down the stairs, make a right and you're in the guest bedroom. You follow?"

"Yeah, straight ahead, down, right, bedroom."

"Under the bed is a nine-millimeter. Get it. The bed's a king; you're going to have to crawl. You're going to need a flashlight to find the damned gun, maybe a broom handle to get it. Bring whatever; just get it. Bring it to Loray Park, the corner in the back. Six o'clock sharp." He gave Heron Silvestri's address, had him repeat it twice, and hung up.

By seven he'd be back to the office, Potelli's men would have spotted Liza Silvestri on one of the freeways north, and he would be done with L.A. and ready to move.

# Nineteen

Liza knew it was ridiculous, but she checked the parking lot for highway patrol cars before getting out of the Camaro and heading toward the restaurant. Too much had happened in too short a time. She felt as if she were walking on bubble wrap. She was steadying herself with the bond of Ellen's friendship. And Ellen wasn't steadying herself at all. She looked gaunt, wobbly and had hair poking in three directions. Her make-up was still in place but she'd turned so pale under-

86

neath that it looked garish, like the last attempt of the elderly to fool death. After what Ellen had been through, of course she'd behave erratically, Liza knew that. She should have expected Ellen could go from animated to mute, buzzed to nearly comatose. But she hadn't, and this shell of a woman shocked her.

She pulled open the restaurant's glass door and all but shoved Ellen into the warmth toward a pink and green booth.

The restaurant was empty except for a couple in their sixties seated on the far side of the salad bar. The man, in a yellow polo shirt, was sitting with his back to her. His royal-blue windbreaker hanging over his chair matched the one around the woman's—she had to be his wife—shoulders. Both of them sat, shoulders hunched, hands knotted, not speaking. Liza jerked her head away. She'd sworn that she and Jay would never come to that. With a start, she realized she'd been right.

"Ellen, what do you want to eat?" She placed the stiff menu in Ellen's stiff hands and beckoned to the waitress. "Coffee. Two."

Ellen was holding the menu but not reading.

"Eggs, Ellen, nice scrambled eggs. And bacon. Toast with strawberry jelly. Breakfast. Food for the beginning of a new day."

"I couldn't . . ."

"Pie, then? Hot, gooey peach—"

Ellen turned white.

Hot and gooey, not the best image for a woman who just escaped being raped.

"Salad. Crisp, healthy—" No. The prospect of Ellen sliding her tray along the salad bar runners, choosing or rejecting cherry tomatoes, bacon bits, chopped green peppers, was as likely as Felton rejecting any of them. "Felton would really like the salad bar. It's what they have in piggy heaven."

Ellen stared over the menu top, eyes wide. Incomprehension? Or disbelief that a friend would think pig chatter appropriate at this time?

"Scrambled eggs, bacon, white toast over there," Liza said to the waitress, speaking loudly to keep the waitress from staring at Ellen. "Here, a cheeseburger, onion rings, and, well,

87

we'll think about pie afterwards, especially if you have chocolate cream pie." She grinned at Ellen, poured milk in both their coffees, pushed Ellen's toward her, and gave the cup a little encouraging pat. "I haven't eaten a cheeseburger in years, all that fat. It's like having your whole day's food in a bun. Okay, so not true about years. Sometimes Jay wants—" wants, not wanted—she couldn't bring herself to talk about him dead—"to go out for a burger and so I order one and eat part, because when Jay's gone—he's away a lot on business—I know I can do a juice fast as soon as he leaves and then—"

"What kind of business?" Ellen looked up and for the first time appeared to really focus.

"Jay? You mean what does he do? He's a venture capitalist."

"Just what is that?"

"He finds funding for businesses, you know."

"I really don't know. What kind of businesses?"

"All sorts, it's not any one kind."

"Uh-huh." Ellen was tapping her teeth together, as if she was pondering a particularly intriguing puzzle. As if she was on the verge of spotting the fatal flaw in it.

"No, see, it's not the business that matters, it's Jay. He's the kind of guy who knows everyone and what they're interested in, what they've got in the way of property and cash, and what they need, or want—" she was talking too fast— "or can be convinced they should want. See, Jay's sort of a business visionary. He can see things—and people—that should come together. He creates wholes greater than the sums of the parts."

Ellen's expression hadn't changed. Liza still couldn't tell if it meant Ellen had zeroed in on some flaw in Jay, or in her, or maybe Ellen was just still in shock.

"What kind of business was he bringing together lately?" Ellen's voice was sharper. She sounded like the lawyers in Juvenile Court and the psychiatrist and the judge, all of them, insisting they were her friends, then once they walked through the hearing-room door, they'd slapped her with questions she couldn't answer, and threatened to send her to Juvie and slam the cell closed.

Liza sat dead still; it was a skill she perfected back then, pulling in tight inside while leaving her shell unaffected. Ellen wasn't one of them, she insisted. Ellen was her friend. But, she realized with a start, she didn't know how far friendship went. She'd never really had a friend.

"Liza, I'm asking because I care what happens to you. I owe you—I don't even want to think how much I may owe you. You called me out here to get some order in things. So let me do that, huh? Trust me."

The music thumped on her skull. Trust her? She hadn't "trusted" since when, when she was three? Four? Before she knew that trust meant giving over control, being helpless, watching someone else stumble over words or chairs or feelings. Years after she'd stopped trusting, she'd still been mopping up mistakes. And Ellen, who hadn't spotted Larry Best for a letch—how could she possibly trust her judgment when her whole life was hanging on what she decided to do next? Ellen didn't know what she was asking.

For the first time she could hear the couple across the room. The man was grumbling about his trailer. No wonder his wife wasn't answering.

The food arrived. With relief, Liza focused full force on her burger. "Could you bring me some mustard?"

"It's on the table, ma'am." The waitress waved a hand at the wicker basket holding mustard, ketchup, salt, pepper, and three kinds of sugar.

"Hot sauce?"

"I'll go back to the kitchen and get you some."

"And salsa? Do you have any salsa?"

"I'll have to check, ma'am."

Liza nodded.

"Will there be anything else, ma'am?" Before Liza could react to her frigid tone, the waitress turned and headed back to the kitchen.

A second later, Liza lifted her hand to call her back.

Ellen grabbed the hand. "Forget her. Forget everything, Liza, except your husband who was murdered, and the police. Why weren't you on the horn to them the moment I told you? Because of a juvenile record? Liza, what's a juvenile record compared to murder?"

Liza jumped up. "I have to go to the bathroom."

"No!"

Ellen clamped a hand on her arm.

"This time yesterday I was home in my own bed. My life was under control. The biggest problem I had was whether to drive to the opera or take a cab." She pressed Liza back down toward her seat with surprising force. "You called me; I dropped everything because I care about you, and because, Liza, I've 'owed' you for ten years. Now, dammit, let me pay up. Let me help you figure out what to do!"

The room seemed like an echo chamber as Ellen repeated, "You're an impulsive person. It's what we love about you. But you're out of your league here. Let me help you make a plan. Tell me what the hell is going on."

Liza sat, still not moving. No one had ever offered this much. She stared at Ellen's face, still gaunt but now flushed, with concern? Or from being pissed off big-time? How could she— "I don't know." That was the truth and it shocked her.

"Liza, I'm not buying that. Now you tell me!"

Liza felt numb. She'd given Ellen the truth and Ellen figured she was lying. Just like the lawyers and shrinks and judges.

"Liza, I know this is hard. Obviously it is. But running away is just going to prolong your misery. Call the police— Inspector Bentec."

Out of the corner of her eye Liza could see the blue-jacketed couple behind the salad bar. They'd given up any pretence of conversation or eating.

Once you talked it was too late. The only safety was in silence. She was surprised to hear herself say, "You want to know why I can't call Frank Bentec?" Her voice was half an octave lower than a moment ago. She took a deep breath, stared Ellen in the eye, and realized that she'd made her choice about trust. "I met Bentec with Jay. He recognized me, from a tattoo I no longer have. He knew I'd been in jail, juvenile hall." Before Ellen could ask, she added, "For holding up a jewelry store." She was not looking at Ellen anymore, not even aware of her reaction. She could hardly make herself go on. Even at the trial they'd had to pull the details out of her. "I was on Wiltshire Boulevard one afternoon with my parents, when they were on one of their sobriety binges. By that time—

90

I was fourteen—I didn't have much hope of success for them, but I knew I'd best keep them moving. Cold turkeying with another drunk is a pretty low percentage prospect. So we were walking along, looking in the shop windows, and I'll say for them, they were really trying to buoy up 'the family outing.'"

She swallowed hard and forced herself to go on. "At a certain point in their drinking cycles they were clever and very funny if you weren't the topic. This day, sober, it was like walking with third-rate actors who hadn't read the script. They got lines out, but their timing was off, the inflection wrong, and it was so clear how much of an effort it was."

"Sounds like it was easier when they were drinking."

"Yeah. Much. These days were torture. But anyway, we came to the jewelry store, Pope's Jewelers. Mom stopped and began to move her head back and forth as if she were really window-shopping. Dad had the easier job of standing behind her husband-like waiting for her to spot one or two items they could spin words around before we moved on. So Mom's looking and suddenly she stops, doesn't say anything. She's staring at a gold pendant. The design just seemed free-flow to me, but she said, 'Don't you see the sports car? Well, not that car so much as the wind in your hair and the open road ahead.' Dad moved in closer and slid his arm around her shoulder and started talking about a trip they took in a convertible right after they were married. I still couldn't see any resemblance to anything in the pendant, but I could see them as they had once been when they were young and fun, and the road rolled out in front of them, before it was all uphill."

Liza reached for her coffee, but the old couple in the matching blue jackets across the rooms co-opted her attention.

"No!" The woman's voice was not loud, but her wiry tone sliced the silence. The syllable was firm, complete, like the final word of a movie before the screen went black. No panic, no fear. The man grumbled something undecipherable. She didn't respond. He grumbled again, then pushed himself up and stomped across the room and out. The woman picked up her cup and drained. it.

Liza eyed the woman, noting her face weathered like red rock in the desert, and the desperately hard clench of her jaw.

Her eyes were closed now. What would this abandoned woman do, a woman so old—in her sixties, at least? Could she even live alone?

"And then?" Ellen prompted.

It took Liza a moment to realize Ellen hadn't even noticed the old couple, and another moment to force herself back into the memory she so much wanted to avoid. "And then the three of us moved on down the boulevard, pausing before other store windows, but after that one burst of real enthusiasm everything we said sounded stale. The next day the sobriety fling failed, and things were worse than ever, and Thanksgiving was coming up, which meant a Hell day with my grandmother.

"What I did made no sense; I knew that even then. But Mom's birthday was right before Thanksgiving and I got the idea the pendant would be a talisman to make her better and then she'd be a talisman for Dad, and, well, you get the picture. It wasn't like me, dreaming up fantasies like that."

"The last clutch of childhood, maybe?"

"Maybe." Liza couldn't stop to consider that. She had to race ahead before she lost her courage. "Anyway, I caught the bus and went down to the store and made a point of speaking to the owner, because I knew if you want to deal you talk to the owner. I asked him if I could pay it off on time, or work in the store, or what I could do. The pendant cost eight hundred dollars. He said we could work something out and I should come back after closing the next night."

Ellen was offering tiny nods; her face was flushed.

"Ellen, this isn't the kind of story you need to be hearing now. Maybe I—"

"No, go on."

"It turns out Jeweler Pope was hot for teenage girls. Seems he was known to the cops, but he was also a wealthy businessman, so you can imagine whose side they were on."

"But you didn't know that?"

Liza could tell for Ellen that was the natural assumption. Why didn't she just go with Ellen's presumption of naïveté? "I had no idea he was a pedophile, but I did assume there would be some price to pay; I mean he did want me after hours." She swallowed hard; her throat caught. This was the part she couldn't imagine Ellen accepting. "I just didn't figure it would be a blow . . . oral sex. I didn't figure he'd get me on my knees. Or that the surveillance camera would be on, snapping pictures of his prick, my mouth and the tattoo between my breasts." She grabbed her coffee and drank. Only when she put the cup down could she bring herself to check Ellen's reaction.

Ellen had gone pale, but not as pale as she'd have expected. In fact Ellen's face was scrunched as if she was considering the logistics. "I thought," she said, "there was a robbery."

Liza nodded.

"Did he say he'd give you the pendant, and then call the police on you? Or did you—"

"Just snatch it while his pants were down? Not quite. Maybe I would have, I don't know. The whole scene was over-whelming and surreal. I didn't know it, but my father had followed me. The shades on the door and windows were down. Suddenly he was banging on the door, and then when Pope didn't answer, he grabbed a newspaper machine and broke the glass. The alarm went off. Pope was shouting, my father was shouting. The pendant was on the counter. I grabbed it and we ran. The cops caught me two blocks away."

"Just you?" Ellen demanded. "What about your father?"

"I ran. He didn't get caught."

"Ever? What kind of man was he?"

"Don't!" It was as if her whole fourteen years with him were wrapped in that one protective word. Ellen understood enough to back off.

Ellen reached for her water glass, drank and drank again. Liza picked up her burger. Her hands were quivering and the lettuce and tomato slices shook loose and ketchup splattered the plate.

Ellen set her glass down in front of her but kept hold of it with both hands. "Liza, I'm so sorry. God, what a wretched childhood you had. I never knew—obviously." She was shaking her head. Her voice was soft, awkward, but full of concern. "Still Liza, bad as that was, it was years ago and it has nothing to do with your husband being murdered now. It doesn't change anything. Your husband is dead and you have to call the police."

Liza felt as if her entrails had been yanked out and thrown

93

back at her before she could get her guard back in place. But it snapped into place now and she was ready to "put it on them" like she'd learned in Juvie. She took a moment to get her fear and anger under control, then said, "Ellen, your boyfriend was talking to Jay for ages in Portland. The two of them looked real serious. What did your boyfriend say about it?"

She spotted Ellen's discomfort before her first word was complete."Nothing. He wouldn't talk about it." Ellen lifted the water glass she'd never let go of and sipped. She set it down with a thump. "I called him from San Francisco and he told me to get out quick."

"Get out? Why?"

"I don't know, I—"

"Well, how about asking him now, Ellen? Jay is dead, but he's alive." Liza pulled her wallet out of her purse and shook out the coins. "Here, you won't even have to call collect."

Liza downed the rest of her water, almost the full glass, as she watched Ellen make her way past the restaurant counter to the phone. Beyond it, the blue-jacketed woman was still sitting in her booth, alone now, fingering her empty cup. Liza kept her head down as she turned back but she could still see shocks of short thick gray hair, "the dust of death" they called it in L.A. Death of love and chance and hope and . . .

Stop it! You should live long enough to have her problems. What about Jay? It'd been one thing to defend him, but she couldn't go on defending him from herself. She had to face . . . whatever. Ellen had a good point about his business. A little two-step outside the law wouldn't have fazed Jay. It would, in fact, have added spice. Like the games.

But a little two-step didn't get you murdered.

# Twenty

Harry Cooper dropped the door key twice before he managed to slide it into the lock. The street was dark now. The trees were winter-bare but the street light stood behind a huge spruce and illuminated only a few feet of lawn on the far side. This section of Kansas City boasted hilly streets of pleasant wood-and-stone bungalows. No sidewalks, no late nights. He mowed his lawn on Saturdays. He had expected Ellen to move in with him. Then the house would have been perfect. When she agreed to come east with him from Portland he had been overjoyed. He just assumed . . . And even when she said she wasn't ready to live together, he did figure that she would rent a house in the neighborhood. It was such a nice area, with all the amenities, and there was no way property values wouldn't rise. It never occurred to him she would choose an apartment she had no stake in, in an impersonal area like the Plaza, when she could reasonably afford a house. She was younger, of course, nearly twenty years younger, but she was so mature, so sensible, so steady.

He opened the door and, from habit, left the light off for a minute, picturing Ellen hurrying to the door, arms outstretched, her eyebrows lifted in question, willing him to come up with a story from the day's annals of railroad freight to connect the two of them in amusement, to remind her that he was more than just a bureaucrat.

Usually he lingered in that daydream and reluctantly snapped it shut with the flick of the light, but tonight he didn't bother with the light at all. The thought of dinner flashed, but although he hadn't eaten since lunch, it was just a thought, no visceral pang, and easy to dismiss. He made a sharp right onto the stairs, and headed for the bedroom. Usually his fantasy ended with Ellen in bed, but tonight he was glad there would be no one lying between him and sleep.

God, he wanted to sleep. He had never taken a sleeping pill in his life but tonight he'd wash down a double dose with a double shot of whiskey, if he had either in the house.

Twenty-four hours ago life had been good. He'd been happy as a tramp in a mattress car. Sure there were people who thought railroad freight forwarding was as exciting as sanding your porch. But they missed the point. Freight routing was always a subtle game. K.C. to Chicago—via St. Louis to add cars and time and income, or send the shipment straight through on the northern route? Which way won the cost efficiency game? And now with the great railway merger there were alternate routes all over. A man could devote a whole day to deciding the cost-efficiency ratio of all the available routes from Chicago to Long Beach. The possibilities filled him with awe. It was like going from black and white to color, from two to three dimensions, from celibacy to sex. He couldn't stop talking about it. He knew ninety, no ninety-eight per cent of the world thought he was bonkers. He'd heard guys, even his friends at the station, mocking him as if he were the twit in a British comedy. They missed the elegance of the system. With all the new possibilities they were overwhelmed. Their goal was to route freight rotely, cost and time be damned.

But for him it was like being sent up from the minor leagues to pitch the pennant game for the Royals. He was having the time of his life.

Until today.

He knew something was terribly wrong but just why, or how it would affect him, to that he didn't have a clue.

He was not a man given to intuition or any of that mushy California stuff, but when he met Jay Silvestri at Ellen's college alumni party, his stomach had gone cold. He'd actually glanced around for the men's room in case he had to lurch to it. Then the moment had passed and he'd felt ridiculous and profoundly inhospitable to this overdressed visitor from out of state who was doing nothing but being polite, in a sort of over-the-top way. But what do you expect from Los Angeles? It would have been unreasonable for him to expect Jay Silvestri to do more than he already was: making an effort to understand the subtleties of freight routing. That was more

96

than he could say for seventy per cent of his colleagues at the Portland yard. He could still see Silvestri putting down his wine glass, milking his smooth chin in thought. Silvestri had picked up the very point that excited him—all the options presented by the merger. He spotted the game. And then he could see all the moves.

Silvestri's mind moved so quickly it awed him, and it scared him. And, he had to admit, here, alone, to himself, the intensity of it all seduced him. Never in his twenty-seven years with the railroads had anyone been so intrigued by it. Silvestri was like a little kid, a whiz kid.

At the end of the event, when Silvestri had introduced his wife, a blonde stunner every other guy in the room had been eyeing, he resented the intrusion. He hadn't realized that he'd snubbed the woman until Ellen chided him in the car: "Liza's not used to men ignoring her like that," she'd said. "It's probably never happened in her whole life."

He could tell Ellen was just mouthing the rebuke. She was amused, and she was looking at him a little differently, as if he was something less drab than she'd thought. Well, he wasn't about to tell her the truth, that he found a beautiful blonde less exciting than moving freight through Pocatello.

"Why would I care about her when I have you?" The words would have sounded corny on Jay Silvestri's lips.

"Why would I care about her when I have you?" He had never had the nerve to ask what went through Ellen's mind in the eternity before she leaned over and kissed him. Whatever, he was sure it was that remark that reassured her she'd made the right decision about Kansas City, about him.

So he had a lot to thank Silvestri for. The angel from the city of angels, he'd thought with a smile as the moving van rolled east. He figured he'd see Silvestri one more time—at his and Ellen's wedding.

It had been a shock to get Silvestri's call, and a bigger shock to find Silvestri, the big L.A. venture capitalist, needed to ship a container of memorabilia from movie lots—he wouldn't be specific—very hush-hush the whole business—to a collector in Richland, Washington.

"I can't be moving hot goods on the rail, Jay." He'd been

97

upfront about it; it wasn't the first time he'd gotten this type of request.

"It's perfectly legal."

What else would he say? This was Silvestri's novice attempt at this conversation. Harry Cooper, Head of Freight Forwarding, was the reigning expert. "You have bills of sale I can show the police?"

"Oh yeah," Jay said without pause. "Oh, hey, you're thinking 'hot' as in stolen." He'd laughed. "The stuff's only hot to the other collector who thought he had an inside route to it. I need to get it to my guy before this other collector knows anyone's thinking about it. To you, Harry, this is freight. To wannabe collectors with viewing rooms in their basements, inviting a guy to watch a screening of *The Philadelphia Story* from the passenger seat of C. K. Dexter Haven's convertible is worth millions. I'm not charging millions, but I'm not running low either. And I'm sure not asking you for a cut rate. I'm calling you, Harry, because I knew you'd enjoy this, and because you're the best router in the business. I need this container to be in Richland, Washington, a week from Monday. And to travel as soybeans."

"Originating in L.A.?"

Jay saw the problem. "Okay, send it through San Francisco and call it sourdough starter."

That was last week. And now Jay Silvestri was dead. Shot down in a way that would make good viewing from C. K. Dexter Haven's car. It was all so Hollywood.

Admit it, he said to himself. Silvestri snowed you. This shipment was only the beginning, Silvestri had said. He was getting more and more orders for memorabilia, particularly from the Silent era. Stuff was going for a fortune and he figured it'd account for more than half of his business soon. He needed a freight router he could trust. "Memorabilia is irreplaceable, Cooper. I can't take the chance of it getting shunted off in Laredo and sitting on a siding till the cloth disintegrates. I've got to have a guy who knows the system and knows its faults. I need the best, and Cooper, you are it. I can't believe my good fortune!"

Harry had pictured his own agency, the trips to L.A. to confer with Silvestri, trips for him and Ellen.

He was an ordinary man with one chance for her to see him as more. He should have known, but he wanted it, wanted her so much.

Sweat coated Harry Cooper's body. His shirt clung to his chest and back and his skin was hot against the icy cotton.

Ellen! Was she still with Silvestri's wife? God, that was the last place to be. He had waited for her to call from her new hotel, waited hours, till his shirt was damp as a dish-towel. She said she'd call and Ellen was invariably reliable. Finally without thought he'd grabbed the phone, and dialed Ellen's hotel. He prided himself on never raising his voice, but when the twerp at the Rosewood Hotel tried to tell him Ellen had checked out, he'd screamed so loud his secretary came running. Then he had to get off the phone and calm her.

Wait till this pothead is off and there's someone respon-sible on duty, he'd told himself. Go home, call from there.

In the bedroom now he walked to the phone. The message light was blinking. Relief flushed him. Everything would be all right; she wouldn't be shot or bombed because of Jay Silvestri and his skittish wife. Ellen had called him back. Maybe she'd called from the airport. Maybe she was already on her way home. He pressed play.

"Cooper, you don't know me. I am an associate of your associate in Los Angeles, the one who just bought it. He had a shipment for me and now he is dead. My shipment is on its way to Richland. Silvestri was supposed to tell me exactly when it will arrive. He did not give me that information before he died. All he gave me was your phone number. What the hell is going on, Cooper? When will my shipment arrive? Listen, I will call you back at seven a.m. your time and you damn well better have an answer." The voice was youngish, male, no discernible accent. And no sense whatever that he was kidding.

Harry played the message four times. It was three in the morning now, four hours before this guy called back. Harry had no answer now and he'd have none at seven.

He dialed Ellen's hotel in San Francisco, again.

# Twenty-One

Devon Malloy stared at Harry Cooper's phone number, ground into the notepad. It baited him. But Malloy did not reach for the receiver. Too soon to call again. He turned back to his computer screen and the game of Free Cell on it. Free Cell, no mindless solitaire, but a card game that challenged the intellect.

Play again? the computer beckoned. Malloy's finger tapped the mouse. He yearned to slip into the closed arena of strategy in diamonds and spades. It would relax him. He moved the arrow to Yes. One game.

No! He clicked the mouse on No. He was too distracted to plan. He could not chance a game now, not and destroy his 100% win record. He turned away from the computer and stared out the window into the dark. Where the fuck was his shipment? Six million dollars of weaponry that would transform twenty smart, committed men into an invasion force, and it was idling somewhere on the rails like an extra caboose. Silvestri was scum, but who could have imagined he would get himself killed? And before he called with the specifics of the shipment!

Malloy chose the transfer spot in Richland. Half an hour before the train sidled through Richland Silvestri was to call him at a Richland number.

Now Silvestri was dead and Malloy had no idea what train his shipment was on, what name it was shipped under, what its contents were listed as, or when it would arrive at Richland grade. He did not have enough data to make his play. All he had was Harry Cooper's number and now Harry Cooper's addresses at home and at work.

He squinted out the window, trying to distinguish one shard of black from another. Dawn would not puff over the mountains in this part of Idaho for another two hours. He had told Cooper seven o'clock Central Time—5 A.M. Pacific Time. Malloy eyed his gray sweats. He could run half way across Coeur d'Alene and back by then. A week ago he would have, just to be seen out jogging just like it was a normal day and he was no more than he seemed, a young lawyer intent on keeping in shape, a guy who moved to Coeur for the lake and the good life. And if anyone noticed the dark circles under his gray eyes they might ascribe them to long hours over law books. No one would label them the result of years in the library, on the Web, driving all night to talk to a retired guard or a guy who drove a truck when the Feds were building Unit B at Hanford. What there was to know about the Hanford Nuclear Power site in Richland, Washington, Devon Malloy not only knew but had cross-referenced.

For years taking Hanford had been a pipe dream. He had assessed it the way he did the Free Cell layout before he moved a card. He kept looking for angles. Early on he had realized he was not likely to blast through the walls and walk into the reactor. But every chain has a weak link. He had read about every nuclear facility, then every secret biotech facility in the United States, in Russia, and as much as he could find on India, Afghanistan, Iran, Iraq, Israel, looking always for their weak link, one that might be duplicated at Hanford.

In his legal practice he took on government cases that got him security clearance. The clearance allowed him to check on shipments going in and out of Hanford. When he spotted the name Orel Jasson, a trucker from Coeur who had retired after delivering to Hanford for forty years, he had his man. For once luck had been with him. Jasson's father had been on the building crew at B-Canyon in the Hanford Engineer Works, as the facility was called in the '40s. It had taken Malloy months of beers and small talk with Jasson, but he had gleaned enough to layer onto what he knew and figure how to stroll inside. Now that the plant had stopped producing plutonium, security had gotten sloppy. They did not figure they were worthy of attack anymore when all they were doing was letting radioactive iodine seep into the ground turning the flies and rats hot.

A few radioactive rats, they did not think that was important at all. Just like when their smokestacks spewed the killer iodine all those years ago.

Malloy took a deep breath. He had trained himself not to get caught up in that. Not now. Just like the beginning of a Free Cell game; this was the time for planning. He picked up the faded Kodak of the little boy, too weak to smile for the camera and let it remind him of his purpose.

Staying in the background pulling the strings was his way. But when he ran into Jay Silvestri called as a witness on a civil trial in Boise, everything changed. Silvestri had been trolling for a buyer, spreading a fine fine net, watching every word as if every salt shaker and ballpoint pen were bugged.

It was a different story three weeks later at the gun show. Silvestri must have assumed Malloy would be taking out armories. All Silvestri said was, "You play your games with the Feds, Malloy, but steer clear of L.A., you hear? I've got a good life down there and I'm setting up this deal with you so I can afford to keep having one. So you do your overthrowing north of California. I'll get you weapons like no one in this room ever dreamed of. L.A.P.D. never heard of some of these till they got real lucky and broke up shipments meant for three of the biggest gangs on the west coast. I'm not talking just guns; these are weapons that can take out the side of a building, missiles, explosives, gas: civil unrest in a box, Malloy, every terrorist's dream." Silvestri had stared him in the eye like he was calling the shots. "Six million. Cash."

But he was not the fool Silvestri imagined. With the cash came the upper hand. He set the transfer point—Richland— and the terms—cash on delivery in two suitcases of mixed bills. Hefty suitcases. He tried for the train and its schedule, but Silvestri was no fool either and the best Malloy could get out of him was that he was using a particular freight scheduler. Silvestri thought he was covering himself by mailing the scheduler's name—Harry Cooper—to Malloy, aiming to get it to him the day after the switch. Mail must go by mule in L.A., Malloy thought smiling, but it moved sharply up here in Coeur, particularly with a friend in the post office looking out for you.

Malloy stared down at the phone. After all these years

planning, it was unbelievable to have the whole operation hang on whether he could get the container numbers, the train number and the schedule out of some guy in Kansas City.

He checked his watch again. Five minutes had passed. Still ample time to jog. Malloy leaned back in his chair. No point in jogging; no need to burnish his image. He would be inside Hanford tomorrow. By nightfall he would be hoisting the Nukers, the vermin who ran Hanford, on their own petards. Petards: farts; Malloy did not see the point of humor but the appropriateness of petards did strike him.

He'd grown up on reports of Hanford: the radioactive wind that had blown for thirteen years from the Hanford Nuclear Site; Green Run, the day in 1949 Hanford decided to see what effect radioactive iodine would have on the people downwind, opened the smokestacks wide and spewed out 225 times more radioactive iodine than the 3-mile Island disaster. People died; not right away—thyroid cancer takes time. The dead were not government officials, who had moved their own families out of danger, but babies who drank the milk from the cows who ate the radioactive grass, babies who breathed the air into their tiny lungs, babies like his brother.

Americans were sheep. They did not want to know the truth. They were too ovine to see that the whole 9-11 sham was not the work of foreign terrorists, but of their own government, designed to control the populace, frighten the sheep. It was a sham designed to divert attention away from the government's own unconscionable crimes, from the poisons of nuclear power and genetically altered food. Herd the sheep by fear, that was the government plan. The terrified sheep closed their eyes to the construction of new nuclear power plants, to the federal vermin pushing China to build nuclear power plants that would spew poison into the air to be carried across the Pacific to the very area Hanford has already poisoned.

But even sheep can be shocked into action.

Hanford would afford him so much more than a bully pulpit. The government had forgotten about all those storage tanks and the mixers that kept the gases from settling. He had not. As soon as he made it inside Hanford he would turn off those mixers one by one. It would take time for the heat to

103

build in the storage tanks. The government vermin would be calling him, wanting to negotiate. He would make his demand: that his call be linked onto all the TV networks. He would tell the world what his government had done to its own people.

Once the fuel in the storage tanks started to heat up nothing would stop it. The tanks would blow anyway, one after another after another after another.

A nuclear waste site blowing sky high would bring Homeland Security racing in from every other state—leaving some of those states easy pickings for the Select to act. The Select were ready. After Hanford, the sheep would know the truth. The sheep would follow the Select. The revolution was about to begin.

He looked from the phone, to the clock, to the Kodak. Three hours was too long to wait for an answer he couldn't control. One phone call would set up a private flight to Kansas City. Devon Malloy picked up the phone.

# Twenty-Two

Ellen stood outside the restaurant bathroom in the beige hallway so narrow the phone box was a major intrusion. Already she'd had to jam her stomach against it to let a waiter pass on his way to the bathroom. Ammonia wafted by when he let the door swing closed. She sighed and punched in O and the number and set up a collect call.

The phone was whirring and hissing before it occurred to her that this was no longer Saturday night. It was Sunday morning and even Harry Cooper might choose to sleep in after six, particularly after his hectic weekend at work. He'd known he wouldn't finish the emergency rerouting in time for the opera. If he'd made it home before midnight she'd have been surprised.

She should hang up before she woke him, she thought, momentarily drawn into the illusion of a normal Sunday. The receiver was shaking in her hand and she could feel the tears she hadn't shed when Larry Best had her pinned on the bed, when Liza saved her, when she knew she was safe in the car; now they were threatening to burst out of her eyes. She had taken Harry for granted. When he'd accused her of it—more a sad statement of fact than accusation really—she'd known there was no way to contradict him. Before she even had distinguished him from the other middle-aged Portlanders in her apartment complex he had yearned for her. Before she agreed to a movie, he'd loved her, so he'd told her and she'd believed him. She'd never loved him; he was never the one she'd lain awake nights thinking of. She'd never had the urge to call to hear his voice. Until now. Now if she could have one ticket for teleportation in her life, she'd use it up to be back in Kansas City lying awkwardly in his arms, listening to his gently rumbling breathing and happily feeling the cold air shoot down the space where the covers spanned the gap between her back and his chest. She'd catch whiffs of the lemon polish his cleaning lady used on the bedside tables, even smile at the sirens from the firehouse around the corner which was what made his house such a steal. She'd know that things too good to be true weren't true and she'd be happy, truly happy with what she had.

Pulling her skin angrily with her knuckles, she wiped at the tears. No need to make a scene. She swallowed and followed it with a deep breath. Okay, now she was better.

The phone was ringing. She'd tell him she missed him first. The receiver was right by his bed; all he had to do was reach out an arm.

She hadn't counted the rings and it shocked her when the operator announced rotely: "Your party does not answer. Would you like to hang up and try your call later?"

"Right. Thanks." She'd almost hung up before it occurred to her that knowing she was gone, he'd probably decided to work through the night, sleep in his office if he had to, and be there to catch any of the unexpected repercussions a massive rerouting always brings. "Try his office number." She repeated the ten digits, listened to the buzz and grumble of the phone, the ringing, the operator telling her that that number had no answer. Yes, she said, she would try later.

The ladies' room was two steps down the hall. She walked

105

in and stood in front of the mirror staring at the detritus of the face she had creamed and penciled, ever so lightly rouged and powdered eight hours ago. Now the make-up was caked, the cheek color gone and she looked like she'd been embalmed. The mirror showed the tan bathroom walls behind her and as she stared she saw the tan hotel room walls. The gurgling of the plumbing seemed to echo Larry Best's friends chortling as they egged him to hurry up. Her stomach lurched and she thought she was going to throw up. And when nothing came up but shame, she tried to force the vomit up and out of her by will. If there were a shower she'd have ripped off the black dress she would never wear again, and scrubbed her skin till it bled.

But there wasn't of course. She yanked a handful of paper towels out of the dispenser, wet them with cold water and scraped every dot of make-up off her face. Tears gushed. She pushed the rough towels up and down her skin for two minutes, for ten minutes or twenty, she had no idea.

When she finally stopped, not because she was done but because her arms were exhausted, her face was red as if she'd had a bad sunburn, a huge scab, a disease. She splashed it with cold water, blotted with a few more paper towels, and walked out.


Liza didn't have to ask Ellen how her call went; she could read it on her face: Nothing good.

"Harry didn't answer." Ellen slid into the booth and pushed her dishes away. The burst of energy that had driven her to the phone clearly was gone. Her hair was limp, her face was limp; even the fabric of her black dress looked like it had had half an hour in the steamer. "He's not at home, not in his office."

"Could he have turned off the phone?"

"Oh, no, Harry would never be that rude. He'd run out of the shower to catch the phone. I don't know—"

"Okay, don't worry. What we do is put some distance between ourselves and San Francisco. We start north—"

"No."

"What?"

"No!" Ellen thrust herself up straight. "No, Liza, we are

106

not running aimlessly. I've done what I can; now you do the same. Call the police inspector."

"I told you why I can't."

"Not good enough!"

"Ellen, police tap phones. If I call him I might as well invite him to pull up a chair."

"Then we'd know what was going on. Now we have no idea. Killers could be anywhere. That old woman on the stool over there, she could be after us. Is this how you want to live? How you want me to have to live because of you? Do you—"

Liza put her hand on Ellen's arm. She didn't look at Ellen; she couldn't bring herself to do that, too. It was all she could do to swallow hard and get her mouth wet enough to speak. "I can't call Bentec. I told you about robbing the jewelry store. What I didn't tell you was Pope, the jeweler, was killed."

Ellen didn't gasp. She looked too shocked to make any sound. Finally, she asked, "Your father shot him?"

"No, Ellen. My father didn't shoot him. I did."

"But how—"

Liza pressed down on her arm to silence her. She had described this night before, but only to people who were paid to judge her. She'd learned to speak without wavering, and not to make eye contact. That connection could pull her over the edge. She started speaking. "When my father burst into the store, the alarms went off. Pope had a gun behind the counter. He grabbed for it. His pants were around his knees. The muzzle got caught in the fabric. Daddy was yelling big sloppy, liquory threats. His breath smelled like something rotting and it blasted me every time he yelled. The alarm was shrieking. Pope was yanking at the gun, trying to get it free, all the time screaming at Daddy that he'd blow his fucking head off."

"Oh my God, Liza."

Liza was back in the jewelry store, on her knees, staring stunned at the jeweler's naked crotch, his limp and tiny penis, the mass of brown fabric swirling on his thighs as she yanked at the gun in futile panic. She felt the hard floor cutting her knees and then she didn't sense herself at all, just the mael-strom around her and the vision of what she had to do. "I

107

didn't even have to take the gun out of his hands; I only had to turn it. His finger was still in the trigger when I shot him." Now she took a long breath. "If I hadn't stolen the pendant the state wouldn't have pressed charges, or at least that's what they said. But taking the pendant thrust me into a whole different class of villain. I wasn't a pretty little innocent lured by a known pedophile; I was a conniving killer just too young to go to the gas chamber."

"But if it was his finger on the trigger—"

"That did help. When the story hit the newspaper two women volunteered to testify that Pope had molested them years earlier. That helped, too." She forced herself to check Ellen's face for signs of disgust and was amazed to find none. It was not her habit to reveal more than necessary, but she went on, "What really saved me was my father."

"His death? The car accident?"

"No accident." She swallowed hard. This she'd never said before and she wasn't sure she could tear it out of herself without ripping off the scar tissue that had held her together for the last twelve years. "It was Thanksgiving, ten days after the jewelry store. Thanksgiving Day with my grandmother was like a contest to see who would break first. She lived to condemn. Her answer to every problem was abstinence. The house was cold because my grandmother didn't believe in heat in California. The food was bland because spices were luxury, and of course there was no liquor. Normally my parents would have been angry or sulking. This day they were just quiet; I assumed it was the result of the murder. They still didn't know what would happen to me, or to Daddy. They were subdued but Grandma was going at it double time, how I had disgraced her, how she'd have to move, how she should have known about me, known when Daddy married a woman he met in a bar, and on and on. Neither Mom nor Daddy answered at all." Liza swallowed. "I should have realized something was off. I used to lay awake replaying the day minute by minute trying to find the time I could have changed things. But the truth is I couldn't have changed anything at all."

"Liza, I—"

"No!" She couldn't deal with being diverted. "Here's what

108

happened. Daddy waited till my grandmother went to the bathroom, grabbed the keys and grinned at Mom. 'Joy ride? Come, my sweet!' he said with a great flourish. It had been hours since either of them had a drink and she was barely holding it together. But at this she gave him a smile that must have been how she looked when she was seventeen. She was halfway out the door when he stopped her and said, 'Kiss the baby goodbye.' Mom thought it was part of the act and gave me a theatrical smooch. But Dad hugged me so hard my ribs crunched." She shivered and shook herself sharply to escape the memories in her chest. "So hard that when the police came hours later I wasn't surprised."

"Oh, God, Liza."

"All in all I spent less than six months in Juvie. But the Jewelry Shop Lolita case was salacious and it made news for months. The area we lived in was like a small town even though it was inside Los Angeles. Everybody knew. Even in other parts of L.A. people recognized my name and eyed me with either a sneer or a smirk. And of course, the cops were drooling over the surveillance photo with my tits, my tattoo and Pope's penis."

"Oh, Liza."

"Right." Liza jammed herself back against the booth wall. She felt naked, helpless with her secrets bared. She swallowed but there was no moisture left. "You can see . . . why I can't trust the Los Angeles police. When they connect me to Elizabeth Cummings, the jewelry shop Lolita, they'll start wondering if I killed Jay. Killed again."

Ellen didn't move or speak. The waitress and the old woman weren't talking. But everything else in the room shrieked—the refrigerator, the coffee machine, the fan. In the parking lot the Camaro stood, outlined in the light from the restaurant window like a star in a spotlight. Why hadn't she thought to park it in the dark? Why—

Ellen shifted and when Liza looked up it was into her gaze. She couldn't decipher Ellen's expression; it was a jumble of sad, resigned, determined.

"Liza, I am so very sorry, more sorry than I can say that this awful thing happened to you. And that you were so alone with it, for so long. I wish I, Mom and I, had known back then when you were so young. I just feel terrible for you." Her voice was scratchy, too, and Liza took comfort in that. "But, well, there's a saying in Mom's family about things like that, that you just have to hitch up your skirt and step over them and not look down while you're doing it. Liza, if you think this cop is going to blame you for Jay's murder, you don't have a choice. You've got to hitch up your skirt and call him and find out what he knows. It's the only chance you have."

Liza slumped down. She was too sapped to argue, and besides she knew Ellen was right. Still it was a full minute before she could make herself look up, nod, and slide out of the booth. She had to brace her hand on the table to get up.

Calling Bentec was a dangerous move. He'd be after her . . . No, wait. He would be after her if she were still driving the car she rented. But Bentec didn't know about Ellen or her car. If she could talk fast . . . Even if he traced the call, so what? They'd get into Ellen's car and drive on, two ladies headed to Healdsburg for breakfast. Okay, this could work. Already she was feeling more herself again.

She dropped coins in the phone, punched in the number, listened to the recorded demand and dropped in more coins. The phone rang and rang. It was the middle of the night. Bentec could have gone home like a normal person, which would mean this was no special case, and—

"Yeah?"

"Bentec?" she blurted out, startled by the gruff syllable.

"Right. Who's calling?" Now he sounded more businesslike and she wondered if she'd caught him on the run, maybe running to go home.

"Liza Silv—"

"Where the hell are you? I told you to come in here. This is a murder case and I don't have all night to sit waiting—"

"Hey! I can hang up." She shouldn't provoke him, this man who frightened even Jay, but she couldn't help it.

"Don't!" He spoke softly as if he didn't need to raise his voice. "Liza, you get yourself in here at nine o'clock. No, better yet, I'll be at your house then. And right now tell me when that container will arrive."

"Container of what?"

"Don't you question me. Do what I tell you. Are you home yet?"

"Aren't you tracing this call, Frank? Don't you know?"

"Yeah, I know. And I know you're driving a Camaro so don't think you can get away. Every sworn officer in the state is after you, Liza. They're holding warnings that say Armed and Dangerous. You want to come out of this in one pretty piece, you get your ass moving. And you can start by telling me what Silvestri said to you before he died."

Don't provoke him! "You want his last words, Frank?"

"Didn't you hear me? What did he say?"

"He said: Fuck Frank Bentec!"

She smashed the phone down and stood facing the wall, barely breathing. Her hip banged the phone tray. Coins bounced up and clattered on the floor.

It was past the time for small change. And not provoking him wouldn't have helped. She picked up her wallet, turned, smacked into a gray-haired woman and screamed. "Oh my God, I'm sorry. I didn't mean to—"

The woman—the blue-jacketed woman whose husband had stalked out, Liza now realized—patted her arm. "Are you okay, honey?"

"I'm. . . yeah." Before she could force out a lie, the woman's arm was around her shoulder.

"You're shaking all over. Here now, come on back inside where you can sit down."

She let herself be led back into the dining room, let herself be lulled by the woman saying, "Let's get you some tea, honey. Something nice and warm to drink. Hot, sweet tea. Here, now you just sit down with your friend and I'll get you some fresh tea."

"What happened?" Ellen was half out of her seat, reaching toward her.

"It's worse than I thought, Ellen. Bentec's a lunatic, and he knows about the Camaro."

"Did he trace the call?"

"What difference does that make? If he knows that I'm with you and you rented the Camaro in San Francisco then he's focused around here. Oh, God, Ellen, I am so sorry I got you involved in this. Maybe I should take the car and—"

111

"And what? Let me walk back to San Francisco?"

"I could drop you at Santa Rosa airport. That's somewhere around here. There must be signs on the freeway. If the Highway Patrol doesn't stop us first. But it can't be that far, and—"

"And you figure Bentec will have cops on the freeways but no one will think of watching a Bay Area airport?"

"But they're not after you."

"Liza, sit still. Think. We've been seen at two hotels in San Francisco. I rented the car. I dropped everything to fly out here to be with you. Do you really think any cop on earth is going to decide I'm not involved?"

"I'm sorry. I am so sorry. I know, fat lot of good sorry does." She reached for Ellen's hand and when Ellen didn't pull away she was surprised, surprised at both of them. "You've been a good friend to me, and, God, now I could get you killed." She paused, in hopes of Ellen interrupting. But Ellen just slumped back. Her lank brown hair hung almost in her eyes and she didn't bother to push it away.

A cup of tea was in front of her. It was a moment before she thought to pick it up. Another before she realized that the old woman had brought it herself. "I thought you could both use tea. Plenty of sugar. Drink it down even if you don't like it that way. This hour of night, you need that before you get back on the road."

"Thanks," she squeaked out.

"Oh, hon, look, whatever this man did to you, it's not worth going numb over, believe me. You feel all empty inside, but you'll fill up again. It doesn't seem like it now, but trust me. I'm an old broad and I've seen it all."

Liza looked up to find her smiling.

"Hon, you just saw my man leave here in a huff. He figures he's got me by the short hairs and it's just a matter of time till I call and beg him to come get me. Well, Gilbert J. Brown's got another think coming. I'll just sit myself on a stool over there till Celia gets off, and get a lift. It probably doesn't seem possible to you now, but someday you'll be as old as I am, and you won't get all choked up; you'll be doing just what I am, shrugging your shoulders and ordering yourself another piece of pie."

Liza found herself almost smiling. She took a sip and felt the hot sweet liquid open her throat. "Thanks. I really mean it. The tea was exactly the right thing. It will keep us from driving the car into a ditch."

Ellen put her cup down and reached for her wallet.

"No, hon. On me."

"But you don't have to—"

"There were hands there to help me when I felt all empty. And more times than one. Filling you girls with tea is my link in the chain." She turned and started for the counter, her shoes thwacking against the floor. Not the soft-soled loafers Liza realized she'd expected, but sturdy brown boots.

The woman turned back and for the first time a look of uneasiness settled on her face. "Where are you girls headed?"

Richland. The word almost fell out of Liza's mouth. But she caught herself. "Portland. Why?"

"Well, I don't want to put on you. But if you're going north, I wonder if you could give me a lift. I'm headed just off the highway about an hour north. Won't take you five minutes out of your way. I'm a good driver. Wouldn't hurt either one of you to rest for an hour."

And if the highway patrol came up alongside, it wouldn't hurt to have a gray haired lady driving. "We'd love to have you," Liza said and finished her tea.

# Twenty-Three

Harry Cooper drove slowly through Kansas City. He wasn't the kind of man who got threatening phone calls. Gangsters got calls like that. Not freight forwarders.

It was in-between time, no longer night-dark, but not yet dawn. The time when the fairies go back underground. Odd, he hadn't thought of that tale from an old aunt in forty years. But now he made his way along the empty street, beneath the great oaks and maples and elms frantically waving their arms like the fairies before they were sucked down into the netherworld of hopelessness and moaning. His headlights made

113

puffs of white, illuminating nothing. The snow that had melted during the day had frozen again, clear and slick. The car skidded every time he braked. He was too tired to drive, too distracted, too damned scared.

Once he got back to the office, he'd be okay. If the threatening lunatic on the phone was the recipient of Silvestri's shipment it'd be easy enough to find it for him. He'd check the Web site, then if there was a problem he could go through the routing for the entire nation west of the Mississippi, check every transfer point that Union Pacific had and Southern Pacific used to have, look at every major carrier and every short line. He knew the majors like the back of his hand. The short lines he'd didn't know so well. Short lines were problems. You couldn't count on them. With the majors you keyed in the bill of lading and a copy was on the receiver's screen before the container left the station. The recipient could log onto the carrier line's Web site, find out exactly when his container would arrive, where it was this instant, and if there was a problem ahead. On the majors the electronic tags from the Automated Equipment Identification System logged in the car every time it passed through a transfer point. Mistakes still happened, but not like they did on the short lines where things were still done manually.

Harry Cooper was the best router in the business—that thought that always gave him a little buzz now only set his stomach quivering.

He made a left and was halfway through the red light before he thought to hit the brake. The car swung wide into a skid. If there'd been another driver crossing the intersection he'd have been crushed flat as a ninety-nine cent burger. Sweat coated his face. Oh God, he couldn't die in a crash now when he might have lost a shipment, a shipment whose unverified weight he had listed as provisionally approved by the Western Weights and Inspector Bureau and stamped through. Never had he bent the rules like that before. "It's just for a day or two, until the paperwork's approved, right?" Silvestri had said. "A day or two, what can happen?"

What indeed.

114

He just hoped Silvestri initiated the papers before he got himself shot. Harry's face flushed. An awful thing to think. But true.

A branch had blown down in the street. He slowed and swung around it.

Jay Silvestri's shipment, a sealed container of Hollywood memorabilia headed to a collector in Richland, Washington, should have been an easy ship. The container, a roll-on-roll-off, should be somewhere north of Dunsmuir, California, by now. Could it have been sent via Fresno despite all his paperwork? Not likely riding on the majors. But still, the human element. Had their AEI code . . .

The light turned red. He slid to a stop. The tall trees and comfortable houses were behind him now. He was near the stockyards now, and the netherworld was filled with the lowing cries of the steer that would be dead within the day.

What had possessed Silvestri to give this lunatic his phone number, his home phone, yet? Silvestri should have given the phone lunatic the Web site information. Why didn't he do that? Maybe he intended to, but got killed first?

Murdered for some totally unconnected reason? As likely as a caboose pulling the engine, Cooper admitted

Maybe it wasn't memorabilia in those cars. Guns? Drugs? Contraband? A chill iced his chest, colder than when he stood listening to the phone message. He'd vouched for the shipment. If it was illegal he was an accessory. He'd never be let near freight again. Anything could be in those containers. Bombs. Oh, Jesus, he'd endangered the lines. And—the realization came so quick he hardly noted it as an afterthought— endangered the engineers, the porters, the people near the tracks.

He pulled into the empty parking lot and headed for the building. Chances were the shipment was on schedule and the lunatic just didn't realize how slowly trains move. But by the time lunatic called back, he wanted to be able to tell him he'd checked everything possible. He wanted this business cleared up before it affected Ellen.

Ellen. Why hadn't she called from her new hotel? He didn't know where she was. Only that she was out there in San Francisco with Silvestri's wife.

Harry Cooper slammed the car door and ran across the icy lot, feet slipping, arms flailing.

At the edge of the lot a tall sandy-haired man sat in a rental car and watched.

# Twenty-Four

Liza watched the old woman, Gwen Brown by name, slide behind the wheel of the Camaro and start the engine. The dark smoothed her face and softened her sharp nose, and determined chin. As she leaned forward checking out the knobs and gauges, she looked like a teenage boy anxious to goose the car forward. Liza barely had the seatbelt latched when she shifted into reverse and the car shot back. Felton squealed.

"Please," Liza said, stroking his head, "a pig expects a smooth ride."

"Sorry, little guy." Gwen grinned at him, reached over and rubbed his stomach, ignoring the road in the process. "We had a pig for a while. Alex, my second son, brought him home when he was no bigger than this. He was a cute little fella, and smart, and I hated to give him up, but I could see the handwriting on the wall, and the second time Gil mentioned bacon, I made sure that little guy 'wandered off.'"

"I know what you mean. The only time I ever argued with my husband was about keeping Felton."

"Only time, huh? This pig must mean a lot to you."

"Odd, isn't it?" Liza was rubbing softly on his belly. "My neighbor was going to take him to the pound, just because he wouldn't be little and cute forever. Jay, my husband, couldn't understand why that got to me."

"Yeah, well, a man wouldn't, would he? Course, now with men dyeing their hair and going in for facelifts, maybe some of them do know what it's like to have a short shelf life." She turned full face to Liza. "But you, hon, you've got good bones

116

and bright eyes; you're going to look good for a long long time. You've got nothing to worry about."

Liza almost laughed. If there'd been a Farthest From the Truth Award, Gwen would be rushing the stage. "Felton's only a piglet now. I don't know what I'll do when he's a porker. But for now he's as safe as I am." She glanced into the back seat. Ellen was stretched out, and if there had been any question whether tension would keep her awake it was gone. In the time it had taken to let Felton out by the restaurant, Ellen had flung an arm over her eyes, and been asleep before the other one slipped off the seat and dangled to the floor. Even the jolt out of the parking lot and the sprint onto the freeway hadn't rearranged her.

Liza leaned back and stared at the dark empty freeway. Two lanes going north now, like 99 had been, was that only last night? It seemed ages ago, making the wrong turns, lost in the fog.

Gwen slowed. "You mind if I cut onto a side road? It won't take but a few more minutes."

"Fine." On 99 getting off the freeway and avoiding Bentec's net had been the right move. And tonight, if Bentec had traced her call, getting off the freeway was a real good idea. "Why, though? Do you figure your husband will be driving around looking for you?"

Gwen laughed. "Not hardly, hon. I'd bet my ATM card that Gil's got his butt settled in the recliner. He's waiting for the phone, watching the door. But if the boys see the light's on they might stop in. I know Gil, been married to the man for thirty-two years. Boys come in, he's going to start telling them about me sitting in the restaurant, waiting for the sun to rise, realizing the error of my uppity ways. They'll decide to do Gil a favor—maybe they'll even think it's me they're helping out. They'll swing by the restaurant. Celia will tell them their mom went off with two girls in a hot car, and the whole thing'll be more than they can stand. By sun-up all their friends'll be on the chase, at least those who don't have the sense to turn their phones off. So, just in case, I say stay out of sight, you know?"

"I know."

In his sleep, Felton was butting against her stomach. She

117

looked down at his black and white head, scratched behind his little ears and shifted him to the left. Outside now, dark shapes of eucalyptus wove and snapped in the wind. There might have been houses behind them along the two-lane road, but Liza couldn't make them out. She leaned her head back against the seat, on the flat part, not allowing herself to ease it into the curve where sleep would be too great a temptation. Gwen reached over and gave Felton another tickle. "If you want to sleep, hon, I can hold him on my lap. He'll be safe with me."

Liza had to jam her teeth together to keep from sobbing at the sweetness of it, of being safe, of Gwen. Sweet, innocent Gwen who she had let into this car and who knew what. She swallowed, breathed and swallowed again. "Gwen?"

"Yeah, hon?"

"Will you be all right when we drop you?"

"Sure. Why?"

"I didn't know how Gil—"

"Gil? Oh. You thought. . . No, see, Gil's going to be pissed and pissed royally, but that's no matter anyway because you're not dropping me at home. I'm headed to my RV. I won't see Gil for a week. By that time he'd better have calmed himself down."

"You're going to drive around for a week?"

"Not 'around,' to Kennewick, up in Washington state. I'm off to my Roving Women's Convergence. Women driving motor homes, you know. They converge every couple months. But I only converge once a year." She grinned just the way Liza remembered Ellen's mom doing when she held out second helpings of the godawful creamed corn from the St. Enid's cafeteria. "The way Gil carries on, it's like as if I was about to converge with Robert Redford, instead of a thousand women on wheels."

Liza looked at Gwen anew. "You just decided to get yourself a trailer and drive north?"

"Not 'just.' I've been thinking about it for years. Gil'd know that if he'd paid any attention. Gil thinks of me as his wife, part of the town like he is. His family's been there three generations. It never occurred to Gil to go anywhere else. But me, I was passing through. It was the Sixties then, lot of stuff going on. Free love and a lot of weed. And, well, you know how it goes. I figured I'd spend the summer there and move on. By the time I realized it was winter it was already February. I was thinking winter, like in Vermont, waiting for the snow. I was coasting. And then I coasted into being pregnant. I got into the whole thing of having kids, doing co-op nursery, raising vegetables, making macramé, whatever, the whole hippie thing. Time passed. Kids grew up, got jobs, had kids of their own. And there I was a grandmother, and that's fine with me. I love those little ones. But, see, I always wanted to travel. Gil never understood that. I don't mean going on vacation and ending up with things the same as at home, just in a different place. I wanted to travel. And I wanted to do it by myself with no one to answer to. I want to step off the end of the world and see what happens. Scares Gil to death."

"How'd you come by the trailer?"

"Waitressed in town. Saved my tips for five years. And I'll tell you, that pisses Gil off about as much as the trailer itself. He can't stand the idea that I had that secret. Not that it was such a secret. I would have told him if he'd thought to ask."

"So you just decided and then you did it." Liza couldn't keep the awe out of her voice.

"Yeah, hon. It's not such a big thing. Only Gil thinks it is. And it won't kill him to be on his own for a week. The boys'll take pity on Dad and get their wives to invite him to dinner. He'll hold forth bitching about me and they won't stop him like they mostly do. So he'll get it out of his system. And me, I'm going to settle in at the Convergence, take some classes, maybe, but mostly just be a woman among women, you know?"

"Right," Liza lied. If there was one thing she did not know it was how to be a woman among women. She didn't even know how to be a decent friend. And the idea of stepping off the edge of the world terrified her. She felt as if she'd spent her life clinging to that edge, trying to get a foot up onto solid ground. She turned the radio on low, shifted and watched Gwen out of the corner of her eyes.

"So you're headed to Portland," Gwen said after a while. "What's in Portland?"

"I don't know. It was Ellen's choice. She used to live in Portland."

"She have a guy up here?"

"She didn't mention anyone."

Gwen was silent. Liza let her head slip back against the seat; she shifted Felton on her lap, and looked out through the waving branches. She felt herself jerk awake when Gwen said, "I guess you girls don't know each other too well."

"Why do you say that?" She could hear the edge in her voice.

"The guy in Portland. That's what girlfriends tell each other. Maybe there was no guy, but from the little bit I saw of your friend she looks like a girl who'd have a guy. My sons' wives are like that, nice, reliable girls. Not as pretty as her, but nice."

"She didn't mention anyone in Portland."

"Course, I could be wrong," Gwen said quickly. "What do I know about Portland, huh?"

Ellen started. "Portland," Gwen was saying. Half–awake, she strained to make out what Liza was revealing about Portland. But Liza doesn't know anything, Ellen reminded herself.

There was nothing Liza could reveal about Portland or Wes Jacobsen. Even half–asleep, Ellen was certain she hadn't mentioned Wes, much less why she hadn't seen him in three years, hadn't spoken of him in two, and hadn't allowed herself a thought of him since she agreed to move to Kansas City. She shifted minutely on the cold, too-short seat, moving slowly, quietly, offering no opening for talk. And just in case, she pulled her jacket over her head.

Not a single thought of Wes Jacobsen, she silently intoned. She hadn't allowed herself one in Kansas City: she'd made that unspoken commitment to Harry. It was her only commitment to him, and how great a sacrifice he'd never know.

When she'd made the No Speak rule the year before, it had been hard, but she was a self-contained woman and she still had the warm refuge of her memories. Then not so much time had passed. Then she could still feel a tingle on her thigh at the spot Wes's hand first lingered over as they lay in the half-zipped sleeping bags with the pine branches holding back the stars. She had allowed herself whiffs of Pinesol that first year of Not Speaking. And she lay in the dark conjuring up the pines they lay in after a day of biking and the musky-sweaty smell of him.

It had been the reverse that first night with him. She could almost smell the odor of the pines and then the smell of him next to her, strong and wild, pulling her into the wild world where past and future vanished and only the scent of him, the feel of his thick curly hair between her fingers, his surprisingly soft beard creeping in around her chin, tickling her lips, tantalizing her. Then his soft, moist lips caressed her till she felt nothing but them, them and the pricking of his tongue creating cravings she'd never had before. Her feet planted against his, her legs taut, her groin sucking up so hard she felt like she would implode. Then the rush up her spine and the frantic meshing rhythm faster, faster till she was one with him and the pines and the stars.

In that year of No Speaking, she rationed that night so she could smell the scents anew, feel his callused palms pulling her butt hard against him. So it wouldn't dull to mere thoughts, to sequential memory. She teased herself then, with earlier bike rides when she and Wes pretended they were focused on mapping terrain for the mountain bike meets. She let her thoughts linger on the afternoon they'd both misjudged a turn, slid down the muddy embankment half-on half-off the bikes and lay in an intimate heap, slowly becoming aware of arms and legs, breasts and breathing, lying unmoving till the other riders clambered down to separate legs from spokes. It had been too soon then, she knew, and he knew well enough that she hadn't had to mention it. Too soon in the Oregonian spring of the serious cyclist. She'd felt like a teenager then, filled with the yearning fantasies, the panting closeness, the sudden pulling away, throbbing from crotch to breasts, face hot with longing, face hot with frustration.

Later, when the year of No Speaking had been replaced by the Edict of No Thinking, she had told herself that their passion had been nothing so special as she'd let herself believe, that she wouldn't have assumed it was unique without the long slow build-up and the certainty that once they made love it would be the beginning of a new grand level of passion that would take them over.

She wouldn't have assumed it without the sudden end.

She wasn't in Kansas City now. She deserved a respite. It would be okay to "see" Wes and—

That was missing the point.

She'd managed to keep him out of her mind for three full months; she had lain in bed at night and read book after book till the letters blurred and there was no opportunity for any thoughts between closing the book and sleep. It was just beginning to get easier. Letting the memories, grown stronger in their exile, take her over again would be disaster. Particularly so close to Portland.

And unfair to Harry. She had tried so hard for Harry; she couldn't give in now. Particularly so close to Portland. The jacket lay on her face, half-blocking her nose; she wanted to move it but didn't dare.

A minute later, or was it an hour, she jerked awake. The car was stopped. Gwen was opening her door.

"Where are we?"

"Oh, Ellen, you're awake." Liza stepped outside.

"Welcome to the Last Ditch Trailer Park, girls."

Ellen pushed herself up and looked outside at varying shades of dark. "Why?"

"Why the name? Some say 'cause it's at the bottom of a slope where it floods every spring. That's how you can tell how fast your trailer will move. But I'll tell you, you look around this place and you won't ask the question twice." She stood, one hand on the top of the door, the other on the roof. "I'd ask you girls in, but truth is, I better get going and so should you."

"'So should we?'" Ellen shifted out of the car and stood beside her. It was lighter than she'd expected and she could see the quiver of the woman's jaw.

Gwen's hand was on the edge of the door and she swung it back and forth, as if it were pacing for her. She looked not at Ellen, but across the roof at Liza. Slowly, she said, "It's none of my business, but you girls did me a big favor and so, well, I've seen enough or life to know you aren't just two friends driving around for the weekend. Something's

122

troubling you two. I don't want to know what it is, but as tired and frazzled as the two of you are, I'd say you need to get yourselves a decent meal, and this time eat some of it, and then figure out what you're doing. There's a café a friend of mine works up this road about an hour, in a hamlet called Max. There's not much on this road most of the way. You go through two little towns—you can miss them if you're not paying attention in the dark like this. Then the road widens to three lanes and the café's about a mile after that, on the left—Café Max. Good food, pay phone, and best of all for you, there's parking behind it so you can get this car out of sight. Like I say, I don't want to know what you're doing, but this boy car you're driving may not have been a problem down in Marin County where people've got plenty of money for hot cars for their kids, but the farther north you get the more of a magnet this car's going to be. Come light, every kid you pass is going to be drawn to it."

Liza came around the car and put a hand on her shoulder. "We're okay, Gwen. It's just been a long time since we travelled together. But listen, thanks for your advice. And you take care, yourself. Get your trailer out of here before Gil and your sons and their friends come looking for you."

Gwen took a breath and gave a little exasperated sigh. "They won't be looking for me in the trailer, hon, they'll be looking for me and two pretty girls in a Camaro. That's what I'm telling you. It's Sunday morning and they've got all day for a 'fox hunt.' You'll get guys all over the county eager to run you to ground. They won't do you any harm, but if they find you they'll sure slow you up, what with them calling all the other guys to crow about it and those guys hightailing it over and all. You could end up with a parade following you."

Ellen could see Liza twitching to move. "We'll be okay." She gave Gwen a quick hug. "You got everything, Gwen?"

"My purse. In the car." Liza reached back in the car, and yanked out a tangle of cloth and leather. More than one purse, Ellen realized as Liza began untwisting them.

Something fell on the ground.

In the dark, she didn't realize till Gwen stooped down and

picked it up that it was a gun. A huge handgun. She slumped back against the car, looking from Liza's frightened face to Gwen's, which revealed nothing.

Gwen stared down at the gun. She was holding it by the butt, looking at the barrel. The light from the car door glistened on the gun and outlined the creases in her face. Her hand, Ellen realized, was shaking.

Gwen looked up, eyeing Liza anew. "Don't you use this gun on my boys."

"What? We're not going to," Liza held out her hand for the gun. "We're not about to shoot anyone. But, you know what would solve that problem, Gwen? Call Gil, leave him a message that you're heading south or east."

It was a moment before Gwen said, "No, hon, better I don't suggest travelling to him at all. That would just get him and the boys chewing over it. Trust me on that, I know my boys."

"Okay. And you won't mention us, right?"

"Course not. But about the gun, you promise you won't use it on my boys? Even if they're being snotty, even if you don't intend to shoot."

"Promise," Liza said and slipped the huge handgun back into her purse.

As Gwen walked into the trailer court, Liza pulled Ellen closer. "Come on, let's move before she has second thoughts."

# Twenty-Five

Frank Bentec settled in his loden-green office chair, lifted a report out of his box. His jaw pouched out at the sides from clenching his teeth and he swung it back and forth as he opened the envelope with the print report. He scanned down over the mandated descriptions: address, time, those present at the crime scene (whose prints had been taken and checked against the latents). Under findings, only two matches were listed. Silvestri was one. The thugs he'd expected to be gloved, but he'd been a cop too long to assume anything so obvious.

The second match was to Liza Silvestri. He lifted the phone and dialed.

The man who answered on the fourth ring was not pleased.

"Martin, Frank Bentec here. Sorry to be playing reveille so early. I haven't interrupted anything more important, have I?" He offered a muted chuckle and hurried on so the old fart didn't have to come up with a lie. "You know I wouldn't have called so early if this wasn't vital. Wouldn't be back down here at the department if it could have waited."

"You're after a warrant, I assume." None of Bentec's banter was reflected in the judge's voice.

"Right. Maybe you saw the TV report on this case yesterday. Victim's Jay Silvestri. Blown away in his love nest downtown."

"The loft love-nest guy?"

"You got it, Martin. The love nest's in an industrial area; not a place you'd spend the night. Silvestri had a house in Malibu, on the ocean."

"Malibu wasn't good enough for nooky?"

Bentec smiled. Now the judge was getting into it. "Not with his wife living there."

"She didn't know about the love nest?"

"That's what Silvestri figured. But nothing's forever, eh, Martin?"

"Apparently not Silvestri."

"Right. And not his secret. His wife found him out. We've got her prints all over the place there. Her prints in his blood. You can't get better than that."

"So, Bentec, then what do you need from me at six in the morning?"

"Taps on Silvestri's phone."

"Done."

"Thanks. I'll have the papers in your office when you get there." Bentec pushed Off, left his thumb on the key for just a moment before shifting the phone and punching in another numbevr and listening to the second sleepy voice of his morning. This time the mention of his name was like a steak bone to a dog. But then that's what cops were to reporters.

125

"Hey, Frank, what're you up to this hour o' morning? The Silvestri case, huh? You got a break in it?"

"Silvestri's wife's prints are in the blood in his love nest."

"No shit! Thanks, Frank."

"Hey, wait a minute. You didn't think that was free, did you?"

"Guy can always hope."

"This is close as you'll get. It's almost free. But in case you don't know, Silvestri's wife is quite a number. Why don't you lead with her picture? She's on the lam."

"Armed and dangerous?"

"Silvestri was shot in the back."

# Twenty-Six

Ellen braced her feet under the dash and clutched the pig on her lap. Liza was driving like a maniac. She pulled back on the road so fast she nearly clipped the trailer park sign pulling out.

"Headlights! Liza, you don't have any lights!"

Speeding through the dark, Liza twisted one knob after another.

"Slow down!"

Liza twisted another knob. The windshield wipers came on.

"Slow down, dammit! Think of your pig!"

The lights came on, and Liza stepped on the gas.

"What are you doing?"

"Getting us out of range of Gwen's fox hunters. It's already getting light. We've got to move."

"We won't be moving if we're picked up for speeding."

"So what's our choice?"

"Let me drive, Liza." She sounded so calm, like the panicked woman holding the pig didn't exist.

Without responding, Liza pulled over. And that panicked Ellen more. Liza should have protested. That would have been Liza. But this—? How wrung-out was Liza to give in like this? Had everything finally caught up with her?

126

Liza was out, walking around to the passenger seat.

Ellen clambered over behind the wheel, adjusting the pig and Liza's purse in the process. Her gun-heavy purse. The engine was still running; she shifted into drive and suddenly they were tooling along the road like two women on their way to a sunrise church service. Liza needed time to get herself together. But there was no time, not now. "Where'd you get that gun?"

"I had it in my purse."

"You always carry a gun? Like you do keys and a lipstick? In case you want to hold up a Safeway? So you still get a bargain when your coupons have expired?"

"Hey, I didn't think of its economic benefits." That sounded more like the old Liza. "But no, I don't carry it all the time. Jay just gave it to me, Friday night."

"He gave it to you the night he was shot?" Ellen couldn't picture that at all.

"He brought it home." Liza's voice was quavering. "He'd said he would bring it from Malibu."

"Why?"

It was a moment before Liza squeaked out, "So I'd be safe."

"Oh my God, Liza! How dangerous is it in Malibu?"

She couldn't label the noise Liza made, but when Liza spoke she'd gotten control and her normal light tone was back. "Oh, Jay didn't get it for there. It's for when I stayed late in the loft because it's pretty deserted there at night."

Ahead was a crossroads. She slowed. Two or three after-thoughts of commercial buildings huddled near the corner before the road turned rural. Spruce, pine and redwood edged in toward the pavement. Puddles of night dew sparkled in the hazy morning light. Way ahead she could see a vehicle coming toward them. Surely it was too soon for "the boys" to be out hunting Gwen in the Camaro. Good she still had on head-lights to shield the car. "If you have a house on the beach in Malibu what are you doing staying in a deserted area down-town?"

"Jay got the loft for business."

"A deserted area that requires a gun, for business? What kind of business was he in?"

"Not for business there. In the house, in Malibu."

"Excuse me?"

"When he finished remodelling the loft and they started selling the other lofts in the building he was going to move his office there. In the meantime we spent some nights there."

"But why were you there alone, late? Liza?"

"Well, he wanted a place for me to go when he was entertaining business clients."

Liza's voice had changed mid-sentence as if she'd started out pitching a story to avoid whatever it was she was avoiding and discovered halfway through that she was spouting a truth she hadn't realized before.

It was like picking at a scab, these prying questions; she couldn't bear to look at Liza but she had to figure out what was going on, had to force Liza to answer. "Why didn't he want you there when his clients were? You must be a superb hostess."

"Yeah, I'm the best." Sarcasm bit into the words. "I can draw out a post. I could make small talk with Hitler, Ben Gurion and Marie Antoinette and have them leave thinking they're best friends. I know the best caterers and the most interesting. So why did Jay want me out of there? Jay said it was so I wouldn't be bored. No, don't bother chortling; I knew it wasn't true either. And don't bother asking what I thought he was up to there. It wasn't other women. Trust me on that."

"With a wife like you why would he—"

"Men do. Even men with wives who are great in the sack want more. Here's what I've learned in my years in L.A., Ellen, guys want more, just more. You know why?"

"Why?"

"Does the universe go on forever?"

"What?"

"Does the universe extend forever? Answer me."

"Liza, we don't have time for games."

"Does . . . the . . . universe . . . go on forever?"

"I don't know."

"Yes or no."

"Okay. No."

"Then what's beyond the end?"

"Liza, what does this have to do with Jay, why he rented the apartment, and what you learned in your years in L.A.?"

The pig made a hiccoughy noise. Liza shifted it on her lap. "Guys want more so they don't have to face the wall at the end of the universe. If they can keep 'getting' they can keep pushing back the end, you know 'sure, there's an end but not until after I get the Mercedes, not till I get the redhead in the sack.' They never have to accept the fact that no matter how much money and power they've got they're going to get sick some day and be helpless and die with a tube up their nose."

In the oncoming lane a car went by. The driver, in beaked cap, slowed long enough for a look at them. Normal for a small town, Ellen assured herself. But she watched him in the rearview till his car shrunk to nothing. "And the end of the universe has what to do with Jay?"

"He knew there was an end. And, I don't mean to brag, Ellen, but he also knew he wasn't going to find a woman better than me."

Ahead a stoplight turned red. Ellen slowed to a stop. "Okay, we agree he wasn't shacking up out there and—"

At first she thought the little squeal came from the pig. "Sorry, Liza, I don't mean to be crass about your husband, especially when he's only been dead for two days."

"'S'okay."

Without looking at her Ellen reached over, and squeezed the spot on her arm where her hand landed. "It's not okay, but things have gotten so bizarre we don't have any choice." Ellen let a moment pass. "So let's say Jay was doing business at the house. What was that business? Before you decide you don't know, think about it. You met some of his venture capital clients, right? You went to some functions, right? So those were safe, legitimate, and—"

"And boring." Liza gave a small laugh. "If the people he had to the house were more boring they must have been dead."

"Boring?"

Liza heard the word but didn't respond. Boring? It seemed like another life when boring was a worry. She leaned her head back, gazing at the collage of colors beyond the windshield. Ellen had stopped the interrogation and the lack of an adversary left her no one but herself to face. She felt like two women, one clinging to her husband, one . . . what?

129

It had all been so innocent in the days of boring business evenings before Jay got the loft and she never had to see his clients again. Of course, avoiding clients had been just a side benefit of the loft. Now she felt the same small warm rush she always did thinking of the erotic nights she'd arranged for him there, the ones Jay had called "sensual even by Hollywood standards." "Why don't we put off the remodelling till next month?" Had he said that after every night, or did it just seem that way? Didn't matter. Nothing had gone in but the receptionist's room, the one she'd made into the beach house. "Because that was the whole point." She was so startled by the sound of her voice, she nearly dropped Felton. He squealed. Stroking his head, she cuddled him, then hoisted him onto the back seat.

"What was, Liza?"

"Nothing."

"Liza, nothing is nothing anymore."

Liza was wringing her hands, actually doing it, hand on hand. She wished she still had Felton on her lap to stroke while she tried to make sense of all this. She pulled her hand tighter over the other, squeezing the thumb into the palm, trying to feel the pain, to concentrate on it, to slip into it and disappear.

"Liza? Goddammit. What was the whole point?"

She looked at Ellen as she drove, a sprig of light-brown hair was sticking to the edge of her eye and Ellen seemed too tired, too preoccupied to feel it.

Liza was expert at rearranging people so they'd be in a position to help her. It was how she'd made it through Juvie, how she'd endured St. Enid's, how she'd created her life in L.A. All her instincts told her to make up a story for Ellen; to give Ellen something that would allow her to remain a friend. Not the truth, not now. She was almost surprised when she heard herself saying just that. "The loft Jay died in we used for sex." She hurried on so she wouldn't hear Ellen's reaction. "Every other week or so we spent the weekend there. Jay was so pleased with the concept of this secret place and the fact that I would spend most of my time hunting down the props for each weekend. I thought it was because our love was so sophisticated, that Jay kept wanting to keep the loft

130

just for us. Other people had to buy excitement, go to Bali or Paris and pretend they were part of the exotic life. but we had it all within us. I gave him what no 'place' could offer. In the loft I gave him total respite, and, well, sex like he'd never had before. At least, that's what he told me." The words caught in her throat, she swallowed, and when she started to speak her voice still creaked. "I thought the loft was special, and he saw clients at the house so he could keep the loft just for us, and all the time he was away on business he was thinking of us . . . there . . . in the loft." She swallowed again. She didn't see Ellen anymore. Her eyes were open but what she saw was the loft, the thrift-shop sofa and the wooden coffee table, the archway, Jay staggering back—

Ellen's voice was like a slap in the face. "But what if he wasn't, Liza?"

She inhaled slowly, trying to find a connection between Ellen's question and the reality she shared with Jay in the loft where they lay long, lusciously as the sun broke the fog in the mornings, listening to the sounds of each other's breathing, feeling each other's thoughts so clearly there was no need of words. "No, that's not the question. I told you, there was no other woman. A guy doesn't come home to a weekend like we had after he's been with someone new. I'd have known. Trust me."

Ellen nodded.

She could tell Ellen didn't quite believe her but that didn't matter. "The question is: What . . . if . . . my husband . . . was just using the loft. . . having me set up these elaborate sensual nights . . . to get me out of the way?"

"Well, that makes sense and—"

"Ellen! You don't understand! I gave him everything I am, there in that loft. I spent my time arranging the most erotic set-ups, games that would tantalize him the whole week when he was away. He'd give me a word: say, Silk, and I created him a harem, six silken chambers, each with its own rules of pleasure. I spent the whole two weeks he was gone creating it. In the loft, he had me, body and soul. We were like one being, like nothing else existed, because nothing could touch what we had. Or . . . that's what I thought." She was shaking; sweat coated her face and back. "I gave him everything I am;

131

and he . . . For him, was I nothing more than an interlude, an amusement when it was convenient?" Nausea roiled through her throat and stomach and mouth, her eyes, her ears, in each breath she drew in. It crowded out thoughts, smashed words to whimpers. What she saw in her mind was the image of a man, not Jay Silvestri but Pope the jeweler.

For a moment she thought she really was going to throw up, but she couldn't even do that. There was nothing in her but bile.

Trees passed. Wind flicked her face. She could feel it cutting away at her skin, carrying it off, leaving . . . what?

"Liza?" Ellen's voice quivered but Liza could tell she wasn't about to be sidetracked by sympathy. "What if you're right, and Jay wanted you out of your house? What does that mean?"

It means that the one man I thought really loved me, fucked me over like I was a naive child on her knees behind the jewelry counter.

"Liza, just what do you think was going on in Malibu when Jay sent you away?"

She started to say "I don't know," but caught herself. She wasn't a child on her knees anymore. "He had business clients or business dealings he didn't want me involved in . . . or to know about because . . . it would make me . . . despise him."

"Or get you killed."

"Or . . . get . . . me . . . killed." She could hardly believe it, but she said the words aloud and listened to herself say them. She unscrewed the water bottle at her feet and shot the water at her face. Then it was all cold, and she was blinking and gasping and wiping ineffectually with her hand as the water ran down her face onto her T-shirt. She was rooting in her purse for a tissue. And she was looking down at the gun. "Jay was involved in something at the house. He had this gun."

"Let me see the gun."

The car stopped. It took Liza a moment to realize they were at a red light. "You want to check it out here?"

"Suddenly you're shy? Yes, here."

Liza pulled it free of her purse.

"Jesus, it's huge." Ellen hefted it. "And heavy. What is it, Liza?"

"A nine-millimeter. What the cops use for personal weapons. See, here on the grip—FB, Frank Bentec."

Ellen looked as if she'd drop the gun through the floorboards. "Let me get this clear, Liza. We've got highway patrolmen all over the state looking for us, and we're sitting here with a gun taken from the Assistant to the Police Commissioner? We've got to get rid of it and quick."

She wasn't looking at Ellen. Her gaze was out the windshield. Eucalyptus lined the two-lane road. Now she noticed the pungent smell that must have filled the car all along. Her nausea settled in her throat. She'd believed she had a tacit agreement with Jay that her past and his business were their own domains, secondary to their life together, and that life was sacrosanct. She had blocked out all questions about his other life and imprisoned herself in her fantasy marriage. But she was not Mrs. Silvestri, Malibu wife, anymore. She never had been, really. She was Liza Cummings, running down the alley with the cops after her and no one to protect her, no one but herself.

All those questions, the unpermitted suspicions, shoved forward now. What had Jay been doing in the Malibu house that left no detritus of lipstick or ash, was so short-lived that she was rarely barred and required so small a space Felton was not freaked by the nearness of threatening strangers? And that left him in possession of Frank Bentec's gun?

Frank Bentec. Jay's betrayal was not in what he was doing, but his doing it with Bentec.

If he knew about Bentec and her past.

Liza's eyes filled. Jay was dead and she'd never know what was real about him and what she'd made up. She stiffened against a sob. No time for anguish, no luxury of regret now. She had to think. What was Jay's business with Bentec? What did she know? Two things: Bentec's demand of her: Tell me when that container will arrive! And Jay's last words: "Richland grade."

She turned, took the gun from Ellen. "I'm not tossing Frank Bentec's gun. Ellen, I'm done with running." A minute ago she'd been weighed down by exhaustion, now she felt as if she'd shed the leaden cloak of Mrs. Silvestri. She felt giddy. "I know. I know. We're driving a car that might as well have

133

a flashing red light. We've got the cops after us, plus maybe Gwen's sons and all their friends. I don't know how Jay got Bentec's gun, but whatever the answer it means they were a lot more entwined than Jay let on."

"Doing business?"

Liza nodded. "Otherwise Bentec would have kicked up a stink about the gun. But if they were doing business like you say, he wouldn't want to call attention to it. He'd figure he'd get the gun back later."

Ellen shrugged. "You led a fast life, Liza."

"Just like the girls at St. Enid's expected, huh?" Ellen didn't reply, which meant that observation was on the money. She leaned forward, half off the seat so she could face Ellen. "Here's what we know. Jay shipped something to Richland but we don't know what, and nor why Bentec is so hot to find it. One container of something. So, okay, here's what we do: stop at the next restaurant, preferably one near a gas station. You call Harry and let him tell us what's in the box."

It was a moment before she realized Ellen wasn't answering. She was staring through the windshield wide-eyed. Liza jerked her head forward but there was nothing but empty road ahead.

"Ellen?"

Ellen's hands tightened on the wheel.

"Hey, you there?"

"Yes. I just can't believe it. It's so simple. Harry will tell us what's in the container. He'll have made sure he knows exactly what it is, because that's how he does business. No one's more precise than Harry." Ellen tapped the gas pedal with each statement. "It's something stolen, right? You agree, right?"

"I guess. Jay was never offended by stepping over the edge of the law. I don't think he'd deal in drugs, though."

"Too evil?"

"Too dangerous. Jay said drug runners were crazy. There are easier ways to make money. So, no to drugs. And definitely not by train. Besides, would Harry—"

"Oh, God, no! So, okay we're talking a product."

"Animal, vegetable or mineral?"

"Liza!" But Ellen was grinning. "A product that belongs

134

to someone. So all we need to do is find out what it is, and contact someone in that field."

"Like if it's a container full of diamonds we call the diamond merchants' association?"

"Exactly, Gold Bullion Society or whatever if it's gold. Then we get them to take charge and vouch for us. And it gets Bentec off our backs."

"What about Jay's murder?"

"You can hire a good lawyer and have him run interference with the police. You said Bentec left threatening messages on your tape at home. Have your lawyer get them. Then you're clear of Bentec. Right?"

Liza tapped out disbelief on her arm. She couldn't find the flaw in Ellen's thesis. Still . . . "It can't be that simple."

"It can. It is. It just seems impossible because of all we've been through." Ellen flipped the wheel to the right and back again, a little dance on asphalt.

Liza grinned. "And all we have to do is call Harry. Okay, Ellen, dial the man up. There, ahead. Turn in there to that restaurant."

"That'll probably be the one Gwen mentioned. She could have called the cops. Still, we have to trust someone."

"It's not a matter of trust. If the cops are watching that place they've already seen us. No matter. You'll use your one call for Harry. And mine for the gold or diamond merchants. Maybe they'll even give us a necklace."

"A reward? Why not?"

"We'll have to go to the opera."

"The opera?"

"To wear our diamonds. Anywhere else a tiara would be tacky."

# Twenty-Seven

Devon Malloy did not feel the cold. He had trained himself to ignore physical feelings as he did emotions. Certainly

135

the chill of a parking lot in Kansas City was not going to get to him.

He checked his watch. Four minutes to go. Give Cooper enough time to get settled inside, to open files, make phone calls that could be redialed. Malloy felt no anxiety; he had trained that out of himself too.

Or almost. And that would be alleviated as soon as he knew the shipment's expected time of arrival at the Richland grade. The whole deal had been dicey from the moment he met Silvestri at the trial in Coeur, then at the gun show, slick Silvestri and his beautiful little blonde wife. He had been worried that Silvestri did not maintain sensible reserve around the wife, as if he did not know women talked. Then he had realized how to turn the tables. He had been specific about the train—a freight with one passenger car and no passengers but Silvestri and his wife. That had surprised Silvestri, his including the wife. Silvestri's condescending smile said, "You want her, don't you? She's mine. But it will amuse me to dangle her in front of you." Maybe in the end Silvestri would have lost his nerve and left her on the beach in L.A.; there was nothing Malloy could have done about that. But if she had been on the train he would have shot Silvestri, taken her and she would have become the perfect poster picture outside the Hanford when the tanks exploded. The yuppie dream girl screaming in terror as she waited to die while the world watched helplessly—it was perfect. Every day he felt the pain of his baby brother's death, but Malloy was not so naive as to think the world would share his grief. They might shove Brian aside. But Liza Silvestri would grab sympathy from coast to coast.

Liza Silvestri made everything perfect. And then Silvestri died and ruined it. If there was just some way to still get her . . .

But there wasn't. He had to be realistic about that.

Malloy shifted in the car seat. The windshield was fogging but he chose not to wipe it. It would shield him from view if any witness was up in Kansas City at this hour. Squinting through it would help to keep him focused.

Obsessed, that was what Caryl had called him before she walked out of their marriage. Obsessed about Hanford, and

136

about Green Run, the day the government chose to open the smoke stacks and kill its own people. She had argued that Green Run was a Cold War phenomenon, that Hanford's thirteen years of spewing radionuclides was over, that the political climate had changed. Like Caryl said, he was a bright guy, a genius, she had called him; any door would open to him. He had lain back, his head in the softness of her lap, and felt the lure of owning two hundred acres of aspen-covered hills, with a house he designed, a boat he built for fishing on the river, with children of his own. "Look," Caryl had said, "the DOE shut down Hanford. They're cleaning up the waste. You say you want change; that's change!"

And then the bastards decided to restart the Fast Flux Test Facility reactor. Their own documents admitted that the reactor posed catastrophic safety risks, that the reactor could melt down or explode. Safety measures? They could notify officials downwind in two hours, they said. In two hours it would be two hours too late.

The windshield was fogged opaque. He was not angry; he did not allow himself anger, not now of all times. He unzipped his jacket and let the cold November air strike his damp neck.

Nothing had changed at Hanford. There was no Cold War now to blame. Only the government and its greedy contractors. And vermin like them would go on forever at Hanford, at other nuclear plants, spewing out deadly radionuclides. He would show them what can happen once and for all.

He checked his watch again. In one minute he would be headed inside. In a few more he would be driving out of the parking lot, with the final bit of data on the shipment. He would be ready to notify all twenty men near Hanford which train to meet and when.

But the sudden blossoming and more sudden plucking away of the perfect accoutrement—Liza Silvestri—gnawed at him. After all these years to see the perfect hostage, the symbol of a nation of hostages, and have to do without. There had to be a way.

There was something, a flicker in his thoughts. What? Women talk, that was it. In bad times they talk a lot. Bad times, like a husband being shot. For the first time since Malloy

137

left Coeur d'Alene he felt a smile teasing his face. Who would Liza Silvestri call at this very bad time but her best friend who was Cooper's, the freight forwarder's, girlfriend? All he had to do was get the woman's name and whereabouts from Cooper.

Harry Cooper was in front of his office computer, standing. He couldn't stay in his chair. Silvestri's bill of lading for his container was on the screen. He didn't need to check it. He'd written it up, taken Silvestri's word on the weight, and—his throat tightened at the thought—created the Western Inspectors Bureau number that allowed the cargo to go through without being weighed. How could he have—

But he'd meant that fiction to facilitate the passage of the container, not conceal some kind of contraband.

Union Pacific, the form said at the top. UP a reliable major. He checked the web page for location—an hour over the Oregon border. He scanned the blocks with the weight in tons—gross, tare, net; the length of car, the marked capacity of car, the stenciled weight of car, the freight bill date, the freight bill number, the waybill date and number. He'd listed the origin road code and the station of origin, Long Beach, CA. Bill of lading date . . . could it be just a week ago? The invoice number was there and the customer number. Consigned to: D. Malloy and Associates. Destination: Richland, WA.

He checked again at the top, where the form offered the option of "STOP this car at"; the goose egg sat in place. No one should have stopped the car; no one should have checked it.

Route Long Beach–Oakland–Roseville–Portland–Richland. If the shipment had been pulled off in the hole, on the siding at one of the interchange points, there'd be a notice on the web page. According to the website, Silvestri's shipment had passed over the Oregon line headed to Portland, just as it should be. Nothing was amiss here. There was no reason for anyone to worry. Certainly no reason for the lunatic receiver to be calling in the middle of the night and threatening him. That frightened Harry Cooper all the more. The only sensible reason for the threats was that the receiver was truly a lunatic, out of control, a madman waiting for a shipment of contraband or drugs or, God forbid, guns.

In the distance metal clanked, cars shifting in the night. Further away, the lowing of a whistle cut the thick winter air and seemed to echo off the empty corridor outside his office. The music of night sorrows. During the day there was ten times the noise, passenger trains whistling through intersections, grinding to stops, phones ringing, computers beeping, young forwarders running in for his advice. Noise thick as tracks around K.C., and he never noticed any of it. But now it was as if he was the only man for a hundred miles, standing on the lone rail in the snows of North Dakota, ears cocked for the howls of wolves.

If he hadn't taken on—no, falsified the bill of lading for Silvestri's shipment, he'd be home in bed right now, with luck with Ellen, and his biggest decision would be how she'd react to being awakened by a kiss. He'd have the weekend off. They'd have gone to Gelia's for dinner and then to the opera. She'd never have thought of jumping on a plane west to . . . oh, God, to Silvestri's wife and who knew what?

If Silvestri's murder was not the sharp corner of a love triangle, if it was somehow connected to this shipment . . . His gut clenched. If Silvestri's wife was involved, then the hitmen would be tracking her down. Her and Ellen.

Things like this didn't happen to people like him, like Ellen. The lunatic wouldn't be threatening Ellen if it weren't for him. If only he knew where she was; he'd fly there in a minute.

Outside in the corridor, shoe leather slapped on the bare wooden floor, shoes rushing, slowing, like an old engine puffing uphill. Cooper's stomach eased up; it comforted him to realize that someone else had reason to be here at this time Sunday morning.

# Twenty-Eight

Ellen leaned back, letting her gaze follow Liza and her pig around the Max Café parking lot. She was too wired to sleep. She could sleep on the plane back to Kansas City. Or in her own apartment, as late and luxuriously as she wanted. In her tiara.

"Sorry. It took him forever." Liza plunked the pig in the Camaro. "Long as he was in the car, you'd think he'd have been happy as the first in line for the Opera House ladies' room at intermission."

"Even if he doesn't have a tiara?"

"We'll get you a diamond collar, huh Felton?" She gave him a final scratch behind the ears. "It's like so much time passed he forgot about that part of his life. They say constipation is a problem for pigs. Who'd figure, huh? But, anyway, he is one empty pig now. Or he would be if he hadn't found the dog's dish over there. Going to be one unhappy hound. C'est la vie, or le chien, eh? Let's go call Harry."

Ellen laughed. "What were you doing while your pig was chowing down? Were you sniffing helium?"

The café was clearly a local hangout. In the minutes it had taken the pig to defecate, the three trucks in front had been joined by a pick-up and a tan-and-rust Desoto, all pulled so close to the fogged picture windows of the diner-sized room Ellen pictured patrons opening those windows and putting their bread baskets on their engines to keep them warm. Two plaid-jacketed men sat at the counter, two in down vests at one table and an elderly couple at another. "Sit wherever you want, ladies," the waitress called from behind the counter.

Liza bounced across the room to the far table by the window and Ellen's own feet felt pretty light. It wasn't over, she reminded herself. But she did feel like a short-timer. She took

140

the seat facing the phone and tried not to glare at the man talking on it.

"Coffee, ladies?"

Ellen nodded.

Liza hesitated. "Do you have herbal— Hell, make it coffee. Not decaf; make it the hard stuff."

The waitress poured and left. Glancing at her ample derriere, Liza muttered, "Food must be okay here."

"Shhh."

"What do you think, she's going to go into a rage and sit on me?"

"Eat some crackers."

Liza laughed. "Keep my mouth busy, huh? And don't comment on that bloodhound in the truck wagging his jowls or the guy at the counter who could be his brother."

"We're not out of the woods yet."

She opened her hands in diva mode and sang, "Over the river and through the woods . . ."

"Stop! You'll get yourself arrested for disturbing the peace. And no lawyer'd be able to talk you free on that."

Liza grabbed her hands. "You know what? A tiara isn't enough! For what we've been through? I don't think so."

"So what're you saying, Liza, two tiaras? With a bracelet tossed in? Of course, then we'd have to do the opera in New York, so we weren't overdressed."

"Two tiaras apiece would stand out even in Manhattan." The waitress brought the coffee and Liza ordered bacon and eggs for both of them. "Maybe we should take the whole shipment and skip the diamond merchants. "Then we'd be really overdressed."

"And we wouldn't be looking at the end of the tunnel, we'd— Oh, rats, look the guy's redialling. Couldn't he have called from home?"

"Why don't you go and poke him with your tiara? Hey, you want onions scrambled in your eggs? I'm going to see if I can catch the waitress in time." Liza was up and out of the chair before Ellen could nod. But it didn't matter, onions or not. She sat relishing the buoyancy even as it seeped away in Liza's absence. Fingering the tines of the fork, she looked out the window at the stand of redwoods across the street. Odd

141

to think that she might never see redwoods again. Redwoods that had been such a part of her life in Portland. She hadn't thought she'd missed the great trees in Kansas City—they had their own great trees there, giant elms with branches swaying in the winds off the prairie, ghost trees in lightning. But not redwoods, taller than one glance could frame, unyielding in flood or storm—until it was too late.

"What're you thinking?"

She started. She hadn't even noticed Liza's return. "Thinking? The redwoods. I haven't seen them since I left Portland."

Liza smiled. "And?"

"And what?"

"That sigh of yours wasn't an agricultural statement. That was a guy-sigh."

"So now you're the all-knowing interpreter of body noises?"

"Nothing special about me. Felton could have nailed that one. If he had, he'd say you were thinking about an old lover in Portland."

"Forget Portland."

"Sure."

"Thanks."

Liza grinned. "I will, if you tell me about it."

"It's none of your business?"

Liza made gimme motions with both hands.

"In a minute you're going to be fingering through my brain."

"So tell me about him. I'm right, there is a 'him.' So, tell. What's the harm? We could use some happy memories. It'll make me happy to know you had fun in Portland."

The fork was still in Ellen's hand. She pressed the tines into her fingertips. She'd been so faithful to the No Speak rule. How could she break it now when she'd be back in Kansas City so soon?

"Ellen, what's the harm in talking about it? Of course I'll never mention it after this, because let's be honest here, it's not like you'll be saving your vacation days to go on another trip with me next year. If I called you again you'd slam the phone down so fast my ear would burn. Right? Huh?"

Ellen laughed softly. "Nah. I'd just have you committed."

"So next to the stranger on the plane I'm the best person in the world. Actually, I'm better than the plane person. You never know how he might react. But me, well what do you think is going to shock me?"

There was a catch in Liza's voice. A great rush of sorrow flowed through and Ellen had to press the tines harder to keep control. What kind of dreary life did Liza have if there was nothing left to shock her? And now she didn't even have that life anymore. Was it so much to tell her about Portland? Slowly, she said, "I've never told this to anyone."

Liza smiled, unconsciously Ellen was sure. The smile was just a slight shifting of cheeks, but it changed her face entirely. She looked like she'd gotten an unexpected gift. It almost made Ellen cry. "There's no one else I would tell. I—"

"I guess that means we really are friends, huh?"

"It does in my book."

Liza's mouth quivered as if she was about to cry. She swallowed, and seemed to hoist a grin out of nowhere and paste it on her mouth. "Okay, friend, tell me your secrets."

Ellen stared down at the table. Emotion wasn't something she was good at and she was way over her head with these two currents washing over her. Even as she shifted back and put the fork down Ellen could feel the tickle of warmth at the bottom of her spine, the warmth she felt each time before the No Thought rule. Still staring at the table, she said, "It's strange to say this out loud. I never thought I would. It never occurred to me I'd trust anyone enough to tell. Sometimes I can hardly believe something that lasted for so short a time wrenched me off my foundations. But I'm not like you. Men would step on my stomach to get closer to you. No man has ever made a beeline to get to me. I grew up gawky, chunky, all the 'y' words that make a girl ignorable. When you knew me in college I divided my time between being efficient and resenting life's unfairness. I guess I could have gone on like that for the rest of my life, if it hadn't been for—" she grinned—"the great gift of my car being totaled."

"Totaled? You okay?"

"Nothing happened to me. I wasn't in it. The car was parked and some drunk plowed into it. But that's not the point."

Liza nodded, a tiny movement that seemed less to signal agreement than to show she was stepping out of the way.

"What happened was I started to use my bicycle to get around. It was a dry year for Portland and the section of town I lived in was pretty flat and so it made sense. I'd never done anything remotely athletic before. I had to borrow my landlady's old bike to begin with. But what I found out was it was fun. So I bought a bike, a new, good bike. I kept making my routes longer, looping around to include a hill, trying— Anyway the point is that I realized that this was something I loved and I, amazing for great-lump me, I was a good rider. When I plunked down six hundred dollars for a mountain bike and equipment I'd made my commitment. I started doing tours and races. My whole life had turned inside out."

The food arrived. Ellen didn't look down at it. The café windows were steamy, giving a misty quality to the redwoods beyond, as if she was leaning on handlebars looking through sunglasses fogged by her hot sweaty face. "My job, which used to be my focus, was just an inconvenience between weekends. I, who used to be an outsider, was a Plum among Plums."

"Plums?"

"Portland Ladies' and Men's Bicycle Society, the Purple Wind. I was part of the crew that made up our first T-shirts— half a dozen purple plums flying in a gust."

"And your guy was a plum?"

Ellen swallowed, eager to clothe him in words, yet knowing the end would be that much sooner. "Wes rode. He started about a year after I did. At first he just rode for the pleasure of being outdoors. But it's hard not to get hooked. And soon he was coming out for tours and cross-country races, too. I'd see him in the beginners' heats."

"He wasn't as good as you?"

Wes, not as good? How could she think. . . "He saw things that I'd never have glimpsed without him. He kept things in perspective. Distance and time and winning didn't matter to him, not in the beginning. . ." Not when they first rode in the redwoods. Or even later, on the routing trip, the two of them stopping in a sun-dappled glade, resting their bikes against

144

the redwood boles, standing in the center of the ring of huge trees, pretending to be absorbed in deciding which path the riders should take, pretending not to notice the heat off his body as he leaned over the map next to her.

God, she couldn't let herself go that deep, not here in a café over yellow eggs and bacon.

"But then?"

She had to swallow so her voice didn't humiliate her. "Then we were at a rathskeller with the Plums after a cross-country I had won—"

"You won?"

"Yeah."

"You beat men and women?"

Ellen laughed. "You can hardly believe it, can you? My life was that different. I wasn't the lumpy kid anymore. I had muscles in places I'd not only never thought of having muscles, but places I'd never thought of at all. And that night I was flying. I had a few beers and I was going on about what it meant to me to win and how everybody should at least try. Wes was just sitting there, drinking his beer." She could see him there, feel him— She pushed the memory away. "But the next time we raced, it was clear to everyone he'd been working out."

"Did he beat you?"

"No." The single syllable thudded between them. Ellen swallowed but it did no good. She could see the reflection of her own pain in Liza's face. "Not then," she managed. "He kept getting better. One race through the redwoods he almost beat me."

"And?"

"And after that day I never saw him again."

"How come?" Liza's egg-laden fork was drooping from her hand.

Ellen stared hard at the Formica between them. She couldn't look at Liza; she couldn't bear to see the redwoods. "Not because I didn't try, Liza. I called him. I had a friend from the club call for me. Finally I wrote a note, and when it came back unopened I gave up. I guess you could say I was a little slow on the uptake."

Liza slammed her fork down. The table shook. "Stupid,

inadequate macho asshole! You can do better than that, a whole lot better, Ellen. You don't have to—"

Ellen swallowed. "Don't! I can't handle that. I know you care; that matters. But I just can't handle— Look, the phone's free. I'm going to call Harry."

"You okay to do that?" Liza gave her arm a squeeze as she stood, and even that touch was almost too much. She squeezed her lips together and hurried the few steps across the room.

The phone was in a cubby between the men's and ladies' rooms, about as private as standing in the YWCA shower with ten other women. But at least her back was to the room. If her face turned three shades of red no one would see. She punched in Harry's number, got the numbers wrong, hung up and punched it again. He'd be smiling when he heard her voice. A hot thick wave of guilt washed through her. Jeez, now her face probably was purple. Nine o'clock Sunday morning; he should be home. He wasn't. His message asked for her particulars.

The guilt evaporated. Where *was* Harry? He had to be home; he was probably mowing the lawn. When he heard the phone, he'd be racing into the house. She took her time telling him she was okay, no longer in San Francisco at all but driving north, taking the scenic route, going toward Eureka. She missed him, she added and realized she meant it. Still he didn't pick up.

She swallowed hard and gave up the pretense. "Where are you, Harry? I need to talk to you. This is important, real important." She paused, strained to hear his footsteps racing across the soft grass two thousand miles away. "Okay, look, I'll call you the next time I'm near a phone. Don't use your phone, don't go out. Oh, and Harry, I miss you."

She put down the phone slowly, as if the wordless air before the click still linked her to him. She wanted to call again, hear his voice again. Maybe he'd heard the last ring of the phone and run inside too late to catch it. She glanced across the room. Liza was gazing out the window at the redwoods, the kind of smile on her lips that said she was pondering Wes and the bike trail mapping. There was no way she could face Liza in that state.

She dialed her own number and punched in the code for

her messages. Old Mrs. Hellman, across the hall loved the opera. She couldn't thank Ellen enough for surprising her with those tickets. She'd found them there slipped under her door when she got up yesterday morning. She hadn't had a wonderful surprise like that since she was a girl. It was such a shame Ellen had to go out of town all of a sudden and miss it, the opera she meant, not the surprise, though she wished Ellen could have seen that, too. But she did so enjoy it and when Ellen got back she'd have to come to dinner—Mrs. Hellman would make her pot roast, Ellen knew she was famous for her pot roast—she added with a little laugh, before another gush of thanks.

The second message was from Harry. He cleared his throat as he always did as if the imminent necessity of speech hadn't occurred to him. She felt her shoulders relaxing and herself smiling. "Ellen, this is Harry." But it wasn't the low, sweet, safe voice she'd been longing to hear. She hardly recognized the throaty tone, the frightened cadence. "El, honey, where are you? Listen, I don't want to worry you but I can't just not let you know. Something's going on. Like I said, I don't want to worry you, but I got a suspicious, well, threatening call, last night. It's connected to Jay Silvestri's shipment. Some crazy man is frantic to find it and threatening me. Sorry, El, you kept asking me about Jay Silvestri and I guess I should have told you, but I just didn't want to worry you. Hon, there's something real strange going on here. I hate to say this about your friend's husband, particularly as he's dead, but I think the man's a liar. There's no memorabilia in Hollywood worth this kind of threat. And if there were he sure wouldn't be sending it to Richland, Washington. There's something else in that container. El, *I* vouched for them. If something happens with this lunatic who's looking for them, I'm going to lose my job. Even after all—" The message clicked off.

She pictured him standing looking down at the phone in his hand, his sweaty hand. Him, threatened, in danger of losing the work he loved, all because of her. Because of Liza. Because of Jay fucking Silvestri.

147

# Twenty-Nine

Devon Malloy slipped in the office door. The old guy, Cooper, was staring at his terminal, so caught up in the computer he would not have heard a tank smashing through the door. Malloy eased across the floor. Cooper did not look up. The sour smell of Cooper's sweat cut through the dull stench of oil and dust. Cooper must have raced in so fast he had not stopped to turn on a light. Only the paler gray from the computer stood out from the gray metal desk and cabinets in the hazy dawn light. Hunched forward, staring at the screen, not typing in, not scrolling down, Cooper himself was part of the gray. Here it was the tail end of the night and the man was dressed in a suit. Just like the bureaucratic vermin at Hanford when they spouted their lies to the media. Cooper's suit was even vermin brown.

He moved directly behind Cooper. "Cooper, when will my shipment arrive in Richland?"

The guy nearly shit in his pants. He spun around in the chair so fast he kicked.

Malloy had the Luger out. He held it an inch from Cooper's face. "Do not cross me, Cooper."

"Wha—"

"The time of arrival! When does my shipment arrive?"

"Your ship—"

Outside the sky was growing light. Men would be coming to work soon. "I do not have time to coddle you, Cooper. When does my shipment arrive in Richland? Which train? What is the container number?"

"How did you get my name? Did Silvestri—"

He smacked him, not hard. He was not done with the man. Blood dripped from Cooper's mouth.

"That is it on the computer, right?"

Cooper was holding his face with both hands, like it was

the only face that mattered, like *his* brother had not mattered. If he had allowed himself to feel emotion— But he did not, especially now when he still needed this man.

The monitor showed a form. He scanned the lines till he spotted a name: Silvestri, J. Location: OR 102. That meant nothing to him. Destination: Richland, WA. Okay. Container number. Too long to remember; he'd have to write it down. Other numbers. Nothing about the time of arrival.

"Cooper, get your ass over here and find—"

"It's headed for Rich—"

"Dammit, do not tell me what I already know. The container is not in Richland yet. It has been en route so long the train could have refueled in Washington, D.C. Where the hell is it now? When will it arrive in Richland? Come on, come on!"

Cooper pushed himself out of the chair. He was bent over, staggering. Blood was running down both cheeks, soaking brown into his asinine brown jacket. He had to prop a hand on the desk as he stared at the screen. "It's guns, isn't it?"

Malloy let go with his backhand. The vermin's head jerked forward and back. A slap of necessity, not from emotion, he noted as Cooper sagged against the desk. Blood coated Cooper's teeth; it looked like his whole mouth was flowing out. "Yeah, Cooper, guns, guns that could blow this building to rubble. Now, when does it arrive?"

"Trains get delayed. No one can tell—"

He smacked the Luger across his face. Bones cracked. "Cooper, I'm giving you one last chance. You want to live?" He looked from Cooper to the form on the screen. "This scrolls down, right?" He pressed the down arrow and the rest of the form appeared. "E.T.A.? Estimated time of arrival? Eleven fourteen—tomorrow—twenty-two forty-eight. Almost eleven P.M. This it?"

"Yeash." The man's words were mushy through the blood.

Eleven tomorrow night, plenty of time for his men to get their trucks to Richland, ready to pull up next to the roll-on-roll-off and roll it onto Hendricks's flatbed, drive to the transfer building Hendricks had found half a mile away, open the container and distribute the weapons. Hendricks objected to abandoning his flatbed there, but he had been made to see the overriding advantage.

Malloy pressed Scroll Up and noted the top of the form again, with the container number. He took a pad out of his pocket and turned to the screen.

Cooper groaned. The guy was lying across the desk bleeding like a pig. His eyes were covered with a disgusting film of red he seemed beyond noticing. Cooper was on his way out and quick.

"Cooper! Where is Silvestri's wife?"

Cooper was already white as paper. But he went whiter, transparent. The man did not even try to answer. Cooper knew where she was. He knew!

Malloy's neck tightened, his stomach knotted, his face burned. He had to struggle to keep his voice under control. "Silvestri's wife is your girlfriend's best friend. Do not pretend you do not know how to reach her."

"I—" he made a gurgling noise—"don't."

Malloy swung the Luger back and barely caught himself before he brought it down on Cooper's nose. He was so close to having her, the crowning touch to Hot Standby. This quivering vermin would not stand in his way. "You tell me, Cooper or I'll get it out of your girlfriend."

Cooper's mouth was open, the blood flowing. Then Cooper fooled him, acted like he was going to answer with that open mouth. Instead, he grabbed a card from his open file and stuffed it in his mouth.

"God damn, you fucking bastard!" The gun went off and he watched the vermin's forehead fly into a thousand pieces. His body slammed into the computer.

Malloy's blood was racing as he focused back on the screen, the blank gray screen. There was data he still needed to copy down! The container number! Dammit, the vermin had made him miss that! Malloy picked up a stapler off the desk and threw it at the red-drenched body. Rage ignited him. It was all he could do to stop himself, to force himself to breathe deeply, to hold himself still and listen for footsteps in the hall, cars pulling up outside. The room reeked of urine and shit from the body.

His fingerprints were all over, but that made no matter. A day from now one more killing would be insignificant.

Noise in the hallway. Were those footsteps? He did not

have time to take out anyone else here. He froze, as he had trained himself to do—freeze and assess. No, not footsteps. Not yet.

Malloy took a last look at the moaning red blob on the floor. It hardly looked like a man anymore.

He bent down, shoved open the vermin's mouth and pulled out the soggy mess of paper. "You thought you could swallow this, Cooper? Too thick. Any fool could see that." He unwadded the disgusting mess. The writing on the address card was almost washed away by the saliva and the blood. All he could make out was, "Ellen Bai."

# Thirty

The crack of the phone against the wall startled Liza. The phone was hanging by its cord and Ellen was leaning against the wall next to it. Liza raced past the empty café tables to her. "Ellen, what's the matter? Did you get Harry?"

"Harry's dead."

"Dead? That can't be. You must be—"

"Crazy? I wish." Tears ran down Ellen's face; she made no attempt to wipe them away. "I called Harry; I . . . got . . . his machine again." A tear dropped off her chin onto her breast.

Liza wrapped an arm around her shoulder and led her into the bathroom. There was only one stall and it was empty. "You called . . . ?" she prompted.

"I was going to call my own messages, even though . . . though . . . they wouldn't have changed in an hour." Ellen's voice was without inflection. "I called Mrs. Hellman down the hall from me, the woman I gave the opera tickets to. I thought maybe Harry had come by. Doesn't make sense, does it? Why would he have come when he knows I'm not there?"

The barrage was to keep away the moment she couldn't face, Liza knew that. She could feel Ellen's panic roiling in her own stomach. Opera tickets? She had no idea what Ellen meant but she didn't interrupt.

"As soon as I said my name, Mrs. Hellman said, 'Harry Cooper, isn't he your gentleman friend?' That's how she talks, gentleman friend. I said yes, and she said, 'He's been shot. An execution-style slaying in his office.'"

"Did you ask—"

"I didn't ask anything. She wouldn't even know what execution-style is, much less anything else." Ellen glared at Liza. "But you know, don't you? That's how your husband died, execution-style. That's why Harry is dead like this, because of you."

Liza gasped.

Ellen shoved her aside and lurched at the door.

Automatically Liza braced the door shut. "No! Ellen, pull yourself together!"

"Harry is dead!"

"You can't go running out of here and have everyone on a counter stool staring and asking each other what's going on with those two girls?"

"I don't care!"

"Wash your face."

"Don't—"

"Ellen, look at your face. It's all red and blotchy. Put some water on it."

"I've got to get out of here. Back home. To Kansas City. I need—"

"Okay. Look, I'll get us to the airport. Let me go outside and make arrangements. You take care of your face. Use the toilet. We don't know how far it is to the airport. Just let me check my own messages to make sure nothing else has happened and we'll go. We can't be that far from an airport. It's just after seven. By noon you'll be back in Kansas City."

She walked slowly out of the bathroom, trying to move like she had some control. How could Harry Cooper—that silly man with no interests but railroads, and no passion but for Ellen—be dead? She could see him at that reunion in Portland, his stubby hands whipping back and forth, illustrating some train thing, his so-ordinary face glowing with sweat and fervor. And then when he turned and saw Ellen, his face lighted up. So sweet. So innocent. How could he be dead?

She leaned against the wall by the phone, her whole body

152

icy and shaking. What had she done to Ellen? To poor innocent Harry? How could this be happening? She felt a great
leaden sorrow for the tiaras, the secrets, for having a real
friend.

She had to pull herself together. The one thing she could
do for Ellen now was get her out of here. The rest she'd worry
about later. She was, she reminded herself, a pro at not thinking
about things.

She walked to the counter.

When she came back ten minutes later Ellen was still
standing at the sink. "Sorry I took so long," she said, knowing
Ellen had no sense whether she'd been gone a minute or an
hour. "The woman behind the counter called a pilot in Eureka
for us. So that's all set up. I checked my messages. There
was only one, and it was from Bentec saying he had something important I should know. I thought maybe it was about
Harry. Though Bentec probably hasn't heard about Harry's
death. A shooting halfway across the country, why would
he? And even if he did, why connect it with Jay and the
shipment?"

Ellen's face was going blotchy white, her face moving in
little spasms as if her mental gears almost caught each time
before they slipped.

"But Bentec's call wasn't about Harry," Liza said quickly.
"Bentec went on forever and then in the end he didn't say
anything except that I should call him right away. Nothing
new. But, look, we'll be in Eureka in an hour. The pilot will
be waiting. It's all set up. Come on, we have to go."

Ellen gave a great nod, as if all the gears had caught at
once. She grabbed Liza's shoulders. "'Bentec went on forever
and didn't say anything.' Liza, doesn't that sound like he's
got your phone tapped? And right now he's running his finger
up the map looking for the town of Max?" She sank back
against the sink. "Liza, how can this be happening? It can't
be real. This is Sunday morning. Friday morning I got up and
my biggest problem was the opera ticket Harry wasn't going
to use. And that it might snow. Now Harry is dead. Your
husband has been gunned down. And we have the police after
us. How is this possible?"

Liza took her hands. "I've been asking myself the same

question. But we're going to have to figure that out later. Now we've got to move. If Bentec really did tap the phone, our only chance is to get out of here quick." She opened the door and half-guided half-shoved Ellen through the café and around back to the Camaro.

As she unlocked the door Felton, settled in the driver's seat, grunted. No way, boy. You had your outing. I know you'd like another, but you're going to have to wait." She held him out to Ellen as a comfort but Ellen was staring straight ahead. So she plunked him in the back, got in and drove the car slowly, with exquisite care out of the lot to the street. She checked both directions—"No cops"—and turned left.

Ellen said nothing and Liza just drove, checking the rearview every minute, eyeing each cross street and when the cross streets ceased and the road became rural again, eyeing each clump of bushes or trees for lurking police cars. She was operating at capacity, driving, trying to make Ellen's last hour here safe. Trying not to think about what she'd done to Ellen. Trying to hide how panicked she was about what the hell she was going to do when Ellen was gone and she was alone. And there was the more immediate problem of money. She only had what was in her purse when she left Malibu and half of that had gone for gas. It wasn't as if she could run to the cash machine. If there was fifty in her wallet it was a lot. That was the irony of it all—Jay involved in some deal probably worth millions and her lucky if she could scrape up gas money. She never planned ahead, always counted on her wits at the moment, but this was asking a helluva lot from just wits.

She glanced over at Ellen. Tears were running down her cheeks, but she was staring straight ahead as if she was too deadened to feel the chill.

"Oh, God, Ellen. How— I'm so sorry. I feel—"

"Forget it," she snapped.

"No, really—"

She sighed. "Liza, I don't blame you. This thing is way beyond blame. All I want is to get out of here. Harry Cooper was the most honest, responsible, law-abiding man on earth. He stopped at yellow lights. The only mistake he made was to love me. And now he's been shot dead. Nothing you can say will make it better. But fortunately, Liza, now nothing can make it worse either."

"Don't say that out loud."

"What?"

Liza realized she had mumbled her appeasement to the gods. Just as well. "Nothing. You close your eyes. Even if you can't sleep it will help you get yourself together. I'll wake you when we get to the airport."

"Hmm."

Liza leaned forward, arms on the steering wheel. She was checking ahead for side roads, behind for cops, she was juggling the pros and cons of staying on this road and hoping Bentec hadn't traced her call, or chancing one of the side roads, heading west, hoping it would link up with 101. "Ellen, sorry to wake you. Is there a map in the back? I want to see how far we'd have to go on the freeway. If Bentec's got cronies watching it, we don't want to chance it too long."

"If they're watching the freeway here, they're probably watching the airport."

Liza nodded. If Bentec traced her call, then by now he'd called back and interrogated the woman at the counter and found out about the pilot in Eureka. And the pilot, would there be cops on either side of him?

"No, pig, I'm not reaching for you. Go back to sleep till Liza can deal with you. Okay, I'm looking, but I don't see any map. Omigod, behind us!"

Liza turned around. A car was coming fast. She couldn't make out anything but shape through the dark-tinted back window. She could feel Ellen's panic radiating, but she was cooler than ever. "No lights and sirens. Look! It must be going a hundred miles an hour." She floored the gas.

"What are you doing! We can't outrun the police, not in a strange car, not on roads they know and we don't."

"Let me—"

"No! If I'm going to die I'd rather take a bullet than be in a wreck and die in sixteen pieces. Pull off up there."

"Hang on. I can do it." The car had to be going over a hundred. She couldn't take her eyes off the road to check the speedometer.

"Are you crazy?"

"It's our only chance."

"You'll get us killed. Liza, you owe me! Pay up now. Stop the damned car."

"El—"

"I'm serious, Liza. You keep saying you're my friend. Do this for me."

In the rearview the car was getting smaller. She could outrun it.

The car jolted. Ellen had shoved her foot off the gas. "What're you—"

"I said, I'm serious, Liza. Pull up over there now."

The car was almost on top of them. It was too late now. "I hope you remember 'your friend' when I'm in jail." She put on the right turn signal, slowed, keeping her mind on her driving, not letting herself think ahead, counting on her wits. Outside, all she could see was dust.

# Thirty-One

Bentec smiled into the phone as a male voice said, "We've got a make, Inspector."

"Where is she?" Bentec said.

"Max. Little town in Humboldt County by Redwood State Park."

"Where the hell is that?"

"Say you're not a nature lover, Inspector?"

"Where?"

"Less than an hour south of Eureka just off one-oh-one. The phone's at eighteen Redwood Avenue."

Bentec hung up. "Damn! God damn, fucking damn . . ." His voice trailed off and even as disgusted as he was by this turn of fate, he felt foolish swearing all alone. He had to get up there to Eureka, get Liza Silvestri before she talked. But he couldn't leave Heron untended. That's the way it always was in police work—you sit in a surveillance car hour after empty hour trying not to drink too much coffee. You do drink and you stay there in the car till you're like a cow before milking, all the time not a thing is happening. When, finally, you open the car door, all of a sudden suspects are running down a driveway, a car's doing a hundred and ten in the street, and shots are coming from every house on the block. All or nothing, every cop knew that.

Bentec called his Homicide liaison, his man in Homicide. "Get on the horn to Humboldt County. Silvestri's wife and companion are at eighteen Redwood Avenue, Max."

"Max?"

"Yeah, that's the name of the town. Tell them in Humboldt not to short on manpower and take no chances. These women are armed and wily. I'm not saying sworn officers up there in Humboldt are naive, but I don't want Liza Silvestri wiggling her way out of this, if you know what I mean. So make it clear to them that they need to keep these two women separate and incommunicado till I get there. Get me on the next flight to Eureka. I can be at the gate by eight."

Eight was cutting it close, but that's the way he liked it. Thank God the waiting was over. Now the whole operation was moving into high gear and he was in the driver's seat.

# Thirty-Two

The other car trailing them screeched to a halt by their front fender, blocking access to the road. Ellen stared numbly.

Liza let out a sigh. "It's not a patrol car!"

"What is he then, a carjacker? Has God run out of locusts?"

The driver loped toward them, hitching up his over-large jeans as he moved. His long bleached hair wagged a bit but it was too wetted down to shift much. He wasn't so much eyeing them as he was ogling the new Camaro.

"This kid's no carjacker. I've handled lots worse than him. Sit back, close your eyes, relax. Don't say anything," Liza hissed. Before she could reply, Liza opened the door and was outside, running her hand through her long blonde hair like

157

a high-school kid herself, standing hips thrust forward, hand on the car. "Like it, huh?"

The boy glanced from the hood to her and back. Then he bent and peered into the car. "Where's Aunt Gwen?" The stud in his lower lip jiggled. In Kansas City he'd be passé, but fashions linger in small towns and he looked like a kid aching to rebel but afraid to do it. He looked, Ellen thought, like one of those unsure high-school boys who flips out and starts shooting. Liza was still grinning. Didn't Liza see how close to the edge he was?

"Aunt Gwen?" Liza repeated.

Oh, shit, Gwen! This kid was Gwen's nephew. Not just a friend in the chase for the hell of us, but a nephew who'd never hear the end of it if he stopped the car and didn't find Gwen.

He'd been saying something. Now his voice rose. "What did you do with Aunt Gwen? You're not leaving here till you tell me, understand? No, till you take me to her."

He was a big kid. Maybe seventeen. A Great Dane of a kid. There was no way they could get past his car or him.

Liza stepped toward him. Hands on hips she declared, "She's not here. You know that. You've already looked inside."

He planted himself between her and the road, almost pinning her against the car. "You take me to her."

"I don't know where she is."

"She left with you."

"We dropped her off an hour ago."

"Then you take me to where you dropped her. I'm not going without her." His face was taut; his hands in fists.

So this was how it would end. There would be no plane back to Kansas City. No escape north for Liza. This boy would force them to drive back to the trailer park, but they'd never get that far south because the police would stop them. The kid looked pumped up and desperate. There was no chance of Liza and her overrunning him. Still she couldn't leave Liza out there alone. She could shove the driver's door open between the two of them, then be out her door, and . . . and she'd see. She reached across the seats.

Liza spotted her and shook her head.

158

The boy was repeating that he wasn't leaving without Gwen. He grabbed Liza's shoulder and said, "My Uncle Gil told me to bring her back and that's what I'm doing. I already called him in Max when I spotted this car. I told him I found her. I'm not going back without her."

Ellen reached for her own door. She glanced back at Liza just in time to see her swing her hand up onto the boy's, one buddy to another. "I hear you. You're not going back and end up having him call you a liar, right?"

"Yeah."

"You're not going to have everyone in the house laughing at you."

"Yeah," he said, and then with a look of surprise, "Yeah."

Ellen took her hand off the door. She'd underestimated Liza. Liza did understand this kid. She was mirroring his sullen look, that make-me stance.

"So you've got to have something to show you really stopped Gwen's car. It's not your fault she's not here. You can't help that, right? You did what they asked you to, you found the car. No one else did that."

"Yeah."

"So what you need is the car, right? You need to bring this car back to Gil."

"Yeah, okay. That makes sense. We drive back and I show him—"

Liza nodded. Her body jerked; her hands slapped her head. "Rats! We can't be driving south now. We have to be in Redding tonight. If it were tomorrow . . ."

"I can't wait till tomorrow. They'll roast me alive tonight. They're never going to believe me."

Ellen almost felt sorry for the kid.

"Wait! It's the car you need, not us, right?" Liza's hands were on his arms. "I'm going out on a limb here. Can I trust you?"

"Yeah, sure."

"I don't even know your name."

"Trent. Trent Hickock."

"Hmm. Well, Trent, I guess I could let you take the car overnight. We could use yours." Liza cast such a disparaging glance at the old Honda, Ellen expected the kid to hit her.

"We'll drive it to Redding and circle back tomorrow and pick up the Camaro from you."

The kid looked skeptical. He eyed the Camaro again and slowly began to grin.

Ellen's stomach clutched. Oh, God, what would the rental-car company do? "If he has an accident I'll be liable."

Liza stared at her, her lips quivering on the verge of . . . of something. Jeez, had she been thinking out loud? About the rental contract? Even the kid looked shocked.

Liza turned back to him and nodded. "Yeah, I guess it is a bad idea. We have our responsibilities to the rental—"

"No, wait. Wait. It could work. I'll be careful."

Liza shifted to the side, a small move physically, but in its import huge. Hers was the stance of control now. "How do we know you'll even be at Gil's house? This is a hot new car. By tomorrow you could be in Canada."

"Uncle Gil would kill me. He expects me back tonight. I told him about this car and all. He's waiting."

Liza crossed her arms, making a show of considering. After a minute, she said, "I'm going to need something from you to show you're serious about being there tomorrow."

"What? All I've got is my driver's license and wallet."

Liza gave a big sigh. "Well, cash isn't really as good as I need, but I guess it'll have to do. Give me what you have?"

"All of it?"

"You can keep five."

He pulled out a wad of bills and handed it to her. A small wad, Ellen noted.

"Okay, Trent, get our stuff out of the trunk. Ellen, get the things from the back." Liza moved around the Honda, opened the driver's door and peered in. Then she was back at the Camaro, scooping her pig up, sticking it in the Honda while the boy was opening the trunk. In a minute the whole trans-action was done. Liza held out the keys. "Okay, Trent, see you at Gil's tomorrow night."

"Hey, you know where Gil lives? You need me to draw you a map?"

"Gwen told us. See you." Liza pulled onto the road.

"Ellen," Liza said as soon as she'd shifted into third, "that was one brilliant comment—about the rental contract. Great

160

reverse psychology. You really goosed that boy along. You know you've got a knack for this kind of thing."

"Idiot savant," she muttered.

"Another term for a natural."

Ellen didn't answer. She didn't even look at Liza, couldn't bear to. Liza was crazy. She was no natural at deception and manipulating and car half-stealing, she was just worried about the car rental and . . . She closed her eyes against the idea she couldn't face, the line she didn't even want to think of crossing.

# Thirty-Three

Frank Bentec's stomach was churning. It always churned when he went into high gear. He left his car in his spot in the parking lot, signed out an unmarked to J. Johnson and light-footed it on the pedal, keeping under the speed limit the whole way to Loray Park. If Heron and his buddy were late he'd have a problem. But Heron was reliable. He was counting on that. The sky was middling gray already, and a distinguished-looking white man in this neighborhood was going to be as memorable as Silvestri's wife's tattoo. But he'd chosen this park, in this neighborhood because it was not an early-rise area. Still, he pulled on a baseball cap to cover his thick graying hair as he sighted the park.

There they were, Heron and his partner, sitting in their shiny black Bronco like a Christmas gift waiting to be unwrapped. Even at a distance he could make out the wary hunch of Heron's shoulders. Heron was no fool; he knew there was no protection there.

Bentec swung left in front of them, and made a swooping loop with his right arm, ending with finger pointing toward a copse of trees in the center of the park. He didn't look back at Heron's reaction. He could picture the scowl on the thug's weaselish face and Heron's buddy grumbling, "What is this, some kinda fucking scavenger hunt?" if he knew what a scavenger hunt was.

161

Bentec took his foot off the brake, letting the car edge forward till he had an unobstructed view of the whole park, and of Heron and friend, driving across the muddy park, the wheels hub deep, the two men almost back to back in the front seat, rotating their heads like dashboard hula dolls.

He eased on the gas, rolling at 10 mph, giving a wave as he neared the center of the park. Heron barely nodded. His weapon wasn't visible, but he'd have it at the ready.

Bentec hung a U, pulled up to the Bronco, driver's window to driver's window, lifted the sawed-off he'd confiscated from some con years ago, and erased two of his problems. That just left his nine-millimeter outstanding. Too bad there hadn't been a smooth way to get that from Heron before.

He eased the car forward and jumped out, ignoring the groans of the dying cons.

Three minutes later he declared the search for the nine-millimeter a failure. His weapon was nowhere in this car, not in the glove compartment, the trunk, under seats or inside door panels.

Dammit, did Heron have it socked away somewhere, or hadn't he bothered to get it out of Silvestri's house? But either place, Silvestri's house or Heron's, that gun would tie him to a corpse.

There was no time to go hunting for it. He'd planned all along to burn his bridges with this operation; he just hadn't expected there to be one moment when the whole fire went up.

He wiped off the sawed-off, tossed it toward the two corpses and headed for the airport.

He'd covered half a mile when his pager beeped. He jumped half out of the seat, and that angered him more than Heron or the gun. He was not a man to lose his cool. He checked the number, and couldn't help sighing with relief. A 707 number. Using the car phone, he dialed.

"Inspector Bentec? Pete Hanks, here. Humboldt County Sheriff's Department."

"You got my suspect, Silvestri, up there?"

"Not yet, sir. I interviewed the waitress at the Max Café. She liked those girls and I had a hard time getting anything out of her, even though I've known her for years, maybe *because* I've known—"

"But you did get her to talk, right?"

"Yes, sir."

"Did she say what road they were taking."

"No, sir."

"Damn."

"But she admitted she made a call for them. Called a pilot in Eureka."

"What'd she set up with him?"

"We're running him down now. In the meantime, sir, I've put a couple of cars in concealment either side of the airport. We'll snatch her up like a fly in a Venus flytrap."

"Good work, Hanks." Bentec pulled the patrol car into a red zone by the arrivals curb and raced for the gate. He'd been cutting it close before Hanks's call—now it was sprint time. Tomorrow or the next day L.A.P.D. would wonder about his car. By that time he'd be on another plane, flying east from Vancouver, a rich man with a new name and a new life.

He made it to the gate as the door was closing, flashed the stewardess a sheepish grin, the kind women loved, and then his shield. He was carrying and he couldn't afford a hassle. But, as he'd expected there was no hassle, not for the Assistant to the Commissioner. His seat was in First Class, the only way he'd travel from now on.

When the plane was airborne, he made a point of huddling with the stewardess in the kitchen, confiding that he was on a high-profile case. Of course he could use the staff telephone, she assured him.

He got Potelli on the first try. "I'm on an airplane, Joe, heading to Eureka. The suspect was spotted less than an hour out of there," he said in officialese. This was an open line. "I've been in contact with Pete Hanks up there, but an update wouldn't hurt."

"I'll get on it, Frank."

"You have any contact at the airport? In security?"

"I'll check around. Give me ten minutes."

Bentec hung up and leaned back against the bulkhead. He could see those little bottles of gin and bourbon and Scotch in the kitchenette. It was way too early for a responsible public

163

servant to be drinking and he wasn't about to blow his good image with the stewardesses. But a bottle or two of something, straight, would have improved the whole morning.

He waited exactly ten minutes and called Potelli back.

"Frank?"

"Right."

"Good news. Listen, the head of security up there is a guy named Dale Evans, of all things. Let me give you his number."

Silently Bentec repeated the phone number, hung up and dialed.

"Evans."

"This is Francis Bentec, Assistant to the Commissioner, L.A.P.D."

"I've been expecting you."

"Listen, Evans, you read about our murder Friday night?"

"The loft love nest? Oh yeah, we've been hashing it over here."

Bentec had been considering which way to go with Evans but now he saw the right play. "Listen, Evans, I'm taking you into my confidence here." Evans would be dining off that alone for a month. "Here's the scoop. The wife is headed for your facility. Driving in a new black Camaro with a lady friend. I'm flying up. I'll be making the collar there. But I'm going to need the help of someone who knows the layout."

"I'm your man, sir."

"Good man, Evans. We'll need back-up—"

"I'll call in guys on overtime. There'll be so many uniforms you'll think there's valet parking. But look, it's a manageable airport here. Trust me, sir, no one slips in here, no one slips out. And two women in a black Camaro, it's a chip shot."

"Good man."

"Anything else I can do for you, sir?"

With another man Bentec would have hesitated to add a layer of icing to the saccharine sweet cake. "Just make sure I've got your card, Evans, so after I've got her in custody I can thank you."

Bentec made his way back to his seat, leaned his head back and let his eyes shut. Everything was back under control.

# Thirty-Four

Liza concentrated on driving, making up the time lost with the car switch.

Ellen would be safe. She would get her on that plane. And afterwards? She kept a smile on her face. It was the least she could do for Ellen, and for herself. She was working at capacity, driving the rickety Honda, smiling, trying to make Ellen's last half hour here pleasant, safe. Trying to hide how panicked she was about what the hell she was going to do when Ellen was gone and she was headed north to the Richland grade alone.

The Richland grade, it had been a beacon, warm and bright drawing her toward it, drawing her out of this maelstrom. Everything would be all right once she got to the Richland grade. Happily ever after.

But now fairy tale time was over. The Richland grade was a real place. At least she knew where that place was from the picnic. But remembering a car picnic was one thing, finding and selling a railroad container of contraband—contraband that might be anything—that was another issue altogether. A big, scary issue. Just thinking of it made her feel four years old.

She took a breath and ran through her "hard-times" litany. She'd been terrified going to face Pope, the jeweler. That hadn't turned out well, but she survived. Terrified about court, but she got off with six months. Terrified about Juvie, about St. Enid's, about living in Malibu as Mrs. Silvestri. Each time she'd managed.

But this? How was she ever going to find the right train and even if she did, how could she get a huge container car off it? And there was the more immediate problem of money. She only had Trent's twenty-eight dollars plus what was in her purse.

165

After a mile or so she said, "Ellen, you're the logical one. Help me with this. Whatever Bentec's connection is, he's sure more concerned about his shipment than about Jay's death. He didn't kill Harry—"

"He didn't? What makes you think that?"

"Because—" Liza took a moment to let her thoughts congeal—"Bentec didn't know about Harry. If he did, he wouldn't be hassling me about the shipment. He'd just pick up the phone and call Harry."

"Harry wouldn't tell him."

"Why not? If Bentec's a partner in this— No, of course, he's a silent partner. If you're shipping contraband and you're a cop, you've got to be the silent partner. But Ellen, that doesn't matter, because if Bentec knew about Harry he would have called Harry and said, 'This is Francis Bentec, Assistant to the Commissioner of the Los Angeles Police Department. If you have any questions about my identity, you can call me back at my office in the police department.' And Harry would have cooperated, right?"

"Of course."

"Which means that there's someone else involved."

"The receiver."

"You mean the person the contraband is going to?"

"That's the term Harry used."

"Then that's the person who killed him."

"What?" Suddenly Ellen was perched on the edge of the seat facing her. "Liza, how do you make that leap?"

"Well, who else? Here's the thing: there are two people, one at either end of the contraband route. They've killed Jay, they've killed Harry. And they are going to walk into the sunset with a fortune. And no one is going to give a shit." She was tapping her fingers on the steering wheel. "Because, Ellen, nobody's going to report the contraband missing, because—ta da—it's contraband."

Ellen braced her arm on the dash. "It won't be contraband if we report it."

"Report what? A container of something, somewhere on some train going to Richland? Sent—stolen—by my dead husband."

"Richland? Where is that?"

"Over the Washington line, above Portland. Jay and I went there for a picnic after the gun show."

"Jesus, Liza, it's guns, isn't it? The shipment. What else would be shipped by a cop to a buyer who your husband met at a gun show? Liza, a container is a railway car. A railway car full of guns. That's like a battalion of guns, bombs, weapons we can't even imagine. . .No wonder—" her voice was barely audible—"no wonder the buyer killed Harry like it was . . . everyday business."

*Just like he'd kill them.* The corollary hung in the air between them. Liza stared straight ahead and drove rotely. There was nothing she could say to Ellen to make the situation any less awful than it was. *Weapons!*

"Ellen, the railroad must have some record of that container."

"There's a web page."

"It lists the container's contents?"

"Yeah."

"And the arrival time?"

"It's got everything."

"How do I get on it?"

"You can't. Not unless you have the password."

Liza sank back. She didn't know how she'd get access to a computer anyway. She'd have to take the human route: just go to the station and get the stationmaster to tell her. Were there pitfalls in that? This planning business was virgin territory to her. But once she dropped Ellen she'd have the length of Oregon to think about pitfalls.

A container full of weapons . . . Jay and Harry murdered. How the hell did she think she was going to survive? "Radio okay?" She needed to blare it.

"Sure." Ellen sounded disconnected, like she was already half back in Kansas City.

She found a Country–Western station. The twang of guitars pricked her skin and one song after another bemoaned heartbreak, abandonment and death.

After a while Ellen asked, "Want me to drive?"

"No. I'm fine. How far to Eureka?"

"Quarter of an hour."

Liza was watching for road signs. The airport lay between

167

Eureka and Arcata on the freeway. She was hoping there was a way of looping around to avoid Eureka altogether and coming down through Arcata. It was the cautious move. If she'd been alone in the car she would have trusted to wits and the camouflage of the Honda. But for Ellen, a little extra caution couldn't hurt.

The trees were enormous; she always found them inspiring, calming. She and Jay had done a wonderful game once where he faxed "cathedral" and she met him at L.A.X. with tickets to Eureka and reservations at a B and B in the redwoods near the ocean and they'd spent the long days and evenings with the mystical light of the sun piercing the deep dark of the fronds and the air so still the soft touch of their feet on the mossy ground seemed an intrusion. Then, she'd wondered whether if she could just stay long enough breathing in the pure scent of the redwoods, she would molt out of her facade and become real.

But now even acres of redwoods and gallons of breaking waves were helpless to quell the sharp buzz in her head. "I need a local map. Check the glove compartment."

"A miracle." Ellen pulled out a map and began to unfold it. "A limited miracle. It must have been in here when Trent bought the car. Which sector do you want?" She held up a piece of map so old the folds had torn through. "The fringe of direction."

"Find a way to Arcata that loops around north of Eureka."

Ellen could be making paper dolls as happily distracted as she seemed with the shreds of map. Mentally she was already back in Kansas City, and Liza knew, she was little more than a memory to Ellen. The road curved sharply to the right, the map flew onto the floor and all Ellen said was "Whoops," before she traced the line off the edge of one rectangle and hunted for its former neighbor.

"I'm going to have to turn soon," Liza insisted.

"Not so soon. Stay on this for another mile till you come to an unbroken gray line—what's that, a two-lane paved road?—and take a left. That will lead west to Arcata."

The road rose leading them out of the woods momentarily. Electric guitars screamed, and then they dipped back into pines, redwood, and static. She turned the radio off. In a few minutes she'd be on the airport connector and Ellen would be gathering up her things, poised to leap out and race for her flight.

"Ellen . . ." She started to say how bad she felt. But sorry was so inadequate. If she could leave Ellen with something of value . . . "Ellen, listen, I've had a lot of experience with men. More than you. Guys do stupid things. They back themselves into corners. They hide behind their pride because they don't know how to do anything else."

Ellen was reaching in the back seat for something. "Yes?"

"Well, my point is, Wes, your guy in Portland. You loved him. Why not give him one more shot? What do you have to lose?"

"Pay attention to the road. We're already in Arcata. There's the connector road up there. Slow down."

Ellen's tone wasn't tart, just practical. Still Liza felt the sting.

Clouds clumped in the sky and then floated on. Felton gave a little snort and settled himself in the center of the backseat. "You're a good travellin' pig," she said to him and he grunted in what she classified as agreement.

They veered onto the four-lane connector south to Eureka. Liza slowed for the airport exit.

On the other side of the freeway just beyond the exit, a highway patrol car perched on the shoulder. She could see the driver, hands on the wheel, eyes doubtless on the rearview mirror, ready to pounce. Like she was a terrorist hauling a load of anthrax. How many cars had the highway patrol assigned to catch a woman who's husband had been shot?

Maybe it was just a speed trap?

Right! In Arcata on Sunday morning.

This was worse than she'd thought.

Did Bentec know about the plane waiting for her? He'd told her he had connections throughout the state.

She looked over at Ellen and a wave of guilt hit her. If she could just get Ellen on a plane out of here, back to safety, then whatever came up she'd handle one way or another.

The airport turn lane was just ahead. She took a deep breath. "Ellen, pay attention. We can't chance the private plane. I'm going to drop you here at the airport. Catch the first commer-

169

cial flight out, to anywhere. Bentec's too busy to worry about you. Get a puddle jumper to Ashland or Eugene, or Reno, whatever. Go right to the gates and take the first plane. Once you're out of state you'll be okay."

Ellen gave a laugh she couldn't interpret. It sounded like Ellen was saying "What is okay?" but she couldn't be sure and she couldn't worry about that. She was eyeing the curb, looking for police, checking for the way back to the freeway north.

"And you, Liza, where are you going?"

"Richland grade."

"But that's so dangerous."

"Nowhere else is any safer."

Liza looked in the rearview mirror and went stiff. After a moment she pulled to the curb. She gave Ellen's arm a squeeze. "You're the best friend I've ever had." Before Ellen could speak, she said, "Go!", reached across her and opened the door.

Next to the main entrance stood a security guard.

Ahead, at the end of the curb, was a highway patrol car. To her left another CHP car was half hidden. They were all over.

She wasn't going to the Richland grade. She wasn't going anywhere. Without a word, Ellen got out of the car. Liza slumped back and let the engine die.

# Thirty-Five

Ellen opened the driver's door, shoved Liza over, and reached for the steering wheel. "Get in the back seat with the pig, Liza. And stay out of sight." She was into the driver's seat and started the car so fast it tossed Liza into the pig. The pig squealed.

"Where's the plane?"

"In the tie-down area by the hangar, wherever that is. But—"

"Never mind that. You've got two minutes to decide what to grab from this car."

"Ellen, don't get yourself more involved—"

170

"I'm up to my ears already. You think Bentec won't suspect you told me about his shipment? You think the guy who shot Harry won't worry about what I know? Grab me sweats and my running shoes."

"Why?"

"Do it!"

The hangar was fifty yards ahead on the right. In the tie-down area by it there were dozens of small planes, single engine jobs, the ones she could make out. And half a dozen highway patrol and security cars.

"Ellen! Behind you! Oh no, and on the curb. They've got cops all over."

The highway patrol car filled the rearview mirror, coming up fast.

"Stay out of sight. You and the pig."

The patrol car was in the left lane. Dead next to her it slowed.

Ellen rolled down the window and called out to the patrolman. "What's going on up there?" She could read his face: officious. "Never mind. Do you know where the—" Oh, Jeez, what was the right term for double-engine plane? Twin!— "twin-engine tie-down is?"

Blood was pounding in her ears; she couldn't hear the patrolman's reply, only read the No in his face and realized that he was pointing not at her but beyond at the security guard blocking the way. *What would Liza do?* In an instant Ellen was out of the car, planting herself in front of the security guard. Nodding in the direction of the highway patrol car, she said, "He said you'd know how to get to the twin-engine tie-down."

"Straight ahead past the hangar and the single-engine tie-down."

"Thanks." She turned, so relieved she felt lightheaded.

"Hey, wait up. You're not from around here, are you?"

The car was so close, the door still open. Not close enough. She turned slowly, trying to make herself smile. "I am now. Just got myself free of the city." Couldn't the man hear her blood slamming against her skull?

"You got a friend with you?"

He knew. It was too late. She had to swallow hard to force out words at all. "No. Just me."

171

The security guard pulled a paper from his jacket, read a sentence or so, looked at her, read a bit more, looked again.

Ellen wasn't breathing at all. Her heart beat like a Taiko drum. Her legs were numb. She couldn't run. Portland flashed in her mind; she had taken a chance there and it ended in disaster. What made her think her luck had changed?

"Sorry, miss." The security guard offered a limp-lipped smile.

Ellen jammed her teeth together to keep her jaw from dropping.

"Thing is, miss, we're looking for two women, but neither description fits you."

"Really?" she blurted out.

"Yeah, one's a five two blonde and the other one has brown hair like yours, but she's six feet tall."

Ellen didn't trust her voice. She nodded, got back in the car and headed toward the hangar to the twin-engine tie-down beyond. When Liza lifted the blanket and stuck her head between the bucket seats, Ellen said, "Looks like Gwen's husband saved face with the cops. Must've said his wife was overpowered by an Amazon. Or maybe Gwen's friend the waitress did us a favor."

"Hey, where are you going? The freeway's to the left."

"Stay down!" Ellen kept the car at 30 mph. The highway patrolman was getting out of his car by the hangar. She waved, and kept going. On the far side of the hangar were two more patrol cars and a group of uniformed men and women talking to a tall red-haired man. "Our pilot. Our former pilot."

"What?"

"Nothing. Stay down."

"What are you doing, Ellen?"

"Waiting for inspiration. Isn't that what you do?" The hangar was far enough behind now to be visible in the rearview mirror. One patrolman was looking toward them but making no motion. Ahead, the road made a sharp left around a maze of larger planes, twin-engines. At the far side she could make out a thin man with a ponytail looping between crafts. She slowed. When she checked him again he was climbing into a plane.

The road to her left probably led back to the freeway, and safety, for the moment. Her heart was still banging in her chest; sweat coated her back. Decisions clicked almost too fast to catch. Safety didn't exist. She'd taken the prudent route all her life—no more. She was sick of being pushed around by men who lost bicycle races, by Larry Best, by the man who killed Harry. If she was going to get herself shot, it damn well wouldn't be in the ass while she was grubbing around for an escape hole.

Portland had been awful in the end. But, till then it was great; it was like being . . . alive.

She stepped on the gas and shot around the planes. "You got what you need, Liza?"

"Yeah, but—"

Ellen dragged Liza's purse onto her lap as she pulled up on the far side of the plane.

"Hey . . . what're you doing?" the pilot yelled.

Ellen took a deep breath to control her shaking. The plane's passenger's door was still open. She grabbed Liza's gun, stepped out of the car and onto the plane's wing and braced herself in front of the doorway.

"Hey, lady, what the hell—"

He was tall, tan under that tight ponytail, and clearly he worked out. His open mouth exposed perfect teeth. He wasn't Larry Best but he could have been. His mouth moved again but all she heard was the snap of the wind against metal, the chugging of her heart like the bellows of a mine miles below the earth.

She raised the gun. "Keep your hands where I can see them. You're flying us out of here."

"What? I can't just fly off anywhere."

"You can if you want to live."

"You're not going to shoot that gun," he scoffed.

She aimed at his groin. "You want a trial shot? I don't have time to argue. You fly or I shoot. Which is it?"

He glared from her through the doorway and back. "Fly," he muttered.

"Get in, Liza."

173

As she adjusted her stance and let Liza slip into the back, she noted the first bit of good fortune they had had—the plane had only one door and it was on this side. There was no way out for the pilot. Keeping the gun pointed at him, she maneuvered into the passenger seat and had Liza pull the door shut and turn the latch on the top.

"Ground control," the pilot put on his headset. "I've got to contact them."

"Wait. Think very carefully before you say anything about us. We've got nothing to lose. If the cops catch up with us they're going to shoot first and ask questions second. Two men are already dead. One more won't make a bit of difference to anyone. Except to you."

He didn't move, but it was clear from the way he was running his teeth over his lip that he was still considering.

"You could get a couple words out before I shoot. Maybe you could even wrestle the gun out of my hand before Liza shoots you. Maybe you'd even survive that and live to take one of the police bullets when they came at us."

"Lady, you are crazy."

She let a moment pass before she said, "Believe it."

"I'll lose my license."

"No you won't," Liza said disgustedly. "You'll tell them you had two crazy ladies with guns in here and what were you going to do? They'll say, 'Crazy fucking broads,' and take you for a beer. So, let's go."

He opened the window and yelled, "Clear." The engines started up. The pig let out a squeal as the pilot made contact with ground control and requested permission to take off.

The pilot was talking about frequencies, requesting permission to taxi for take-off, and checking gauges. Replies came through the headset, inaudible to her. The plane rolled forward, made a sharp turn at the end of the runway and stopped.

"Eureka Tower, Four-Four-Delta, at the hold line. Request permission for take-off." He checked gauges and controls, nodded, apparently at some comment on the headset. "Roger. I've got the E.L.T. on."

He eased in the throttle and the plane picked up speed, jostled them, and then they were climbing in air.

174

Ellen waited until they leveled off to say, "Turn north."
"Where are we headed?"
"North, out of California." For the first time she took her eyes off the pilot and glanced back at Liza. The two of them smiled.

# Thirty-Six

"**B**.L.T.?" the air traffic controller scratched his chin. "Why the hell would Four-Four-Delta want to activate his Electronic Locating Transmitter?"

"He wouldn't. Not unless he's trying to tell us something."

"Hey, what's that car doing out in the middle of the field? That's where Four-Four-Delta came from."

"I'll call security. Let them deal with it." He picked up the receiver, just as it started to ring, murmured, "Uh huh, uh huh, gotcha." He was still holding the phone as he said, "Security just told me the damnedest thing. You know those two babes the C.H.P.'s after? That's them there in Four-Four-Delta. That was their car out there on the field. Chips are fit to be tied. Getting heat big time from some brass in L.A. Do you know where they're headed?"

"North. Fourteen forty-four's in Oregon now. He's on radar track."

# Thirty-Seven

**F**rank Bentec felt a strange calm infuse him. It was as if he was not entering Oregon but stepping onto a movie set. None of the rules of real life, of California, held. Here in this world it was all fiction.

He could have blown a gasket half an hour ago when he got the word from Pete Hanks that Liza Silvestri had escaped, and worse that she was in Oregon, and worst of all that Hanks had taken it upon himself to call in the Feds.

For a moment he saw the whole fucking deal slipping through his fingers. California was webbed with his connections. In Oregon he was nothing. Even if he had been, the Feds wouldn't care. He had been so steamed he nearly choked.

But nineteen years on the Force had taught him to keep his cool, to flip the scene and see if it played better bottom up. California authorities hadn't connected him to any crime yet. The Feds weren't going to be at every landing site in Oregon; it would take them time to deploy men. Meanwhile, he'd be landing on Liza Silvestri's tail.

For Dale Evans in Eureka the debacle had been a personal indictment. His one chance to catch a high-profile fugitive and he blew it. It was Evans's gush of contrition that shoved Bentec back to practicality. "No time for regrets, Evans. We're all professionals here. Have a charter waiting for me, a plane faster than Liza Silvestri's, and we'll nab her at the next stop." Evans had liked that "we" stuff.

He was half an hour behind Silvestri, Evans told him in the thirty-second drive to the charter.

Things were under control. In Oregon he'd still be the Assistant to the Commissioner of Police, Los Angeles, with all the rights and privileges. He'd have time; just less than he'd thought. The window of opportunity was closing, but it was still a window and he was the only one sitting on the sill.

When he landed in Oregon he'd be the charming, competent police official eager to exploit his years of experience to make every local cop look good, willing to take the chances and give them the credit, eager and willing to be on the front lines.


# Thirty-Eight


Liza came awake in the back of the plane. The drone of rotors clobbered her ears. She was freezing except for her chest, which was warm. Hot. For a moment she thought the coarse hair rubbing her chin was Jay's beard and it was Sunday morning in the apartment and they were dragging themselves up after hours of sleep and lovemaking. But it was Felton, snuggled close.

To her left the sun was slipping fast and low into the fog. God, how long had she slept? Where were they now? She sat up slowly, moving with exquisite care so she didn't wake Felton. No matter how bad things were they could be made worse by pig shit. To her right it was almost night. A wave of guilt and fear overtook her. Ellen was the one who needed to sleep, but there she was in the front seat staring straight ahead.

"Where are we, Ellen?"

"Eugene."

"Eugene, Oregon?"

"We don't have enough fuel for Portland," the pilot declared, clearly anxious to talk. His neck was so tight it was bunched above his collar. She wondered what Ellen had said to keep him quiet all this time. "We're fueling here."

It was dusk and the lights of the airfield below were barely brighter than the surroundings. There were roofs and roads, a river winding through town, but everything was dusted by the impending night. Even the tall pines around the town seemed closer to shadow than trees. The pilot contacted the tower and spoke official-sounding phrases into his headset. A jet landed and another was taking off. Ahead of them was a plane about the same size as theirs.

"So we're not going to the terminal at all then?" she asked.

"Nope. No need. Just to the pumps."

"How much farther is Portland?"

"Little over a hundred miles. That's not counting if we get stacked up in a holding pattern," he added quickly. Too quickly.

Did Ellen catch that? Ellen's face revealed nothing and Liza couldn't decide whether Ellen didn't read men well enough to catch this kind of thing or she was just too zonked out. The memory of Ellen commandeering the plane seeped back into her mind; she was as amazed now as then. Had that been like a tornado in L.A., a one-time burst before everything went back to normal? Or was the woman holding the gun one helluva new chick? If this was what friendship wrought, it was damned well okay. Maybe Ellen would come along to Richland. There had to be a way to get control of the shipment. Then the world would be theirs.

The plane ahead of them touched down. They were making a lazy circle above. Through the angled window Liza could see easily the plane turning off the runway as if it was headed beyond the terminal to the hangars. Cars raced out from both sides of the hangar. She could just barely make out the light bars on the roofs. At what looked like the last moment the plane made a sharp turn and headed to the terminal. The cars moved back into the hangar.

The pilot said, "Four-Four-Delta. Thanks for your help tonight."

Thanks for what? she was tempted to ask. It was making her real uneasy, him talking into a headset and getting answers in it she couldn't hear.

He dipped the nose of the plane and she watched as the white lights of the runway jumped up at them. The terminal was over to the side. "Where are the gas pumps we're going to?"

He didn't answer. Either he was listening to words in the headset, or pretending to. Ellen was looking out her side window like a tourist enjoying the landing.

Frantically, Liza checked the area near the hangars. Patrol cars were lined up in front, eight of them. The police weren't even making an attempt to hide. Ellen glanced at them and turned to gaze out the front window, like the police cars were no more startling than roses in June.

"Roger." The pilot's sudden smugness filled the cockpit like thick foam blocking out the roar of the wind. For a moment the world was deadly silent.

The snapping of metal against metal cut through the silence. The click of the safety. Ellen held the gun chest-level, pointed at the pilot. "Make a hard right."

"Wha—"

"Don't talk. Sharp right. Now!"

He didn't shift. The plane was moving fast, toward the hangars. They were fifteen yards off the ground.

"Now!"

178

He kept going.

The bullet skimmed his nose; he screamed and grabbed his face. The plane shuddered and for a moment Liza was sure they were going to crash.

"Now!"

He swung the plane hard to the right.

"Speed up. Fast."

"Where are—"

"Don't talk! Keep going."

"Traffic."

"Go faster." The plane shot across the macadam, across lights and lines that could be runway markers. "That's it, keep going."

"We're going to crash into those trees."

"Lift off."

The pilot looked too scared to argue.

Behind, across the field, cars were moving, red lights, blinking, sirens starting up.

The plane barely cleared the low trees. A quarter mile beyond was what looked like a moonscape. A golf course.

"Over there." Ellen pointed to the left, to a fairway.

"I can't just—"

With her free hand she grabbed a protruding knob. "Then I'll do it." She sounded dead calm.

"Okay, okay, just get away. You're going to get us all killed in here. Just let me land."

"Do it fast."

The plane was skimming the grass. Liza couldn't believe how calm Ellen was. She scanned the golf course. There had to be a maintenance truck around. Or even a golf cart someone forgot. But there wasn't. Just sand and grass, and trees ahead. Nowhere even to hide but the trees. At least Felton would be happy there. The plane was almost stopped. She clutched him hard, but she could tell he was too frightened even to squeal.

"Sharp right!" Ellen ordered. "Okay, stop." The plane jerked and slammed her into the side, but Ellen seemed unaffected. "We're getting out. You are going straight down that hill. Get out, Liza. And you," she wagged the gun at the pilot, "you can turn off the Emergency Location Transmitter now."

"You knew we were on radar all along? How'd you know that?"

Ellen climbed out. "Downhill. Hurry, I may just shoot you to rid the world of one more asshole."

Liza was already running toward the trees when she heard Ellen yell, "That's it, straight on, Liza."

She ran across the short grass. It'd rained here and the wet grass grabbed at her feet. She was clutching Felton to her chest. The tote bag was banging against her leg. Sirens in the distance squealed louder than Felton.

The trees were too thin. They weren't a forest. In a hundred yards there was a paved path. She stopped, panting. There was no place to hide. No sign of Ellen. She ruled out the path, and the woods. On instinct she headed back toward the airport.

# Thirty-Nine

Captain Raymond Zeron screeched the patrol car to a stop at the edge of the woods just south of the Eugene airport. "Where the hell are they going? I thought they were out of fuel. Get on to the tower, Unsel."

Unsel took the mike.

Zeron kept on talking. "Dammit, the Feds call us at the last moment, like we've got nothing on our plates up here except duck. 'Pilot changed his mind,' they say, as if that makes everything okay. They're all set up at Portland. *They* can't get their men down here. Do I hear any 'we're sorry' or 'we goofed?' Not hardly. They dropped the ball, but now it's all on us to go scrambling after it. What the hell's going on with the tower?"

"They say the plane lifted off."

"Hell, we know that."

"Then it dropped out of sight."

"Like in the golf course?"

"That's what they think."

"Let's go. Get everyone on line two."

"Everyone?"

"Every free car in town."

Unsel relayed the order to the dispatcher, but Zeron kept talking. "Here's the thing, Unsel. We've got a two-pronged case here. A woman who murdered her husband in cold blood. She kills him and flees, steals a car from a teenager, kidnaps a pilot and shoots at him; we're talking death penalty case here. This is a university town, Unsel, I don't plan to have a crazed killer running loose in the girls' dorms here."

"Ready to go, sir," Unsel said, handing him the mike.

"Take us around the edge, Unsel." He motioned to the rough ground beyond the line of the trees. Cut over to the path."

"Okaaay." Unsel hit the gas.

Zeron braced against the dash. He clicked on the mike. "Who's dispatching?"

"Queen, sir."

"Everyone on line two, Queen?"

"All accounted for."

"Okay. We've got two female fugitives in a small plane on the golf course. Pilot's a hostage. Get there, lights and sirens. Spread out. I'm at the south end of the airport runways. I'll be hooking around, coming up on the far side of the park. I'll be handling the inner cordon. Mioki, set up an outer cordon a mile around the golf course. Check every vehicle coming out. Units one to five, you're on the inner cordon. Meet me at the east end of the course. Move. The rest of you are outer cordon. Mioki take line three for that."

"Queen, get the canine unit out. And call Portland. Have them fly their dogs down here. Hell, they can put the dogs in the plane with the Feds."

"You want me to tell them that, sir."

"Hell, no, Queen, use a little common sense. Tell them to send down a sharpshooter."

"Roger. Will do."

He clicked off the mike. "And here's the other thing, Unsel, the thing I'm not putting out over the air. We got a hotshot administrator flying in from L.A. We got Feds. This case has

181

already been all over the news in California, and it takes plenty to rise to the top of weird and wonderful down there. What we got here is one big, splashy sex case and if we don't mop this up pronto we're going to have Dan Rather standing on the courthouse steps laughing at small-town cops. You got the picture, Unsel."

"Got it, sir."

"So we are going to do what it takes to neutralize these fugitives. Whatever it takes."

# Forty

The sirens were coming from all around. For the first time in her life, Liza literally couldn't move. There was no Plan B. Nothing. All she could think of was Felton. She had to turn him loose, give him distance away from her, but she just couldn't. He was the only creature who ever cared for her no matter what.

Behind her, branches crackled. "Over here, Liza."

"Ellen?"

"Hurry! Come on!"

"Where? Ellen, there are cops coming from every direction. Listen? They know where we are."

"Shut up and come." Ellen set off running and it was all Liza could do to keep her in sight. She never pictured Ellen as an athlete, but Ellen was moving out now. Hugging Felton to her chest, Liza panted with each step.

The woods opened on a wide, paved path. Ellen ran across and into trees and underbrush on the far side.

"Ellen, there's no point in running. The cops are all around us."

"Hurry. Run, Liza."

"Where to?"

A siren shrieked to its peak and cut off.

"They're right here!" Liza's thick breaths sounded like waterfalls, momentarily blocking out the screech of the sirens.

182

She couldn't think at all. She ran from inertia, her legs pumping as if they were foreign objects. Ellen was going down an incline. She disappeared. Liza kept running, sweat dripping into her eyes.

At the bottom of the bank, Ellen was rotating slowly like a ballerina on a child's music box with the battery running out. She stopped abruptly, pointed to the thick brush and pulled a mountain bike out with a helmet hanging from the handlebars. "You take this one."

Liza looked from the bike to Felton.

Ellen pulled another bike from behind the bushes. "Liza, you don't have time to stand and gawk. Here, give me that bag. I'll put the pig in there. I'll carry him. You just get on the bike. Put your hair up under the helmet."

"Where'd these bikes come from?"

"There's a bike club rendezvous over the rise. There are always bikes here. I've ridden with the Eugene club. I could take you to ten other bike spots like this."

"People just leave them?"

"This isn't L.A., Liza. People are more trusting up here." One after another sirens screeched and cut off. "Check the bike bag for clothes." She was hauling a purple windbreaker out of the pouch on her own bike. She put it on, pushed her dress up under it, and yanked her own sweat pants out of the tote Liza was carrying. Ellen yanked the bag from Liza's bike, grabbed Felton out of Liza's arms and plopped him in. "Come on, Liza! Move!"

Liza gasped. Her stomach roiled—she couldn't focus. All she could feel was the cold on her breasts where Felton had been.

"Liza! Now!" Slippery cloth hit her face. She jolted. Panic filled her, but this time *move*-panic. She donned the sweat-shirt—chartreuse with a purple stripe—and grabbed a bike.

"Keep up with me." Ellen flung a leg over the bar and bounced down a narrow dirt path.

Liza could barely reach her bike pedals over the bar. There was no chance at all of sitting on the seat. She braced her feet and arms and headed down the rough path. Only fear of losing Ellen entirely in the growing dark kept her going.

And going fast. Ellen had told her about mountain biking

183

with the guy who dumped her in Portland. But that hadn't changed Liza's notion of her. The Ellen Baines of college days had been no athlete, but the woman spewing dust ahead certainly was. No wonder she beat the Portland whiner. Clutching the handlebars, shifting side to side, Liza pedaled as fast as she could. The path started to climb. Liza pressed harder, standing on each pedal as much as pushing it down. All of a sudden she was out of the woods and on the paved path. Ellen was a hundred yards ahead. If it hadn't been for the moonlight shining off a silver stripe in her windbreaker she wouldn't have been able to keep her in sight at all.

Liza pedaled faster, no longer feeling so wobbly as she shifted side to side. The wind on her face was cool. Going all out on a path she could barely see left no time for worry or regret.

Suddenly she noted the quiet. All the sirens had stopped. Men's voices cut the air but she was moving too fast to discern words. She didn't need to; she knew what they were after. And right on the path was the worst place to be. What could Ellen be thinking of? She shoved the pedals down as fast as she could, taking an extra push with her toes to connect one downstroke with the next. Each breath seared her ribs; her throat was dry as potato chips. Her hands cramped on the rubber grips but she didn't dare stretch her fingers. She was drawing closer to Ellen but not fast enough.

A guy on a racing bike shot out of the dark, passed her without a look. She kept her eyes down, but he didn't even glance as he swept past. Ahead, running up a slope was a couple, looking around as if they were checking the path. Were they part of the bike group? After their stolen bikes? Their stolen clothes? Liza leaned forward, trying to pedal faster. There was no surge left in her legs. She made a wide circle left almost into the trees, pressing her arms forward to shield the big purple stripe on her sweatshirt. Right, she thought, as if they won't notice the chartreuse.

They didn't yell as she passed. It would have been smart to just keep going but she couldn't resist turning her head to make sure they weren't running after her. They weren't. They'd slowed down and turned their attention to each other and she, clearly, hadn't entered into their consciousness at all.

184

Her wheel hit something. She snapped forward and just had time to stop behind Ellen, who was watching a police officer running out of the trees.

# Forty-One

Ellen watched the cop approach. He was in a coverall, like he was with the S.W.A.T. team or the morgue. Sweat streamed down her face; her back and chest were coated. She'd ridden just far enough to overcome her initial stiffness. Her hamstrings and adductor muscles were nowhere near taut like they were when she rode ten miles a day and fifty on a weekend. They were stinging with life. The night air smacked deliciously her hot damp face. The helmet felt so right on her head and yet it had that familiar heaviness that made her want to unbuckle the strap, hang the helmet from the handlebar and run her fingers through her hair. Like waiting between heats in Willamette Park with twenty guys panting behind her and the knowledge that she could tear into the course and beat every one of them. She hadn't felt this way in years and it felt good, real good.

"Can you make it quick? I'm losing my heart rate," she insisted as the officer came up. "I've only got a few more minutes till it's too dark to ride."

"Sorry, Ma'am. We're looking for two women with a pig. They crash-landed on the golf course."

"Are they injured?"

"Not necessarily. They could be, though. Have you seen women limping like they were hurt?"

Her euphoria faded. The strap of the pig-heavy sack gouged her neck. Suddenly she was no longer an importuned racer, but a fugitive with a pig. "No," she muttered, "no women limping."

"We're advising you to clear the area. These women are armed and dangerous. You don't want to get caught in the crossfire."

The pig squirmed and let out a squeal. She forced a cough, doubling forward over the bag.

"Officer!" It was Liza behind her. The cop turned to Liza. He wasn't thinking they were together, not yet. Liza was so wrung out, who knew what she'd say? She had no reserve tank to fire up her brain.

The pig squirmed; in a minute he'd be poking his snout out of the bag and they'd all be fried. "Okay, officer, I'll keep my eyes out." Eyes *open* she meant. Still hunched, she coasted off, dying to look back at Liza, knowing she couldn't.

"Officer," she heard Liza say, "hurry. There's a woman injured. Her friend's with her, but she says she's not a doctor. The woman looks awful."

Ellen was too far ahead to hear his reply. She slowed as much as she dared and soon she heard Liza coming up behind her. She checked the bushes and then gave up caution.

Liza coasted up. "He's racing back, looking for an injured woman."

"Back where?"

"Back around where we got the bikes."

"Great. In a couple minutes he'll discover two bikes have been stolen, no one's injured and who's he going to think of, huh, Liza?"

"Then we need to move fast."

The pig's head was exposed and Liza wheeled closer to scratch it. "Ride as hard as you can, Ellen. Give me a location in case I can't keep up."

"Quarter of a mile ahead we're going to cut right between two posts. Paved path. That will take us to a road. Go left and keep going. If you come to a Seventh Day Adventist Church, stop."

"How far?"

"'Bout ten miles. Past three or four major intersections. There's a Catholic Church across the street. But don't go there. Stay in the Adventist parking lot. They're Saturday people and it will be empty tonight." She looked at Liza, as sweaty as she was, her T-shirt hanging loose, her spindly arms sticking out like white canes. She reached toward her.

Liza caught her hand, and squeezed it. "Go!"

# Forty-Two

Frank Bentec took the mike from the driver as the Eugene patrol car sped along dark lazy streets. "Bentec here."

"Captain Raymond Zeron, Eugene Police."

"You got them, Zeron?"

"We're on their trail."

"That's a No, right?" Bentec forced an understanding laugh. "They're slippery, these two. We came within minutes of getting them in San Francisco. Ditto Eureka. And how they got out of your airport—" He was veering precariously close to disdain. "Like I say, they're slippery. But you're on their tail, and I gotta tell you, Zeron, the one I met had a very fine tail indeed." He held the mouthpiece away from his mouth and waited to see what that last gambit would draw in.

"You met the suspect?"

All business, this Zeron. "L.A.'s a small town sometimes. Silvestri was a slick character and Liza, the wife's, quite a looker, cunning, too, in an off-beat way." He paused to let Zeron assume he was thinking. "Maybe I could be some use to you. I'd like to get this cleared up before the Feds get themselves entrenched."

"Right you are on that one, Bentec."

Bentec read the surprise in Zeron's voice—*not the kind of L.A. asshole I expected.*

"We've got the pilot they kidnapped. They're traveling with a pig. The pig's the key."

"The pig," Bentec said to nudge the hick along.

"This is a college town. Two young women could split up, pick up guys, wander into parties and disappear. If they hit a party with enough liquor even their own dates wouldn't remember them. In the daytime they could slip into lecture halls like any other older student, hide out in the library—"

"I get your point, Zeron. With the pig they can't."

187

"Right."

"Ah, so then you have a lead on where they went?"

"They're on bicycles. Stolen bicycles."

"You got descriptions?"

There was another pause before Zeron said, "You bet." But this time he didn't sound at all so confident.

"Like I said, Zeron, I met one of them."

It was a moment before Zeron bit. "Why don't you start here at the command post and let us see what we can give you. Sounds like you're our spotter."

Which was just what Frank Bentec had in mind.


# Forty-Three


Safe! Ellen leaned the bicycle against the Seventh Day Adventist Church back wall and stared at the six-foot hedge between the parking lot and the one-story clapboard houses behind. No one would see her here. She should feel safe here, if anywhere; the place brimmed with good memories of bike rides, of races, victories. And of Wes.

But safe? Where was Liza? Was she lost? Crashed? Or caught? Ellen was desperate to. . .there was nothing she could do but wait. The pig squeaked; she plucked him out of the bag, put him down, and watched him trundle unsteadily to the hedge and throw up. Nonplussed he trundled on, his wide little butt jiggling with purpose.

Liza? She was just slow, surely. Liza wasn't a good rider, nowhere near her own level. Or Wes's. She'd be here any minute. No need to worry. Police sirens weren't shrieking, tires weren't squealing, no guns poked through the hedge. Things were okay. The damp air cooled her sweaty body as it had here so many times after meets . . . when she and Wes had rolled into this parking lot after their doubles victory . . . Wes leaping off his bike, grabbing her, sweat running over their kissing, his hands sliding down her back till someone doused them with a bucket of water.

Streetlights were coming on; shadows wavered in the breeze. She eyed each of the hedges, methodically checking for too-dark shadows, light shining on metal. She was still safe. There was one more memory of this parking lot, that never arose on its own. She stiffened and forced it up, feeling rather than seeing herself panting after a race with the other Portland riders, captive to each who asked where Wes was, why they hadn't seen him in a month. Her face reddened as it had then with each *I don't know*, with the roar of her breathing in the silence as each rider backed away into small talk, to other riders, more water, just away from her. As if they'd known Wes was bored with her, had a floozie, whatever. She hadn't ridden again.

But now, dammit, she wished she had had one more race to leave them in her dust. For the first time she understood that it was not just Wes she had missed, it was the woman who had won races.

She'd already won a couple laps of a helluva race tonight. And the race wasn't in the wilds of California anymore; it was on her turf now.

The grind of brakes jolted her. Liza rolled the bike in. "Oh . . . Ellen . . . thank God." She bent full over. "I'm . . . gonna . . . die."

Ellen caught her bike before it banged down. "Did anyone stop you? Follow you?"

"No. I thought I'd . . . taken the wrong road. I thought . . . I'd missed it for sure," she got out between breaths.

Ellen pulled a water bottle from the bike. "Here, drink. Then we need to get going."

"Going? I can barely stand. Wouldn't we be safer staying put here?"

Ellen laughed. "No, we wouldn't. Drink."

Liza drank till she was gurgling air, stood up in a shaky attempt at briskness, and snapped the bottle back on the bike. "Okay, refueling finished, Monsieur Legree."

The wind rustled Ellen's wet hair, just as it had when she'd snapped the tape at the finish line. She grabbed both of Liza's arms. "Liza, we are doing it. Maybe we can do it all."

"*It all?* As in *escape with our lives?*"

"We can show the bastards. You were headed to Richland;

189

you were already planning to find their shipment and ride off into the sunset. So how about cutting me in?"

"Ellen, the shipment . . . it's weapons. Bentec and the receiver are killers. If I'm very very lucky I'll ride off with my life; there's nothing else to ride off with."

"Sure there is. The weapons must be worth millions, right? Millions would make my life a lot better. We can take the shipment and leave Harry and Jay's killers to deal with the consequences; what better revenge? We'll worry about the details later."

Liza nodded slowly.

"We've got to go. We've got miles to ride and money to grab."


# Forty-Four


Captain Raymond Zeron had the mike in his hand when the call came.

"Lenz here. I'm at the northwest perimeter. We got a witness who saw a woman on a bicycle headed into the Seventh Day Adventist Church parking lot."

"How long ago?"

"Ten minutes, he said, but that was ten minutes ago. So twenty."

"He see where she went after that?"

"No, but, Captain, we got the dog here and he went crazy."

"The dog, Lenz, is he still on their trail?"

"He had it headed north out of the lot."

"Good work, Lenz." Zeron clicked off and back on to the dispatcher. "Shift the perimeter. Stretch it ten miles north of the Seventh Day Adventist lot. A mile on either side. Get the bike patrol over there." He tapped his finger on the mike. That drove the dispatchers crazy and normally Zeron made a point of avoiding it, but tonight he didn't care.

"Sir, are you through?"

"No, dammit. If I was through I'd have signed off. Get those damned sirens off. We don't need to bellow our location."

"The sharpshooter from Portland's at the airport, sir."

"Is the helicopter ready for him?"

"Fueled and ready to hover."

Zeron turned to Bentec. "You have any ideas, Frank?"

Bentec nodded. "You know where I'll be most use to you, what with my being able to spot Silvestri so easy? In the copter with the sharpshooter."

# Forty-Five

Liza panicked every time a car passed. She'd have pedaled into overdrive if she'd had any reserve. That had been used up hours ago. She'd lost track of distance, direction, scenery, everything but pedaling as she struggled to keep up with Ellen. Her body ached in places she hadn't known she had. She smelled of sweat, and mud from times she'd fallen. The bicycle seat rubbed her crotch each time she tried to sit and she was sure she'd never have sex again. Ellen must have changed direction ten times, leading her through parks and bypasses, over hilly rises, down unpaved trails, under branches so low her chin scraped the handlebars, through trees so dense she had to jump off and run the bicycle. They even forded two streams. Anybody who knew her would be amazed she'd kept up. Foremost in that category would be Ellen, though Ellen could have left her in the dust any time.

No matter how much her legs ached, and each breath tore at the lining of her lungs, she could not fall behind, not and make Ellen stop. It was more than just obligation that kept her moving at maximum. She still felt an inner warmth distinct from the sweat of exertion, and a wonderful amazement that Ellen would wait for her, chance her freedom, her life for her.

The sirens had stopped. She hadn't seen a police car in an hour. It was night now and there were no more children cycling in the streets in front of their houses, no more bike commuters dragging home from work. She hadn't even heard dogs barking in ages. She was outside town now. Houses along this rutted two-lane road were small, set far back and wide apart, interspersed with the occasional mobile home on blocks. There was no safety here. If a patrolman came up behind her he'd be calling for back-up before she realized he was there.

And despite the jolts of terror, her eyes kept easing shut. The roadbed rose. She leaned forward, almost standing on each pedal, but she was barely moving. She chanced a glance up from the pavement. Ellen was growing smaller in the distance.

"I will not. . .let her down!" She stood and pressed her full weight each time. Her head was far forward. The rise was turning into a hill, a Himalaya. She had to . . . she had to . . . she had to . . . She was over the top, coasting, panting, scanning the downslope. No Ellen. She pedaled faster than ever, racing downhill, trying to keep ahead of the spin of the gears. The air iced her face, her shoulders. She kept checking ahead but the road was empty.

"Hey! Liza. Stop." Ellen was standing beside a low stone wall.

It took Liza a hundred feet to grind to a halt and then she had to lean on the handlebars as she put foot numbly in front of foot as she walked.

There was no road behind Ellen, not even a gravel driveway. Ellen's bike was against the stone wall and she was cradling Felton. Liza rubbed his head. "Ellen, why did you stop? There's not even a truck here for us to steal."

"That's okay; we should leave a couple vehicles untouched anyway. There's an old stone outbuilding behind the house. We can hide inside."

"I don't see any house."

"About fifty yards back along the road."

"How do you know about the stone hut or whatever?"

"I've ridden this road."

"I don't see anything."

"Liza, do you want to call the Diners' Club? Trust me. We've got to sleep. Do you have a better plan?"

"Lead on." She was afraid Ellen would make her climb back on her bike and follow over the rocky ground. But Ellen was walking her bike, and doing it no more steadily than she was. The underbrush led to denser woods. The outbuilding was behind a rise. No police cruiser was going to spot it.

And Ellen hadn't seen it pedaling by, either. Liza could have confronted her about that, but she was way too tired.

The eight-by-ten leaf-and-moss-covered building probably had been built as an above-ground equivalent of a root cellar. The deep earthy smell of decomposition filled the place. Felton waddled in, flopped down and within seconds was snoring softly. Liza propped her bike against the wall and collapsed back next to him on a bed of vines, underbrush and things she chose not to consider.

If she let her eyes close she'd be asleep before her next breath. She propped herself on her elbow and continued to look at Ellen. She wanted to savor this moment when it was just the two of them—friends—against the world. Maybe together they really could have taken the shipment, evened the score, gotten the money. She loved the idea of them with a ton of cash, catching a sleeper car from Brussels to Siena, looking down at the world from a mountain outside Kathmandu. Her face was still wet from sweat or maybe it was tears, she didn't know. She didn't have words to marvel within herself at the wonder of friendship. She took Ellen's hand before she could go to sleep. "Ellen, I can never repay you for all you've done, for all I've done to you . . . I don't know what to say."

"Say goodnight, Liza."

Liza squeezed her hand and Ellen squeezed back. She stayed still, savoring the feeling in her hand because she knew this moment, this communion of friendship would never come again. She waited till Ellen's breath was almost regular, and said, "This is Wes's place, isn't it?"

"Mmm . . . Don't worry. We'll be out of here before dawn. He'll never know."

Forcing herself to stay awake may have been the hardest thing she'd ever done. But she had to take care of Ellen. She dug her nails in her palms and waited till Ellen's breathing became longer, smoother, then pushed herself up slowly, quietly and made her way out of the hovel and back to the road to find Wes.

It seemed like midnight, like an eternity beyond midnight. But her watch said only ten thirty. She brushed the leaves and dirt off her windbreaker and started up the road, trudging stiffly, straining for the first sound of an approaching car, clambering into the brush until each passed. She wasn't thinking; just moving. It wasn't till she had Wes's house in sight that she hesitated. She reminded herself that she was a woman who didn't hesitate, and that, with a few glaring exceptions, reading men was her strong suit. But Ellen knew the guy; maybe Ellen was right about getting out of here before he discovered them. If this guy was an arrogant poor loser who stalked off because he couldn't stand being beaten by a woman, turning Ellen in to the cops would be the Superbowl of victories for him.

A winter's worth of wood was piled next to the house, much too close. The house was log, one of those prefab deals with big windows on each side of the door and a porch that ran the length of it. Light formed muted creamy squares behind the shades in both windows. A staccato male voice inside was muted, too. A guest? Radio? Police radio?

If there was an open window— But she'd make too much noise in the dark. Better to trust her skill.

She was at the porch step, but she couldn't move. Fear was choking her, the fear she'd been out-riding for hours. She was risking everything with this guy. If she was wrong— He could grab his cell and call 911 before she opened her mouth. She and Ellen would be the lead story on the news here—murder, kidnap, plane hijacking. How could she possibly convince even the most decent guy—

She was knocking on the door.

Nothing happened. Fear vanished; she didn't feel at all. In the stillness she pictured Wes, the dry stick, the brittle loser.

The door opened.

"Wes?"

"Yes."

She realized she was wrong. "Omigod."

She stared.

She'd blurted out the absolutely worst thing but she couldn't make her mouth work and her mind was blank with horror.

194

Wes looked stunned. Then he let out a huge guffaw. "I've had people stare at my stump and turn away. A lot of them pretend I've still got both legs. Some try not to look at all. But no one's ever greeted me with Oh my God. It's a safe guess that you're not in door-to-door sales."

Her gaze was aimed straight ahead but all she could see was the right leg of his sweatpants, hanging loose with no foot at the bottom. She forced herself to note the rest of him. Tall, thin—too thin—sinewy shoulders and arms. Big, wide hands. Curly light-brown hair that was beginning to recede, craggy face—too thin—high cheekbones, high-arched nose, wide mouth that looked like it was left over from better days. Now, with him laughing, that thin face was impish. So this was what Ellen had seen in him. He was a sexy man and blunt in a way that made her want to trust him. And made her loath to do so.

"Would you like to come in?"

"I'll just stand and gawk."

He slid his foot back and shifted the two canes, and she hurried in. Both windows were lighted, she realized, because the place was essentially one big room. The big stone fireplace at the south end called out for great leather chairs and a hooked rug, but Wes had furnished with straight-back armchairs, a sofa, and wall-to-wall carpet. Easy access, sure footing. A practical man.

"Drink?" The quizzical smile was still on his face. A radio played music now. There was no television; he wouldn't have seen her picture. But . . . ?

She nodded and watched him stride to the sink in great vaulting steps. He was like a crane looking for the right spot to light. Where was his phone? Not on him; his sweats had no pockets.

"Sit. You look like you've been to every door on the road, all the way from Eugene. Sit on the left side of the sofa."

She sat. The couch was firm but comfortable, a nap couch. She didn't dare lean back. She couldn't get a make on him. The leg thing; her awful comment; her mind was a whirlpool. Oh, God, she really could not think. Time was running out.

"Look next to you."

She picked up on the irritation in his voice. Quickly she

checked the couch.

"Other side."

"Oh!" A miniature train had pulled into the "station" on the end table. Its freight was her drink and a bowl of mixed nuts. It must have made train sounds coming but they didn't penetrate. With her eyes she followed the tracks back to the wall by the fireplace and around to the kitchen.

"I had a few spills before I built the Household Local Line." He was in a straight chair on the other side of the end table, leaning back as if he had her in his custody and could wait forever for her explanation.

She couldn't read him; she was too tired. Playing for time, she gobbled nuts, washed them down with the drink. The glass was empty when she put it down but still no verbal move occurred to her.

"Another drink?"

She sat forward and listened as the words came out of her mouth. "My name is Liza Silvestri. My husband was murdered yesterday in Los Angeles. The police think I killed him. I need your help."

The phone was on Wes's far side. He made no move. He was watching her, assessing. The fireplace was dark and a draft blew in from the chimney and curled under the neck of her windbreaker. Behind her a clock ticked. She could shift the balance, tell him about Ellen, but she would not. That much she could do for Ellen: find out if he was trustworthy before exposing her. Finally he said, "Did you?"

"Kill him?"

He nodded professorially as if he'd asked for elucidation of an oral exam answer.

"No, I didn't kill him. Of course, I didn't. They shot him in the back. They burst in, and shot him." Her eyes welled. "I was right there. I felt him die."

Wes nodded again. His skin was tan and there was a white margin around his hair line as if his creator drew the deep S-curves to mark where to put hair. She couldn't read him.

"Why didn't they kill you?"

"They didn't see me."

"They couldn't spot you in a loft room?"

Liza started. "You know?"

196

He laughed. "This is the biggest manhunt or womanhunt we've had probably ever. You're responsible for making two or three broadcasting careers. They even cut into *Sixty Minutes*."

She was shaking all over. "What did they say?"

"That you shot him in a love nest."

Her breath caught. She could barely force out words. "And you don't believe them? You believe me?"

"No and maybe."

"No?"

"This is a helluva manhunt for a love triangle."

"And the maybe?"

Wes grinned and leaned toward her. "Come on, asking me to swear allegiance on the basis of what you've given me is a big leap of faith."

"So why aren't you calling the police?"

"It's worth the risk."

"Why?"

"Because, Liza, I want to see Ellen."

# Forty-Six

"We're getting low on fuel, sir," the helicopter pilot said for the second time. And now Zeron was on the horn.

"Frank, you're putting us all to shame up there. But, look, you can't see worth shit, can you?"

Bentec squinted harder, but he was doing well to tell the color of a car, much less the make, much less spot a cyclist under the trees.

"Frank, look, it's raining down here, too. These women have been on the run over twenty-four hours. They're not going anywhere. They're hunkered down somewhere waiting for the weather to let up. Only makes sense. Them and their pig"

Bentec fingered the mike but didn't speak. He'd been right about Oregon: all doors opened for the Assistant to the Commissioner of the Los Angeles Police Department. It would

197

be the same with the railroad. Once he got the container number, railway officials would find him the train, give him the schedule, and make sure he had ample time to get aboard before it left Portland. Liza Silvestri had the container numbers; why else would she have high-tailed it up here? He had to find her.

"Sir, the fuel gauge is on empty! We've got to land."

Bentec clicked the mike on. "Have the Feds arrived?"

"Not yet. They're saying morning now."

"Then we have time for another shot before they get here?"

"You got it, Frank."

"Okay, we're on our way down." Bentec turned to the sharpshooter. He was the best marksman in the state, the shooter had assured him. There would be ample time for the 'copter to land and Bentec to squeeze a statement out of the suspect before she bled out.

Bentec tapped his arm and shouted over the beat of the rotors, "Be at the airport half an hour before dawn."

# Forty-Seven

Ellen rolled over again and pulled the blankets up to cover her head, but this time her eyes opened halfway. The sheets were so warm, the bed so soft, and even awake, her body was still closer to sleep. Rain thudded on the roof, tinkled against the window panes, gurgled down spouts. A hard rain. A morning to sleep in.

If it was still morning. She could have checked her watch, but that required such effort. Her body felt like cement, her chest a hollow of fear, and she knew if she opened her eyes all the way it would be to face something awful. She eased onto her back feeling the sheets slide over her breasts and realized she was naked. Oh, Jeez, this was bad. And the room . . . where was she? Was she a prisoner? This wasn't the sty she'd hauled the bicycle into.

Now she remembered Liza poking her awake, and the

twigs and leaves clinging to her hair and something crawling down her collar, and Liza telling her she could sleep inside where it would be safe, telling her no one was home, that Wes's mother didn't live here anymore, and telling Liza she *was* asleep and to leave her the hell alone and . . . and Liza yanking at her and her figuring if she was ever going to sleep again she'd be better off going along with Liza so she'd leave her alone. And Liza dragging her in through a kitchen door and then insisting she take a shower when it was all she could do to stand up and finally . . . finally falling into bed. This bed.

No one was home but Wes's mother didn't live here anymore? Last night she didn't question that, but now it made no sense. How would Liza know that if no one was home? This bed, was it Wes's mother's bed? But she didn't live here anymore. *Wes's* bed?

But that couldn't be. This was a dream. She should never have allowed herself to dream of him again. Now her dreams were branching out from familiar memories to a kind of speculation that was going to drive her out of her skin. In a minute she would wake up from this dream of him, like always . . . But maybe, just this once, she could let herself roll over and get back into the dream, just this one time she could make it go on until Wes walked into the room, over to the bed . . . She shifted onto her side and pulled the pillow on top of her head, ignoring the creak that could have been a door or anything else.

"Ellen?"

She rolled slowly back, still sure she'd be opening her eyes in Kansas City, bracing herself against the disappointment.

But there he was. Wes. She couldn't believe it—Wes! Real! Alive! Wes! Her heart was pounding so hard it was shaking her body. She couldn't talk, just stare. Wes looked older, thinner. Much thinner. But that drawn quality suited his hungry look. His brown eyes seemed larger now, his brows arched with the same questioning need he'd had the first time he asked her to dinner, not sure the race winner would deign to dine with a novice like him. His mouth was opened a smidge as if to ask a question that never came. He was, still, the sexiest man she had ever known. Suddenly she was aware of her breasts, her thighs, her stomach, her groin against the sheet. She felt very naked.

"This is your house now?" she said to say something.

"Yes . . . after the accident . . . Mom moved to San Diego." He was putting in words too, like a chess player moving a pawn.

"How did you know about— Oh, Liza. Where is Liza?"

"Eating. With her pig, eating. I'm going to have to make a run to the store. I live alone. I wasn't prepared for a pig to drop in." He flashed the grin she'd pictured in the dark night after night, the grin that created mounds high on his cheeks. She could see that he was holding it out to her, that smile, warily.

This moment—she dreamed of it so long, and then no longer allowed herself to visit even in dreams—she wanted to hold it like an opal, turning it so she could see it from every side, to note how the light caught it and made it sparkle, how it glowed afterward in the dark. She wanted to put it in a velvet case where nothing could scratch it or make it shatter as its predecessors had.

Her arms ached from holding them back, from not reaching out to him, drawing him against her, feeling him soft and warm, hot and eager, steeped from the years of absence, pulling him so close she couldn't think. *Take him now like a gift from the fates, a last meal on this death row trip of Liza's. Take him, pretend nothing's changed in four years.*

The last thing she wanted was to ask the question that could smash this moment. But despite her cherished dreams about Wes Jacobsen, she was not a dreamer. She was a realist.

He stood beside the bed, leaning forward, not so much eagerly as tentatively, like a marionette, or as if he was propped on something she couldn't see. How many times after the bike crash had she gone to the hospital, even driven all the way down here to go past his mother's house—this house—like a teenager hoping for just a glimpse of him? How many more times had she called, desperate to hear a sentence on the phone, a laugh, a groan even?

"Why—"

"Why didn't I answer your calls? Was I such a poor loser—"

200

"But you weren't losing. We were both knocked out of the race. And it was only a bike race, it wasn't the end of the world." She patted the bed. "Sit down. Tell me."

"I'll stand." His gaunt face was flushed; he looked as nervous as she was. "Maybe you won't want me sitting near you."

A draft shot down her bare back but she didn't move to shift the blankets.

Wes shifted his weight. His arms were stiff as canes. "After that crash," he said slowly, as if reading intricate instructions, "you were back at work in a couple days. By odds I should have been, too. But I landed a lot harder than you did. My shinbone broke in three places, messy breaks. They did surgery; it got infected. Then I picked up a staph infection and nearly checked out with it, and when I came to—" he took a breath and hurried on—"I didn't have a leg. Well, more accurately not much shin and no foot at all. Except when I put it in my mouth, of course."

"Oh, Wes, I never—"

"Of course, you didn't know. I made sure you didn't. It sounds ridiculous now, after all these years, but I didn't know you that well then, and I sure didn't know myself, and . . . well . . . I felt like I'd been through so much I couldn't face losing anything—anyone—else."

Memories, dreams, and memories of dreams tumbled over each other so furiously she could barely think. "But why? What could possibly have made you think I wouldn't want you?"

He took a deep breath. His ashen face seemed even paler. "I was depressed, I didn't realize how depressed till I got medication and came out of it. I couldn't get out of bed, couldn't deal with the prosthesis or the crutches, couldn't eat because food made me sick, and when my mother forced me to see relatives I resented them asking about my leg and hated them if they ignored it. If you'd asked me before the crash 'How would you react to having an amputation?' I don't know what I'd have said, but I'll tell you, Ellen, 'I'd fall apart' would never have occurred to me. But that's exactly what I did."

She reached for him but he still refused to sit as if he hadn't

201

yet given the password.

"Didn't I think of you, Ellen? Yeah, I thought of you every day. What I thought was: How could I expect a top-class athlete like you to spend your time with a cripple?"

"What?" She sat up in amazement, and had to make a grab for the sheet. For the first time she saw the canes on which he was leaning.

"It sounds stupid now, but in that gulch of depression it made perfect sense. It gave me an image of nobility to hang onto. Like I was the hero in some melodramatic black and white movie. I couldn't do much of anything, I thought, but at least I could make this sacrifice for you. Your whole life was biking. What would you have done with me, waved as you rode by?"

"The one year in my life I did anything athletic—" She shook her head in amazement at the ludicrousness of it all. "Dammit, why did you think I kept calling you, so I could tell you whether I'd won or placed?"

"I know—"

Her face was flushed and the heat of her welling fury battled the cold on her bare back. "You could have—"

He put up a hand to silence her. "Not then. I couldn't anything. I might as well have been in a straitjacket. When I came out of the depression I couldn't believe the things I'd done, and the things I had not done. But that was seven months later and you'd stopped calling and someone said you were dating someone, and I just, well, figured it was too late. Even then, it was all I could do to admit I didn't have a leg anymore. Now I know it's not the worst thing in the world. I've got a good prosthesis and when I'm using it you wouldn't notice anything more than a slight limp. I ride again, though—" an uncertain smile flashed on his face—"I'm not better at it than I was before."

"Why aren't you—"

"Occasionally it irritates the contact spot."

"Oh." Ellen didn't know what to say, about the irritation, about him, the years gone, the stupidity of it all. There was so much to say, nowhere to begin. The failure of speech hung between them.

He shifted his weight onto the crutch. "Well, listen, like I said,

I'm going to make a run to the store. Tell me what you need. I'll deal with food, and I'll pick up some quilted plaid shirts and caps for you both for camouflage. I've got a rifle—"

"No!"

He jerked back as if she'd hit him.

"No, please, don't talk about shooting. I know . . . I know we could die . . . I know that, and I'll have to deal with that, but please, not yet. Not now." She was shaking, tears pouring down her face. And he, he was next to her holding her.

"Oh, Ellen, I'm so sorry. Don't worry; we'll work it out. It has to work out. It can't not."

She tried to speak, but she couldn't form words. She held him to her, blocking out thought and fear with the reality of his flesh. Rain pounded on the roof like rifle shots; the air chilled her bare back. She couldn't believe she was here with him. She couldn't believe she could die. She pulled him closer. Last week she would have held her grievances before her like a shield, demanding explanations like tolls on the road to trust. But life had lost its grounding, and time had accordioned to nothing. "Don't go. You can shop later. Be with me now."

She smiled, feeling as if he were pulling her back toward him in slow motion, acknowledging the slight scratch of his not quite shaven beard before his hard moist lips were on hers. She remembered the last time, and then didn't as he eased closer to her, and she stretched her arms back around his chest and let her head drop to his shoulder and stayed motionless in amazement.

Finally she scrunched back and pulled the covers free, and he stood.

"For a guy using a couple canes you're damned fast dropping your clothes," she said as he slid in.

"It's that extra shoe that takes the time." He pulled her to him.

She nodded and let herself be carried toward him, let herself notice the exquisite touch of her nipples against his chest, the first warm feel of his moist penis on her thigh, the raw neediness of her stomach, her breasts, her groin. His mouth was hard on hers, his body meshing frantically into hers, and all thoughts disappeared. She ran her hands around him, pulling the mounds of his butt into her. His desperate groans gouged deep, mining down to her marrow. She dug her fingers into his back, but she couldn't pull him close enough, till the barrier of skin disappeared and they became one being.

And afterwards she couldn't have described the passion she had so long dreamed of. The feelings resounded in her body but there were no words attached to them, nothing to anchor them in memory.


# Forty-Eight


Raymond Zeron closed off his mike and rubbed his eyes. It was almost dawn. The patrol car felt like a box, and the air in it like styrofoam pellets.

The radio buzzed.

"Zeron."

"Wilkes here, sir. Hey, we got us a lead. Guy driving home last night almost clipped a girl on a bike out Route three-sixteen."

"This case was on every newscast. Why didn't he call us last night?"

"He was driving home from a bar. He sounds like he just staggered up."

Zeron pulled himself together. "The witness, he seem credible to you?"

"Yeah. I don't think he's to the point of seeing things. He says he almost hit one girl and then passed another. I believe him."

"Where on three-sixteen?"

"About five miles beyond the Seventh Day. Beyond the stream. Heading north."

"Good work, Wilkes." Zeron switched back to the dispatcher. "Patch me through to all units." He could have added Bentec and the Fed to that list. He hesitated. "Make sure Bentec's on the channel." The Feds he'd worry about later. "Okay men, and women, we've got a spotting out three-sixteen five miles north of the Seventh Day. These suspects have been on the lam for two days. Even if they're Superwomen they've got to sleep. They could have taken hostages and be holing up in their house. They could be in an outbuilding snoring away, or even in the brush. I want someone at every door along three-sixteen and every road off it. Get yourselves inside each house and look around. Get into every garage, every garden shed, play house, doghouse. Get those dogs into the fields. Those women are still in Eugene and we will damned well get 'em before they leave town."

He looked around for Bentec and spotted him finger-combing his L.A. gray hair. He couldn't decide about Bentec, but that didn't bother him. If the case went bad it was good to have a goat. When the Feds started throwing barbs, a goat was good also. And up in the copter with the sharpshooter, Bentec wasn't going to cause him any trouble.

# Forty-Nine

Liza stoked the fire. Felton was stretched out in front. She rubbed his cute little black and white head and he gave a cute little snort in his sleep. She'd split an omelet with him that could have sated a village. If eating and sleeping were numero uno and duo in the porcine world, Felton was finally one happy pig.

The fire was crackling and she had that delicious feeling of heat on her back and cool on her front. She'd found Bisquick in the kitchen and made old-fashioned biscuits. Now she was drinking good, strong coffee with cream. She'd slept till eight—nine hours. She was still tired, but it was that day-after tiredness when the party was over, the glasses were washed and her biggest decision was whether to read Sunday's paper or go for a swim and probably she'd leaf through the paper because the ocean would always be there.

She settled on the leather couch and sipped her coffee. The fire was crackling. The smell of burning pine logs meshed with the aroma of coffee. She had another biscuit waiting on the model train's flatcars in the kitchen and she considered whether to call up a delivery, taking her time puzzling over the pros and cons of this decision of no importance.

She couldn't stay here, of course. It was odd sitting on this leather sofa in a stranger's house not knowing how soon she'd have to scurry out, or even how long she'd have charge of this room before Ellen and Wes emerged from the bedroom. She smiled. She was proud of that little mitzvah. Too bad she couldn't have seen Ellen's face when Wes walked in, but she was free to imagine how unmitigatedly good she felt. There had to be some way for them, some future.

*Don't get caught up in that now!* This safe, peaceful moment wasn't unmitigatedly good, but it was as good as it was likely to get. No need to let the future bleed into it! Half an hour ago—maybe an hour—she'd turned on the local news and was horrified to see her own face and hear herself described as a deranged jilted wife, armed, and of course, dangerous. With a pig. The broadcasters hadn't had Ellen's picture then, and if they knew of her connection to Eugene, they weren't saying. But it was only a matter of time.

"Inspiration," she said aloud. "Where is my vaunted inspiration?" She flicked the switch on the model railroad and watched the engine chug along the wall, curve left at the corner, make another left at the fireplace and shoot into Sofa Station. She hit another switch and watched the train back up.

The bedroom door opened. Ellen and Wes came out together and it was hard to say which of them had the bigger, blowzier grin. Their faces were flushed, their hair finger-combed and none too expertly, their eyes were watery and only for each other. If this were Hollywood, schmaltzy music would be hitting a crescendo. But these two were so real it made her want to cry.

"Thank you," Ellen said to her in a still half-in-bed voice. She stopped, looked her in the eye and said again, "Thank you."

She nodded and felt a wave of warmth and ease, of having evened the ledger. Of, she realized, no longer being the beggar. "Have some coffee before we talk." She waited, no short period because they couldn't keep their hands off each other and with what was left of their attention their coffee-pouring acumen was on a par with Felton's. She was grinning as she watched them.

She hated to destroy this glowing moment, maybe their last, but there was no choice. She said, "We can't stay here and wait till they find us. We have to make decisions."

Ellen was the most controlled person she knew, but Ellen looked cow-eyed at Wes, then glared at her. In a moment Ellen had her face under control; she took a swallow of coffee and nodded in acquiescence. "We wait until dark—"

"Which gives us all day." Wes grinned and wrapped an arm around her waist. He must have been wearing his prosthesis now; he was standing on both legs and looked perfectly normal.

"And after dark, Ellen?" Liza prodded.

"I don't know. Clearly you've been worrying about this, what do you think?" There was a whiny quality to her voice, but that was understandable. For Ellen planning a getaway had to be the ultimate lose-lose situation.

Liza refilled her cup. "The obvious escape route is the freeway, north and south. But it is obvious. Is there an east–west route, Wes?"

"Hour and a half to the coast, eight or nine hours to Boise. That's if you can drive on a two-laner."

"What, a little L.A. bashing?"

He toasted her with his cup, then smiled down at Ellen, not saying anything more, just smiling.

Liza took her coffee and settled next to Felton by the fire. Roads in all directions, but no vehicle. The coast was a dead end, too easy for them to find her there. Inland, then. There had to be back roads connecting small towns. But if they were spotted—two women and a pig would stand out—all the advantages would be with the cops.

The answer was obvious. Tears welled up again. She swallowed hard against them, lost the battle and swiped at her eyes with her knuckles. It was the answer she'd really known for hours but just hadn't been able to face. Ellen and Wes were still by the coffee pot. They probably hadn't realized she'd moved away.

"What do you drive?" she asked, walking back to them.

207

"A pick-up, and old yellow Chevy."

"Okay, here's the plan. You drive me and a bicycle to the other side of town, maybe twenty miles beyond."

"And?" he prodded.

She swallowed again. "And you take care of Felton."

"And?" Ellen said.

"And I ride off into the sunset with my newfound thigh muscles. The police won't be looking for a single woman. But if they find me, that's the chance I take. You stay here. If anyone asks, you're Wes's wife."

Ellen eyed Wes questioningly.

He gazed down at her, his eyes widening, his mouth stretching slowly into a half smile. He looked like a man in a dream afraid to move lest he wake himself up. "El, you know, it could be a go. I work at home. No one comes in. There's no neighbor near enough to know who's living here."

Ellen eased back against him. A contented smile settled onto her face and her eyes closed.

A gush of pleasure, of pride even, washed over Liza. Underneath she felt so hollow her skin could implode. She'd planned to make herself scarce and leave them alone. But now that they were going to have the rest of their lives together she didn't bother. She snagged the biscuit on the flatcar, slathered on jam and ate.

She'd finished the last bite when Ellen hooked her arms around Wes's neck, leaned hard into him, and sighed. With one arm he pulled her close, and there she stayed, so still it was eerie. When she pushed back there was no sated glow in her face; she looked as wary as Liza. "It won't work, Liza. I'm sorry, really sorry. I'd throw you to the wolves in a minute if it meant I could stay here. That's the kind of great friend I am. But I don't have that choice. I'm no innocent bystander now; I hijacked an airplane. Oh, shit, and the pilot, that's kidnapping. They send people to the electric chair for that." Ellen was still leaning into Wes, but now she looked unaware of him, as if she felt nothing but the awakening horror of how very bad things were.

Wes's mouth was actually hanging open and Liza was sure he never imagined Ellen as the hijacker. He gave Ellen's shoulder a squeeze. "Damn, El, that's so like you."

208

Ellen straightened up.

This, Liza thought, was what she must have looked like at the bike races. This was who she must have been. This Ellen so foreign to her was the woman who grabbed the wheel, took the plane, found the bikes, and outran the cops. This was sure not the woman who would have settled for Harry Cooper.

Liza squeezed her eyes shut and when she opened them she saw things about Ellen she ignored before—the muscles in her forearms and her thighs, how she'd pushed her hair behind her ears to get it out of the way, the lines of determination just beginning to etch into the skin around her mouth. She recalled Ellen's comments in the church parking lot. Then she credited them to Ellen's euphoria or exhaustion; it hadn't occur to her that Ellen would really take the big chance. But now she reconsidered. "So, then, we take the money?"

"What?" Wes turned to face Liza.

But it was Ellen she was speaking to. "In for a lamb, in for a sheep? I mean, just how much do we have left to lose?"

"Are you wacko, Lady?"

Liza ignored him, moving to face Ellen directly. "Bentec could shoot me— He will shoot me if he gets the chance, me and you, because we know about his illegal weapons shipment. Even if he's unmasked and carted off to jail before he can get us, we're still fugitives and no jury is going to say, 'Yeah they were justified in stealing every form of transportation on wheels, plus kidnapping.' Best scenario is we go to jail till we're too old to care. Ellen, we're already in for a damn big lamb."

Ellen nodded. "A black sheep."

A moment passed before Wes said, "Illegal weapons! What are you two involved in? How are you going to—"

"Jay and Bentec figured out how to orchestrate their sale. There's nothing to stop Ellen and me finding a better deal. We'll figure out how to get the money, and worry about the shipment after."

# Fifty

Liza nodded when Wes said, "If you ladies are going to steal a fortune, are you going to cut me in?"

"We're dealing with killers. Our odds of survival are miniscule."

"I know." He smiled down at Ellen. "I'm in."

For a moment they all stood there in the kitchen watching the rain drops meandering down the window. It had been cold when she took Felton out earlier, but it was toasty in here now. The bowl she'd stirred the biscuits in was soaking in the sink and the everything's-okay aroma of hot biscuits still filled the air. When she'd first seen Wes, with his El Greco-esque body and his angular face she'd been afraid he'd be stoic. But he sure wasn't.

Ellen said, "Let's start with what we know." Her voice was crisp and shaky, like an overcooked biscuit in danger of crumbling. "Liza, how do you think this scheme started? Did Jay know Bentec? Did he—"

Liza fingered her coffee cup. She'd already had way too much coffee but the buzz seemed appropriate now. "Jay insisted on coming to Portland for that reunion. A St. Enid's reunion was the last place I wanted to be. It made me real uncomfortable. Oh, sorry, Ellen."

Ellen shrugged.

"And any reunion is the last place you want to bring a husband. I mean, either you spend the whole time making sure he's not bored, or if he isn't bored it's because he's hearing something about you you don't want him to know. So, I pulled out all stops to derail this plan. I suggested Banff. Too far, he said. I got a special on a weekend in San Francisco. Too close. Finally, he said he had some business up here and I gave up. I don't think he planned to connect with Harry; that was just luck for him."

210

Wes refilled cups and said, "So, lady-now-in-the-know, what was he coming for?"

"Trolling for a buyer for his shipment, that's my guess. We were only there for the weekend. Friday night we checked into the Benson Hotel, had dinner and walked around town. Saturday we went to a gun show in Idaho. It was so unlike Jay I thought it was a joke. But there we were, looking as out of place as two buffalo on the Venice boardwalk. We'd both made an effort to dress down, but still our jeans were creased, Jay's jacket was new black leather, and the sweater I had on was about half the size of what any child in the building was wearing. We couldn't possibly have stood out more. We were like Queen Elizabeth and Prince Philip visiting the colonials, except that colonials always seem pleased to see them. At the gun show people weren't rude, just wary." She sipped the hot coffee; it was bitter now this fourth or fifth cup, but she didn't care. "At the time I thought Jay didn't notice how L.A. we were; but he did, of course. Jay never overlooked appearances. No, he intended to play the hotshot Angeleno, and me in tight jeans and skimpy sweater, I was part of the show. He strolled around the whole show, stopping at each booth, picking up the biggest weapon he could find and shrugging as if it were nothing. I thought he was behaving like an ass, and doing it in the worst possible place. I'll tell you, I was relieved when we made it back to the door. I was already figuring how long before we'd be back in Portland. Then he said he wanted to ask a couple of guys a couple of questions and would I get him the map out of the car so he could ask about the best route back to Portland."

"So you left?" Wes asked.

"Not hardly. I knew Jay was getting rid of me—and normally I would have gone along with his plan, but I was worried that without me there he would provoke some local and get himself killed. So I tried to make myself as inconspicuous as possible—no small task—and keep an eye on Jay. He didn't meet a couple of guys; he walked directly over to one guy, a tall sandy-haired man in a sports jacket, the one I would have called the most normal-looking person in the place."

"Would have called?" Wes prompted.

"Until I saw him outside later. It was on the road out, a narrow two-lane job with cars and trucks parked on the bank on either side. His truck was behind a rust-splotched blue Chevette. Both were on the edge of a ditch. The bumper of the Chevette was against his. He had about eighteen inches free behind him. He could have squiggled out—it would have been an effort, but doable. Instead he went forward, and slowly, as if he were cleaning off his windshield, he pushed the little car into the ditch. Then he backed up again and left. The little old car sank farther in the mud than I could have imagined, up past the doors. Even if the engine was in the rear and it wasn't a total loss, the seats were on their way to being soaked and the poor person who owned it—and it had to be a poor person, miserable vehicle that it was—was looking at towing out a smelly heap, spending money he didn't have, hitching rides, and who knew what all inconvenience. All because it was in this jerk's path. I saw his expression again, cool, righteous, consumed, like he would crush a man and it'd all be in a day's work."

Ellen slipped her hand into Wes's. "And that," she said in a stunned voice, "is who you think is Jay's buyer?"

Liza nodded, keeping her eyes lowered to avoid Ellen's gaze. "Because he was the one person Jay didn't want to joke about after."

Ellen started for the sofa but Wes caught her, put both their coffees on the flatcar and sent it ahead. His arm was tight around her waist as they walked to the sofa and sat so close together Liza could almost have stretched out on the remaining cushions. She hunkered down next to Felton by the fire.

Ellen set her cup down. "Harry was shot because he was routing Jay's shipment, right Liza? Because the killer, this guy, got what he needed—" she swallowed and for a moment Liza didn't think she'd be able to force herself to go on—"and then he shoved him into the ditch."

Liza nodded. It was all she could do.

Wes rubbed Ellen's shoulder and said softly, "The only thing his killer would want would be the 'when and where' of the shipment arriving. Would Harry have that?"

"Of course. If Jay's shipment left L.A. say, uh . . ."

"Friday," Liza offered.

"Friday, why Friday?"

"Because Jay died Friday night. Bentec wouldn't have had him shot before the shipment left. There'd have been no point. It had to be after the shipment was beyond Bentec's control that he panicked and . . ." Liza stiffened against the memory of the loft and Jay staggering back against her. Even if she survived all this, she knew that scene would never fade. "So the shipment left no later than Friday—"

Ellen nodded. "And going along at nineteen miles per hour—"

"Ellen, I think Jay would have sent it express."

Ellen caught her eye and smiled. "Nineteen miles per hour is express, freight express. That's the average speed of a freight train, in good times. Admittedly, it's counting in stops at weigh stations and regular stations, at crossings and the occasional shunting off onto the wrong track."

"But if it didn't—"

"Liza, you're missing the point! All that stuff happens. With Harry's best-laid plans, routing cargoes through the best-run transfer points, avoiding the black hole hubs of the freight world, still cargoes got shunted off onto side rails and there they sat full of rotting melons while their computer tracker clicked on with the rest of the train."

Wes leaned forward. "Computer tracking?"

"Oh, yeah. All the engines have numbers, all the cars, all the containers. A.E.I. . . . Automated . . . Equipment . . . Identification, I think. And there are sensors along the way. Still, if a container is shunted off into a siding at the rail yard in Eugene, chances are the loss won't register till Salem, maybe even Portland."

"Register on?" Wes was almost out of his seat.

"The sender can check the carrier's website and track his cargo, just like Harry could."

"So Silvestri could have done that?"

"I guess so. No reason why not. But my point—"

Wes was just about shaking her. "So both the sender and the recipient can check on the cargo's progress?"

"Sure."

"But Silvestri didn't trust the recipient, so he didn't give

213

him the key to check on the shipment, maybe not the shipment numbers or something—"

Liza smacked down her empty cup. "Because the recipient hasn't paid up yet."

"Yeah. Good, Liza. And then he hears that Silvestri's been eliminated and he figures he'll just grab his shipment for free, that is, if he can get enough data to find it—"

"Which means we can feed him whatever data we want, right? We can off-load our shipment somewhere in Washington, and give the buyer the number of a container of corn."

"For six million dollars he just might want a peek first."

"So we'll get half before and let him think we'll wait around for the rest. Harry wouldn't have given him the right data, would he, Ellen?"

"No! I know Harry. He'd die before . . ."

An icy cold shot down Liza's back. She looked up at the two of them sitting so close a germ couldn't squeeze in. "Wouldn't everything the buyer needs be on the web page? Wouldn't he just have to have gotten Harry to pull it up?"

Ellen nodded stiffly. "Poor Harry, to die in the midst of his corruption."

"Ellen, I am so sorry that Jay—"

"Forget it. You're not responsible for your husband, not anymore. So, the shipment. It left L.A., say, forty-eight hours ago, at nineteen miles per hour."

"C'est tout, mes femmes. Let me find that web page on the ol' computer." He circled his arms behind Ellen's back and pulled her closer, planting a goodbye kiss worthy of heading off in a space capsule.

It was almost an hour before Wes rushed back in, his expression an uncoalesced mixture of delight and shock. "Here's the scoop: the Los Angeles Police Department is missing all the weapons that were being sent to be melted down. Six million dollars worth. The kind of weaponry the Marines use to storm buildings."

Liza sank onto the sofa. "Six million dollars of weapons worthy of a Marine invasion. All of it headed to the jerk who pushed the rusting Chevette into the ditch. I don't want to think of him waiting up there in Richland, Washington, ready to unload—"

"Richland?" Wes was staring open-mouthed.

"Yeah, Richland. So?"

"Liza! Do you know what's there?"

"No."

"Richland is the home of the Hanford Nuclear Power Plant. Or the remains thereof. We're not talking about grabbing six million dollars now, we're talking about blowing up the world. Liza, this is way bigger than us. We don't have any choice. We've got to call the police."

# Fifty-One

Frank Bentec had gotten enough sleep during the night and he was all wound up and there was nowhere to go to. Rain pounded the tin roof of the outbuilding Zeron had chosen for command. Zeron's men and women kept running in and out the door, slamming it, sending waves of soggy air all the hell over. The whole room reeked of mud and coffee. Little towns like Eugene didn't get big-time manhunts like this and these guys were pumped so tight they were bouncing off each other. The young ones were barely controlling their excitement; the old ones were eager to see years of training sessions pan out into something. Serious business, they kept saying to each other, but it didn't take a mind reader to see to them it was a fox hunt.

Rain sheeted windows and even he had to admit heading up in the copter would be a waste of time. He couldn't commandeer a patrol car because he didn't know where the hell to go.

Railroad computer records, the idea teased him. If only he could have gotten Liza Silvestri to find Jay's shipping papers. If he had a support unit. If only—shit. But he didn't and there was nothing to do but down coffee, study the map, pace and wait for the Feds to arrive. And search his memory for some

215

clue, some slip on Silvestri's part that would tell him what train his container was on.

The door smacked open. A drenched Fed in a sopping suit burst into the office, grinning like a normal guy.

"Kryczalski?" Zeron asked.

"Got it! The address!" Kryczalski shouted. "Forty-two eighty-seven, Route three-sixteen. Road's just this side of the freeway." He was waving the soggy paper he'd just read off, like a final lap flag.

"That where Silvestri is?" Bentec asked with forced calm. He needed to keep the situation under control here.

"I ran the friend, Ellen Baines, the one from Kansas City. Seems she just moved to K.C. three months ago. Want to guess from where?"

He stared at Kryczalski, who had to be right out of the academy. This was one Fed who never would have passed J. Edgar's sweaty palm test. "Where?"

"Portland. And what did she do in Portland?"

"What?"

"She belonged to a bicycle club. One of the members then was a guy who lives in Eugene now."

"At the Route three-sixteen address?"

"Right."

Bentec sighed. "Worth a check, but—"

"Wait, wait! The two of them were hospitalized at the same time, in the same crash."

"Still, that's not even circumstantial evidence."

"It's darned well worth following up." The kid looked positively outraged. "Are you saying you can't be bothered?"

"Not hardly, man," a local insisted. "Here's what we do—"

"Look, we need—"

"Hey, just a minute there, all of you, this is a federal case, a federal collar."

The bubble of Kryczalski's youthful trust had burst. He was frightened he'd blown it, and now he was all rules and regulations. Bentec could have played the rest of the argument from memory of his own encounters with the Feds. He stepped back, leaving it to Zeron. Map in one hand, keys to the patrol car in the other, he slipped outside.

He eased the car away and didn't hit the lights and siren

216

till he was into traffic. Zeron knew his own town way better than a stranger from L.A. could hope to. Even allowing time for Zeron and Kryczalski to fight it out back there, Bentec knew he wouldn't get much of a lead.

But he didn't need much time, just long enough alone with Silvestri, to get her to spill which train the shipment was on and when it was due in Portland. That was the easy part. The hard part would be disposing of her, and her friend, and the guy in the house before they tripped him up. The hard part would be doing it with a different MO than he'd used with Heron, something that would keep Zeron and the Feds off his tail for twelve hours—enough time for him to get the money and clear the border.

He sped past the Seventh Day Adventist Church, swinging the car into oncoming traffic or onto the sidewalk when the siren didn't clear the road. He hung a left on Route 316 and flicked off the lights and sirens. The silence smacked him. The rain muffled his movements.

It wasn't till he saw the wood piled outside the house, so well protected from the rain, that he realized how easy things would be.

# Fifty-Two

Liza sat on the floor. The fire threw out heat that merely pricked her skin; it didn't warm her. Have to go to the police. She couldn't chance the police. Neither could she let the guy who pushed the Chevette in the ditch steal a carload of weapons and head for a nuclear power dump. There was no good answer, only wrong choices. She sat, shivering, watching Ellen, waiting.

Ellen didn't move. Her eyes were open but Liza could tell she was seeing only what was inside her head, aware of Wes next to her, aware that once she spoke the safety of this moment would be gone.

Finally, Ellen shifted away from Wes. "It's too late," she

217

said. "The police aren't going to believe us. We could come up with facts and speculations till we turned to stone and they'd still think we were two crazy broads making up a bizarre tale to cover a crime spree. If the train left L.A. forty-eight hours ago, it's almost here now." She leaned forward, holding up a finger as if she was about to explain a math theorem. "Best possible scenario: We convince the cops. But that convincing would take hours. And by that time the weapons would be off the train at Richland and pointed at the nuclear waste site. And the radioactive waste would be all over Washington, Oregon and Idaho."

"What's the alternative?" Wes demanded.

Liza and Ellen looked at each other but neither spoke. They both knew the answer, Liza realized, but neither of them could bring herself to say, "We'll derail a carload of assault weapons while battalions of police and terrorists look on." She asked, "Can we find out exactly when the shipment is due in Richland? And who it's going to?"

Wes shook his head, a motion of disbelief, but he was pushing up from the sofa and his eager expression belied the seriousness of their plight. "Let's just see where that shipment is. Ellen, do you know what we're looking for?"

She followed him toward a room next to the bedroom. "Harry showed me a sample form with all the info, including container numbers, train numbers, shipper data and destination. Once you've got that you can call up the location."

"*Anyone* can call it up?"

"Harry could. The shipper or receiver can if they've got the password."

"And the guy who killed Harry could have taken that info off Harry's screen?"

Ellen had that stricken look she'd gotten each time Harry's name came up, but she nodded. "The bastard could have seen everything on Harry's screen, but he wouldn't know how to call it up again."

"I can get into Southern Pacific's database, but it'll take time and luck. It'd be a lot quicker if I had a password."

"Harry's you mean?"

"Yeah."

Ellen took up her post looking over his shoulder at the

218

screen. "Try—" she sounded like she could barely get the word out—"Ellen."

Tears gushed down Liza's cheeks before she could catch herself. She scooped up Felton, walked to the back window and stood looking out at the underbrush and the trees, and the rain. Felton, awake now, squeaked. "I need to take him out," she announced, knowing neither of them was listening.

On the back stoop she watched Felton sniffing seriously and rooting fervently. The rain walled her in and the cool damp brought out the fresh scent of the pines. An earthy smell wafted up from where Felton was rooting. Inside the house she heard the whistle of the Household Local Line.

The whistle blew again. She almost laughed. It wasn't inside at all, but coming from some place beyond the trees. A real train.

"Liza, he's got it. Come on."

She gathered up Felton and checked the monitor screen. Before she could decipher the boxes, Ellen said, "Here's Jay's shipment, one container car. Here's the destination: Richland, Washington."

"Okay," Wes said. "This triangle—Richland—Pasco—Kennewick—is pretty close over the Washington line."

"Kennewick, isn't that where Gwen was going?"

"Look here, mes femmes. The train's due in Portland this afternoon at three seventeen."

"Whew!" Liza nearly dropped Felton. "Three seventeen! It's almost noon now. That's too soon. Way too soon." She plunked Felton on the floor. "Wes, you're into the website, can't you slow the train, put a cow on the track in Eugene or a blizzard this side of Portland?"

"Sorry. I can read this report. I can't run the train."

"Wes . . . Ellen, do you see what that means? We've got less than three hours to come up with a plan and get ourselves to Portland. It can't—"

Ellen put a hand on her shoulder. "And the alternative is?"

"We run . . ." She chucked the rest of that option before it left her mouth. "Right, run and leave the crazy Chevette pusher to blow up the nuclear dump or do whatever it is he's getting six million dollars of weapons for."

"And Liza, that means we let him add Harry's murder like

a notch on his cane. We let Bentec go free. Maybe we'd even be letting him kill Gwen. And we never know who's still after us."

Liza took a breath. This was what she was good at: changing gears, thinking on her feet. "O . . . kay. How do we get the money and keep him from the weapons?"

"Here! Look!" Ellen pointed to the screen. We've got a phone number for the recipient."

"Really? That's amazing. Would he take the chance of someone calling a number and hearing, 'Hello, Montana Militia. Death to liberals, non-whites and uppity women. Have a nice day.'"

"Maybe it's not the Montana Militia, Liza. Let's see." Before Liza could protest, Ellen was dialing.

*You've reached the law offices of Devon Malloy. Please leave your name and number and a good time to reach you.*

Ellen hung up. The room was so silent the buzz of the computer sounded like a speeding freight.

It was Wes who said, "Makes it real, huh?"

Ellen nodded slowly. "Well, Hon, at least we'll be dealing with a lawyer, not a flock of guys who haven't been out of the woods since Vietnam."

Odd, Liza thought, how matter-of-factly the issue was solved. *We're dealing.* "Is there anywhere right before Richland where the train stops long enough for him to get on?"

Ellen nodded again, her mouth half open as if in thought. "Harry worked this stretch of track a lot when he was in Portland. There's a long grade about five miles west of Richland that Harry always worried about. The train slows to a crawl there. If a man's waiting, he can hop on. Harry worried about that."

Liza could see the spot. She'd seen it through the rain-slick windshield of Jay's rental car, cushioned by the smell of deli ham sandwiches. The memory of that picnic of Jay's shifted and she saw him dying on the loft floor. "The Richland grade?"

"Right."

Liza took a breath. She could feel the switch happening in her body, as if a gale had been growing into her chest, and suddenly the wind died, and now it was the instant before she took the first giant step ahead. "Okay, call Malloy back."

"Now?"

The odd unreality vanished. Ellen was panicked, she could tell that, but Liza felt totally alive. "Here, I'll do it."

"No, Liza, let a man speak with the boys in camouflage."

"I'm not catering to those sexists, Ellen."

"They're not going to take orders from a woman, believe me. That's why they're call supremacists."

"They will if they want their guns."

"Hey, you two, enough. Liza, do you want to raise their consciousness or take their money?"

Liza stalked to the far side of the room and back. "Okay," she forced out. "Go ahead, Wes, call."

Wes punched in the phone number and held the receiver an inch from his ear while it rang. The ringing stopped and the silence seemed like styrofoam filling the space between them. The phone rang again, stopped and rang a third time before someone picked it up.

Wes said, "I want to think you're bright enough to know who your supplier is by now. If not check yesterday's *L.A. Times*. Your shipment is waiting. Be at the top of the grade five miles west of Richland tonight at ten forty-eight. The spot where the train slows almost to a stop. There's one passenger car. Get on it. Come alone with the money. Do this and the shipment is yours. We're watching the tracks." Wes hung up.

The three of them stood as if frozen. It was as if all of life has been frozen around them.

The phone rang. Liza gasped, and laughed to cover it.

The phone rang a second time. Wes reached for it. Hand over the receiver he eyed each woman as if for an okay, and picked it up just as the third ring began. He held it out for them to hear.

*You're going to feel real silly if this is your mother*, Liza was dying to say.

The voice on the phone said, "I am bright enough to know who you are. I also know the train arrives at ten forty-eight. My people will be watching the tracks, too. If

221

you want the money, have Liza Silvestri on that train, alone. Is that clear?"

Wes held the phone away from him as if it were a hot iron. She was afraid he'd drop it. Ellen was slowly shaking her head No. The picture that filled Liza's mind was the man shoving the Chevette into the ditch.

*Why does*— Ellen began to mouth.

Liza grabbed the phone. "This is Liza. You remember me. I'm not a giant. Bring the money in two suitcases so I can handle them. See ya later," she added with a flourish, and hung up.

Ellen clutched her arm. "Are you crazy? You can't go alone."

It was a moment before Liza could speak. "And the alternative is? You figure he's going to shoot me, right? Getting shot has always been one of the alternatives. Only the shooter has changed." She poured coffee and took a swallow before she could go on. She was trying to sound matter-of-fact and not succeeding any too well. "Like you said, Wes, this is bigger than us. We have to do everything we can to keep Malloy from getting these weapons. So our best shot—no pun intended—is if only one of us is on that train, right?"

She made a point of taking another swallow of coffee as she waited for them to object. When Ellen finally said, "We'll talk about it on the way to Portland," her voice sounded hollow, and that plan sounded pretty flimsy—because it was flimsy.

"Hey, we'll figure this out. Wes, you download the railroad map and we'll have the whole ride to Portland to decide which siding to slip our container onto. Ellen, I'll bet you know twenty times more about how that's done than you think. Once you start remembering all the things Harry talked about when you were half tuning him out, it'll all be there." Even to her own ears she sounded perky. Ellen and Wes's expressions labeled her a Pollyanna. "Hey, take some responsibility, huh! You deal with getting the guns off the train before the terrorists get on, then I'll only have to worry about snatching the money and saving my ass."

222

One glance at Ellen and Wes told Liza her pep talk was a disaster. And they hadn't yet given a thought to what would happen *after* they got the money, assuming there was an *after*. "What about the bicycles? And—and Felton?"

Wes nodded, all business. "I'll take the bikes to the freeway, leave them in the grass on the southbound side. I've got a friend with kids near there. They'll love Felton. I can let him wander onto their place. He'll be in hog heaven."

"No . . . pig . . . jokes." Liza swallowed. Felton was sniffing at a recycle bin. Automatically she started toward him.

"Three kids, Liza. Small girls with rabbits and hamsters."

She nodded and quickly turned so Felton was no longer in her line of vision. "Okay, so back to the train, the first question is how I'm going to get on."

Now Wes reacted. "There's got to be a better way than just you—"

Ellen held up a palm. "No! Not now! We discuss this in the car, too. Who gets on and more to the point how we get away when we get off. Now we've got to clear our stuff out of here, because, Wes, honey, we can't come back. *You* can't come back."

Wes looked down at his train with the empty cup and biscuit plate on the flatcar. He pushed a button and the little train's whistle blew as the engine headed back toward the kitchen.

Liza walked across the living room. The rain had let up and she could hear Felton's trotters tapping on the linoleum, the little train chugging, and a car stopping.

A car? Liza hurried to the window, shifted the blinds and peered out.

A police car! The red lights on the roof bar were pulsing on and off. A man was getting out of the driver's side.

It was so reasonable that it should end like this and yet the shock was overwhelming. All their plans . . .

For an instant she couldn't move. She was a pillar of ice. Then what she had to do was clear. She turned to Wes and Ellen. "Pull the plug on the computer and get out of here."

"What?"

"Bentec's outside."

"How could he—"

"He's got a patrol car. He's walking up the path."

"Liza, you can—"

Liza shouldered her purse, opened the door. As she stepped out she forced a smile and said, "Frank, I've been waiting for you." She shut the door behind her.

# Fifty-Three

Ellen couldn't move. Wes took her hands but she felt only pressure. How could it end like this? She was so stunned she didn't walk to the windows till she was jolted by the rasp of the car pulling off. Then guilt washed over her and the words seemed to drip slowly from her mouth. "I just let him take her away."

"There was nothing you could do. Nothing either of us could."

She slammed her fists into his shoulders. "There can't be nothing. We can't just let a murderer drag her off and shoot her on the train. We have to do something. Oh, God, poor Liza." She trudged to the sofa and flopped down. He moved right next to her, their thighs touching. "Liza didn't think I saw her looking at us, Wes. We were sitting here, like this. She glanced over and her whole face collapsed. It wasn't jealousy, as much as shock, like we were a mirror on the emptiness of her life. She—"

He squeezed her hands. "Ellen, don't."

She inhaled and sat up straighter. "I'm not going to 'dissolve in tears.'"

"El, Liza's given me the biggest gift in my life. She knew what we have and she's given us the chance to keep it."

Ellen swallowed hard, but it was a moment before she could make herself agree out loud.

"The least we can do for her is make sure when the cops come back—cops are like ants, if one finds you, you can count on there being a line of them in half an hour—there will be nothing to incriminate her. I need to get the railroad's web page off the computer screen."

Ellen nodded but didn't move. "We . . . can't . . . just . . ."

In a minute he was back. "We've got to get out of here."

Ellen nodded again, but still made no move to get up. "I'm not abandoning Liza. We have to get to the train."

"I hate to say it, Ellen, but what makes you think she'll live long enough to be on it?"

Ellen pushed back hard into the sofa. Her teeth ran hard over her lower lip. It was a moment before she could translate the jumble in her mind into words. "I could say because she'll be smart enough to not give Bentec the train's time of arrival in Portland till she gets there. I could tell you when she gets to the station she'll come up with a reason Bentec can't do without her. She'll make sure she's on the train when it pulls into Richland grade, because Bentec's not going to stop those weapons going to Hanford. He'll either take his money and run, or he'll be killed. The only one who's going to stop those guns going to the nuclear power site is Liza. She'll make sure she lives long enough to do that. I saw that in her face. Two days ago she wouldn't have had it in her. She does now." Ellen stood up. "That's my logic. But the real answer is, I know she'll be on the train because she's Liza."

"I hope you're right."

Ellen was halfway across the room toward the bedroom. "The real issue, Wes, is not how Liza gets on the train, it's how we get her off."

He followed to the bedroom door. "What are you doing in there?"

"Packing. We've got to get going, and you know, Wes, we can't come back here." Ellen poked through his closet. The black dress she'd worn for two days was no prize when she hiked it up under her windbreaker as she biked. She took a step toward the fireplace, thinking of the satisfaction of watching it burn. But she had overstated things with Wes. Maybe *he* could come back here. If so she didn't want to leave any incriminating evidence to prove he'd harbored fugitives. She stuffed it in a duffle.

She pulled on sweat pants, a long underwear shirt like her grandfather wore, and a sweater worthy of the Arctic. When she checked the mirror the image startled her. With her hair unstyled and slicked behind her ears, no make-up or hope of it, and these thick baggy clothes she looked like a stranger from— No, not a stranger, what her face reminded her of was a picture taken of her at the finish line of the last race she won. Except then she was exultant; now she looked terrified.

She plucked tissue after tissue out of the box, stuffed them in the pants pocket and headed for the kitchen. "Look, we know the transfer point is the Richland grade, at ten forty-eight tonight. We know Malloy will get on the train no later than that. And if he gets on and sees Bentec with Liza— Oh shit. He'll kill her."

Wes tossed another thick sweater at her for the duffle. "No he won't."

"Why not? Are you just trying to make me feel—"

"No, listen. Malloy, he needs something. If he didn't he wouldn't have bothered to call back here. He made such a big point of wanting her on the train, why? If he's off to blow up Hanford he's not insisting on having her there because he wants a pretty lady along for the ride. He thinks she's got something he needs. He's not going to kill her till he gets it."

Ellen stuffed a blanket into the duffle. She grabbed a handful of underwear, a couple balls of socks from his drawer and tossed them in. "If you have an anorak, stick that in. And a couple of wool hats. And gloves." She handed the bag to him and headed for the kitchen. "Okay, so we go to Portland and hope that we can parallel the train and keep it in sight till it stops."

"That's a pretty thin plan."

She'd opened cabinets and was stashing raisins, nuts and bread in a bag. Now she stopped and leaned back against the counter. "I'm open to better."

"I wish I had a great plan, even a good one. You know, Ellen, as little time as I've been with Liza I could tell she's something special. Even besides being your best friend." He turned and headed to the bathroom.

Ellen filled two bottles with water. Then the solution struck her. "Wes," she shouted through the closed door. "The schedule!"

As he emerged, his face was pulled into a quizzical grin.

"Jeez! All the time I spent with Harry and I didn't even

226

think of the schedule! Here's the plan. We drive to the station in Portland and get the schedule of where that freight is going to stop before Richland grade. It's not like a regular passenger train, but still the station agent will have its scheduled stops. Then we make sure we're at each stop first. If no one gets on, we go to the next place."

"And then?"

"Do you have a gun?"

"A rifle."

"How good a shot are you?"

"Good enough." Now he grinned unequivocally. "Shooting tin cans was something I could do during my convalescence. I kept neighbors for five miles in each direction busy emptying beer cans for me. There's not a six pack in Oregon that doesn't fear me."

Ellen put the bag by the door. For the first time since Liza left she felt some hope. "You'll have to be dead on with both barrels. We'll have to have a lifetime's worth of luck, but, you know, we can do it. Really, I think we can."

He nodded, then hugged her so hard she let out a squeal, kissed her hard, and grinned. "Damn right we can."

Recovering her breath, she said, "Do you have a heavy box we can put this stuff in in the back of the truck?"

"The truck?"

"*Your* truck, Wes. Where is it?"

"Out front. The old yellow Chevy."

"There was no truck in front last night. Are you sure—"

"Oh, shit. Goddamn fucking shit!" He sank back against the counter.

"What?"

"The truck. It's in the shop."

# Fifty-Four

Devon Malloy did not indulge in emotion. But if he had, he thought, he would be outraged at the puerile threat on the phone. We're watching the tracks. As if Liza Silvestri and her male mouthpiece would suddenly have access to an army. Did they think he was born yesterday?

For an instant the specter of the police crossed his mind. The police did have an army; the police could station units at every stop of the train. If Liza Silvestri was fronting for the police— Malloy shrugged off the waft of fear. If the police were involved they would simply stop the train and check every car till they found their weapons.

The puerile threat meant nothing—nothing except an admission that this lie was the best Liza and her man had, and it was nothing. Maybe the man would hide on the railroad car with her, planning to burst out of the bathroom or from behind the seats. If he was so naive as to think anyone in Malloy's position would come alone, the man deserved to die. And he would die. Malloy had no need for two hostages.

No indeed, no need for more than Liza Silvestri, the perfect hostage. Little enough to handle easily, pretty in that pouty little-girl way. With her out there waiting to die, the whole world would be watching.

Malloy leaned back and let his eyes close, picturing her in that skimpy little sweater, those poured-into jeans. There was a little smile on his face; quickly he yawned to remove it. This was business, an integral part of the plan. There was nothing personal in it.

An enclosure, he decided. Like the zoo. He would have one of the men find him some hurricane fencing. Orel Jasson, the retired driver, had said there was a ton of it in Hanford, lying out around Unit "B." He would set up an enclosure like they do for the apes, small enough that there was nowhere to hide from the television cameras. He would make an announcement about the tanks, the countdown to when the tanks would blow. He would make sure she heard it, that she knew how long before she was scattered into ash. He would let the cameras record the terror on her face.

Maybe she would try to escape—there would be no way of escape, he would make sure of that—but an attempt would be good, very good. Up the ante for the viewers.

She was the crowning touch on his perfect plan. At Hanford they said no one could overrun the facility. But they forgot the human element. The combination of willing guards and a long-forgotten roadway Orel Jasson had used, would get his men to the inside before the droopy-eyed security force realized its perimeter had been broached. His big weapons unit would create a camouflage disturbance—ear shattering explosions, plumes of smoke—in the 100 Unit by the "retired" nuclear reactors. Security forces would fall all over each other getting there. He would break through the low-level security at the underground tanks and he would turn off the mixer, let the gases build inexorably, and he would blow them sky high. There was no smile of triumph on his face, no raised fist, no fast-beating heart. He had trained himself well; he felt nothing—almost nothing.

He needed only one thing—the container number. His container should be the last one on the train, the one that could be rolled off. That was the only sensible arrangement. But he could not go on trust, not and find himself at the Hanford gate with a container of baseballs or hog bellies. There was no feasible way to check the container. He had to get the container number from Liza Silvestri.

Suppose she did not have it? A chill spiked his back.

Of course she had it. Why else would she come here if not to get the container? How would she know her own container if not by number? Of course she had it.

Devon Malloy prided himself on being a realist. He knew he would never walk out of Hanford. They would pretend to bargain with him, just as they had pretended they were not emitting radioactive iodine into the air. When the waste storage tanks exploded he would go up with them. His statement would be powerful. And pure. Then he would let himself feel. He would feel pride. He was only sorry he would not be alive to see Liza Silvestri die.

# Fifty-Five

Liza's head throbbed. Bentec had hit her so hard when he shoved her in the car she must have blacked out. She didn't know where he'd been or what he'd been doing or how long he'd been doing it. Her vision was blurry. She felt for the door handle.

Bentec yanked the patrol-car door open on the driver's side, swung onto the seat, slammed the door. "Where's the train, bitch? Which train? Where's my shipment?" Before she could open her mouth, he grabbed her shoulder and smacked her head against the door.

The car reeked of smoke and stale vomit. His face was the color of cold cooked beef, eyes wild; he was out of control, yelling words she couldn't make out over the ringing in her ears. She'd expected back-up cops, at least a partner in the car, but Bentec was alone.

He was going to kill her.

But she had led him away from Ellen and Wes and that was what mattered. Them together—she had to clasp that picture like an amulet to get her through.

Behind her, the sky was turning dark.

"Where? Dammit, Silvestri told you. I know he told you." Her head hit the window again; she could barely think. She wanted to cry, but she'd be damned if she'd give him that satisfaction.

"Huh? Come on, bitch, talk!" He was yanking her hair, pulling it loose from her scalp. He slammed her into the window; glass cracked. She didn't even feel the cuts on her cheeks until she saw the red dripping on her shirt. Cold gusts blew through the broken glass, stinging the edges of her cuts.

230

He shoved her out of the way, reached for the window, broke off a shard of glass and poised the point against her nose. "I'll turn your face into a map. The best plastic surgeon in L.A. won't be able to sew you back together again."

She no longer felt anything, even terror. She looked straight ahead through the rain-veiled windshield at the deep green beyond. When she spoke her voice was low and cold; she hardly recognized it. "My husband slid down my body and died at my feet. My life is over. There's nothing left to threaten." Warm drops hit her chest. She didn't look down. "Throw the glass away. I'll take you to the guns." When he moved his hand she added, "For Jay's share."

"What, bitch, you expect me to give you a million dollars?"

"Three million."

"Hey, even he didn't—"

"So kill me and get zip." She picked up a towel from the dashboard and wiped away the shards of glass on the window sill. "Take your time. But don't take too much. The train won't wait."

He was staring at the blood on his hand, watching it drip. Wind poured through the window, searing the cuts on her face but she doubted he even felt his own wounds. Finally, he said, "Okay. Tell me where the guns are."

"Drive north."

"Just tell me, Goddammit!"

"I'd prefer to live long enough to see the money. Drive north."

She sat, smelling the car, smelling Bentec. She'd thought she felt nothing, but now she realized that the swirling cold that filled her chest and stomach was rage. She didn't dare speak. The windshield wipers turned the glass from mottled green to trees and sky, road and trucks. The car rattled, the wipers splatted, the steering wheel squeaked on left turns. Bentec's breaths were thick, labored, and she could hear the maelstrom of fury in them.

A huge blast shattered the tension.

"What was that?"

There was a smile on Bentec's face. "Sounds like an explosion to me. A mile or so back. A damn big send-off."

Sirens screamed behind them, headed back in the direction of Wes's house. She turned, stared out the back window, looking for patrol cars.

Bentec laughed. "That siren's not police, Liza."

"What then?"

"Fire engines. Sounds like two, three alarms. Ah yes, biiiig fire."

"The house? You set the house on fire?"

"Well, Liza, how could I resist, tell me. With those piles of dry wood by the walls? So easy. And it blew so fast. Anyone inside, well . . ." He chuckled.

She lunged at him. He grabbed her by the neck and slammed her back. He was laughing, holding her at arm's length, watching her flail and gag. His hand tightened; she couldn't breathe. She gagged. He gave one great howl of laughter and let go.

She slumped back against the broken window, her buttocks half off the seat. She had to brace her leg to keep from crumbling to the floor next to her purse.

Her purse. She let herself slip down, reached for the purse and pulled out the gun.

"Don't!" Bentec roared. Before she could get both hands on the trigger, Bentec swung his arm and smacked it out of her hands.

She waited for him to shoot her. But he just smiled. Not the manic laugh of a minute earlier but the relieved laugh of a man back in control.

"My nine-millimeter," he said. "I thought this was in Silvestri's house." He held it in both hands like a great and fragile gift, but it was her he was watching. His smile shifted, his eyes narrowing. "I thought I'd left this under the bed in Silvestri's house—your house—when he brought in the whores."

His throat quivered as if he was salivating. He was waiting for a shriek or moan, an oath, some sign that he'd delivered the final outrage. They sat unmoving for a moment before she saw the disappointment in his eyes. By now, her dead husband screwing another woman in her bed was not worth a shrug.

Bentec focused back on the gun, turning it over, smiling.

232

"I thought this would send me to jail. But here back in my hand, it's going to get me my money." The desperate red was gone from his skin. When he pulled her purse from the floor, dropped his gun back in, and slid the purse between his hip and the driver's door he had the look of a man revitalized.

She slumped, ignoring the flames of pain in her hands and shoulders and throat. The throbbing in her head shoved out thought. But through it, somehow—she had no idea how—she vowed she would do one thing. Whatever it took, she would make sure Frank Bentec never saw his money.

# Fifty-Six

Captain Raymond Zeron pulled up near the suspect house. The place was a blackened shell. Flames shot out the windows. Despite the downpour, branches of the nearby pines and eucalypts were sparking. The pulsar lights on the fire trucks turned the macadam brick red and the fire fighters looked like they'd been roasted alive. Engines raced, men yelled orders, incoming sirens screamed in the distance. It was all Zeron could do to find the captain in charge. He'd worked with Jake Mason before. Eugene was a small town.

"Arson," Zeron stated. No need to pretend it was a question.

"Oh, yeah. Blew like Vesuvius. Owner had nice dry wood-piles on the porch. Convenient for him. Fucking invitation for any arsonist driving down this road."

"Nah, Jake, no spur-of-the-moment ignite here. This is the house where the L.A. love nest wife was hiding out. Anybody alive in—"

"Not a chance. See that black twisted lump by the door?"

It took Zeron a few moments to make out which particular blackened item Mason meant. "Yeah?"

"That's a fake leg—prosthesis. *Was* a plastic leg before the

233

blast shot it out the window. Guy doesn't leave home without his leg."

Zeron nodded and started back to his car. This was one big, messy case and there were going to be a lot of loose ends to tie up. Feds would be demanding everything and in triplicate. Then there'd be Bentec.

Zeron settled in the car and stared sadly at the cataclysm. He'd deal with Bentec and the Feds when he damned well got around to it.

# Fifty-Seven

Liza's head throbbed and the buzzing in her ears was like an army of leaf blowers. She'd always prided herself on not thinking ahead; now she couldn't even figure out how to move her head to a less painful angle. Bentec was being careful not to exceed the speed limit, but he jerked the car at every turn and she caught him glancing over to see her wince. He'd be in hog heaven if she moaned or screamed. She gritted her teeth and settled in for the ride to Portland.

She never planned, but she did observe. Bentec's watching the speed limit said he was a maverick now. He'd stolen this Eugene patrol car but he wasn't taking back roads, worrying about the local cops; he just didn't want to force the issue. By the time the locals focused on Bentec, she'd be dead. Like Ellen and Wes.

Wes and Ellen. She saw them again, on the sofa, sitting so close their breath came in unison. Ellen with that soft, awed smile Liza couldn't have imagined on her square face. Wes pushing the button to call the Household Local Line. She shut her eyes tighter and listened to the Household Local chugging in from the kitchen. She saw Felton's cute little black and white head, his pink nose wrinkling eagerly as he rooted in the bend of her elbow. Poor little . . .

Bentec slammed to a stop.

Liza looked up and saw tracks, overhead wires. The railroad station was at the other side of the parking lot. Rain splatted hard on the metal roof almost blocking out the sounds of a train. She squinted her ears, trying to hear only the train, chugging louder, slower, coming nearer.

"That's the train, right, Liza?"

She looked over in time to spot a freight coasting in on one of the middle tracks. "Should be." Metal jammed into her ribs. His gun! Oh, God, now that he had the train, he didn't need her anymore. He'd parked at the farthest possible spot not so no one would help her, but so no one would hear the shot. "Malloy will be expecting to deal with me. He insisted I come." She was amazed at how calm she sounded.

"Who's Malloy?"

"You don't know? Let me tell you then, Frank. Malloy is the lunatic head of a survivalist cult you're arming. How do I know that, that's what you're going to ask, isn't it? I called him. From Eugene. I got his phone number off the web page just like you could have done if you hadn't been so busy killing people." He couldn't have, not without the password, but he didn't know that.

He rammed the gun into her stomach. She struggled not to throw up, forced herself to breathe so shallowly she barely moved. Sweat coated his face; he was crazed, mouthing words without sounds, but he hadn't shot her and she knew she had him—for the moment.

"We don't have . . . all day, Frank. The train's pulling out."

# Fifty-Eight

Devon Malloy drove west. The wipers squeaked on the windshield. He turned them off, waited to see if the dredges of the storm coated the glass. The glass stayed clear. Malloy nodded. Broaching the Hanford defenses would be easier in a downpour but Malloy was glad the sky was clearing. When the Hanford tanks blew he did not want the explosion curtained by rain. And he certainly did not want a wall of rain blocking shots of Liza Silvestri in her cage, screaming with panic.

He was careful to keep the speedometer just above the speed limit. His white pick-up was standard issue, nothing to draw attention. In it he carried only the registration and a bottle of water. No fake plates, no phony license, no weapons. If he should get stopped he was just an Idaho lawyer on his way to Spokane to shop. He did not indulge in emotion but it warmed him to think of the twenty trained men in trucks heading to the Richland grade, one of them in an eighteen-wheeler ready to take on the container. He would have more weapons than men, but for this operation more men would only mean more danger of leaks. Twenty men armed to the hilt was plenty.

It had not taken Malloy long to discard the option of boarding the train in Oregon or some spot well before Richland. He needed to shunt the container car onto the siding in Richland. This was no time to go hunting for alternate sidings miles from Richland and Hanford. Even if he found a suitable one, that would mean carting a container of highest-grade weapons over hill and dale. More exposure. And the scene in the passenger car itself—what was he going to do, shoot Liza Silvestri's accomplice and ride for hours with his corpse? Toss it out and have a kid walking his dog discover it? And Liza Silvestri? He would have to deal with her whining and begging the whole way.

No, he would do just as the guy said, get on the train at the top of the Richland grade, and be gone before the vermin's body rolled into the station. One small adjustment. There was a spot the train stopped, more of a pause than a stop—he did not know why, did not care why. That spot was not at the top of the Richland grade, but at the bottom, two miles before. That spot—*his* spot—was where he would get on.

# Fifty-Nine

Liza made a point of not sitting as far away from Frank Bentec as possible in a passenger-train seat. He had shoved her in the window seat and put her purse with his gun on the seat across the aisle from him. She stared out the window into the dusky woods. Sundown came so much earlier this far north.

The passenger car, the only one on the train, was six down from the engine and empty except for them. It was cold. The floor was covered with a thin sticky dust that suggested the car had been sitting on a siding in some desert and the dust had blown in around the window seals and settled onto the amorphous goo of neglect. A couple of lights had burned out and the whole car resembled a sepia-toned photo. The train swayed back and forth, back and forth . . .

There wouldn't be anything to see till they came to the grade before the bridge in Richland and the train stopped—in eight hours! But Bentec would start in on her long before that.

The train crossed the Columbia River. They were in Washington now and somehow that seemed like a big step, into the state of the Hanford nuclear waste site. She could feel Bentec tighten up. The train picked up speed.

He shifted to face her. "Okay, Liza, where do we meet the buyer, this Malloy?"

"I don't know." She expected his slap but that didn't help. His hand smashed into her jaw and she couldn't keep her head from hitting the window.

He grabbed her shoulders shaking her till her teeth actually rattled. "You answer me, you bitch."

She didn't say anything; she couldn't—he was shaking her too hard.

237

"Don't you stonewall me like that shifty little shit of a husband of yours. Think about him. Remember how he died. You tell me the truth! Where do we meet Malloy?"

Her head was jolting back and forth; she was terrified her neck would snap. She couldn't think. "The train," she blurted out. He let go and her head banged hard against the seat back.

"When?"

"I don't know."

He grabbed again, but didn't shake. "When, bitch?"

She was tempted to say: in Idaho. "In Richland."

He nodded. "This Malloy, why's he so hot to have you in on this deal?"

His nod was so perfunctory she realized he knew the train's destination. He knew about Richland, so now he assumed she was telling him the truth. Okay, one for her. What exactly had she told him about Malloy? Malloy had told her to come *alone* but she hadn't told Bentec about the alone part. "Malloy wants me as a guarantee. Jay and I met him at a gun show in Idaho. Now that Jay's dead I'm the only one who can assure him that the deal's still going through, that he's not handing six million dollars to some guy who hopped a freight."

"How many men does Malloy have, Liza?"

"What do you think, that Jay discussed every detail of every client's business? I have no idea."

He jerked toward her then restrained himself. She knew the danger, but taking a punch or a cut was better than giving him time to concoct a plan that didn't require her. "I'd say this, Frank, you don't buy a railroad container crammed full of weapons for five people. Six million dollars is a lot of money to these guys up in the woods; they'll have enough of an army to make this purchase pay off."

Bentec leaned back against the seat, too tense to slump. The news took him by surprise. Obviously, he hadn't concerned himself with where the weapons would end up. He was used to having maneuvers mapped out by lieutenants or captains. But now he was on his own and he was worried—with good reason.

Still, the logic of her own conclusion horrified her. How many soldiers would Malloy have? How was she possibly

238

going to secure the container of guns from an army?

She stared at the window. The dark beyond created a mirror reflecting the railroad car back on itself as if this was a capsule rattling through eternity. The clackety-clackety shifted her into almost a daze, a nightmare of uncontrolled visitations pulling her back into the moment of Jay's death, thrusting her forward to Ellen's funeral; shriekings that might have been train brakes or Felton's plaintive squeals. She shook her head to wake herself and it felt like a bottle of loose screws and bolts. She was almost relieved when Bentec demanded, "The Richland grade? What kind of area is that?"

"Didn't you even check a map? Were you expecting limo service?"

"I was expecting your husband to handle this."

"Too bad, Frank. That's the price you paid when you had him killed."

He reached toward her as if to strike, but seemed to lose interest mid-way. Not a good sign. He was thinking too much. "The Richland grade?" he insisted.

She tried to remember the spot from the day of the picnic-in-the-car. She could see Jay staring through the rain-blurred windshield. She could almost smell the ham sandwiches, feel the squishy roll bottom wet with mayonnaise and tomato. Her shoulders tightened as they did that day the third time she asked if he wanted to stop for coffee here in the state of serious coffee drinkers, and realized he wasn't listening but staring into apparent nothingness. Staring at the tracks, of course, but that didn't occur to her then. She remembered the scene inside the rental car so well she could paint it in oils. She'd been so absorbed in it she noticed neither the tracks nor a thing about the area around them.

But clearly Bentec knew less than she did. She said, "It's a suburban area."

"You mean houses?"

"Houses on one side. The other side of the tracks have factories, light industry. And places like maintenance garages . . ." She was in her element now, creating out of whole cloth, taking each of his questions as a challenge, careful not to get too fanciful, careful to include options

239

and questions in each answer, creating a fictional town with many roads out and choices on them all. He paused after answers, took time planning his route or concocting a back-up plan.

For her there was nothing to plan. Thoughts were useless; she stared into the dark, acutely aware of every change in the woods, every sound from the train, the roads they passed, Bentec's breathing, the chill of the air on her chilled skin, of the smell of the dust, of the feel of the dust in her throat. Time passed without notice. She was oddly relaxed and yet ready to jump out of her skin.

After a while—hours—Bentec grabbed her arm. "The train's slowing. Is this it?"

"Trains slow; otherwise they'd be called airplanes."

"Hey, don't smart-mouth me."

The train jerked forward, tapping them back against the seat as it picked up speed.

"You know," he said sounding more reasonable than at any moment since he grabbed her outside Wes's house, "if Jay hadn't stonewalled me none of this would be happening. If he'd just played it straight."

He was making an offer. A couple of complaints about Jay and she could be Bentec's ally. If Jay had played it straight with *her*, well lots would be different. He'd lied about their whole life. She owed him no loyalty. This offer was the reward for her hours of fictional town building.

Bentec was waiting, offering her ample time to cross over. So why couldn't she take it and give herself a little edge? In her mind she saw not the house in Malibu but the loft the moment Jay recognized the Point Pleasant Beach room. She could hear him calling out, "Ohmigod, Liza! A Philco, Liza, how did you find that? Oh my God!" Had he been faking it then? She'd never know. It didn't matter. What she would not betray to Bentec was not Jay at all but her own self, the woman who'd created that room, and who had loved Jay Silvestri whether he deserved it or not.

She looked Bentec in the eye. "If he'd played it straight? Like you, you mean?"

He slammed her hard into the window. Pain blinded her.

240

Blood filled her mouth. She had to stop taunting him. She couldn't; not anymore. She was a short-timer now.

She swallowed the blood and squinted till her eyes focused. Bentec glanced at her in disgust, got up, carried her purse half a car away to the seat second from the front, then turned to survey the aisle. He paced to the back, and forward again, never taking his eyes off her. After a while he sat back in his same seat. There was a good six inches between them but she felt the heat off his body. She was dying to get up and pace, too, but she didn't bother to ask. She added the latest bit of data revealed by his moving her purse, with his gun. He was comfortable with that because he had another weapon on him. Of course. She leaned back listening to the clackety-clackety and watched time pass.

Bentec flew out of the seat. "It's stopping!"

Outside her window were black woods. The road was probably on the other side. She looked across the aisle, but the windows only mirrored back the railroad car.

Brakes creaked. Scraping wheels flung sparks into the night.

"Malloy wants you; he'll get you. Get over by the window where he can see you." Bentec yanked her up and shoved her across the aisle.

He raced forward and positioned himself by the front end door.

Brakes ground, metal clanged, the car swayed and jolted as the train slowed to a stop.

"Perfect. The perfect victim," Devon Malloy said, admiring the blonde woman in the train window. He allowed himself a smile.

# Sixty

Ellen squinted through the windshield, but in her mind she could still see Wes standing at the back door, arm blocking her way back in, rain running down his face unabated. "Get the bike and go, El. The cops'll be here any minute. They may have dogs. Go on!" His body had been stiff, his hand quivering against the door frame, as if it alone was keeping him from grabbing her and not letting go. She could have—should have—leaned forward and pulled him close. She'd have felt him against her one more time, kissed him one more time.

Instead, she had said, "Wes, if I can't come back here—"

"Meet me."

"Where."

"As far away as we can get. Maine."

"Where in Maine?"

"Brooksville, a cabin by the sea. Ask for Foucault. Now move. Go." He'd kissed her again.

She'd squeezed his hand and run for the shed, grabbed her bike and, as if making up for her restraint with him, headed not for the woods and streams, but for the road. She'd have sworn her legs were too stiff to ever bike again, her butt too sore to come near the slicing little bike seat. She'd ridden the three miles to the repair shop, through the barrage of rain, with the siren squealing behind her. Her legs had gone numb and she'd pedaled from will alone, concentrating on stroke after stroke. She hadn't looked out for cops or questioned the siren. She'd had no thoughts but: ride.

At the repair shop, she'd snatched the old yellow Chevy pick-up with its beat-up shell, shoved the pile of newspapers to the floor, glanced in the glove compartment for a map and found only a flashlight and a cigarette lighter. She lit out east, warmed by the memory of this morning with Wes—making love frantically, and then so tenderly it almost made her cry for joy. It had been magic. A gift from Liza. She wanted to caress every second of that time, recall each touch of his lips, each luscious moan, to make plans for their long dark nights at the Maine coast.

But there was no time. It was already too late to check the railroad station in Portland. The hour it had taken riding the bike, starting the truck, and finding a through road had ruined that plan. Now it was a question of how long till the police connected Wes's truck to her. The ancient yellow Chevy would

242

be a cinch to spot.

With Wes beside her, saving Liza had seemed possible. Now there was only her. How was she going to divert a policeman while at the same time heading off a militia? Liza would count on inspiration. Ellen needed a plan.

She turned on the radio and listened inattentively till she heard: "Los Angeles sex-loft chase ends in inferno." Inferno! The announcer's description of the chase, the street, the burning house blended and words became just sounds pounding against her head, until he paused and added, "In a bizarre twist, thrown out of the inferno, police found the tenant's artificial leg, almost contorted beyond recognition by the extreme heat. And in Washington State the issue—"

She snapped off the radio, but it was too late to block the picture of Wes dying, his flesh burning so hot that his leg exploded off— "No!" Her scream filled the cab. The steering wheel slipped out of her hands; the truck sidled onto the bank and she sat in the cab on the empty road and screamed and screamed till her throat went dry. Then she just shook.

Eventually it was the cold that pierced her and she started the engine. She drove on rotely, putting no names to the waves of sensation that passed through her body. This was how people went insane, she thought.

She just drove, east till an intersection, then north, then east again, not looking at signs, not stopping. The gas gauge was broken. After an hour the engine coughed and she bought fuel and drove on.

She couldn't bear to think of Wes; instead, she pictured the pig. Silly little animal. She squeezed her eyes hard against tears and felt foolish.

And Liza? Was Liza dead already? Common sense said Bentec would find out when the train was due in Portland, then kill her. Common sense insisted he'd dump her dead body and keep moving.

"But this is Liza," she said aloud and the hollow ring of her voice mocked her.

The car ahead slowed to a stop. A traffic light. She looked up at the sign and turned north to Richland. Goddammit, she would not let these men who killed Wes

243

and Harry walk away. No, not even *walk* away, drive off with weapons to blow up the nuclear power site and spew death for decades.

When the train stopped outside of Richland, she had to be ready to hop on. And? Liza would say: you'll know when you get there.

But she wasn't Liza. *She* needed to plan. If she had Liza's gun . . . But she didn't. Nor did she have Wes's rifle. All she had was an ancient truck full of newspaper.

The truck? Okay, she wouldn't get on the train at all. She'd wait for Bentec to jump off. She'd floor the gas and crush him against the train. He'd die; she'd die, the train would stop and the police would find the weapons. Not a perfect plan, but one that could work. She stepped harder on the gas. The pick-up rattled and when she hit sixty the whole thing shimmied.

It was almost 10 P.M. when she crossed into Washington. The train was due in Richland at 10:48. She focused on the road signs. She couldn't afford to get lost. Common sense said: make no contacts. Common sense had been her protection all her life. Now it seemed like a cloak from another person's closet. She turned off the freeway in Richland, pulled into a gas station, gassed up and asked how to get to the railroad tracks at the Richland grade. For a moment she was afraid the Richland grade was a term known only to railroad men. But the boy at the gas station knew the spot.

10:24. Plenty of time for a five-mile drive.

"Take the first left," the boy said. "It's a two-lane road but you'll stay clear of the city traffic. Keep on it straight past the fairgrounds. It'll deadend at the tracks. Couldn't be easier."

She hung a left onto the two-lane road and headed through the dark. One mile down, two.

How odd, she thought, this last hour of her life. She would have expected something different, something more. She wasn't afraid now. From her days at St. Enid's a voice reminded her that it wasn't good to smash a man into a train right before you meet St. Peter. She shrugged. When ol' Pete saw Bentec he'd understand.

Three miles down, two to go. The truck rattled like thunder;

244

the engine groaned. She opened the window all the way and let the wind smack her face.

Red lights ahead. Police? Did Bentec have crooked cops helping him way up here? She slowed, her foot stiff on the brake.

The light multiplied, four pairs, eight, more than she could count, and they slowed, clumped. Their vehicles blocked out the right-side light. They weren't police lights at all. They were tail lights. She laughed with relief, and shook her head hard. "Stupid! Pay attention!"

In front a house trailer inched forward. She edged to the left to where she could peer around the edge.

A line of tail lights as far as she could see; they were barely moving.

She slumped back into the seat. This was worse than police lights. Them she might get past, but this, this was a solid wall between her and the tracks. All the running and planning and hope, and it came down to this: stuck behind a line of boxy trailers. The headlights shone off the bumper sticker ahead: *Roving Women Convergence, Kennewick, Washington.* There had to be a hundred women in a hundred trailers ahead, roving slowly, converging into a solid mass, blocking the only road to the railroad tracks.

# Sixty-One

Captain Raymond Zeron was jerked awake by the phone. "Zeron."

"Rouch, here. Sorry to wake you, Captain."

Zeron looked at the clock: 10:29 P.M. He had been in bed exactly twenty-four minutes. He said nothing.

"Thing is, sir, the stationmaster at Portland called and said one of our cars is in their lot. He said he knows you don't leave cars in his lot overnight without notifying him. He asked me to check. He sounded pissed. I mean, otherwise I wouldn't have woken you."

Now Zeron was alert enough to recall that final problem in the L.A. loft-sex case, the missing patrol car. "Any word on Bentec, the inspector from L.A.?"

"No, sir."

"Well, not our problem. Maybe since he didn't have any suspects to escort back south, L.A. told him to take the train. Anyway, like I said, it's not our problem. Tell the station-master thanks and that I'll send someone after the car tomorrow."

# Sixty-Two

*Nuclear plant blows up while woman sits in traffic.* It couldn't end like this!

Ellen's foot cramped on the clutch pedal. The engine rattled and groaned and an ominous burnt rubber smell came from somewhere around her feet. She thrust the truck into neutral and stamped her foot on the floor boards.

In the distance a train whistle sliced softly into the night. Liza's train? With Bentec on it? Malloy waiting in the bushes? It had to be the right train. The whistle sounded again, cutting through her thoughts. *The* train—and she was still two miles away. She leaned on the horn.

Ahead of her nothing moved.

She could almost see Bentec standing over Liza, Bentec telling her about the fire that killed Wes, Bentec waiting for his six million dollars and a ticket to Tahiti or to Paris. The clang of metal on metal cut through the night. Could she really hear that this far away? Was she imagining it? The clang resounded in her head, background music to the question of the train. Was Liza on it? And the weapons?

She leaned on the horn. The trailer ahead jerked forward an inch. A redheaded woman stuck her head out of the cab and threw her hands up. Southbound traffic whooshed by.

The train whistled louder, closer. How long before Malloy

got on? How long before Bentec got the money and jumped off?

Ellen hit the horn. "Emergency," she yelled. "Let me out of line."

The red-haired woman shrugged and inched forward.

Six minutes, and two miles to go. She hit the horn again. The trailer in front sat tight. She thought of Harry; she could still feel the warmth of Wes's body against hers. She reached for the car door and was halfway out of the seat when the truck behind her backed up. Across the white line cars sped by.

With one hand hard on the horn she cut left through the oncoming traffic onto the far shoulder, shot forward. Horns blared. Cars dodged right and left. She weaved forward missing them by inches. Headlights glazed her vision. At the corner the traffic light was amber; she shot through.

She saw the huge, high headlights first, an eighteen-wheeler coming at her, guttural horn roaring. The shoulder might have been big enough for her; she didn't look. She kept her foot on the gas, her eyes straight at the truck.

It swerved, clipping her bumper. The pick-up bounced. She yanked the wheel sharp right. Her window was open. "Biiiiittch!" cut in through the wailing of horns and wind and the sound of her own breath. "Damn right!" she yelled as she pulled around the truck and two trailers to the front of the RV line into the clear northbound lane.

The dark and the silence startled her. There was nothing to do now but drive. She expected police sirens; none came. There was no train whistle, just silence. 10:46. Two minutes to go almost two miles. The road was empty; she floored the pedal, but the old truck barely jolted forward. Sweat poured off her face, ran down her back; her breath was thick and short, her hands stiff on the wheel. She rattled forward, looking neither right nor left, barreling through intersections, swinging around a station wagon, her foot jammed against the gas pedal.

The road ended without warning at a T. On the far side were woods, and nearer the road, weeds and railroad tracks. Empty tracks. 10:52. No train. No Malloy getting on. No Bentec hopping off. Just trees, and naked tracks. Could the train really have come four minutes ago, on time, and be gone? She followed the tracks to the left a quarter mile or less. It wasn't empty there.

She turned and drove slowly by the clutch of vehicles. Pick-up trucks sat parallel-parked very legally. There had to be a dozen, all in a line facing east. At the head of the line was one flatbed big enough to haul away a railroad container. In every truck a man sat in the driver's seat, as if ready to go. The drivers could have been buddies fresh from a bar across the street. Sitting in their dark cabs, the men could have been taking a moment to get themselves oriented before driving home. No one but her would guess they were waiting for the train.

A train whistle up the track cut her speculation. She was beyond the trucks when it struck her she was going down-hill, down the Richland grade. The men were waiting at the top, the spot where Malloy would get off. But where would he get on the train? She stepped on the gas and headed slowly west, paralleling the track, unsure now just what her plan was.

The whistle shrieked, louder now, closer. The road dropped downhill. She downshifted the old truck and swung left around a curve.

In the distance one startlingly bright light shone on the tracks. The train's engine light. The train was stopped.


# Sixty-Three


A s Liza stared out the window into the blackness, a tall, sandy-haired man—Malloy—materialized into the rhomboid of light from the window and strode toward the front steps into the car.

She nodded toward Bentec. He moved into a defensive position. When Malloy stepped into the car he'd see a four-foot-long compartment to his left; he would not see Bentec flattened against its far wall. When Malloy moved down the aisle Bentec would pounce. It was her chance; she had to be ready. She stooped behind the seat halfway down the aisle, five yards beyond Bentec.

Malloy pulled the door open. Cold wind shot through the car. "Liza," he demanded. "Come here."

She froze. Bentec smiled and she felt colder yet. Peering through the hand hold at the end of the seat she watched as Malloy stepped inside, and scowled in her direction, unsure just which seat she was hiding behind.

She didn't move, barely breathed. She had to get Malloy moving slowly, checking seats, give Bentec time to strike.

Malloy eyed the middle of the car. He started forward. In three more steps he'd pass the compartment wall and Bentec would move. She braced to move.

Bentec's voice rang out. "The money? Where is it?"

Malloy jerked to a stop. "Who the hell are you?"

"I'm the deal breaker. Bring me the money or it's off. Got that?"

"First give me Liza Silvestri." A whine of excitement undercut Malloy's small-town cadence. His voice terrified her almost as much as his demand.

"She's all yours, Malloy. Do whatever you want with her. As soon as I get the money."

Each man could see the other's hazy reflection in the windows now. Neither moved: Bentec tense at alert; Malloy, icy, figuring his odds. Bentec just wanted her dead. With Malloy it would be much worse. With him she'd have no chance.

Malloy waved a hand in the doorway. A brown duffle, huge, slid in behind him. "One of two," Malloy offered. "Now where is she?"

Bentec smiled. "Get your ass up here, Silvestri."

If she didn't move; made him move through the car looking for her . . .

"She's hiding in the middle, Malloy."

There was no use in putting it off. She took a breath, and stood up.

Malloy's face tightened in suspicion. "Silvestri! Move!"

She strode slowly forward, aware of each foot striking the floor, of Bentec's impatience, Malloy's suppressed triumph.

249

She kept them both in sight, alert for her chance, careful not even to glance at the second seat across the aisle where her purse lay. By the front seat she stopped, waited. Bentec's breath soured the air. She could smell the dust on Malloy's shoes. A cold wind shot through the door. In the distance car engines roared to starts. A crossing bell sounded, ringing for the train that wasn't moving.

"The other suitcase?" Bentec demanded.

"First the container number. What is it?"

Bentec stayed silent.

"The number!" Malloy yelled. Malloy assumed Bentec knew the container number. Malloy needed Bentec alive. The power shifted; all three of them knew it.

Bentec moved into the aisle, stood arms crossed, as if he had all of L.A.P.D. backing him up. A yard separated the men. "You produced a suitcase, I produced her. You want the number, pony up the rest of the money."

Her throat closed. The number had been her only currency. Bentec didn't know the number; she did. But Malloy would never believe that. She had nothing.

"The suitcase, Malloy." Bentec shifted into an easier stance. The veteran negotiator. "Look, I know you've got men out there, what do you think I'm going to do, grab these cases and sprint off while your guys diddle themselves?"

Malloy stiffened, stayed dead still, then turned and nodded toward the door.

Another suitcase—a satchel—came through the door.

The satchel smacked down on the floor. In that instant, Bentec drew his gun. Malloy reached into his jacket.

"Don't even think about it, scum. Keep those hands where I can see them."

Malloy poked his arms straight forward.

"Good boy. Now nudge those bags forward, toward me. Use your feet."

Malloy slid his foot forward, toe and instep under the satchel and kicked. The bag sailed into Bentec's shins. Bentec jumped back. Liza watched Malloy reach under his sweater and begin to pull out a gun. It happened fast, but she was watching in slow motion, and because of that there was an

250

instant in which she could have yelled out, warned Bentec, the man who had burned Wes's house with Wes and Ellen in it.

She watched in silence as Malloy shot him.

Bentec howled, "No!" He sounded not surprised but outraged. His scream drowned out the train whistle. He banged to the floor.

Malloy glanced at him, shrugged and motioned her away, back toward the middle of the car.

She reached for the duffle.

Malloy put out a hand. "Do not worry about the money, Liza. You will not have any need of that in Hanford."

# Sixty-Four

Liza sat on the arm of the second seat in the dimly lit passenger car. Malloy had stepped over Bentec's body and walked ten feet down the aisle. He was standing three seats away from her. He'd said nothing more and she had made no move to prod him. His whole body was quivering like a truck ready to burn rubber. He was staring toward her, his gray eyes squinting, his forehead crinkled. A small, satisfied smile pulled against the lines of his face. As he looked her up and down his face shifted, the smile changed revealing the greed beneath it. She could tell he wanted her, but not in the way any other man had lusted after her.

She sat, using the width of her body to shield the purse on the seat behind her. To her left, in the space by the door, Bentec lay silent, just a corpse now. His silver gun had fallen inches from his fingers. The cash-stuffed satchel and the duffle were on either side of him.

Malloy paid no mind to the corpse or the bags or even Bentec's gun.

Behind her in her purse lay Bentec's nine-millimeter, the weapon that had failed to keep Jay safe. Small chance of

251

turning around, rooting between tissue and wallet, extricating the gun and shooting. So many guns, so little time, she thought, and in the surreal atmosphere of the sepia-lit car, she laughed.

Malloy's forehead bunched in what might have been disgust or pleasure. "You will photograph well. The television cameras will have zoom lenses. The wire of your cage will not be a hindrance. Yes, you will be the perfect victim."

She tried to block his words, but she couldn't block the icy terror in her chest.

The train jolted forward.

Ellen sat stopped at a traffic light by the railroad crossing, a two-lane road to her left. Behind her, tiny in her rearview, stood the parked trucks. Ahead were small buildings with dim lights—bars, she guessed. Across the street was a wide dark shoulder dotted with discarded cans that sparkled in the light from passing cars, and beyond that the railroad track. She could see the train, moving slowly up the grade toward her as if it had just started, the engine's headlamp creating a moving oval of day. It was little more than a quarter of a mile away.

She had had a plan. But now she didn't know if this was even the right train. She was a practical woman and no practical woman made a decision on data like that.

And yet, if Liza—

If the guns—

The train was picking up speed.

If it got to the top of the grade, with Malloy's men there—

The whistle blew. In a minute the engine would be in the crossing. All thoughts of planning vanished. She hauled the crumpled newspapers up onto the seat beside her, pulled the cigarette lighter out of the glove compartment and set the papers ablaze. Flames leapt up so fast they startled her.

She hung a right, onto the tracks, pulled on the brake and jumped clear.

Running all out, she raced across the tracks, away from the street. Metal shrieked against metal—the train's brakes fighting hundreds of tons of metal, the engineer fighting to stop before he hit the burning truck. The great horn blared

252

panic; the vibrations smacked her. Under the trees, she turned back, panting. The cab of the old yellow truck was burning red. Flames reached out the window like arms of wild children.

Without waiting to see if the train could stop in time, she raced alongside. In the dark she slipped on a jumble of rocks and barely righted herself. Her breath was coming in bursts as she ran, looking up at blank-walled container car after container car.

Wheels squealed; the train lurched to a stop.

The railroad car jolted forward, boomeranged back, slinging Bentec's corpse against the front seats. Luggage flew. Metal shrieked on metal. Liza smacked back into the seat. Sirens screamed. Malloy stumbled back against a seat. He caught himself. Liza rolled onto the floor. Her purse shifted but the heavy nine-millimeter held it on the seat. The butt was sticking out. If she could pull the purse after her—

Malloy yelled, "Don't!"

He stepped closer. His gun was still in his right hand. He braced that arm against the seat back, and reached for the purse.

The train gave one more great jolt. Malloy grabbed the top of the seat, his eyes fixed on her purse. Metal scraped, clattered. Bentec's silver gun was sliding down the aisle. On the far side of the aisle. Too far. There was no chance— She reached toward it. Malloy looked from her to it, and lunged for it.

Liza turned, grabbed the nine-millimeter, still half in the purse, and shot with both hands on the trigger. Shot again and again and again till the clip was empty.

Malloy shifted. He looked merely uncomfortable, then his bent knees collapsed and he fell back against the seat and slid to the floor. He uttered no cry.

Ellen yanked the passenger-car door open. Bodies. Blood, redder than blood should be. And Liza, lying in it like a rag, pale, lank, two-dimensional, that huge gun Jay had given her in her hand. "Oh, no! Liza! No!"

Liza pushed herself onto her side. "Omigod, Ellen. I thought

253

you were dead. The fire Bentec set? I thought you died. You and Wes escaped!"

"I escaped."

Liza pointed to Malloy's body. "He's dead. I shot him till the gun just clicked."

Ellen pulled her onto the seat, hugged her hard and felt Liza shaking in her arms. The gun was still in Liza's hand. Ellen pulled it free, wiped it as best she could, and tossed it near Bentec. "We've got to get out of here. Those bags, are they the money?"

Liza nodded.

"Grab one." Bentec's body blocked the way. Ellen looked down at him, the man who killed Wes. She braced her hands on the seats, swung her foot all the way back, and kicked him as hard as she could. It wasn't enough, not nearly. "Come on, Liza, we've got to move."

She opened the outside door. Sirens shrieked. It sounded like every police car and fire engine in Washington. Brakes squealed. Car doors slammed. She jumped to the ground and dragged the duffle after. Now, in the dark she could make out people running across the street forward toward the engine, toward Wes's old yellow pick-up that was sending up spumes of red and black.

"It's gonna blow," a man yelled. "Hurry."

She turned to see Liza jump from the train and lurch as the satchel yanked her toward the ground.

Metal doors banged—trucks. Where had all these people come from? Now she could see men running not toward the engine but back toward the passenger car. Terror spiked down her spine. "Oh, Jeez, Malloy's men."

Liza nodded. She pointed to a dark van. "Over there, get behind it. Hurry."

Ellen ran around the bumper and crouched down.

Liza dropped the satchel next to her and stood panting, staring down at it. "The bags, they're too big. We can't run with them. You're going to have to bring the truck here."

Ellen collapsed against the van. "I can't believe it. What was I thinking? Oh, Liza, I'm so sorry."

"What?"

"See the fire up in front of the train? That's our truck."

254

She didn't know what she expected from Liza then, but Liza merely glanced toward the fire and said, "No, Ellen, that was our *old* truck. There are trucks all around us. You'll find us a new one."

"Right. I *will* find us a new one." She moved clear of the van and fell in behind a man with a dog headed toward the fire. She shifted toward the road, eyeing pick-ups, checking for empty cabs, listening for engines idling.

She slowed, letting the sightseers pass.

"Get back!" a man yelled ahead, but men and women still rushed toward the fire.

A dark pick-up idled. She skidded to a stop, checked the cab. Empty.

She reached for the driver's door, then caught herself. This wasn't right. Ahead was the right vehicle. She ran three yards to a pick-up with a shell on the back. The engine was idling and the truck was facing her, facing in the direction of the train's passenger car, facing west. She stepped up into the cab, pulled off the emergency brake and shifted the truck forward till she came to Liza. "Hop in."


# Sixty-Five


Ellen hung a U in front of a van and headed back east, barely missing three stragglers lopping toward the fire. At the intersection the light turned red. She ran it.

"Hey, show some restraint!"

"This from you, Liza?" Ellen squeezed her shoulder. "God, I'm glad . . . I'm just so glad you're alive."

"Alive and likely to be in jail if you don't watch the speed limit. Just because you stopped a train you think you're invincible?" There was a wildness to Liza's voice.

Ellen was just as ungrounded. "We just need to put some distance between us and the train. Then we're okay. No one's going to report this truck stolen."

"Oh yeah?"

"Yeah. That's why I chose this one. Pointed west, with the engine running. And Idaho plates. This little truck belongs to one of Malloy's men and you can bet he's not going to the police."

Liza let out a laugh. "Ellen, I am proud of you." She was wedged in between the duffle bag and the satchel. She clambered over one and planted a kiss on Ellen's cheek. "I can't believe it, that we're really here, alive, we're free, together."

Tears gushed down Ellen's face.

Liza stretched awkwardly over the luggage and hugged her. Behind them a bus honked. Liza jerked back but Ellen held her there a moment longer, feeling her breath on her face, her arms quivering around her, the warmth of her.

The bus honked again. Ellen gave her a squeeze and let go.

Liza slumped back and the wildness was gone from her voice as she said, "Wes would be proud, too. You really did stop the train with the weapons on it. You did that. He'd be real proud." Her voice cracked. "Oh, God, Ellen, I'm so sorry. He was such a great guy. He was . . ."

Ellen swallowed hard. "The best." She reached over and took Liza's hand. It was ice cold. She had to keep her eyes on the road and now she was glad of it. She had never considered herself an emotional person, but she felt so much—love, misery, fear, and the beginnings of hope. She really was on the verge of losing control. Beside her Liza huddled between the bags and said nothing.

A light turned red. The car ahead stopped and there was no question of running this light. "One good thing, Liza," she said, taking comfort in facts, "we don't need to worry about the container on the train. In L.A. they know all those weapons are missing. Once the cops ID Bentec they'll look for the guns."

"And for us."

"They don't know what we're driving."

"But they do know where we are."

She shot a glance at Liza, this woman who was suddenly thinking ahead, watching out for pitfalls, this practical woman. But the bedraggled blonde nestled amidst the luggage looked almost like a child. The aura of sophistication that had surrounded Liza from her first step onto St. Enid's was gone.

256

The traffic light turned green; cars moved, and oncoming headlights flashed on Liza's face, showing it wan, slack, as if the muscles no longer connected in the same way, as if they were balanced precariously between her past and future.

An eighteen-wheeler lumbered into the intersection making a left. Ellen cut a hard right in front of it. The bags banged forward; Liza hit the windshield.

"Yeow! Ellen, what are you doing? You afraid the cops won't find us fast enough?"

"Hang on, you'll see." Ellen hit the gas and the truck rattled down the road. "I cannot let us dawdle behind a truck. We cannot get caught. We owe it to Harry and to Wes. Hell, we owe it to us."

"Felton." Liza's voice was so soft she almost missed the word. But she was sure Liza had said only that one word, Felton. Not Jay.

The street was dark, and if there were signs, they were too small, too high, or maybe too old and drab to be deciphered, but Ellen recognized the road she had come in on and hung a left. It was the same road, but she was driving in the opposite direction, not speeding in panic to likely death, but doing 35 in a 35 zone, heading into the future. In a mile she spotted the row of tail lights, and this time as she pulled in behind the last RV, she felt her shoulders relax and her jaw unclench.

They sat silent, Liza not even asking her plan. An RV moved in behind, shielding them. The line inched forward. They should be making plans, she knew that, but there was time, and the shared silence was too comforting to break.

Liza must have realized it too. She shifted the bag between them, pulled her knees to her chest, and sighed.

The RV in front moved forward. Ellen let out the clutch and the truck jolted ahead, as if tossing them into the future. "So, Liza," she said, "there's money in those bags, right? Take a peek, huh? Chances are there's a knife in the glove compartment."

"I'd expect no less of one of Malloy's trusted men. Ah ha! Right you are. He's got a knife, a flashlight, and hey, a Hershey's bar." She broke the bar and handed Ellen half. "God, I am so starved," she said through a mouth of chocolate. "I

257

thought I'd never eat again, and now I'm ready to stop at every fast-food joint between here and Portland. If it were up to me there'd be no deep fry left in the entire Pacific Northwest. But okay, onto the money. Should be three million. That's three million, each."

"Three million dollars? I can't believe it. I know we said we'd take it. And we did take it. But I still can't believe it. Three million dollars. What are you going to do with yours?"

"Buy food. No, seriously, it's hard to imagine that much money could be in these bags. But—" she slit the side of the duffle and pulled out a bill—"this is a hundred dollar bill."

"A hundred dollar bill! Let me see!" She held it near the windshield, but the intermittent glow from the streetlights flashed and was gone before she could make out the figure on the bill. No matter. Plenty of time to get to know Mr. Hamilton or Mr. Grant. "So after you eat, Liza, then what are you going to do with the rest of your life?"

Liza wrapped her arms around her knees. It was a minute before she said, "The rest of my life. God, what a gift." Her voice was thoughtful, but there was still an undercurrent of wildness. "You know I've never thought beyond tomorrow, I guess because the future just held fear—you know, like with Felton—what will I do when I'm not a cute little piglet anymore? When I'm just good for bacon—or whatever other use they have for over the hill pigs and women? My whole life has been directed by men: my father, Jay and even Bentec. I've been so busy pleasing them, or outrunning them, or keeping their protection that all I've done is maintain a good facade."

The RV in front turned left. Ellen eased her foot off the brake and let the truck roll a couple yards and into the turn. When she stopped it again, Liza was facing her.

"But that's over. The rules are different now, Ellen. They're *my* rules." Liza shoved the suitcase to make more room for herself. "Here's what I'm going to do. As soon as we get into the campground I'm going to stride over to the bulletin board and see what's for sale. Then I'm going to buy me a trailer, one with the engine in it. I'm going to drive it into the country and park where I can't see anyone. There'll be no one's reaction for me to check to see how I'm doing or who I should be. Just me. Then I'm just going to sit on my steps till I know who I am." She let a moment pass and added, "After that I'll decide on the rest of the rules."

Ellen's throat clutched. She swallowed hard and just at the moment she thought she had herself under control she blurted out, "What about me?" She felt like a fool.

Liza reached over and rubbed her shoulder. "I know, it's so much harder for you. I don't have anyone to lose now, but you, with Wes . . . God, I am so so sorry, Ellen. Sorrier than I can ever say."

"I didn't mean—"

"I know. But, look, three million dollars can take you anywhere. It can buy you a passport, a summer in London, a flat overlooking the Seine, a houseboat on the Nile. Anything."

"That's not what I meant, dammit. You want to buy a trailer and head into the woods alone. Well, what about me? I steal you an airplane, and a bicycle, and stop a whole goddamn freight train for you. And I'm not part of your plans at all?"

Liza stared. She let out a laugh. She grabbed Ellen's head with both hands and planted a kiss. Then she laughed again. "Wow! I can't believe it. You really want to stay together? I knew things had changed, but, still, I figured you'd light out of here as fast as possible and you'd never want to see me again. I, well, I didn't want to presume."

"Presume." The kiosk was two cars ahead. She reached in her pocket for cash.

"Allow me." Liza pulled a few more bills through the hole in the satchel. "A hundred okay?"

Ellen took the money and let the subject drop. She needed to pull herself together, but so much had changed she didn't know how to pull or where to pull it.

The RV ahead rattled off, leaving a clear view of the campground with its irregular lines of trailers, trucks, campers, vans and vehicles that defied description. Lots of whites, but sunflower yellows, a sky print with clouds à la Georgia O'Keeffe, a couple lavenders, one striped, and a red tartan print that looked like a kilt on wheels. Ellen rolled the truck forward to the entry window.

259

"Reservation number?" The woman wore a billed cap, a plain blue sweatshirt, and a no-nonsense expression.

"Four-oh-eight." Beside her she could hear Liza's muffled gasp.

"Four-oh-eight's already been taken, are you sure—"

"Hey, we've driven twelve hours straight. If you double booked that's not my problem. Four-oh-eight's what they told me."

The woman jerked back as if slapped.

Liza gave a small windy whistle of approval.

Ellen softened her voice. "Listen, I don't care where you settle us. I just want to park and get out, and find the bathroom, you know?"

"I hear you on that, sister. Head over to the left. Park at the end for now. Someone won't show and you can move to a better slot later if you want."

"Thanks." She held out the bill and waited for change.

"Hey, El," Liza whispered, "whatever happened to the cautious daughter of the creamed-corn woman? You really are a natural at this."

Ellen pocketed the change. Being a natural, it didn't horrify her anymore. She let a smile creep across her face and headed the truck beneath the welcome sign, hung a left, then a right, rumbled down the irregular lane between vehicles.

Halfway down the aisle, Liza yelled, "Stop. This must be the bulletin board area." She wriggled her legs over the bags and reached for the door. "I'll go see if there's a for sale list. Maybe I can get one tonight so we don't have to be quite so together in the back of this truck."

Beside the roadway five or six women in jeans were laughing. The sound seemed so foreign, so oddly normal. Ellen leaned back. She was way too tired to think. She just watched Liza walk across the parking lot, her hair pulled back tight, the curls yanked straight on her scalp, and bushing out below the rubber band. Wes's brown wool sweater hung loose on her and halfway to her knees. But it was her walk that marked the difference in her: heavy, solid, despite the dirt-coated tennis shoes that looked so flimsy here. She looked, Ellen realized, like she belonged.

260

When the rattle of the door woke her she had no idea how long Liza had been gone.

Liza climbed in, grinning like a kid with a present.

"You bought a van?"

"Not yet. I got sidetracked by all those women and the excitement. It was like a reunion, a real reunion of real friends. I mean, Ellen, what a high. Women calling out to each other, hugging, shifting to make room for more friends. A dozen conversations going at once. You want to know what they're talking about?"

"All of them?"

"They're talking, Ellen, *laughing* about a story on the news. Seems, my friend—" she grabbed both of Ellen's hands— "that there's this guy in Eugene kicking up a fuss, threatening to sue the pants off the cops and the F.B.I. because they burned down his house. Fire devoured everything including his spare leg. The locals are blaming it all on a rogue cop from L.A." She squeezed Ellen's hands. "What do you think? Think Wes may not need our millions?"

Liza started shaking her.

Ellen felt like her head was going to burst. She pushed Liza off. "Omigod, he wasn't in the fire? Really? Can that be true? Wes is alive? How could he not. . ." She was grinning so wide she could barely speak. "Felton, your wonderful wonderful pig. Wes said he'd make sure Felton was safe. He must have taken him to those friends with the three little girls before his house got torched. Wonderful pig."

# Sixty-Six

Rain began around noon Tuesday. It rained all day and into the night. Wednesday morning the rain stopped just as the lines of RVs headed out past the gate, endless lines of women honking, waving, calling goodbye to old and new friends. Women headed south to San Diego, north to Canada, east to Ohio, to North Carolina, to Brooksville, Maine. They had their water bottles, their maps, their apples and trail mix. Some had the news on the radio, some were singing along with tapes they'd bought at the gathering. They drove for the first few miles like an unstoppable train, bumper to bumper, silver airstream to handmade wooden tent over pick-up bed. Police officers—women—grinned and waved them through intersections and they tooted their horns. When they turned onto the freeway and the gathering of women began to dissipate like incense in a breeze they felt the clutch of sadness, but also the thrill. They were travelling women and the road rolled out before them.

Liza grinned at Ellen, pulled her cap down and headed east into the sun.